THE
BONE
HOUSE

ALSO BY BRIAN FREEMAN

The Burying Place

In the Dark

Stalked

Stripped

Immoral

WRITE TO BRIAN AT

brian@bfreemanbooks.com

OR

JOIN THE MAILING LIST AT

www.bfreemanbooks.com

FIND HIM ON FACEBOOK AT

www.facebook.com/bfreemanfans

THE
BONE
HOUSE

BRIAN FREEMAN

**Doubleday Large Print
Home Library Edition**

MINOTAUR BOOKS

NEW YORK

THE BONE HOUSE. Copyright © 2011 by Brian Freeman. All rights reserved. Printed in the United States of America. For information, address St. Martin's Press, 175 Fifth Avenue, New York, N.Y. 10010.

ISBN 978-1-61129-494-1

**This Large Print Book carries the
Seal of Approval of N.A.V.H.**

**For Marcia
and in memory of
Gail Foster**

"I'll be judge, I'll be jury,"
said cunning old Fury:
"I'll try the whole cause,
and condemn you to death."

—LEWIS CARROLL

THE
BONE
HOUSE

PROLOGUE

Six Years Ago

Glory Fischer lay atop a mattress on the floor with her brown eyes wide open, smearing the mosquitoes that landed on her face and listening to the moths beat their wings madly against the screen. Her skin was filmy with sweat. Her nightgown clung to her scrawny legs in the dampness. She waited, chewing her fingernails, until the house was dead still. At one in the morning, she finally decided it was safe to sneak away, the way she had done for the past five nights.

No one would hear her leave. No one would hear her come back.

Her mother slept alone in a bedroom across the hall, with an electric fan grinding beside her pillow that drowned out her snores. Her sister, Tresa, and Tresa's best friend, Jen, were finally sleeping, too. The two girls had stayed up late, acting out stories from a vampire fanzine in loud voices. It was a Tuesday in mid-July, and bedtimes and school nights were a long way away. Usually, Glory didn't like Jen sleeping over, because the ruckus of the girls on the other side of the wall kept her awake. Tonight she didn't care, because she needed to stay awake anyway.

Jen lived in the house across the road, but Glory didn't think that her sister's friend knew what was hidden in the loft of their garage. Nobody did. Not Jen's mother, Nettie, who was in a wheelchair now and rarely left the house. Not her father, Harris, who was on the road most days, traveling around Wisconsin for his job. Not Jen's two older brothers either. Especially not them. If they'd known, they would have done something cruel, because that was who they were. Cruel boys.

Glory sat up cross-legged, with her pink nightgown bunching above her knees. The hot wind gusted under the curtain and made the room smell of cherries, which were squashed all over the county roads like dots of red paint at this time of year. Leaning over, Glory slid open the bottom drawer of her dresser and dug beneath her underwear for the stash she had deposited there after dinner: a warm, unopened carton of milk and a paper bag stuffed with crumbled potato chips, sunflower seeds, mushed banana, and hard-boiled egg.

The ten-year-old girl stood up and stuffed her bare feet into sneakers. It was time to go. She bent back the broken screen from her window until she could fit one leg outside the house, then the other. She held the paper bag between her teeth and squeezed the milk carton under her arm. She jumped awkwardly, landing in the dirt five feet below. Her mouth opened with a loud *oof,* and the bag fell and spilled. She picked it up and checked inside. There was still plenty of food.

Glory bit her lip and peered at the messy weeds in the yard and the nearby woods. The world felt big, and she felt small. The moonless sky glistened with stars. The pines swayed like giants and whispered to each other. Swallowing down her fear, she sprinted through the tall grass. She figured if she went fast enough, the ticks and the box elder bugs clinging to the green shoots wouldn't land on her. Her arms pumped, and her long hair flew behind her. She reached the dirt road, which was rippled with tractor ruts, and she stopped, breathing hard in the stifling air.

The rural lane looked lonely. There were no cars and no streetlights, just a crooked row of telephone poles beside her, holding the bowed wires like jump ropes. The two-story house loomed across the way, sheltered by oak trees down a long driveway. Glory ran again but slowed to a nervous walk when she got close. The chipped paint and hanging shutters gave her a creepy feeling, and when the wind blew, the house sighed. She'd asked her mother once if the Bone house was haunted. Her mother had gotten a strange look on her face and said there were no such things as ghosts or monsters, just unhappy people.

Glory crept to the garage, which was in the midst of a grassy field. A rusted padlock held the side door closed. She knew where Mr. Bone kept the key, on a hook hidden underneath the window ledge. She undid the padlock, replaced the key on the hook, and opened the door. She always got a lump in her throat creeping inside. She reached for a heavy flashlight on the shelves next to the door, and when she turned it on and rattled the batteries, it struggled to make a tiny orange glow across the floor. She could see mouse droppings littered at her feet. Parked in front of her was a pickup truck with a dirty tarpaulin stretched over its bed. At the rear of the garage was a wooden ladder leading to the loft.

"It's me," she called softly. "I'm here."

Glory tiptoed to the ladder. The rotten steps sagged as she climbed, and splinters poked her fingers. Ten feet over the floor, she crawled onto the bed of the loft, which was strewn with paint cans and moldy blankets. She saw nails jutting down through the roof shingles and a huge papery growth under the eave that was really a hornet's nest.

"Hey," she said. "Where are you?"

She heard the scrape of claws and a wispy squeal. When she turned her flashlight toward the sound, she saw the wide, curious eyes of the kitten squeezing out of its hiding place. She gathered the little animal up into her arms and was rewarded with a rumbling purr that was loud in her ears. The kitten's spiky fur was mottled with tan and black, striped like a tiger.

"Look what I have," Glory said. She poured milk into the lid of a dirty glass jar, then dumped the food from the paper bag onto the floor and let the kitten attack it hungrily. She stroked its back as it ate noisily and then picked it up with one hand and deposited it near the milk, where it drank until its mouth was damp and white. When it was done, the kitten climbed up her bare legs with wobbly steps, and she put it back down on the floor of the loft. As Glory watched happily, it hopped in and out of the flashlight glow, slapping at a black beetle with its tiny front paws.

Glory was so caught up in the antics of the kitten, so much in love with it, that she didn't realize immediately that she wasn't alone anymore.

Then her heart galloped in her chest. She heard footsteps treading on the gravel outside the garage.

Glory sucked in her breath, covered the

light, and shrank back from the edge of the loft. *Don't come inside, don't come inside, don't come inside,* she prayed in her head, but she heard the bang of the metal plate on the door lock as the side door opened below her. Someone stole into the garage. Someone was with her, moving about in the darkness, the way a ghost would, the way a monster would.

She hugged the kitten to her chest and flattened herself against a blanket on the floor. In her arms, the kitten squirmed and mewed. She tried to bury the sound by keeping its little body against her chest, but whoever was below her heard something in the rafters and stopped. There was a moment of horrible quiet, and then a flash-light beam speared through the dark space. It swept like a searchlight around the corners of the garage and traced the wall of the loft just above her head. Hunting for her among the spiderwebs.

She thought about calling out. Whoever it was would be surprised, but they'd laugh to find her here. There was no reason to be afraid. Even so, she kept her lips tightly shut. She didn't even want to breathe. It was the middle of the night, and no one should be here now.

Somehow Glory knew in the hollow of her stomach: Something bad was happening.

The light went black. Below her, she heard labored breathing as the stranger dragged something heavy off the metal shelves. She heard an odd burp of plastic and a hiss of air. Something bounced on the floor like a bottle cap and rolled, and the intruder didn't bother to retrieve it. As Glory listened, stiff with fear, she heard the outside door open. The lock rattled, and the garage fell into a deep quiet again. It was over. She was alone.

She waited with no sense of time ticking away. She didn't know how long she lay in the loft, not moving, wondering if it was safe to escape. Finally, when she felt bugs crawling over her bare legs, she grabbed the kitten with one hand and navigated backward down the wobbly ladder. She jumped the last few feet to the floor and took blind, tentative steps toward the window so she could stare outside. She spied the dark square of glass, which looked out toward the west wall of the Bone house. The bottom of the window frame was almost higher than she was tall. She had to stand on her toes to look out.

The glass was punched with BB holes shot by the Bone boys. Air whipped in through the starbursts. Before she pushed her head above the ledge, she smelled an odor that was both sickly sweet and over-powering.

Gasoline.

A drowning, drenching wave of gasoline.

Glory didn't understand, but the foul smell made her want to run. Run fast, with the kitten sheltered in her arms. Run home to her bed. Get away.

She poked her eyes above the window frame. When she did, she had to clap her hand over her mouth not to scream. A black silhouette stood immediately on the other side of the glass, not even a foot away. She couldn't see the person's face, but she squeezed her own eyes shut and stood stock-still, as if becoming a statue would make her invisible. Fumes of gasoline crept into her nose, and she swallowed back a cough. When no one came running, she peeked through her eyelids and dared to look again. The person didn't move. She heard loud breathing, the way an animal would pant. Before her brain could process what was happening, she saw the smallest flick of a hand, saw bare skin, and saw the tiny eruption of a flame.

A match.

The hand cupped it and dropped it. The flame descended to the ground in a flash of light like a falling star. It was a simple thing, someone lighting a cigarette and then stamping out the match.

Except there was no cigarette.

Glory's world blew into pieces. The flame struck the earth, and a cannon of fire erupted, filling the window and blowing her backward like a punch to her chest. She shielded her eyes with her hand, and through her slitted fingers, she watched the fire leap like a circus acrobat toward the Bone house. The flames sped along scorched, intersecting paths, greedily licking at the walls and climbing for the sky. In seconds, fire was everywhere, consuming the frame of the house as if it were nothing but a few branches of kindling stuffed under the grate. She smelled wood blackening and heard knots pop like knuckles cracking. Through the house windows, she saw the yellow glow of flame blooming inside, and soon she couldn't see the house at all; it disappeared behind a tower of smoke and fire. The heat was so ferocious and so close that her hands and face began to sear. She backed up and gagged as poison billowed through the window and filled the garage.

Crying, coughing, Glory bolted for the door, but it was locked. Locked on the outside. The rattling hinges refused to give way. When she touched the doorknob, she burned her fingers on the hot metal and screamed.

It was now bright as day inside the garage, but the white haze gathering in the air was as impenetrable as the darkness. Glory ran from the fire toward the wide automobile door, but she pulled and tugged on the handle and couldn't move it at all. She could hardly breathe now. The smoke infiltrated her eyes and lungs. She crumbled to her knees and wept as an orange dragon crackled through the wall and began to devour the garage itself. The sound was loud and terrifying, a roar, a hiss, worse than any monster she'd imagined living here.

Glory backed up, scraping her knees on

the floor until they bled. She retreated into the farthest corner of the garage, and when she could go no farther, she curled up into a ball. She clutched the kitten to her cheek, kissed its face over and over, and whispered in its ear, "Baby, baby, baby, baby." She closed her eyes as the fire ballooned over her and poked at her with its evil tongue like a spitting devil.

She prayed the way her father had taught her to pray before he died.

She prayed that God would lift her up in his arms and take her back home, where she would awaken on her mattress on the floor of her bedroom. The humid night would be still again, the mosquitoes would be buzzing in her ears, and the kitten would be purring in her arms.

She prayed.

Even when part of the wall collapsed around her body in a cascading spray of sparks and debris, and left a gaping hole where she could escape, Glory prayed.

Even when she crawled away over a trail of burning embers into the safety of the grass, with the kitten nestled in her chest, she prayed.

She lay with her hands covering her

ears, but she couldn't shelter herself from the awful noise. Over the howl of the fire, she heard the agonized wails of the people dying inside the Bone house, and in her desperation, she prayed that God would make this night unreal. Make it go away forever. Wipe her memory clean until she forgot everything, even in her worst dreams.

Please, God, let me forget everything, Glory prayed.

Forget everything.

Forget everything.

PART ONE

Death's Door

1

The girl in the bikini pirouetted on the wet sand.

She was a hundred yards away, and all Mark Bradley could see was the sheen of her bare skin in the moonlight. She danced like a water sprite, with her head thrown back so that her hair swept behind her. She had her arms extended like wings. The dark water of the Gulf was as calm as glass, barely lapping at the beach. The girl splashed and kicked at the surf, sometimes running deeper into the warm water until it rose to her knees.

He could hear her singing to herself.

She had a sweet voice, but it wasn't perfectly in tune. He recognized the song, which
he could remember playing on his Walkman
while jogging through Grant Park in downtown Chicago as a teenager. To the girl on
the beach, the song must have been an
oldie, something from her mother's genera-
tion. He heard her chanting the chorus over
and over.

It was Billy Joel's "We Didn't Start the
Fire."

As he got closer to the girl on the beach,
Mark couldn't help but admire her. Her
body was mature, and the flimsy strings of
the red bikini showed it off, but she still had
the gangly gait of an adolescent, all arms
and legs. She was more girl than woman,
with an innocence about her near naked-
ness in public. He was still too far away to
see her face, but he wondered if his wife,
Hilary, knew her. He assumed she was
one of the girls who had competed in the
dance tournament at the resort, and now
that the competition was over, she was
enjoying a few sleepless moments on the
beach before going home.

Mark couldn't sleep either. He dreaded
the return to Wisconsin. The vacation in

Florida had been an escape for a week, and now he would have to face the reality of his situation at home. Shunned. Jobless. Angry. He and Hilary had avoided the subject for most of the past year, but they couldn't avoid it much longer. Money was tight. They would have to decide: stay or go. He didn't want to give up on their dream, but he had no idea how to put the pieces of their lives back together.

That wasn't how it was supposed to be. They'd left Chicago for rural Door County because they had wanted a quieter life in a place where they could join a community and raise a family. Instead, it had become a nightmare for Mark. Suspicion now followed him everywhere. He was marked with a scarlet letter. *P* for Predator. All because of Tresa Fischer.

He pounded a fist against his palm. Sometimes his fury overwhelmed him. He didn't blame Tresa; she was just a girl in love. The others, though—the teachers, the parents, the police, the school board— they had ignored his denials and picked apart his life, leaving him with his career destroyed. He wanted revenge for the injustice. He wanted to hurt someone. He wasn't a violent man, but sometimes he wondered what he would do if he met the principal of the school in a deserted county park, where no one would see them and where no one would ever know what he'd done.

Mark stopped on the beach. He closed his eyes and breathed deeply until his anger washed away. The waves came and went, and he felt the sand eroding beneath his feet. The peace of the water calmed him, which was why he was here. He smelled the briny, fishy aroma of the Gulf. The mild, damp March air was like a tonic compared to the cold weather back home, where temperatures were still in the thirties.

He could have stayed here forever, but nothing lasted. He knew it was time to go back to the hotel. Hilary was alone, and she'd wonder where he was if she awakened. He'd slipped silently out of bed when he couldn't sleep. He'd shrugged on a swimsuit and a yellow tank top and walked out their patio door, which led directly down the flat stretch of sand past the palm trees to the water. The sea had helped clear his head, but the relief was temporary, as it always was. Things never changed. They only got worse.

Mark heard the voice again. "We didn't start the fire."

The teenaged girl in the bikini wandered closer to him. She had a wine bottle in her hand, and he watched her drink from it like a runner downing Gatorade. Watching her swaying motions on the beach, he realized she was drunk. She was only thirty yards away now, her skin bronzed and damp. She tugged at the bottom of her swimsuit and adjusted it without self-consciousness. Her wet hair had fallen across her face, and when she pushed it away, their eyes met. Hers were wild and unfocused.

He knew who she was.

"Oh, son of a bitch," he murmured under his breath.

It was Glory Fischer. Tresa's sister.

Instinctively, Mark looked up and down the beach. The two of them were alone. It was almost three in the morning. He eyed the tower of the hotel, and in the handful of rooms where he saw lights, he didn't see the silhouette of anyone looking out. Even in the moonlight, it was dark enough that no one could see them here. He hated the idea that his first thought was self-protection, but he felt guilty and exposed being this close to a young girl. Especially this girl.

She took a long time to realize who he was, but then she offered him a teasing smile as she recognized him. "You," she said.

"Hello, Glory. Are you okay?"

The girl ignored the question and hummed to herself. "Did you follow me here?" she asked.

"Follow you? No."

"I bet you followed me. That's okay."

"Where'd you get the wine?" he asked.

"You want some?" She looked at the bottle and realized it was empty. She over-turned it, and a few red drops sprinkled onto the sand. "Shit. Sorry."

"You shouldn't be out here," he said. "Let me take you back to the hotel."

Glory wagged a finger at him, and her torso swayed unsteadily. "Tresa wouldn't like that, would she? Seeing you and me together. Troy wouldn't like it either. He gets so jealous. If you want to do it with me, we should do it right here. Do you want to do it with me?"

Mark's body tightened with anxiety. He knew he shouldn't be here. He had to get away before this got worse, before anyone saw them together.

"Come on, let's go," he told Glory. "I don't want you on the beach alone. It's not safe. You've been drinking."

"What's the problem? You'll keep me safe, won't you? You're big and strong. No one's going to mess with you."

He reached for her arm, but she spun out of his grasp. He ran a hand back across his short hair in frustration. "I'm not going to leave you out here by yourself," he said.

"So don't leave. Stay. I like being here with you."

"It's late. You should be in bed."

Glory grinned and stuck out her tongue at him. "See, I knew that's what you wanted."

"You're drunk. I don't want you hurting yourself."

She hummed again. The same Billy Joel song. "Tresa saw you on Friday, you know."

"What?"

"She saw you and Hilary in the auditorium. That's why she choked. She was really upset. She couldn't concentrate knowing you were there."

"Not winning isn't the end of the world."

"Yeah. I know." Glory didn't look distressed by Tresa's failure. Her face had a drunken brightness to it, as if she were drowning her sorrows. "Hey, I read a poem once that said the world would end in fire."

"Robert Frost," he said.

"You know it? Oh, yeah, duh, English teacher." She looked at him like a broken toy. "I mean, you used to be. Tresa felt bad about what happened."

"Let's go, Glory."

"Tresa never thought they would do anything like that."

"We should get back to the hotel." He put his hand out.

Glory took his hand in hers, but then she slid a damp arm around his waist. Her face came up to his neck. She tilted her chin toward him. Her breath smelled of alcohol, and her white teeth were stained darker by the wine. "Kiss me."

He reached around his back to disentangle himself. He looked over his shoulder toward the hotel again and felt an uncomfortable sensation, as if he were being watched from the darkness. Or maybe someone was testing him.

"Stop it."

"Tresa says your lips are soft," Glory whispered.

Mark pried her hands away from his body. He took an urgent, awkward step backward in the sand to separate himself. When Glory reached out to hold him, she was too far away, and she stumbled and sank to her knees. Her stringy brown hair fell across her face. Her skin was pale, and he saw disorientation in her eyes.

"Are you okay?" he asked.

Glory didn't say anything.

He squatted in front of her. "Glory?"

She looked up at him. Tears streaked down her face. She wiped her nose with the back of her hand. On her knees, crying, she looked like a pretty, lost girl again. A typical teenager with blemishes on her forehead. A kid pretending to be an adult. He reached to touch her shoulder but pulled his hand back, as if her skin would be on fire.

"What's wrong?" he asked. "Why are you out here by yourself?"

"I don't want to go home," she said.

"Why not?"

She shook her head. "I don't know what to do."

Mark started to press her for details, but he realized he was letting himself get sucked into this girl's life and problems. That had always been his weakness. He was a fixer.

"I'll take you back to the hotel," he murmured. He took her elbow and helped her to her feet. Her legs were rubbery, and she grabbed him for balance, clinging to his neck so tightly that her nails dug into his skin. He guided her into the dry sand with an arm around her waist, but she yanked free and skipped unsteadily back into the water. Trails of sand clung to her knees and thighs. She held her arms out to him.

"Let's swim," she said.

"I don't think so."

"One quick swim, then we'll go."

"No."

"Oh, come on." She was a coquette again. Her moods changed like clouds passing over the moon. "I won't bite. Unless you're into that."

"Get out of the water," he told her sternly. "You're drunk. You could hurt yourself."

"I think you're afraid of me," she said. "You want me."

"Stop playing games, Glory."

"You think I'm too young, but I'm not."

"What are you, sixteen?"

"So what? All the parts work."

Mark didn't feel vulnerable to her, but he remembered what Hilary had told him about teaching teenaged girls. *You think they're kids. They're not.* He wanted this encounter to be over. He wished he had never gotten out of bed and never taken a walk on the beach. Nothing good could come from being here with Glory.

"It's okay to play with fire," the girl said.

"I'm leaving."

Glory scrambled out of the water. She sprinted up to him and stood, dripping, in front of him. Her voice was young now. "Don't go."

"We're both going inside."

"Why don't you want to have sex with me?" she asked. "Is it Tresa? I won't tell her."

"Oh, for God's sake, Glory," he muttered in exasperation.

"I'm not a virgin," she went on. "Troy wasn't even the first. You know what the boys call me at school? My nickname? It's Glory Glory Hallelujah."

"You shouldn't brag about that," he said, before he could stop himself. He didn't want to lecture her or be drawn into a discussion of her sexuality. He just wanted to turn around and go. Things were getting out of control.

He saw her eyes focused on the palm trees over his shoulder, and he flinched. He turned, expecting to see someone watching the two of them together. He knew it would be the same as last year if they were discovered. Suspicions. Accusations. *You're a predator,* they would say. Instinctively, he thought of ways to explain his behavior, to defend himself, even when he'd done nothing wrong.

Instead, he saw no one. They were alone. Weren't they?

"I'm leaving, Glory," he insisted.

"If you go, I'll just tell everybody we had sex anyway," she said. "Who do you think they'll believe? If you stay, it can be our secret."

Glory reached behind her back. He didn't realize what she was doing, but when her hands came forward, they held the strings to her bikini top, which dangled at her hips. She tugged the ties at her neck, undoing the knot, and shrugged her torso, letting the red top peel away and fall to her feet. Her eyes were serious and confident as she cupped her naked breasts.

"No one will ever know," she whispered.

2

You're quiet this morning," Hilary Bradley said to her husband.

They sat at an outdoor table by the pool with plates filled from the hotel's breakfast buffet. It was early morning, just after seven o'clock, and the patio café was sparsely populated. Both of them were early risers. Hilary sipped her orange juice and watched her husband, whose blank eyes were focused on the wide stretch of beach and the placid Gulf water.

"Anyone in there?" she asked when he didn't answer her.

Mark's head snapped toward her. "Oh, sorry. I'm not quite awake yet."

"Drink your coffee."

He sipped from a ceramic mug, not saying anything more.

"You okay?" she asked.

"Sure. Fine."

Hilary didn't push him to talk. She tried the jalapeño-laced scrambled eggs, which were spicy and delicious, and she picked up a piece of crispy bacon with her fingers. The buffet meant an extra hour on the treadmill tomorrow, but the trade-off was worth it. Hilary was tall, and she would never be thin. Even when she'd danced in school, she hadn't been a waif; instead, her muscular physique had been an asset in winning competitions. That was a long time ago. Now she was only two years away from forty, and she found herself waging a daily battle to maintain a weight where she could look at herself in the mirror and not wince. Each year the battle got a little harder, but she wasn't about to starve herself.

She studied her husband, who had shown surprising willpower at the buffet this morning. Mark was a rugged man, the kind

who turned women's heads. She felt satisfaction when she thought about his toned
body, but she also felt mild jealousy and
annoyance. He carried his own weight well,
but he had the advantage of being three
years younger than she was. He was a man,
too, and a lifelong athlete. When he gained
ten pounds on a vacation, he added half an
hour to his weight-lifting regimen, and the
pounds miraculously vanished on the second day.

Annoying.

Hilary followed Mark's eyes to the beach,
where she saw a large cluster of people half
a mile away near the water. They weren't
dressed like swimmers. She thought they
looked like police. "I wonder what's going
on," she said.

"I don't know." Mark sounded distracted.

She leaned back in her chair, brushed
her long blond hair away from her face,
and adjusted her sunglasses. Even early
in the morning, it was already warm on the
patio. She tried to read her husband's mind
and decipher what was bothering him. "If
we have to move, we move," she said.
"We've done it before."

"What?" he asked.

"Home. Money. I know you're worried. So am I. But what's the worst that happens? We pack up and go somewhere else."

Mark dragged his gaze from the sea. He rubbed his chin, which was stubbled; he hadn't shaved yet. He picked up a fork to eat his breakfast and then put it down. "Who says it'll be that easy? Any high school district in the country looks at a male teacher released after two years, and what do they think? Inappropriate behavior."

"Not necessarily."

He set his mug down sharply on the glass tabletop. "Let's not kid ourselves, Hil."

"I'm just saying, budgets are tight everywhere. We're coming out of a big recession in a small district. People get let go. It doesn't have to raise red flags."

Mark shook his head. "You don't think there's a back channel between principals? You don't think they talk to each other off the record? 'What's the deal on Mark Bradley?' 'Forget about him, he was banging one of his students.' Face it, wherever I go, I'll be blacklisted."

"You don't know that."

"The hell I don't."

She saw in Mark's face a bitterness that

had grown and deepened over the past year of joblessness, until it was a constant fixture in his eyes. She couldn't blame him. He'd been treated badly, convicted without a trial or an appeal. He was in an impossible situation, and he was angry about it. The trouble was that his anger didn't change the reality or make it better; it only threw a shadow between the two of them. When they were together, when they were in bed, his anger was always there with them now.

She let the silence linger, and then she changed the subject. "Did you see the bulletin board in the lobby? Amy Leigh's team from Green Bay did really well. They got first runner-up for small ensembles."

"Good for her."

"I wish I could have seen their final performance, but that was the day we drove to Tampa. Amy was one of my favorites in Chicago. Bubbly girl, really sweet."

"I remember her."

Hilary had coached Amy Leigh in dance for four years while she taught in the northern Chicago suburb of Highland Park. Amy didn't have natural grace but compensated for it with practice and enthusiasm. They'd become friends. Hilary's last name had been

Semper, not Bradley, until Amy's senior year, and Amy had been among the students who were most excited when Hilary had announced that she was getting married.

"I called Amy's room to congratulate her," Hilary said, "but the Green Bay bus left early. I missed her."

"You can post on her wall on Facebook when we get back," Mark said.

"Yeah." Hilary yawned and worked the crick out of her neck by stretching her arms. "I hope I can sleep on the plane. I'm still really tired. You must be, too."

"Why do you say that?"

"You didn't sleep well, did you? I woke up at one point and you weren't in bed."

"Oh," Mark said. "No, you're right, I couldn't sleep. Sorry, I was obsessing about the job again. I know you think I should just let it go."

"I never said that. I just don't want it destroying our lives, okay? Look, we'll get home, and you can focus on something else. You can paint."

"I'm not going to make any money that way."

"Who knows? That gallery in Ephraim

talked about selling your stuff. Anything will help right now." She frowned when she saw Mark's face. He thought she was chastising him. She tried to make it better, but she only made it worse. "Or you could do golf lessons this summer. A lot of women are looking for a sexy pro to help them stop shanking. A lot of men, too."

"We've talked about this."

"I know, I know. I'm just saying."

She let the subject drop. On some issues Mark was stubborn, and you couldn't get him to change his mind. Golf was a big one. He'd spent several years in his twenties on the pro circuit, working his way up the ladder and into the money, until a shoulder injury ended his career. As an ex-pro, he could have made a decent living giving lessons or working in the business, but Mark had an all-or-nothing attitude. If he couldn't be competitive as a player, he didn't want to be part of the game. She'd never been able to help him past it.

Still, she couldn't complain. When he gave up golf, Mark had gone in a new direction and taken up teaching. That was how they'd met, when he was a substitute teacher in the Highland Park system. If he'd never been injured, he would have been on the Golf Channel, and she would probably still be single. So maybe it was fate. On the other hand, she knew it made the current situation even worse for Mark, because it meant that a second career had been stripped away from him in circumstances beyond his control.

"So what did you do?" she asked.

"What do you mean?"

"When you couldn't sleep. Where did you go?"

Mark hesitated. "I took a walk."

"On the beach?"

"Yes."

"That must have been great. It was a beautiful night."

"It was," he said.

"How long were you gone?"

"I don't know. An hour maybe."

Hilary pushed her chair back and stood up. "I'm going to get some more orange juice. You want anything?"

Mark shook his head. He'd picked at his food but left most of it on his plate. It made her feel guilty eating everything she'd taken. If she'd been alone, she probably would have treated herself to another scoop of scrambled eggs, but instead she wandered over to the buffet and poured a second glass of juice over ice.

She noticed the cluster of police on the beach again. The handful of patrons in the café watched them curiously. Several guests had stood up and were shielding their eyes to get a better view of the activity near the water. A white-uniformed waiter passed Hilary with a fresh tray of cut fruit, and she smiled at him.

"Do you know what's going on?" she asked.

The waiter shrugged as he positioned the fruit on the buffet. "Somebody told me they found a body out there."

"A body? What happened?"

"Don't know. That's all I heard. Somebody died."

"Do you know who it was?"

"A hotel guest, I think."

"Here? At this hotel?"

"I guess so."

He slid the empty tray under his arm and left without waiting for more questions. Hilary looked around the patio for someone she knew, but she didn't recognize anyone among the morning guests. She was concerned, because she and Mark had traveled to Florida this week specifically to watch the dance competition, which included several of her former students from Chicago. She had good friends among the girls and the coaches, and she hoped they were safe.

Hilary brought her juice back to the table. Mark saw the anxiety in her face.

"What's wrong?" he asked.

"Those are police out on the beach. The waiter says they found a hotel guest dead out there."

Mark reacted immediately. "Dead? Who was it?"

"I don't know." She saw his eyes dart to the water, and she asked, "Did you see anything last night?"

"What, like a body? Of course not."

"Well, I wonder if you should talk to someone," she said.

"And tell them what? I didn't see anything."

Hilary shrugged. She saw the glass doors open on the other side of the patio, and she knew the woman who emerged from the hotel lobby. It was Jane Chapman, the mother of one of the dancers from

Chicago. Hilary waved at her, and she made a beeline for their table. Her face was distraught.

"Hilary, it's terrible, did you hear?" Jane asked breathlessly. "I can't believe it."

"I heard that somebody from the hotel died. Do you know who it was?"

Jane nodded. "A teenaged girl. She was murdered."

"One of the dancers?"

"I don't think so. I heard she's from your area, though. Door County."

"Who?" Hilary asked. Instinctively, she felt a wave of nausea and fear.

"A coach told me the dead girl's name was Glory Fischer."

Hilary's breath left her chest. She felt dizzy. She heard Jane asking if she was okay, but the woman's voice was at the end of a long tunnel, muffled and distant. Hilary tried to speak and couldn't. She knew. Somehow she knew, without looking at Mark, without saying a word, that this event was a tornado that would suck in her and her husband. Her head swiveled slowly so that she could stare at him. She didn't want to see the truth, but their eyes met, and his expression confirmed all her fears.

She saw emotions in his face she'd never seen in him before. Panic. Terror. Guilt.

Mark, what did you do? What happened last night?

She hated that her first thought had nothing to do with trusting him. She hated that her first thought had nothing to do with protecting him. It didn't matter that she would never believe for a moment that Mark Bradley could ever harm another human being. It didn't matter that she had faith in his willingness to stare at temptation and walk away from it. Her first thought had nothing to do with his innocence.

Instead, she stared at the man she loved, and all she could think was *Not again*.

3

Detective Cab Bolton didn't notice the Gulf wave riding up the beach until he felt salt water lapping at his two-hundred-dollar Hugo Boss loafers. The surf rose above his ankles like a margarita in a blender and soaked inside his shoes before he had time to leap out of the way. As the wave retreated, he squatted in the sand, removed the loafers, and peeled off his wet socks. He shook his head in exaggerated dismay.

"Every time I buy a new pair of shoes, we get a beach body the next day," he complained.

Cab rolled up the trouser legs of his

navy blue silk suit. With his bare ankles and size 13 feet on display at the bottom of his six-feet-six frame, he resembled a great blue heron. His long neck and spiky blond hair and the ski-jump slope of his sunburnt nose contributed to the impression of a bird on stilts.

Lala Mosqueda, who was the lead crime scene analyst, didn't look sympathetic. "It's Florida, Cab. You ever hear of flip-flops?"

"I'd sooner wear Crocs," he said.

The damage to the leather was done, but he took a handkerchief from his breast pocket and wiped the sand from his shoes and blotted the excess water. He hooked the shoes on the fingers of his right hand and let them dangle. With his other hand, he stripped off his amber sunglasses and squinted at the tower of the hotel.

"So what do we have in this place, five hundred rooms?" Cab mused. "Maybe more? You'd figure somebody had to be up there staring at the beach at three in the morning. Somebody saw something."

Lala shook her head. "No way. Too far, too dark."

Cab pointed a long, crooked finger at the floor-to-ceiling windows, where at least a dozen gawkers followed the activity near the water. "Look at the binoculars spying on us right now. Beachfront voyeurs are always looking for people humping by the water in the middle of the night."

"Well, we've got uniforms interviewing guests in the lobby," Lala told him. "It's Sunday, and half the hotel is checking out. We're trying to catch people as they leave."

"Good." Cab eyed the narrow strip of Gulf Coast sand, which stretched along the water like a ribbon for several miles in both directions. Even in the early morning, there were already bathers sunning themselves up and down the beach. "If you strangled someone in the surf, what would you do next?" he asked Lala.

"I'd walk along the water and head up the beach where there are a ton of footprints in the sand," she said.

"Exactly. I hate beach bodies." He replaced his sunglasses on his face, covering up his sky blue eyes. "Okay, Mosquito, what do we know so far?"

Cab saw her dark eyes flash with annoyance. He knew she hated it when he used her nickname, but he couldn't resist pushing her buttons. He'd never been a master of social graces; his mouth was always getting him into trouble. That was one of the reasons he'd gone from the FBI to the police to private investigative work and back to the police in half a dozen cities over the past twelve years. His colleagues also resented his born-in-L.A. style. Unlike most cops working for a pension, he had a bulging trust fund thanks to his Hollywood mother, and he did what he did because he enjoyed it, not because he needed a paycheck. That didn't fly with most cops, and particularly not in Naples, which was a sun-soaked resort town of rich snowbirds and spoiled spring-break college students. If you had money, you were supposed to be on the other side of the social divide.

He wasn't fooling Lala with his jokes, though. He was deliberately keeping her at a distance, and she knew it. They'd had a brief affair not long ago that was the equivalent of a supernova: supercharged, blindingly bright, collapsing with a big bang. Their attraction hadn't gone away, but what was left between them was a black hole, with both of them fighting against the pull of gravity.

"Okay, *Ms. Mosqueda,* what do we know so far?" he asked her.

She had a very pretty Cuban face, but there was definitely no light escaping from it now. Black hole.

"A jogger found the body before sunrise," she told him. "She was facedown in the water, topless, with her bikini top wrapped around her neck. He pulled her out of the water and tried mouth-to-mouth, but she'd been dead for a while. Preliminary estimate on time of death is between two and four o'clock. From the ligature marks on the neck and bruising on the backs of the shoulders, it looks like someone held her down and strangled her in the water. The ME isn't sure yet whether asphyxiation resulted from the rope of the bikini top or the water itself."

"She didn't just get drunk and do a bellyflop in the surf?" Cab asked.

"No, she definitely had help. The girl had been drinking, though. We found an empty bottle of Yellow Tail near the body, and her teeth and tongue show discoloration from red wine. We won't know how much she had until we get the blood analysis back. Maybe she was drunk, maybe she wasn't."

"Did she have sex?" Cab asked.

"She was still wearing her bikini bottom," Lala replied in a monotone, "and the fabric wasn't ripped or otherwise disturbed. There was no bruising, blood, or external injury consistent with vaginal or anal rape, at least based on a visual inspection."

Cab wasn't convinced. "You're talking about a teenaged girl who's drinking and topless on the beach. That sure smells like sex was involved."

"I'm not saying she didn't have sex, but there isn't any evidence yet of sexual assault."

"Fair enough. I get it. Did you find anything else near the body?"

Lala gestured up and down the beach with frustration. "We're combing the sand, but you've got a few thousand people along here every day. We'll bag and test what we find, but don't get your hopes up."

"How about the body itself?" Cab asked.

"We're checking for DNA under her fingernails, but her hands were lying in the water. Even if she fought back, I'm not sure what we're going to find."

"See, this is why I hate beach bodies," Cab repeated.

Lala opened her mouth as if she had more to tell him, but he held up a hand to stop her as he let the details soak into his mind. His way of approaching an investigation was to add layers of fact to his brain like coats of paint. He liked to let one coat dry before slapping on the next one. Lala was different. She preferred to blurt out her whole report at once and sort through the puzzle pieces.

Lala was dressed all in black. Black T-shirt, black jeans, black sandals, all of it matching her shoulder-length black hair. She was in her midthirties, like Cab, and had spent her entire career with the Naples police. She was intense about everything that Cab wasn't. Her Cuban family. Her Cuban politics. Her Catholic heritage. Her job. Her temper. She was fire; he was water, always flowing downhill, always running away. Still, she was about the only cop in Florida he considered a friend.

Not that he would ever say so to her face.

"Cab?" Lala asked impatiently.

"Yeah, okay, keep going. Do we know who this girl is?"

"We got lucky about that. Her name's Glory Fischer. Sixteen years old."

Cab exhaled in dismay. "She's just a kid."

"Sixteen's older than you think these days."

"Yeah, yeah, thirteen is the new eighteen, sixteen's the new twenty-one. How'd we make the ID?"

"Her sister and Glory's boyfriend were looking for her on the hotel grounds when we showed up. The sister said Glory wasn't in their room, and when they heard about the body, they both freaked. The sister confirmed Glory's ID from a photograph. We've got them with a policewoman now. A counselor's on the way."

"What about a parent?"

Lala shook her head. "The girls are from rural Wisconsin, an area called Door County. Mom's back home, Dad's deceased. The sister already called the mother and gave her the news. She's flying down here today."

"Wisconsin," Cab said. "Remind me, that's north of Michigan, right?"

"No, the place north of Michigan is called Canada, Cab."

"Same difference. What were these girls doing here, anyway?"

"The hotel is crawling with college dancers," Lala told him. "There was some kind of competition this week with student teams from all over the country. The sister—her name is Tresa, T-r-e-s-a—she goes to school at the University of Wisconsin at River Falls. She came down here on a bus with her teammates. Her mother couldn't come, so it sounds like Glory and her boyfriend—his name's Troy Geier—drove down here separately to cheer for Tresa during the program. They were all supposed to be heading back home today."

"The victim, Glory, she wasn't part of the competition?"

Lala shook her head. "Nope."

"Did you get any more info about Glory out of the sister or the boyfriend? Do they have any idea what she was doing on the beach last night?"

"They say no."

"Do you believe them?" Cab asked.

"If one of them was involved, they put

on a good act. Most of the time, you can see through kids if they're lying."

"I pretty much assume everybody's lying," Cab said.

That was part of his legacy growing up with a mother who worked as an actress. If someone was moving their lips in L.A., they were probably lying. Being a cop had done nothing to change his conviction that people were dishonest at heart. He'd learned that lesson the hard way.

"How old is the sister, Tresa?" he added.

"Nineteen. She's a freshman at River Falls."

"How about the boyfriend? Did you pick up anything about his relationship with Glory?"

"Nothing about Glory," Lala said. He saw a self-satisfied smirk on her golden face. She knew something. She'd been aching to tell him from the beginning.

"Spill it, Mosquito," Cab said. "What did the boyfriend tell you?"

Lala didn't blink at the nickname this time. "Troy followed me so we could talk in private. He didn't want Tresa to hear what he had to say, because she wouldn't let him talk about it."

"About what?"

"Apparently there's another couple from the same part of Wisconsin staying at the resort this week. Mark and Hilary Bradley. I checked, and he's right. They have a room that opens right onto the beach. It's not even two hundred yards from where the murder took place."

"Okay," Cab said, waiting for more.

"Troy told me that we needed to talk to the husband before he skipped town. He claimed that if there's anyone in the hotel who might have done this to Glory, it's Mark Bradley."

Cab raised an eyebrow. "Yeah? Based on what? Does this guy have some kind of connection to Glory?"

"Not to Glory," Lala told him, "but to her sister. According to Troy, everyone in Door County knows Mark Bradley. He was a teacher at the high school until he was let go under a cloud last year. The police couldn't bring statutory rape charges, because Tresa wouldn't say a word against him on the record, but the story is, he was having sex with her."

4

Hilary Bradley sat motionless on the sofa in their hotel room as Mark paced in and out of the dusty stream of light through the patio door. They hadn't spoken. She studied the stricken expression on her husband's face. His breathing was fast and loud through his nose; he was scared. It was like a rerun of the previous year, when they'd sat together in their Washington Island home and confronted the rumors about Mark and Tresa.

Not again.

They didn't need to talk to each other to know what was going to happen. Hilary could see it all too clearly. Accusations were about to rain down on Mark like a storm. There would be a knock on the door. Questions. Suspicion. This one would be even worse than the previous year because Mark's name had already been linked to teenaged girls and sex—and because there was no doubt this time about whether anything bad had really happened. There would be no he-said, she-said this year.

A girl was dead on the beach. Someone killed her.

Mark stopped in the middle of the carpet. He'd closed the glass door to the beach, and the air in the room was cold and sterile. Their eyes met. She saw anger and anxiety fighting in his face. He took two steps in his long stride and knelt in front of her. He took both of her hands and squeezed them hard. "I need to say something."

Hilary was calm. "Go ahead."

"I didn't do this," Mark said. "I never thought I'd have to ask this again, but I need you to have faith in me. You have to believe me."

"I do."

He stood up again, relieved, and she

hoped he didn't doubt her sincerity or wonder if she was hiding something behind
her face. She wasn't lying.

A year ago, her friends had called her
naive when she told them that she didn't
think that Mark had slept with Tresa Fischer.
He denied it; she believed him. They'd both
been foolish in letting Tresa get closer to
them than their other students. It was a
mistake Hilary had always sworn to herself
she'd avoid as a teacher, but she and Mark
were new to Door County and anxious to
fit into small-town life. Tresa was sincere,
smart, quiet; she was pretty, but she wasn't
wild or sexual like her younger sister, Glory.
They'd paid attention to her, and Tresa, who
didn't get much attention at home, thrived
on it.

Hilary had realized quickly that Tresa
was developing a schoolgirl crush on her
husband. It wasn't the first time. Women
young and old were drawn to Mark, but
he'd never shown any inclination to cheat.
She hadn't seen Tresa's emotions as a
threat, because she knew the girl too well
and didn't believe Tresa would ever try to
act on her feelings. Her affection for Tresa

made her forget her first rule of teenagers, which was that they weren't girls growing up to be women; they were women in girls' clothes. She also never expected that Tresa's fantasies alone could get her husband into trouble.

Then Tresa's mother, Delia, found her daughter's diary.

When Tresa wasn't dancing, she was writing. Mark was her English and art teacher. He'd encouraged her to write short fiction, and he and Hilary had both read several of her stories, in which she'd created a teenaged detective who was a lot like herself. What neither of them realized was that Tresa had been writing other stories, too. On her computer, she'd invented an imaginary diary in which she related the details of her passionate sexual affair with her teacher. It was erotic and explicit. She described their trysts, how he touched her, how her body responded, the things he told her, the things she told him.

It was Tresa's sexual awakening on the pages of her diary, and it was convincing enough to be real. When Delia Fischer found it on Tresa's computer, she leaped to the obvious conclusion: Mark Bradley was having sex with her seventeen-year-old daughter.

Delia confronted Tresa, but the girl's evasive denial persuaded her mother that Tresa was covering up the truth of the affair. She didn't confront Mark about their relationship; instead, she went directly to the principal, the school board, the police, and the newspapers. In the face of allegations of criminal sexual misconduct, Mark's own denials meant nothing. No one believed him. The intimate detail in the diary spoke for itself. The only thing that saved him from prosecution and jail was Tresa's stubborn insistence that the diary was a fantasy, that there had never been any sexual relationship between herself and Mark. Without her testimony, there was no case to bring to court.

Even so, Tresa's and Mark's denials didn't change many minds in Door County about what had really happened between them. When Tresa talked about Mark, everyone who listened to her could tell that she was in love with him. Her face glowed when she talked about him. To her mother, and to the school authorities, that meant she was protecting him.

Mark escaped without criminal charges, but the principal, teachers, and parents of Fish Creek High School weren't about to leave him in front of a classroom. As a second-year teacher, without tenure, he had essentially no rights under the union contract. At the end of the year, he got what he knew was coming. The ax fell. The nominal excuse was budget cuts, but everyone on the peninsula knew the real reason. They all knew what kind of man Mark Bradley was, and no one was going to let him take advantage of another teenaged girl.

In the wake of Mark's dismissal, Hilary had wanted to quit, too, but that would have left them with no income at all. She also didn't want to give anyone at the school the satisfaction of turning tail and running, as if somehow that would justify what they had done, like an admission of guilt. She stayed. Since that time, though, it had been a long year of hostility. She was nearing the end of her third year in the district, and she knew her own tenure decision would come down soon. Even if they granted her tenure, she and Mark were struggling with the question of whether they wanted to leave. He had no job prospects. She was tired of living under constant suspicion.

What kept them where they were was the fact that they loved their home on Washington Island. They loved Door County. They'd moved from Chicago to the peninsula because it was exactly where they wanted to live. She just didn't know if they could stay in a place where they would never be welcome.

Then there were the doubts. The questions. They followed her everywhere. Even the handful of friends who'd remained on her side sometimes lapsed into awkward silence, as if to say: Are you sure?

Are you sure it was just a fantasy? Did you read the diary? It was so detailed, so precise, so explicit about their sexual encounters. *What if it really happened*?

That was a question Hilary refused to entertain. She never even allowed it to enter her mind. She knew her husband. If he said there was no affair, then there was no affair—but she also knew that Mark was afraid that in the end she'd begin to believe the lies. They would both be consumed by the cloud of judgment.

That was why she'd told him how she felt on the first day and never again. If you have to say it more than once, you don't mean it.

"I trust you."

"Tell me what happened," Hilary said.

Mark shook his head. "Hil, I don't know. I wish I did."

"Start at the beginning. Did you see Glory on the beach?"

He nodded. "Yes."

"Did you talk to her?"

"I did, but it was just for a couple of minutes."

"Why didn't you tell me at breakfast?" she asked, keeping her tone even. She didn't want him to hear an accusation in her voice.

Mark hesitated. "I should have, but I wasn't ready to drag up everything for you again. Or for me. I didn't think it mattered, because nothing happened. I saw her, and then I walked away. As far as I knew, that was the end of the story. I have no idea who killed her."

"What went on between the two of you?"

Mark sat down next to her on the sofa and stared at the carpet. "Glory was drunk. I didn't think it was safe for her to be out there like that, so I tried to persuade her to come back to the hotel with me. She wouldn't go."

Hilary saw the tension in how her husband was holding himself. His body was taut, like a coiled spring. There was something else that he was reluctant to tell her, and she made a guess about what it was. "Glory came on to you, didn't she?"

Mark exhaled in a loud hiss. "Ah, shit."

"Tell me."

"Yes, she kept asking me to have sex with her. I said no."

"I get it," Hilary said. "Look, we both know Glory is the wild one compared to Tresa. I'm sure she liked the idea of trying to seduce the man her sister was in love with."

"Nothing happened," he insisted.

"You already said that."

"Most of it was just talk, but the one thing she did—she took her top off."

Hilary closed her eyes. "What did you do?"

"Nothing. That was it. I gave up trying to get her to go back to the hotel with me. I left." He added, "Things were getting out of control, Hil. I just needed to get away."

"Don't blame yourself," she told him.

"I do. I should have told someone she was out there, but she was threatening to say we had sex. She said no one would believe me, and she was right. I couldn't take the risk, not after last year. I couldn't put myself in the middle of it. Or you."

We're in the middle of it anyway, Hilary thought, but she didn't need to say it out loud. Mark knew the score.

"They're going to come after me," he said. "They know I'm in the hotel. The police are going to paint a bull's-eye on my chest."

"You're probably right," she acknowledged, "but let's not panic, okay? Did anyone see you leaving the room? Did anyone see you on the beach or see you when you came back?"

She watched him mentally retrace his footsteps. "I don't know. There may have been a hotel employee on the patio when I left our room, but that's a couple hundred yards away. I'm not sure whether he saw me or whether he would recognize me."

"Did you see anyone with Glory on the beach?" she asked. "Someone killed her. Whoever it was may have been watching the two of you."

Mark shook his head. "I didn't see anyone."

She heard hesitation in his voice. "But?"

"I don't know. I felt like we were being watched. I felt like Glory saw someone, but I didn't see anyone there."

"Did she talk about anyone else?"

"Just Tresa," he said, "and her boyfriend. Troy Geier."

"What did she say?"

"She talked about Troy being jealous, and she said—well, she said Tresa saw the two of us during the competition, and she got rattled. That was why she didn't do well."

Hilary nodded. She'd actually felt guilty being in the audience during Tresa's performance. Despite everything that had happened, she still liked the girl, and she hated to see her do poorly.

Mark leaned back into the sofa and

stared at the ceiling. The room was gloomy and cold. "So what do I do?"

"Right now, nothing," Hilary said.

"I should tell the police what I know," Mark insisted. He paused. "Or do you think I should shut up? I mean, if no one saw me . . ."

He let the thought drift away, but she knew what he was thinking. If no one saw him on the beach, should he really put his head into the lion's mouth by admitting he was out there with Glory?

"We need to talk to a lawyer," she said. "Right now. Today. Until we do, I think you shouldn't say anything. We don't lie, but we don't volunteer. Okay?"

Mark nodded. "Okay."

"We'll get through this," she said.

He frowned and said what she was thinking. "It's going to be just like last year, Hil, you know that. Everyone's going to think I'm guilty."

"You're not."

"I'm not sure how much more of this we can take."

"I know."

Mark leaned over to embrace her, but

before he could, their heads snapped around. Someone rapped sharply on the door of the hotel room.

Without looking through the peephole, Hilary already knew. It was beginning.

5

Cab Bolton had to knock twice before the attractive blond woman answered the hotel door. When she did, he made a show of checking his notes. "Mrs. Bradley, is that right? Hilary Bradley?"

She smiled politely at him without saying yes or no. "May I help you?"

"My name is Cab Bolton. I'm a detective with the Criminal Investigations Division of the Naples Police Bureau." He flipped open the leather folder for his badge and handed it to her to review, which she did.

"What is this about?" she asked.

"You may not have heard, but there was

a serious crime committed on the beach outside the hotel overnight. A teenaged girl was murdered."

He looked for surprise in her face and didn't see any. She knew exactly why he was there. You could always see intelligence in the eyes, like a window onto the machinery of the mind. Hilary Bradley was a smart woman.

"That's awful," she replied, "but I'm not sure how I can help you."

Cab pointed one of his absurdly long fingers over her shoulder at the glass doors leading to the beach. "Your room looks out on the area where the crime took place."

"I see. Well, come in. I don't have much time, though, and I don't believe I can help you."

Cab ducked his head as he went through the doorway, which was what he had to do with most doorways. Behind him, Hilary Bradley let the heavy door swing shut. As he walked into the center of the room, he was conscious of the closed bathroom door and the noise of the shower. He noted two open suitcases pushed against the wall, half-filled with clothes. Laid messily on top of one suitcase was a bright yellow men's tank top with a logo that read D.C. He continued past the unmade king-sized bed to the far end of the room, where he had a view through the patio doors out on the Gulf. The beach was sheltered by a web of palm trees with drooping fronds. He saw the crime scene team at work near the water. He recognized Lala's jet black hair.

"Beautiful view," he commented.

Behind him, Hilary said nothing. He slid open the door and stepped onto the square stone patio, which was dusty with sand and featured two lounge chairs and a metal table. From the patio, you could walk down two steps to a walkway that led to the beach. He eyed the hotel rooms on either side of him, which all had similar waterfront access. It would be easy to come and go undetected in the middle of the night.

When he went back inside the hotel room, he noticed that both suitcases were now closed. Hilary Bradley waited with her arms folded over her chest. She made a point of not sitting down and not suggesting that he sit down. She wasn't interested in prolonging his visit.

"The guests in this wing are all potential

witnesses," Cab told her. "We're interviewing everyone."

"I'm afraid I didn't see anything."

"Nothing at all?"

"No, I didn't look out overnight."

"Did you hear anything?"

"I was asleep."

"Did you get up at all during the night? Did you go to the bathroom?"

"No, I didn't."

Cab nodded and let the polite dance play out between them. He wanted to put her at ease and not imply that there was anything special about his visit. She and her husband were two of many guests looking out on the beach, not suspects with a connection to the victim. Even so, he had little doubt that she'd already seen through him and was waiting for the other shoe to drop.

He studied the woman in front of him. Hilary Bradley was smart, and she was pretty, too, in a mature, self-confident way. He figured she was a few years older than he was, maybe forty, or maybe knocking on the door. Her face was rounded, with blue eyes and thin black glasses, and dangly earrings that looked like red sour balls. She wore a simple burgundy top, tan slacks that emphasized her long legs, and sandals. Despite her shoulder-length blond hair, she wasn't a classic bombshell, and he didn't imagine she ever had been one, even when she was younger. Nonetheless, she had the sexiness of a woman who knew she was two steps ahead of you in just about everything.

She looked up at Cab. Based on his height, almost everyone did. He could feel her taking his measure, even as he did the same to her. Most people underestimated him. They thought he was a spoiled beach bum; he didn't look like a man who'd graduated from UCLA in three years. They saw the pomade in his hair, the exfoliated complexion, the earring, the suit, all of it on top of a lean body that made the ceilings look low, and they wrote him off as a shallow metrosexual. He didn't care. He also didn't think Hilary Bradley was the kind of woman who would make that mistake about him. Her face was a mask as she stared at him, revealing nothing, but she had the look of someone who didn't misjudge an enemy.

Cab glanced at the hotel roster in his hand. "You're not here alone, are you, Mrs. Bradley? Your husband is with you?"

Her voice was cool. "That's right."

"His name is Mark?"

"Yes."

"Is that him I hear in the shower?"

"Of course."

"I'd like to talk to him, too," Cab told her.

"I doubt he saw anything either."

"How do you know? You said you were sleeping."

Hilary got a little frown on her face, as if she were annoyed at being outfoxed by his question. "If my husband saw anything overnight, he would have told me."

"I still need to speak to him myself."

"We'll try to find you before we leave, Detective," she said, with a glance at the door to the room. Her meaning was clear: She wanted the interview to be over.

Cab stroked the point of his protruding chin and stayed where he was. "Do you mind if I ask what you two are doing in Naples?"

"We're on vacation. I'm a high school teacher, and it's spring break. We had some hotel points on our credit card, so we used them to get a free week here."

"Nice. How did you happen to choose this hotel?"

He watched her think through her response, as if she were trying to understand his motives in asking. Or maybe she was trying to assess how little she could say without lying. "In addition to my academic teaching, I've been a dance coach for many years," she explained finally. "Some of my former students were performing in a college competition at the hotel this week."

"So when you're not coaching dance, what do you teach?"

"Math."

"Math was never my subject," Cab said, which was a lie. He'd aced every class in school. Except geography. His brain didn't process directions. He needed a map to find his own bathroom. "Where do you teach?" he continued.

"It's a high school in Door County, Wisconsin."

"Where exactly is that?" he asked.

"If you look at a map of Wisconsin, Door County is like the state's pinky finger. The peninsula juts out into the water between Green Bay and Lake Michigan."

"Sounds like a pretty spot."

"It is."

"Do you know a family named Fischer living in that area?"

Hilary's blue eyes turned cold. Cab figured that Lake Michigan was probably cold, but it would have felt as balmy as the Gulf compared to this woman's eyes.

"Do you think I'm stupid, Detective?"

"I'm sorry?"

"I know you're not here because we happen to have a room that overlooks the beach. I don't imagine the lead detective on a murder investigation does the grunt work of interviewing hundreds of potential witnesses."

Cab smiled. "There's a lot more grunt work than you might imagine."

"Someone already told me that the dead girl is Glory Fischer, and someone obviously told *you* about me and my husband."

"Yes, your husband's name did come up."

"Mark had nothing to do with this."

"Maybe not, but you can understand my concern, given his relationship with the Fischers. Particularly the dead girl's sister."

"There was no relationship," Hilary insisted. "The accusations against him were false."

"I don't really care," Cab told her. "It raises suspicions about him either way."

"My husband didn't kill Glory Fischer."

"Except we've already established that you were sleeping, Mrs. Bradley, so you really don't know what he was doing."

"I know Mark."

"Nobody knows anybody," Cab said.

"Maybe you don't, but I do. I'm not going to see my husband subjected to another witch hunt, Detective."

"I don't do witch hunts. I don't believe what anyone tells me, good or bad, until I can prove it one way or another. So right now, what I'd really like is for your husband to stop hiding behind the bathroom door pretending he's in the shower, and instead have him come out and talk to me."

"I'll let him know you stopped by," Hilary said.

"If your husband has nothing to hide, let him answer a few questions."

"You've already lied about your reasons for coming here, Detective," she snapped. "So spare me the 'nothing to hide' speech. Mark and I don't trust people any more than you do. We've learned that we can only trust each other."

"I've seen a lot of wives who think that," Cab told her. "Most of them wind up disappointed."

"Do I look like a naive twenty-five-year-old to you?"

"No, you don't," he said.

"Then don't treat me like one."

Cab dug in his pocket. "Your husband is going to have to answer questions sooner or later. Here's my card. Have him call me. Don't bother leaving town today, because you'll just have to fly back here again."

"Are you finished?"

"No. If your husband won't answer questions, then I'll ask you. Did you know Glory Fischer and her sister were here at this hotel?"

"I've said all I plan to say for now," Hilary told him.

"You're painting a target on your husband's back. You're both acting guilty."

"You've already said you won't believe me, so why should I say anything at all?"

Before he could answer, Cab heard his phone ringing in the inner pocket of his suit coat. It was Lala on the other end of the line. He listened to her, and he knew that the Cuban cop's voice was loud enough to be heard throughout the room. He didn't care. When he hung up, he noticed the changed expression in Hilary Bradley's eyes. She'd followed the thread of his conversation, and she was uncomfortable now . . . and worried.

"I don't think you were sleeping, Mrs. Bradley," he told her. "I think you woke up, and your husband was gone."

"Good-bye, Detective."

"That was one of my investigators on the phone. You heard what she said. We have a witness. A hotel employee who saw Glory Fischer going out to the beach. The question is, what else did he see?"

Hilary said nothing.

Cab rapped his foot against one of the suitcases on the floor, which had been open when he first arrived. "I saw the yellow tank top. Is that what your husband was wearing? That's hard to miss, even at night."

She folded her arms again and was quiet. Her face grew flushed.

Cab walked past her toward the hotel room door. As he passed the closed door to the bathroom, he pounded on it loudly.

"Don't think you can hide behind your wife forever, Mr. Bradley. The sooner you talk to me, the easier this will be."

When there was no answer, he left the room.

Mark waited until he heard the hotel room door slam shut. He emerged from the bathroom, fully dressed, and found his wife sitting on the end of the bed. Her face was tired and stressed. He'd seen that look for weeks last year, as they'd both faced his accusers at the school.

"You heard?" she asked.

Mark nodded. His frustration bubbled over, and he felt like punching the wall. "He's right. I should have come out and talked to him. I don't like to hide, Hil. That's not me."

She shook her head. "He was just pushing your buttons. He was trying to goad us into saying something stupid. Look, I'll call my father and get the name of a defense attorney here in Naples. There are probably Chicago snowbirds all over the place down here. We'll talk to him and then decide what to do next."

"Guilty people hire lawyers."

"No, smart people do," she told him. "This is about protecting ourselves."

Mark glanced at the suitcases on the floor. "We can't leave."

"I'll call the desk and see if we can stay another night."

"Does he really have a witness? Or was that just a mind game?"

"I don't know. I heard the person on the phone say that someone at the hotel saw Glory, but they could have staged the call."

"If someone saw me with her . . ." Mark's voice trailed off.

"If someone saw you with her, maybe they saw you leave, too. Maybe they saw who really did this."

6

Lala Mosqueda had added black sunglasses to her all-black outfit as the sun got higher over the resort. Her skin had a glistening sheen of sweat. It was Florida, and there was nothing you could do to escape the humidity. Cab had assumed he would get used to it over time, but in two years, he never had. By the time he was done shaving every morning, his skin was already damp. Every surface he touched felt moist and swollen. When he left his high-rise beachfront condo, his clothes stuck to his body, and he felt the thick air draining his energy. The only creatures that thrived in the damp climate were the cockroaches and spiders, which grew like mutants.

Lala leaned against the trunk of a palm tree near a wide tiled walkway that led toward the water. The sky overhead was postcard blue. On the hotel terrace, Cab saw a goateed hotel employee with greased black hair sitting alone at a patio table, nervously pushing around the floral centerpiece and swigging water from a plastic Aquafina bottle. The man shifted and crossed his legs uncomfortably in the deck chair. White cuffs jutted out from the sleeves of his red hotel jacket, and he wore black slacks. He was in his early twenties.

Cab met Lala, who was texting on her phone. "That our witness?" he asked.

"Yeah, his name's Ronnie Trask. He's a bartender at the pool bar."

"He looks ready to pee his pants. Is he feeling guilty about something?"

Lala holstered her phone and pushed up her sunglasses, which were slipping on her sweaty face. "The other employees tell me he's a smooth operator with girls who like to party too much. The younger the better. But if he was involved in what happened to Glory, I think he would have kept his mouth shut rather than stick himself in the middle of our investigation."

"Have we found anyone else who saw anything?"

"Not yet."

"What about cameras? Don't they have any cameras out here?"

"Not too many spring breakers want hotels with eyes in the sky, you know? What happens on the beach stays on the beach. The only place they've got a camera is the lobby. We're looking at the tape." She added, "What about Mark Bradley? You get anything from him?"

Cab tugged the buttons of his dress shirt away from his sticky chest and adjusted the gold chain on his neck. He smelled chlorine from the nearby hotel pool. "He ducked me. I talked to the wife."

"And?"

"And they're not crazy about answering questions. Let's dig up whatever we can about this incident in Door County last year. Call the sheriff up there. I want to know more about it before I talk to the sister and the boyfriend, okay?"

"Sure," Lala said. Cab turned away toward

Ronnie Trask, but Lala called after him. "Hey, Cab?"

"What?

"I saw your mother in a movie last night."

It was an innocuous comment for her to make, but every time they deviated from work talk, he felt gravity again, as if the two of them were circling the black hole. He recognized it was a big leap for Lala even to say it, and he wondered if she had an ulterior motive.

"Yeah? Which one?"

"Sapphirica."

Cab nodded. "That was twenty years ago. I was on set with her when she filmed that one in Italy. It won a special jury prize at Sundance."

"Did you travel with her a lot growing up?" Lala asked.

"Yeah, it was like being an army brat without the guns."

"You look a lot like her," she told him.

"Thanks."

"So why aren't you an actor like her, anyway? You've got the looks for it."

"My head kept getting cropped out of the frame."

Lala laughed, but it was hollow. She went back to her phone as if he'd dismissed her with an expletive, rather than a joke. He thought about saying something more, but he didn't. He was his mother's son.

Tarla Bolton was a fierce loner, and so was Cab. She'd never married and never even acknowledged the man who got her pregnant. He didn't know who his father was, although he had narrowed the field to a few likely candidates based on the film she was making at the time he was conceived. He'd never asked her for the truth.

Cab had never married either, although he'd gotten close. Once. Her name was Vivian Frost. Vivian was the reason he made a point of never trusting anyone. She was the reason he was always running.

Cab took a seat at the patio table opposite Ronnie Trask and pushed the chair back to make room for his long legs. He squinted up at the sky and wiped his forehead with his handkerchief. "God, this heat, huh?"

The bartender sucked on his lower lip and drummed the glass tabletop with his nails. "Yeah."

"I'm Cab Bolton. Naples police."

"Ronnie Trask. Naples bartender." He added, "What kind of a name is Cab?"

"Born in one," Cab said.

"Oh."

"You work here at the hotel, Ronnie?"

The man drained a last swallow from his Aquafina. "Yeah. I work nights, I work afternoons, whenever they slot me in. Crappy schedule. I sleep somewhere in the middle."

"You always work at the bar?"

"Yeah."

"So tell me what happened last night."

Trask shrugged. "I closed up the pool bar at one o'clock. I was cleaning everything up. It must have been close to one thirty when I saw a teenaged girl in a bikini on the far side of the terrace. She went through the palm trees out to the beach. End of story."

"Was anyone else around? Employees or guests?"

"Nah, once the booze shuts down, the guests go to bed. I was the only one out here."

"Tell me about the girl."

"What about her? She was a cute kid. Young."

"Was she alone?" Cab asked.

"Yeah, she was alone."

"Did you talk to her?"

Trask scowled and got defensive. "Hey, I told you, she was on the opposite side of the terrace, didn't I? How was I supposed to talk to her?"

Cab let the man stew before he went on. "You could see her clearly, though?"

"Clear enough, sure."

"Could you see what she had in her hand?"

"Like what? She wasn't carrying anything."

"So where'd she get the wine, Ronnie? We found a bottle of wine with the body."

Trask tugged at his goatee. "Oh, yeah. She had a bottle of wine with her. I forgot that."

Cab slid a pen from inside his suitcoat pocket. He reached across the table and rolled Trask's empty water bottle toward him with the cap of the pen. "We're testing the wine bottle we found near the body for fingerprints. I think we'll test your water bottle, too."

Trask cursed under his breath. "Shit. Okay. I sold her the wine."

"She was sixteen."

"I didn't know she was underage."

"You already said she looked young."

"Fuck it," Trask breathed. "So what, man? She gave me thirty bucks. These kids down here will always find a way to score booze, you know? Why shouldn't I get a slice? The hotel writes it off as breakage, and everyone's happy."

"Not Glory Fischer. She's not happy, she's dead. Had she been drinking before you sold her the wine?"

Trask shook his head. "She looked sober enough."

"Did you help her drink it?"

His eyes widened. "Say what?"

"Did you have a drink with her? Did you go with her to the beach?"

"Shit, no," he hissed.

"Word is, you do well with the girls who come down here, Ronnie."

"Yeah, well, I don't do jailbait."

"So you did know she was underage."

"Oh, for Christ's sake, sure I did. Big deal. I didn't go to the beach with her. I took her money, opened the bottle for her, and she went off by herself. That's all. That is *all*."

Cab heard the panic in Trask's voice. "What did the girl say to you?"

"Nothing. She wanted a drink. That's it."

"Did she say why she was out there?"

"No, man, no."

"How did she behave?"

"What do you mean?"

"I mean, how was she acting? Upset? Happy? Angry?"

Trask ran his hands over his slick-backed hair. "Oh, hell, I don't know. She was kind of flirty, you know, the way teenagers are. Smiling at me. Adjusting her swimsuit. Acting all girlish. I think she figured she could tease the wine out of me."

"Did you take that as an invitation?"

"Huh?"

Cab leaned across the table. "Did you assume she wanted sex?"

"Look, whatever she wanted, I didn't give it to her."

"Okay, Ronnie. How long was she at the bar?"

"A couple minutes, no more. She bought the wine, and she headed down to the beach."

"Did you see anyone else after the girl

showed up?" Cab asked. "Did anyone else follow her?"

Trask shook his head. "Nobody."

"You didn't see anyone else outside?"

"I left right after the girl did. My shift was over. I locked up, and I cleared out."

"What about before she arrived? Did anyone go past you out to the beach during the half hour you were cleaning up?"

Trask stared at the sky, as if he were hoping he would remember someone, but he came up blank. "I didn't see anybody."

"So you were the only other person out there with the girl who was murdered."

"Hey!" he barked. "I'm telling you, I left. I didn't follow her, and I didn't see anybody else. The clerk behind the desk saw me leave through the lobby. You can ask her. Hell, you've got hotels up and down this beach. Anybody could have done this."

Cab knew that Trask was right. That was what worried him. Beach bodies meant thousands of suspects. If you didn't get lucky with forensics or witnesses, it was almost impossible to make a case. He thought about Glory Fischer on the beach. About Mark Bradley. He'd hoped Trask would have spotted Bradley outside, or at least someone matching Bradley's description. He could have prompted Trask by mentioning the yellow tank top, but he guessed that the bartender would take that tidbit of information and spit it back the way jailhouse informants do, to give Cab whatever he wanted to hear. Yellow tank top? Yeah, come to think of it, I did see someone out there wearing something like that.

"Did you recognize the girl?" Cab asked Trask.

"What do you mean?"

"She was at the hotel for several days. Had you seen her before last night?"

He nodded. "Actually, yeah."

"You sound pretty sure. This place was crawling with teenaged girls this week."

"Well, she almost knocked me over."

Cab cocked his head. "When was this?"

"Friday night. I was bringing a case of wine to the pool bar from the restaurant, and out of nowhere, this girl sprints past me. I mean, there I was big as life, but it was like she didn't even see me. I almost dropped the bottles. Pissed me off. You want to shout at these kids sometimes, but the hotel won't let you do that."

"Why was she running?"

"I don't know."

"Did anyone else run after her?"

Trask shook his head. "Nope. There were people milling around down by the event center, hitting the bathrooms, going outside to smoke, that kind of thing. No one paid any attention to the girl, as far as I could tell. She just came at me down the corridor past the outside windows like some bat out of hell."

"She came toward the lobby from the event center?"

"Yeah."

"That's where they were doing all the dance competitions, right?"

"Yeah, I guess."

"Did she stop and talk to you when she ran into you?"

"No, she kept going. I dodged out of the way, and she didn't apologize or anything. She looked really freaked."

"Excuse me?"

"Freaked," Trask told him. "Scared. She was crying. It was like she'd seen a ghost."

7

———————

Oh, man," Amy Leigh announced. "Did you see this?"

Amy sat in the next-to-last row of the Green Bay team bus. The window beside her was cracked open, and Amy could smell exhaust fumes as the bus sputtered through the foothills of southern Tennessee. Unlike the Wisconsin campus, where winter had barely loosened its grip, the trees and mountains here were lush green.

When her roommate kept typing on her laptop without responding, Amy nudged the girl with her shoulder. "Hey, look at this."

Katie Monroe glanced away from the

screen impatiently. "What? I've got to get this article done. I need to e-mail it to the paper by three o'clock."

"Yeah, but check this out," Amy insisted.

She held out her iPhone to her friend, who squinted at the online news feed. After reading the first couple of lines of the story, she took the phone from Amy's hand and scrolled to the next paragraph. "Wow. Is that where we were?"

"Yes, that was our hotel. A girl was murdered there last night."

Katie blew the bangs out of her eyes with a quick puff of breath. "It says here she was drinking on the beach in the middle of the night. Jeez, not smart."

"It still sucks."

"Of course it does. Life sucks."

Katie handed back the phone and returned to the document on her laptop. Amy wanted to talk more, but when her roommate was writing, you didn't interrupt her. Amy reclined her head against the musty foam of her seat cushion and stared into space down the dimly lit aisle of the bus. Her body jolted with the bumps of the road. Her eyes felt heavy, but she couldn't sleep, unlike most of the other girls, who were draped over the seats. It had been an adrenaline-packed week, and she hadn't come down to earth yet. Her dance ensemble from Green Bay had taken first runner-up in the competition—almost the winners, but not quite. She figured they would nail the prize next year, because the hotshot team from Louisville that beat them would be losing most of its first-string girls when they graduated in June.

Amy was a junior. One more year to go.

She tried to clear her mind, but the image of the girl dead on the beach outside their Naples hotel intruded on her brain. That was who Amy was. She was a psychology major, always analyzing people and trying to figure out what made them tick. When she thought about the girl, she imagined the world through her eyes, seeing the empty stretch of Gulf sand. Here was a teenager four years younger than Amy was, alone, assaulted, killed. Katie was right; it was dumb to go off by the water and drink in the middle of the night. Amy had done stupid things, too, though.

"Hey." Her roommate waved a hand in front of Amy's face, breaking her trance. "You okay?"

"Yeah."

"You still thinking about it?"

"Yeah."

"You can't take on the whole world's problems, you know," she chided her.

"I know."

"So knock it off."

Katie was the reporter, who looked at the world like a black-and-white encyclopedia of facts. Amy was the eye candy with the soft center, the one who felt too much, laughed too much, and cried too much. She secretly believed that her roommate would make a better therapist than she would herself, because Katie didn't let people get to her. She kept her distance, cool and objective. Amy dove in headfirst.

"She was from Wisconsin," Amy said.

"Who?" Katie asked, dragging her eyes away from her article. She'd tagged along with the team to write about the competition for the Green Bay newspaper. It made for a free spring-break trip, with the paper picking up the hotel tab and her parents not worrying about what they didn't know.

"The girl. Glory Fischer. The one who was killed. She was from Wisconsin."

"Okay."

"Door County," Amy added. "That's not even an hour away from us."

"Where are you going with this?"

"I don't know."

"Did you know her? Was she on one of the dance teams from the other schools?"

Amy shook her head. "No."

"Then what's up with you?"

"It's just a feeling."

Amy took out her phone again and ran a Google search to see if any other newspapers had picked up the story. She saw that the Milwaukee paper had already filed a report on the murder. Local girl killed on vacation—that was big news back home. The *Journal Sentinel* reporter had tracked down a yearbook photo of Glory Fischer that was posted with the article. Amy stared at the dead girl's face, and her sense of unease grew. She told herself that she'd made a mistake and that she was confusing Glory with someone else, but she didn't think so.

Glory was the girl she'd seen. The one Gary was talking to. She'd seen them together that Friday night.

"What's wrong?" Katie asked.

"I recognize her," Amy said.

"The girl who was killed?"

"I saw her. I remember her from the hotel."

Katie looked dubious. She grabbed Amy's phone again and eyed Glory's picture herself. "Are you sure? Yearbook pictures make everybody look like everybody else."

"I know, but I think it was her."

Katie closed the cover of her laptop and shifted in her seat so she was sideways, pulling her skinny legs underneath her. She was medium height and lean compared to her roommate, who had a big-boned, muscular frame. Katie poked Amy in the shoulder.

"Okay, so you saw her. I know it's creepy."

"It's not just that. It's who I saw her with."

"Who?"

Amy opened her mouth and closed it. Her eyes darted around the bus to see if he was nearby, and her full pink lips sank into a frown. "This is crazy. I must be wrong."

"Come on, you're freaking me out, Ames."

"It's nothing," Amy insisted. "Write your article."

"Tell me."

"There's nothing to tell. I'm a dork."

"You think that's news to me? Spill it. What did you see?"

"Forget it. You've got a deadline. I'm going to sleep."

Amy gave her a hollow smile. She waited until her roommate was typing again, and then she closed her eyes. Her blond curls splashed across her face. She tried to convince herself that she was being stupid. She wasn't sure of anything; she'd made a mistake. Or if she hadn't made a mistake, maybe it didn't mean anything at all. What she'd seen, what she'd heard, was a misunderstanding.

She breathed slowly in and out. She was certain she wouldn't be able to sleep, but the vibrations and noise worked on her brain like a drug. Glory Fischer went away. The bus went away. She was back at school in Green Bay.

In her dream, Amy practiced a dance routine, solo, in the center of the gymnasium, moving to the beat of a song by Kristinia DeBarge. She knew her moves were feline and sexy, and she wished she had a crowd to admire her, but the gym was almost deserted. She could see only one person in the uppermost row of the bleachers, almost invisible in the shadows, and she realized it was her old dance teacher from high school in Chicago. Hilary Bradley. She hadn't seen Hilary in years, but she looked the same, still pretty and confident, exactly the kind of woman Amy wanted to become. Hilary waved at her and cheered.

Seeing Hilary made Amy want to hit every step, to show off how good she was. She wanted to dazzle her and make her proud. Instead, she felt her body lose the rhythm of the music. Every motion felt awkward and clumsy. It was as if she couldn't remember dancing before in her life, as if her mind had erased every move she'd ever learned. She stuttered. Tripped. Stopped. Her face grew hot and red with embarrassment. She stood in the center of the lacquered floor, frozen.

The music ended. The gym had an echoing silence. She stared up at Hilary and wanted to shout an apology to her for failing, but Hilary was gone. The bleachers were empty.

She heard sarcastic clapping, slow and

mean. She realized someone else was with her in the gym. She wasn't alone.

It was him. Her coach. Gary Jensen.

Gary walked toward her. He wore a black turtleneck and gray slacks. His black dress shoes tapped on the floor. He smiled at her, but his smile was like the snarl of a wolf. She heard herself begin to explain and ask for another chance, but he said nothing at all. He came up to her until he was so close that she smelled burnt coffee on his breath, and then, still smiling, he wrapped both hands firmly around her neck and began to choke her. His fingers were strong. Amy struggled. Pushed back. Fought. She tried to scream and couldn't. She waved at the bleachers, but no one was there to rescue her. Amy sucked for breath and found nothing. Her eyes closed.

Then they opened.

Amy awoke with a start, lurching forward, her heart racing. She was back on the bus, which rattled on as if nothing had happened while she was gone. Outside, she saw highway signs for Nashville. She'd been asleep for almost two hours. The other girls on the bus were still sleeping, too, their tousled heads dipping off the seats into the aisles. Beside her, Katie dozed, her article finished, her laptop closed and packed away.

Amy cupped her hands over her face. The dream had unnerved her.

"You okay?"

Amy jumped as a hand touched her arm. She looked up and saw Gary Jensen standing over her, and she recoiled. He smiled at her, and it was the same hideous smile from her dream. His hand on her bare skin was warm. She had to remind herself that it wasn't real. He hadn't been trying to kill her a moment ago.

"Oh," she said. "Oh, yeah, I'm fine. Bad dream."

"Take it easy, Amy," he said. "We'll be stopping for a break soon."

"Good."

"Great job in Florida. You were a star."

"Thanks," she said.

Gary winked. He continued toward the front of the bus, and she watched him go. She wondered if he knew how much she disliked him. He'd been the dance coach and a physical education instructor at Green Bay ever since she'd arrived at the school three years ago from her high school in

Highland Park. He knew his stuff, and as a coach, he had an eye for what worked and what didn't in their routines. That wasn't the only thing for which he had an eye, though. The girls on the team all talked about it in the locker room. The coach was a flirt. A lech. He was in his middle forties, widowed, with a balding crown of brown hair that she knew he colored. He biked. He stayed in shape, and he made sure everyone knew it with his tight shirts and jeans. He was the kind of teacher who never made an overt pass, because the university frowned on teacher-student relationships, but you got the signal in his attitude and his grin. She'd felt the come-on when she was a freshman in the way he looked at her and touched her. If you wanted more, he had more to give.

Gary sat down near the driver and glanced back down the dark aisle of the bus and saw Amy watching him. Something in her expression obviously made him uncomfortable. Normally, she had warm blue eyes and an easy, infectious laugh, but not now. He looked as if he were about to come toward her again, with a question on his lips. Instead, he turned away and sank into his seat.

"What is it?"

Amy glanced at her roommate, who had awakened and was staring at her. *It's nothing,* Amy told herself—but she didn't think it was nothing.

"I saw Gary talking to the girl who was killed," she murmured.

"Gary? Are you sure? When?"

"Last night. Late, around eleven o'clock. I saw them on the terrace of the hotel. At first, I thought it was one of the Green Bay girls, but then I realized it wasn't."

"Did you hear what they were talking about?"

"No, but Glory looked upset." Amy shook her head. "If it was really her. I just don't know."

"All the coaches talk to the girls from different schools," Katie reminded her.

"But this is Gary."

"I know you don't like him, but that doesn't mean anything. I profiled him in the paper last year. He didn't seem like such a bad guy."

"What about the thing with his wife?" Amy asked.

"Wasn't that an accident?"

"There were rumors."

"I think you're getting paranoid."

"There's more," Amy said. "There's something else."

"What?"

Amy could see the back of Gary's head. A reading light bounced off his shiny pate. It was almost as if he could feel her stare, because he looked up into the driver's mirror. She saw his pupils glow the way a cat's eyes shined at night, and she felt a shiver of fear as their eyes met. He reached up and turned off the light above him.

"My room was next to his," Amy said.

"Yeah, so?"

"I couldn't sleep last night. I was awake sometime after three in the morning, and I heard footsteps in the hallway. I didn't look out, but I heard Gary's door. He was going back into his room in the middle of the night."

8

Cab sipped a Starbucks iced latte through a straw and watched Tresa Fischer and Troy Geier behind the window of the interview room. It was late afternoon on Sunday, and the police headquarters building on Riverside was uncomfortably warm, the way it usually was. The counselor who had been with the two teenagers for most of the day had departed ten minutes earlier, leaving them alone. Cab had received word that Delia Fischer, Glory's mother, had landed at the Fort Myers airport, and he wanted a chance to sit down with Tresa and Troy individually before Delia arrived. He knew that once the victim's mother was in the building, the two kids would be more guarded with their answers.

He took his coffee into the interview room, where Tresa and Troy waited in silence, ignoring each other. Tresa sat at the interview table and drank a can of Diet Sprite. Troy, who was a fleshy sixteen-year-old, drank root beer and leaned against the wall. To Cab, the silence between them felt hostile. They weren't friends.

"Your mom's on her way," Cab informed Tresa. "She'll be here in an hour or so."

Tresa didn't look happy with the news. Cab guessed that the girl would bear the brunt of guilt and blame when Delia arrived. As the older sister, she'd failed. *I trusted Glory with you, and now she's dead.*

"Troy, I'm going to ask you to wait outside," Cab told the boy. "Hang around, though, because I need to talk to you, too. Ask one of the officers to fix you up with some chips or a sandwich if you're hungry."

Troy grunted and pushed himself off the wall. He put down his empty bottle of root beer and left the room without a word. Tresa's eyes followed him, and Cab thought his first impression about the two of them was correct. Tresa didn't like her sister's boyfriend.

Cab sat down at the interview table opposite Tresa and gave the girl a reassuring smile. At nineteen, Tresa still had a naive way about her that made her look younger than she was. She was extremely skinny for her height, which made Cab wonder if she had an eating disorder. She played with her straight red hair between her fingers and stared vacantly at the wooden table. Her pretty blue eyes were rimmed in red, and her face was dirty with streaks of tears. In talking with her earlier, Cab had found her to be painfully shy, a loner without a support network of friends. He'd offered to ask some of the other dancers from River Falls to stay behind with her, but Tresa hadn't given him a single name of someone who was close to her. It was also obvious in her answers about her family that her sister, Glory, got most of the attention from their mother. Tresa, who was clearly artistic and smart, had been left to live in her own world.

"I know it's been a long day," he told her. "I appreciate you being patient with us. It probably seems like we cover the same stuff over and over, and you know what? We do. But that's usually how we find the details that help us figure out what really happened."

"Do you have any idea who did this to Glory?" Tresa asked. Her voice was barely louder than a whisper.

"I wish I could say yes, but we don't, not yet," Cab admitted. "I'd like to make sure that we haven't missed anything important. Okay?"

Tresa nodded without enthusiasm. "Okay."

"You came down on a university bus from River Falls with the rest of your team last Monday and Tuesday, is that right? And Troy and Glory drove down from Door County on Tuesday and Wednesday?"

"Yes, they took turns and drove straight through," Tresa answered. "They got here around ten o'clock Wednesday morning."

"Did anyone else from Door County come down at the same time?"

"No."

"Did Glory and Troy bunk with you in your room?"

"Uh-huh." She added quickly, as if her mother were already listening, "Glory and I shared the bed, and Troy took the couch."

Cab noticed the girl fidgeting. She was hiding things, and she wasn't good at it. "Tresa, I need to know who your sister was, even if there's stuff that wasn't so good. Understand?"

Her eyes narrowed. "What do you mean?"

"I mean, teenagers do things that their parents don't always know about. I don't care about that. I just need to know if Glory was involved in anything that might have gotten her into trouble. See?"

"Yeah, I get it."

"So it doesn't matter to me who slept in what bed, but I would like to know if Glory and Troy were having sex while they were here."

Tresa hesitated. "What difference does that make?"

"Maybe none at all," Cab admitted, "but I need to get the whole picture."

"Okay, yes."

"You know that for a fact?"

"Yeah, I came back from practice once,

and they were in bed together." Her tone was pinched and unhappy.

"You sound like you didn't approve," Cab said.

"It wasn't any of my business."

"Did you not like the idea of your little sister having sex, or did you not like the idea of her having sex with Troy?"

Tresa shrugged. Her grief couldn't overcome years of sibling rivalry. "Glory's been having sex since she was thirteen."

"With Troy?"

"No, Troy's just the latest."

"What about drugs?" Cab asked.

"Yeah, Glory liked to do grass. That was her, not me. I'm not into it."

"Okay. How about this week? Did Glory use any drugs while she was here?"

Tresa nodded. "She and Troy scored some on the way down. I told her not to use it in the room, because I didn't want to get in trouble, but I smelled it. I told Troy to get rid of it, but I don't know if he did."

"You don't like him, do you?"

"Who, Troy? He's okay, just dumb. He's a stupid puppy dog, and Glory liked to yank his chain."

"Was it serious between them?"

"He thought it was, but I don't think she did."

"Did you see Glory with anyone else while she was at the hotel? Did she hook up with any other boys?"

"Not while I was around, but I wouldn't put it past her, either." Tresa lowered her eyes and looked guilty. "I shouldn't talk like that. I'm sorry. You must think I'm a shitty sister."

"No, I don't. I asked you to be honest with me."

Tresa nodded. She wiped her nose with the back of her hand.

"Would Troy get jealous if he saw Glory flirting with someone else?" Cab went on.

"You mean, would he hurt her? I don't think so. Troy's a big kid, but he's a wuss. Everybody treats him like dirt."

Cab thought that was an interesting comment. In his experience, when you poked the bear long enough, eventually it poked back. "When you woke up early this morning and Glory wasn't in bed, was Troy in the room?"

"Yeah, he was zonked out on the couch, snoring away."

"Was he there all night?"

"As far as I know."

"Could he have left and come back without waking you up?"

"I don't know. I guess. I don't think he did, but I can't be sure."

"Let's start at Saturday night and move backward, okay? I know we've covered some of this before, but bear with me. Was Glory in your room when you went to sleep?"

Tresa sighed. "No. Last time I saw her on Saturday, she was swimming in the hotel pool. That was around nine o'clock. I went back to the room to read. Troy came back about half an hour later by himself, because he wanted to watch a movie on HBO. I crashed around eleven thirty, and Glory wasn't back yet. Troy had already fallen asleep in front of the TV."

"Were you worried that Glory hadn't come back?"

"No. Glory stays out late a lot."

"Was she hanging out with anyone else at the pool?"

"Not while I was there. There were a few girls from the various teams in the water. Some guys, too. Glory didn't know any of them, but I don't know what happened after I left."

Cab nodded. They were still trying to identify the other teenagers who'd been in the pool on Saturday night, but so far, they'd had no luck. "You told me earlier that Glory was acting strangely on Saturday."

"I guess so. Yeah."

"Describe it again for me, okay?"

Tresa rubbed her eyes with both hands, fighting off exhaustion. "She looked upset. Kind of angry, too. She snapped at Troy a lot during the day. I wasn't really paying attention. I was upset, too, because I choked during my performance on Friday, so I kept to myself that day. I just figured Glory was pissed off because we had to go home, you know? No more sunny Florida, back to dreary cold Wisconsin."

"Did she say anything to you about what was bothering her?"

"Glory wouldn't do that."

"What about on Friday? How did she seem to you then?"

"During the day, fine."

"And at night?"

Tresa shook her head. "I don't know. I didn't see her in the evening. I mean, I saw her right after I blew it in the competition, but I didn't want to talk. She gave me a hug, but I needed to get out of there. I don't know what she did after I split. I went off on the beach by myself, and I didn't get back to the room until real late. She was already in bed."

"Was Troy with Glory at your performance on Friday night?"

"Troy? At a girls' dance show? No way."

"Where was he?"

"In the room, I guess."

"I talked to a hotel employee who saw Glory at the event center on Friday night," Cab told her. "He said she ran past him, and she was crying, and she looked scared. Do you have any idea why?"

"I already told you, *no,*" Tresa insisted. She twisted the loose fabric of her T-shirt into a knot, and her eyes grew teary again. "Don't you think I'd tell you if I knew what happened? When I left her, she was fine. I was the one who was upset."

Cab eased back in the chair, his long legs stretching out, his arms behind his head. He watched the girl in front of him, and he thought about all of the messes, insecurities, fears, jealousy, pettiness, and traumas of being young. There were so many nicks and cuts that felt deep even when they were shallow and left scars that you could pick at years later. To him, Tresa looked like a typical teenaged girl, screwed up in all the ordinary ways, but looks could be deceiving.

He brought his arms back onto the table and leaned forward. "Tell me about Mark Bradley," he said.

Tresa recoiled in surprise. "What about him? How do you know about him?"

"It doesn't matter."

"Troy told you, didn't he? That stupid jerk."

"I know Mark Bradley and his wife were here at the hotel this week. I know you and he have some history together."

Tresa pushed her chair back, physically adding distance between them. "That was all a misunderstanding."

"He was a teacher accused of having an affair with a seventeen-year-old student."

"It didn't happen like that!" Tresa retorted. "God, all of you are so stupid. No one listened to me. No one believed me."

"He lost his job."

"Yes, and it was my fault!"

"Are you in love with him?"

Tresa's face flushed. She tugged at her dirty red hair. "That's none of your business."

"Mark Bradley was at your performance on Friday night, wasn't he? Is that why you didn't do well? Did it make you nervous having him there?"

"I choked. The pressure got to me. That's all."

"What was Mr. Bradley's relationship with Glory?" Cab asked.

"None. There was no relationship."

"Did Glory believe that you and Mark Bradley were having an affair?"

"No! That was my mother. That was all her stupid idea."

"Did you or Glory have any contact with Bradley this week? Or with his wife?"

Tresa shook her head fiercely. "No. I didn't even know he was there until I saw him on Friday. We didn't talk to each other."

"Are you protecting him?" Cab asked.

"From what? He didn't do anything." She hooded her eyes and stared at her lap. "Are we done? I need to find my mom."

"Sure. I understand. You can go."

Cab watched her as she gathered up used tissues from the table in her fist and left the room. Her face was a pouty mask. He realized that he'd reached a roadblock with Tresa anyway. The girl was shutting him out. What frustrated him was that he still didn't know a thing about Mark Bradley, and he didn't have any evidence about the man, only rumors.

He was an enigma. Was he an angry predator with a predilection for teenaged girls or an innocent victim?

Maybe Glory Fischer, drunk, sexually promiscuous, had met Mark Bradley on the beach on Saturday night. Maybe it was an accident or a deliberate rendezvous.

Maybe.

If Glory did meet him, what happened next?

9

It was him," Troy Geier insisted, bolting out of his chair. "Bradley. He did it. I know it was him. That son of a bitch."

Cab held up his hands. "Sit down, Troy. Okay? Take it easy."

The burly sixteen-year-old paced back and forth between the walls of the interview room and then slumped heavily into the chair again. "Sorry."

"You did the right thing by telling us about Mark Bradley. I appreciate it. Right now, though, I want to talk about Glory."

Troy's big head bobbed. "Sure. Okay."

Cab sucked out more of his iced latte,

which had melted and was mostly warm. He gave Troy a minute to calm down. The teenager was a beefy kid with a broad face dotted by pimples. He had wavy brown hair covered by a baseball cap, which he wore backward. His flabby chest and huge fore-arms stretched out the green fabric on his Packers T-shirt. As Cab watched, Troy stuck an index finger between his teeth and chewed on the nail.

"This is my fault," Troy murmured, his mouth full.

"Why do you say that?"

"I never should have left her alone."

"You're being pretty hard on yourself," Cab told him.

"Yeah, but we argued, and it was stupid. She wanted to stay and swim, and I really wanted to see this Will Ferrell movie on TV. I told her to come with me, but she wouldn't, so I just left. Then the movie sucked, and I fell asleep anyway."

"You never realized Glory hadn't come back?"

"I was out like a light. The bartender snuck me a couple beers for a few bucks. I crashed."

The bartender. Ronnie Trask obviously

had a thriving business funneling alcohol to minors. It was a spring-break tradition in Florida.

"Tell me a little more about Glory, okay?" Cab went on. "How long have you known her?"

Troy shrugged. "Pretty much all our lives. We go to school together. Both of our families have been in Door County forever. We're natives, but now it's all rich fibs moving in, buying up the land."

"Fibs?" Cab asked.

"Fucking Illinois bastards."

Cab smothered a smile. "When did the two of you start dating?"

"Last year. She had a bad summer breakup. She was dating an older kid who was staying on the peninsula for the summer. A tourist. She figured he loved her, but he was just in it for the sex. After he dumped her, I think she decided she wanted someone who really wanted her. That's me."

"What was Glory like?" Cab asked.

"She was super cute. Really outgoing, doing things a mile a minute. Me, I'm pretty shy, and I always felt like I was running to keep up with her."

"Was it exclusive between the two of you?"

"Oh, yeah. Definitely."

Cab was dubious. "Are you sure it was exclusive for her?"

"Absolutely. After school, we were going to get married."

"Was that your plan or hers?"

"Mine, but Glory wanted it, too."

"Most girls aren't looking for a serious relationship at sixteen," Cab told him.

"Well, I loved her, and she loved me," Troy insisted. "We weren't thinking about college. You go to college, and they ship your job overseas these days. I figured we'd both work at my dad's restaurant after we graduated. That's where Glory's mom works. When my dad retires, I figure I'll take it over, although he tells me I can't handle it."

"Why does he say that?"

Troy frowned. "Oh, he never thinks I can do anything right. He still thinks I'm a dumb kid."

Cab thought about what Tresa had said. Troy's father didn't treat him well, and neither did Glory. Despite his size, Troy looked like the kind of boy who got kicked in the head and came back on his knees for more punishment. At some point, all the kicks probably felt like love.

"I heard that Glory was a wild child," Cab told him. "Sex, drugs, drinking. Is that true?"

"Sure, Glory liked to do crazy stuff sometimes. Drugs once in a while, but nothing heavy. She'd get me to sneak some wine from my dad's restaurant on the weekends. So what?"

"Sex?"

"Yeah, we had sex. Glory was cool about it."

"It sounds like you two were pretty different, though."

"I told you, I had to run to keep up with her, because she was always going two hundred miles an hour. It was like I was along for the ride sometimes."

Or maybe you were just the designated driver, Cab thought. He understood the attraction for Troy, who had obviously worshipped Glory for most of his life. It wasn't as clear to him what Glory saw in Troy. The teenager was plain, and simple in a farm-boy way, but he had the attraction of being utterly pliable. Cab guessed that

Troy's role in their relationship was to do whatever Glory wanted him to do.

"Whose idea was it to go to Florida?" Cab asked.

"Glory's," Troy said.

"To see Tresa dance?"

Troy shrugged. "Yeah, that's what she told her mom so she'd say yes. Really, she just wanted a vacation in Florida, you know? Swim and sun."

"How was it for you two hanging out with Tresa? Big sister, little sister. Did that slow you guys down?"

"Tresa's pretty low-key compared to Glory. Always with her nose in a book. We didn't spend much time with her. She was practicing a lot for the dance thing anyway."

"Were there any arguments?"

"Between Glory and Tresa? No."

"How about between you and Glory?"

Troy flushed. "Just on Saturday. Glory was really pissy with me. I don't know why. That's one of the reasons I left her at the pool. She'd been giving me shit all day over the stupidest things."

"Did something happen?"

"No, that's the thing. We'd been having a great week."

"When did it start?" Cab asked.

"I told you, it was Saturday."

"Not Friday night?"

Troy stopped. He chewed his fingers again. "Well, that night she went to see Tresa dance, and I stayed back at the room watching basketball. Glory came back around ten thirty."

"How did she seem?"

"She was quiet," Troy said.

"Upset? Angry?"

"I'm not really sure," Troy admitted. "I was watching the game. I know I should have paid more attention, but I didn't. I found out the next morning that Tresa hadn't done well in the dance competition, and I figured Glory was just disappointed for her."

"What did Glory do when she came back to the room?"

"She took a shower. I remember thinking she was in there a long time."

"Then what?"

"She came out and sat down next to me. She had a towel on, and I thought, maybe she wanted to have sex, but when I tried to kiss her, she pushed me away. I asked what was wrong."

"What did she say?" Cab asked.

"She said it was nothing."

"That's all?"

"She told me that she saw someone she knew." Troy blinked nervously, as if he realized he'd forgotten to share something important.

"Someone she knew?" Cab leaned forward. *"Who?"*

"She didn't say."

"Did you ask?"

"Yeah, but she didn't answer me. She didn't make it sound like it was a big deal. She just said she was going to bed. "

"Did you ask her about it the next day?"

"No, she didn't say anything more about it."

Cab laid this nugget of information down in his head and stared at it. *Someone she knew?*

Not a stranger. Someone who sent her running through the dark corridor of the hotel in tears, nearly colliding with the hotel bartender, Ronnie Trask.

The next night Glory wound up dead on the beach.

It still could have been a random assault. Boy meets girl, boy rapes girl, boy kills girl. Sometimes it happened that way, but Cab was beginning to wonder if Glory's death involved a more personal motive.

"Did you see anyone you knew during the week?" he asked. "Anyone that Glory would have known?"

Troy shook his head. "Nobody," he said. "Nobody except Mark Bradley."

10

Cab found a bag of organic plantain chips in the drawer of his desk. He ate them one at a time as he reviewed the interview notes gathered by the police with guests at the hotel throughout the day. He also reviewed the crime scene photos, and as he studied the body and imagined how Glory Fischer had ended up in the surf, topless, strangled, he found his memory going back to Vivian Frost.

The girl he'd asked to marry him. The girl who had said yes.

It wasn't a big leap from Glory to Vivian,

not that they looked alike or had anything in common about their lives. What they shared was the similarity of their deaths.

Glory, a dead body on a beach in Florida. Vivian, a dead body on a beach north of Barcelona.

A dozen years later, he could still picture her face, vivid both in life and in death. He'd always assumed that the memory would fade, but it didn't work out that way, no matter how much he tried to outrun her. She followed him as he moved from place to place and job to job. Whenever he felt the urge to let down his guard, Vivian was there, reminding him that trust was a dangerous thing. Lala and the other women in his life since then had paid the price.

That was another reason he hated beach bodies. They came with a lot of baggage.

Vivian Frost. His mother had warned him that he was falling too hard and too fast. Tarla Bolton was a Hollywood actress, which meant by definition that everyone was trying to screw her. She'd tried to protect her son with an emotional suit of armor, but back then, in his early twenties, Cab was still young enough and naive enough that he hadn't accepted her view of the world. He hadn't been burned as a cop or as a man, and he didn't want to end up as disillusioned as his mother. Vivian changed all that.

He'd gone to Barcelona as a newly minted special agent with the FBI, dispatched to Spain to liaise with local authorities in the search for an American fugitive named Diego Martin, who'd been caught on videotape in a bar on Las Ramblas. The waitress he'd interviewed at the bar, a divorced woman ten years older than he was, languid and sensual, was Vivian Frost. She was a British expat who'd married a Spanish computer executive and been kicked out of his estate after she got tired of his cheating. Like most Londoners who moved to Spain, she had no interest in going home, even after she'd found herself alone and mostly penniless in the city. She worked long hours. She smoked incessantly, the way everyone smoked there, and it gave her a husky voice. She had bone white skin in a city of golden faces. She glided where everyone else walked.

After an interview in which Cab decided that Vivian knew nothing about the man he was chasing, he went back to the bar that same night and sought her out again for his own purposes. She professed to be utterly uninterested in men, and the more she rejected him, the more he returned to the bar like a moth to a flame. He became obsessed with Vivian. He fell completely under her spell.

The fruitless investigation dragged on for weeks, then months. There were no more leads. The American fugitive, Diego Martin, had gone underground or left the city entirely. Cab's superiors in the Bureau wanted him back home if the trail was cold, but he gave them hope where there was mostly no hope at all. What he wanted was more time with Vivian. His lies bought him three more months, and slowly, cold indifference on her part gave way to a few casual dates and then to their first night of sex in her cramped, smoky apartment, with the neighbors listening on the other side of the thin walls. He found her to be uninhibited, making love with abandon, unlike any other woman he'd known. After that night, they were inseparable.

When the Bureau finally ran out of patience with his delays, he quit. He walked

away from the job he'd sought from his
earliest days out of college. His mother told
him he was insane and that he didn't understand women or how manipulative they
could be. He told her he was in love. Madly
in love, and that was the truth. He told her
he was staying in Spain and getting married. Looking back, he remembered those
days as the one time in his life when he'd
been innocent enough to be happy.

Vivian Frost. Beautiful, funny, intense,
wicked, graceful, faithless, and treacherous.
Vivian Frost, who'd wound up dead with a
bullet in her brain on a deserted beach north
of the city.

Unlike Glory Fischer, though, there was
no mystery for Cab about who had killed
her.

He'd done it himself.

"Someone she knew?" Lala Mosqueda
asked as she sat down next to Cab's desk.
"Troy said that Glory recognized someone?"

Cab sat with his hands cupped over his
nose and mouth. He didn't hear her. Instead,
he heard a roaring noise that sounded like

the Spanish surf, and he saw Vivian's face again, eyes open, entry wound in her forehead.

"Hey, Cab?"

He blinked as Lala said his name and heard concern in her voice. He rocked back in his chair and reached for the bag of plantain chips, but it was empty. He forced a smile onto his face. "Moh-skee-toh," he said, drawing out her nickname, talking loudly enough that others in the department turned to watch them.

Lala shook her head in disgust, then leaned closer and hissed under her breath, "Why do you do that?"

"What?"

"Push people away."

"Is that what I'm doing?" he asked.

"You know damn well it is."

She was right. He'd become an expert at keeping women on the far side of his safety zone. Those he liked, like Lala, were the ones he worked hardest to alienate.

"Fine," she said, when he didn't reply. "Be an ass. I don't care."

Cab wanted to apologize, but he swallowed it down. "Yes, Glory saw someone she knew," he said. "That's the story. Troy thinks she was talking about Mark Bradley, but he's just guessing. Glory didn't say who it was."

Lala waited before she said anything else. When she spoke again, the softness in her tone was gone, replaced by cool detachment. She'd opened the door; he'd slammed it shut. That was his pattern.

"Do you think Troy is telling the truth?" she asked calmly. "Did Glory really say anything like that, or is he simply trying to point us toward Bradley?"

Cab shrugged. "I don't believe Troy is enough of a deep thinker to come up with a plan like that. He says he's certain that Bradley killed her. If he was going to lie, I think he'd just say that Glory said she saw Bradley on Friday night."

"What about Tresa? Did Glory say anything to her about recognizing someone?"

"Apparently not."

"Well, Troy backs up what Ronnie Trask told us," Lala pointed out. "Glory saw someone she knew, and for some reason, she freaked and ran."

"Too bad, I was hoping Trask made the

whole thing up," Cab said. "The question is who Glory saw."

"Could it be Mark Bradley?"

"Sure it could. Troy's guessing, but he may be right. What did you find out about Bradley and the Fischers?"

"I called the sheriff's department in Sturgeon Bay, which is the county seat for Door County," Lala told him. "I talked to the sheriff himself, tough old goat named Felix Reich. He said that pretty much everyone in the department believed Bradley was having sex with the girl. That would have been a misdemeanor assault in Wisconsin given their ages, but Tresa was adamant in denying the affair. No witness, no charges. Even so, Bradley wound up losing his teaching job. Tresa's mother kept calling for his head. The district called it budgetary, but no one expected the school to keep him on. He hasn't found another job."

"So he's got reason to be pissed off."

"Yes, but I'm not seeing any motive for him to kill Glory," Lala pointed out. "No one accused them of having an affair."

"That doesn't mean they weren't."

"You're pretty cynical, Cab. For what it's

worth, the sheriff had some things to tell me about Glory, too."

Cab raised an eyebrow. "Such as?"

"She was a troubled kid. Multiple arrests going back several years."

"Several years? She's only sixteen."

"Yeah, her first drug possession bust was at age twelve, and it wasn't her last. The local cops think she may have done some selling, too, although she was never actually charged. She was involved in vandalism, shoplifting, B&E. It's not a happy picture."

"Have there been any problems reported at the hotel this week?"

"The usual minor stuff. Glory's name didn't come up."

"If we can pin this on someone, the defense is going to say Glory got involved with the local drug scene or hooked up with the wrong crowd."

"That may be what happened," Lala told him.

"Yeah, I know. Maybe. Let's keep talking to everyone we can, but put an emphasis on girls who were at the event center on Friday. I want to see if we can find someone who saw Glory before she went running toward Ronnie Trask. I want to know who she recognized."

"The Bradleys are the only other people in the hotel from Door County," Lala said.

"I know, but it sounds like this is a tourist area in Wisconsin. If Glory saw someone who *visited* the area, but doesn't live there, that opens up a lot more possibilities. Particularly with a bunch of college kids staying at the hotel."

"We're looking for a needle, and the haystack just got a lot bigger," Lala said.

"There were a lot of people at that competition. Someone other than Ronnie Trask is bound to remember a girl running through the hall crying."

Lala shrugged. "Teenaged girls do that all the time."

"Yeah? I don't picture you doing that, Mosquito."

"I was tougher than most," she replied. After a moment, she added, "You have a nickname, too, you know."

"Catch-a-Cab Bolton," he said, nodding.

"You know about it?"

"Sure. I know about the betting pool,

too. When will Cab quit and move on? It's been two years. The welcome mat is wearing thin."

"It's nothing to be proud of, Cab."

"Did I say I was?" he asked.

"You never say anything."

Cab opened his mouth to fire off a sarcastic reply, but for once, he let it go. Then he asked, "So what week do you have in the pool?"

"Next week, actually," she said without smiling.

"That soon?"

"I know you better than the others."

It was as if she'd given him a terminal diagnosis. "Well, if anyone's going to make money on me, I'd like it to be you."

Lala didn't answer. Behind his shoulder, someone gestured to her, and she climbed out of the chair and chatted with a uniformed officer in the doorway of the investigation division. When she returned, she was all business again. There wasn't time for anything personal between them, and he wondered if she was relieved by the interruption.

"You've got a visitor in the interview room," Lala told him.

"Delia Fischer?" Cab asked, checking his watch. "She's right on time."

Lala shook her head. "It's not her. It's Mark Bradley—and his attorney. They want to talk."

11

Hilary Bradley emerged out of the Naples police headquarters building into the bright sunshine. She slipped sunglasses onto her face. She stopped on the circular brick walkway and hesitated, unsure where to go. Mark was upstairs, and she assumed the police would interview him for an hour or more. At least he wasn't alone in facing their questions. She liked the attorney they'd hired; he was a bulldog, according to her father. It was the smart thing to do to get help, but she knew Mark was right about perceptions. The police would see him with a lawyer, and one word would jump into their heads.

Guilty.

She'd heard it in her father's voice, too. Her parents had stood behind Mark last year, because Hilary had convinced them he was innocent. Now she'd gone back to the well, and this time, there was an unspoken doubt in their reactions. They didn't know what to believe anymore. They probably wondered what *she* believed and whether she was being honest about her suspicions. Still, they had stayed silent.

Hilary stood in front of the pink stone building and saw a police cruiser glide up to the curb twenty feet away. The front passenger door opened, and she stiffened with dismay as she recognized the woman climbing out.

It was Delia Fischer. Glory and Tresa's mother.

Delia's head swiveled as she looked up at the two-story building, and her eyes were vacant, as if she were lost and overwhelmed. Her stare passed over Hilary without recognition, and then, slowly, horribly, it came back and landed on her and froze there. They confronted each other across the sidewalk. Hilary took off her sunglasses and nodded at Delia. There was no point in pretending.

Glory's mother approached without saying a word. She was several inches shorter than Hilary. She looked beaten and exhausted, with deep worry lines furrowed in her brow and around her mouth. Her cheaply colored blond hair was tied in a ponytail. She was rail thin, a woman in her midforties who looked ten years older than she was. She wore spiral earrings made from aluminum cans; that was one of the eBay businesses she used to earn extra money in the off-season. If you weren't rich in Door County, you always had something going on the side to make ends meet. Hilary had bought some of Delia's jewelry as a gesture of friendship the previous year, before everything erupted over Tresa.

Despite their history with her, Hilary had never been able to hate Delia. She understood the emotions that drove her. Delia was a single mother struggling with two teenaged girls, fiercely proud and protective. Hilary could easily imagine the stunned fury Delia had felt in reading Tresa's diary, believing that her child had been exploited and abused by a man she trusted. All of that anger had landed on Mark's head, regardless of Tresa's denials. If Hilary had been in her shoes, she probably would have done exactly what Delia did—launch a crusade to destroy the man who had stolen her daughter's innocence.

Hilary didn't expect that Delia had ever suffered a pang of doubt. She was convinced she was right and would never believe otherwise. In her eyes, Mark was a child molester who deserved the ostracism he'd received. Now, like a bad dream, he was back in her life, violating her family again in an even more terrible way than before.

"Mrs. Fischer, I'm so sorry," Hilary began. "Mark and I—"

"Don't you dare." Delia cut her off in a voice hoarse with bitterness. "Don't you dare defend him. Don't you dare speak his name in front of me."

"Mrs. Fischer, please. I understand your grief."

Delia's cheeks flushed. "You don't know the first thing about my grief, so don't pretend that you do. Everyone says how smart and attractive you are, and all I see is a woman who's a fool. You're married to a monster, and you won't admit it to yourself. Maybe if you'd opened your eyes last year, my daughter would still be alive."

"Mark didn't do this," Hilary told her, but she knew her words were useless, and she almost regretted saying them.

Delia flinched, as if she might slap Hilary's face, but then she closed her eyes and breathed heavily. When she opened her eyes again, Hilary felt a wave of violence breaching the small space between them. The policeman coughed, like a gentle warning to draw their attention, but Delia ignored him.

"I almost feel sorry for you," Delia said, "trying to convince yourself that he's not evil. But then I think, you must know, and you just don't care. Because you're *not* a fool, are you? You really are as smart as everyone says. So I guess you've just decided you'll protect him regardless of what he's done."

Hilary noticed other people coming and going from the police building who had begun to stop and watch them. She felt a burn of embarrassment. It was familiar; she'd learned to expect stares from strangers. She knew that Delia was lashing out in pain and desperation, and she knew that there was no way for her to bridge the divide with this woman. If anyone could comfort her, it wasn't Hilary. Her presence just made it worse.

"I should go," Hilary told her. "You may not believe me, and it doesn't matter, but I'm very sorry about Glory. You're right, I can't understand your grief. I can't imagine losing your daughter. It may mean nothing coming from me, but I'm hurting for you. I really am."

Delia's face was impassive. Hilary hadn't expected to reach her. The policeman approached Delia and touched her elbow in order to guide her toward the door of the building. Delia allowed herself to be led, but she pulled away abruptly and jabbed a finger at Hilary's face.

"Do you have any idea what he took from me?" she shouted. "Glory was my baby! I almost lost her once, and I thought I got a second chance. Now I've lost her all over again because of you and your husband. He took her away from me. It wasn't enough what he did to Tresa. He had to go after my baby, too."

Hilary said nothing. She stood there and let the woman vent her despair.

"Mrs. Fischer," the policeman murmured. "Let's go inside."

"Well, you know what?" Delia continued, screaming at Hilary now. "He's not going to get away with it! I promise you that. Not again. This time I'm going to make sure he pays for what he did to us!"

Troy Geier sat on a concrete bench in the lobby of the police building. His back was slumped as he leaned forward, and his hands dangled between his thick thighs. Tresa sat next to him, as straight as a board. They both watched the altercation outside between Delia Fischer and Hilary Bradley, and the noise of Delia's screaming cut through the glass windows, clear and shrill.

Tresa didn't look at Troy. "You told my mom, didn't you? You told her you thought that Mark did this."

"What the hell was I supposed to say?" he muttered.

"You bastard. Mark would never hurt Glory."

Troy blew out his breath in a disgusted sigh. "Shit, Tresa, listen to yourself. You're more concerned with your teacher boyfriend than you are with your sister. Glory's dead, and you're still protecting him. What do you think? He's going to leave his wife for you?"

"You don't know anything," Tresa snapped.

"No? Who the hell else do you think did this?"

"It wasn't Mark."

Troy shook his head. "You're actually jealous, aren't you? Jesus. The fucking pervert was stalking Glory, and all you can think about is yourself."

"You have no idea what you're talking about. There was nothing between Mark and Glory."

"Oh, come on, Bradley obviously had a hard-on for her, the son of a bitch."

Tresa shoved him, which was like pushing against the trunk of a tree. "Shut up, Troy, just shut your mouth. You think Glory was so sweet? Do you have any idea how many boys she slept with?"

"Don't talk like that!"

"What, I'm supposed to pretend she was a princess because she's dead? Sorry, I won't do that. She probably came on to some biker on the beach, or she tried to buy drugs from the wrong person. Wake up, Troy. Glory used you like she used everyone."

"I loved her," Troy murmured.

"I loved her, too, but she got a free pass for everything. Mom's probably out there right now wishing it was me that died."

"That's crazy."

"Yeah? For the last six years, I've been invisible. Everything's been about Glory. Ever since the fire."

"She almost died," Troy protested.

"I know. She almost died. Poor Glory, she's screwed up because of the fire. Well, fuck her."

Tresa bit her lip, knowing she'd gone too far. It had always been that way between the two sisters. Sometimes you didn't know they loved each other because of all the bitterness and jealousy. Troy watched tears slip down Tresa's face, which she wiped away with her shirt. He felt like crying, too, but he hadn't been able to squeeze out any tears since he heard the news. He was just numb—and guilty.

He saw Glory's mom storm into the foyer. When she got angry, you didn't want to be in Mrs. Fischer's line of fire, because she had a temper. He cringed to see her, because he knew what she would say. Their eyes met, and he could feel all of her grief and rage unloading silently on him across the room. Before he could say anything or explain, she gestured to Tresa and opened her arms. Tresa ran to her, and the two of them embraced and sobbed together. A minute earlier, Tresa had been bitter about Glory; now, she moaned into her mother's shoulder as they shared the loss.

Delia stroked Tresa's red hair. Troy sat there, ignored. It was probably better that way, with her not looking at him. Eventually, though, Glory's mom detached herself and told Tresa to get her a glass of water. Delia Fischer waited until Tresa was gone, and then she descended on Troy.

He climbed to his feet, and the tears finally came. "Mrs. Fischer, listen, I—"

"Don't make excuses with me, Troy," Delia said, practically spitting at him. "You promised me, didn't you? What did you say? You said you'd protect her. You said I didn't need to worry."

"I know, it's just that I didn't—I mean, Glory didn't come back—" Troy's voice cracked. He hated himself for being weak. He hated himself for having failed her.

"You knew that pervert, that rapist, was right here at the resort, and you left Glory alone? Are you crazy?"

"Tresa says she doesn't think that Bradley would have done this," Troy protested meekly.

"Tresa? What the hell do I care what Tresa thinks about Mark Bradley? That man brainwashed her into his bed. I know men like him. I know what they do to teen-aged girls. This is about you, Troy. I trusted you. *I trusted you.* You told me you'd protect my baby, and she's dead. You let her die."

For a husky kid, Troy felt himself getting smaller and smaller, until he thought he could shrink into the tiniest hole in the earth and disappear. "I'm so sorry, Mrs. Fischer," he pleaded. "Really."

Glory's mom slapped him. Her fingers clapped against his cheek so hard that he stumbled backward. His hand flew to his face, which stung like he'd been attacked by wasps. He opened his mouth to say something, to say anything, and he had nothing to say to her at all.

"Your father's right about you," Mrs. Fischer sneered. "You are completely fucking useless."

She turned on her heel and stalked away, leaving him alone and in tears. Troy sank onto the bench again and covered his face in his hands. He thought about Glory, and he realized that everyone was right. Mrs. Fischer was right. His dad was right. He'd had a chance to prove himself, and he'd failed.

He really was useless.

12

Cab found Mark Bradley inside the interview room, along with a rotund older man who sported a lion's mane of curly gray hair and a devilishly pointed goatee. He was impeccably dressed in a gray suit with a buttoned vest and a pink tie. As Cab entered, the older man jumped to his feet with a spry bounce, hopped around the wooden table, and extended a hand. Cab shook it and felt his finger bones groaning under the man's iron grip.

"Archibald Gale," the attorney announced. "I don't believe we've had the pleasure before, Detective Bolton."

Cab sat down and studied the man's eyes, which twinkled behind tiny owlish glasses. "Meeting a lawyer really isn't my idea of pleasure, Mr. Gale."

"Ah, you're funny, Detective. I like that."

"Are you new to Florida, Mr. Gale? I thought I knew all the local criminal attorneys." Cab said the word "criminal" with a small smile directed at Mark Bradley.

"I've just begun wintering here. My other home is in Duluth, Minnesota."

"I'm not familiar with that area," Cab admitted.

"It's a beautiful place, but we've had an unusually high murder rate in recent years. That's a mixed blessing if you're a lawyer." Gale put an arm around the shoulder of a well-built man seated beside him, whose face was smoky with caged anger. "Detective Bolton, this is Mark Bradley."

"Mr. Bradley, I didn't recognize you without the shower going."

Cab smiled, and Bradley shot him a look of naked resentment.

"Detective, we're here as a courtesy," Gale interjected. "I hope we'll all be polite."

"It's just that I'm anxious to hear Mr. Bradley speak," Cab went on. "Whenever

I'm around him, he seems to have other people talking for him."

"This was a mistake," Bradley said, getting out of the chair.

Gale put a gentle hand on his shoulder and eased him back into his seat. "Don't worry, Mark. Let's just focus on the unfortunate business at hand and provide whatever information we can."

Bradley didn't hide his impatience. Instinctively, as a result, Cab proceeded slowly. He pushed back his chair, crossed his long legs, and picked up a yellow pad of handwritten notes. Under the guise of reviewing them, he studied Mark Bradley over the top of the pad. Bradley wore a red collared polo shirt and tan dress slacks. He had the easy, unconscious grace of an athlete when he moved and looked like a man who was comfortable in his own skin. He was attractive, but not in a Hollywood way like Cab or in the macho way that some athletes exuded. He was simply good-looking without thinking about it. His brown hair was cut short without much care. He wouldn't have been caught dead with an earring or a gold chain or cologne. His forehead and nose were so pink with sunburn that he may as well have said, *I like the sun. Screw cancer.*

"You look familiar, Mr. Bradley," Cab told him. "Do I know you from somewhere?"

"I was on the PGA tour for a few years in my twenties," Bradley replied.

"Really? Why did you give it up?"

"I injured ligaments in my shoulder in a car accident about eight years ago. It doesn't restrict my day-to-day activities, but I no longer have the precision I need to be a pro."

"I'm sorry to hear it," Cab said. "Why go from golf to teaching? I assume you could coach or give lessons or something along those lines. You'd make a lot more money, wouldn't you?"

"I was a professional golfer, Detective. When you've done that, the idea of helping fifty-something investment bankers go from a thirty-six to a twenty-eight handicap doesn't sound too attractive."

"And teaching?"

"I like working with kids. I like the flexibility of having my summers off. You may not think there are athletes who enjoy painting on the beach or talking about Henry Fielding or Chaucer, but you know what? Some of us do."

Without changing the expression on his face, Cab struck like a snake. "Tresa Fischer ended all of that for you, though, didn't she?"

He saw Gale's hand lightly cover Bradley's wrist, as if to send his client a message. *Stay calm.*

"That wasn't Tresa's fault," Bradley said.

"Whose fault was it?"

"I'm not sure it was anybody's fault. If you're a male teacher these days, people have a bias to believe just about anything bad that gets said about you. It doesn't matter whether it's true."

"That must be infuriating. I mean, first you lose one career, then another. I'd be pissed off at somebody."

Gale leaned forward. "Excuse me, Detective, but this doesn't seem to have a lot to do with your investigation."

"I'm interested in your client's state of mind, Mr. Gale. I think if I were in his shoes, I'd be angry at how I was treated."

"I was," Bradley admitted before his lawyer could stop him. "I am. That has nothing to do with Tresa or Glory."

"Did you have a sexual relationship with Tresa Fischer?" Cab asked, watching Bradley's face.

"No."

"What about Glory Fischer?"

"No."

"Have you ever had sex with a girl under eighteen?"

Bradley cocked his head. "What, in my life? Do you want to know when I lost my virginity? Do you want to know everybody I dated in high school?"

"I think we'll skip that question, Detective," Gale interjected.

"I'm suggesting that athletes and teachers both have to deal with underage girls, Mr. Bradley," Cab went on. "You've had girls making passes at you your whole life. You've had girls trying to manipulate you. Come on, it must happen all the time. It has to feed your ego."

"I'm married to a mature, beautiful, independent woman who's a hell of a lot smarter than I am," Bradley retorted. "*That* feeds my ego."

Cab pursed his lips in surprise. He hadn't expected that response, and it sounded sincere. However, he'd known some accomplished liars in his life. Starting with a girl in Barcelona named Vivian Frost.

"Many athletes look at women with

contempt, Mr. Bradley. You figure if they don't respect themselves, why should you?"

"I wanted something more meaningful, Detective, and I found it. I hope you're as lucky as I am."

"Well, here's my problem. Glory Fischer is dead. You lost your job, and you're pretty much hated in the community where you live, all because of the Fischer family. You had a room overlooking the beach where Glory was killed. Those are big coincidences."

"Wrong," Bradley snapped. He ticked off his responses on his fingers. "The Fischer family did not fire me. The principal and the school district did. I bear no ill will at all toward Tresa or her mother, and certainly not toward Glory. It's no coincidence at all that I'm at the same hotel as Tresa, because she's a dancer, and my wife coaches dance. As for my hotel room, half the rooms in the building overlook the beach."

"But you were out on the beach last night, weren't you?" Cab asked. "You met Glory Fischer there."

Gale jumped in quickly before Bradley could say a word. "Sorry, Detective, that topic is off-limits."

"Excuse me?"

"Mr. Bradley will not answer your questions about where he was overnight," Gale informed him sharply. "I've instructed him to say nothing. We're not saying he went out on the beach, we're not saying he didn't. We're not saying he met Glory, we're not saying he didn't. No info. No answers. Nothing."

"In other words, he was out there," Cab retorted.

"In other words, if you think he was out there, then you better be prepared to prove it," Gale said. "We're not going to do your work for you."

"We have a witness who saw him."

Gale wasn't fooled. "Good for you, Detective. If you have a witness, you trot him out. In the meantime, Mr. Bradley isn't answering any questions about his actions last night. The most important thing is that Mark did not kill Glory Fischer."

"If he was out there, then he may know something that can help our investigation," Cab reminded him. He looked at Mark Bradley. "Did you think about that, Mr. Bradley? A girl is dead. If you didn't kill her, someone else did. If you're the kind of man you say you are, then I'd think you would feel a moral obligation to tell us anything you saw."

Cab saw a genuine conflict in Bradley's face. The man wanted to talk. Or maybe Bradley thought he was smart enough to deflect suspicion by appearing cooperative. It didn't matter. Gale shut it down.

"We're done, Detective," the lawyer announced. "Obviously, if Mark knew anything that would be relevant and important to your investigation, I would have advised him to share that information with you. You can conclude from his silence on this matter that he doesn't."

"Neither of you is in a position to make that call," Cab told him. "Mr. Bradley, if you saw Glory Fischer on the beach and you did *not* kill her, then you can give us a time at which we know she was alive. That will help us pinpoint the time of death."

Bradley glanced at Gale, who shook his head.

"Give me some help here, Mr. Bradley," Cab insisted. "I think you're a man who stands up and does the right thing."

Gale got out of his chair and reached for Bradley's arm. "Let's go."

Bradley remained seated, staring calmly at Cab. "Theoretically," he began.

"Mark, *stop*."

"Theoretically," Bradley continued, ignoring his attorney, "on nights when I can't sleep, I sometimes get up and clear my head around two thirty in the morning. If I do, I'm usually back by a few minutes after three."

"Did you do that last night?" Cab asked. "Did you arrange to meet Glory?"

"No, I didn't."

"But you did see her on the beach."

"That's it, Detective," Gale interrupted. "Mark, we're going. Now. Come on."

Bradley got to his feet, still staring at Cab. He was sending him a message, and it was obvious to Cab that his suspicions were correct. Mark Bradley had been with Glory Fischer in the middle of the night.

"I'm going to send a police officer to your hotel room to make sure nothing is removed. Based on your responses today, I'm sure we'll be able to get a search warrant."

"My responses?" Bradley asked.

"I think a judge will conclude what you and I both know to be true. You left your room last night. You met Glory Fischer."

"Mr. Bradley isn't changing his travel plans to accommodate your fishing expedition," Gale told Cab. "Tomorrow, he and his wife are going home to Door County."

"Running away won't get you off the hook, Mr. Bradley," Cab said.

"I never run away," Bradley snapped.

"I'm glad, because I may just follow you back to Wisconsin. If you won't talk to me, I'm sure there are people who will."

Gale smiled at him and steered Bradley toward the door. "If you go, enjoy the view, Detective. Just don't have any conversations with Mr. Bradley. I'm sure you know that anything he tells you wouldn't be admissible, now that he's represented by counsel."

"Of course." Cab added, "Tell me one other thing, Mr. Bradley."

Bradley stopped and looked at Cab suspiciously. "What?"

"Exactly why do they call it Door County?"

Bradley laughed without humor. "The peninsula juts out into the water between Lake Michigan and Green Bay. The area where the waters come together at the tip of the land is extremely treacherous. A lot of people have lost their lives in those waters. So the passage got the French name *Porte des morts*."

"I'm afraid I studied Spanish and German, not French," Cab said.

"It means Death's Door."

13

Sheriff Felix Reich drove his Chevy Tahoe off the Washington Island ferry, and the vehicle clanged over the ship's metal gate onto the mainland at the tip of Door County in Northport. The crossing through the Death's Door passage had been rough, but Reich had made the journey thousands of times in his life, and he was immune to the jockeying of the waves. Most of the travelers on winter weekday mornings were locals who had iron stomachs even in the worst weather. On this crossing, Reich had shared the ferry with only three other vehicles bound for the peninsula.

Reich turned off Highway 42 beyond the port onto a gravel road known as Port des Morts Drive. He drove between winter trees that clawed for his truck with bare branches. Through the web of trees, Reich could see secluded, expensive waterside houses hugging the cliff tops, but there was hardly anyone in residence to admire the panorama below them. Most of the owners only arrived during the high season, leaving the empty land to the small tribe of year-round residents in other months. Even in summer, most tourists didn't venture beyond the main highway or travel north of the shopping towns like Fish Creek, Ephraim, and Sister Bay. When you got as far north as Gills Rock and Northport, you were usually alone.

He drove to the very end of Port des Morts Drive, where he parked in a sheltered turnaround. He got out of his Tahoe and walked up a muddy dirt driveway toward Peter Hoffman's log home. It was a small house on a large lot that was thick with mature oak trees. Pete had lived there since he and Reich returned from Vietnam together. His friend kept it impeccably maintained; the house was his hobby and his passion. There was not much else in Pete's life, not since the loss of his wife to cancer seven years ago. Not since his retirement.

Not since the fire.

Reich rang the bell, but the quietness of the house told him that Pete had left for his morning hike. He knew where to find him. He got back in his truck, retraced his path for a quarter mile, and turned toward the water at Kenosha Drive, which led into the county park. Toward the end of the short road, he could see the bay through the grove of towering spruce trees, and under the dark sky, the water was so blue it was almost black. He parked in the dormant grass, where remnants of snow clung to shaded patches of earth. Ahead of him were two gray benches, angled toward the water. Sitting on one bench was Peter Hoffman.

Reich climbed down from his truck. He could see his breath. The morning was cold, with a gusty breeze that had tossed the island ferry like a whale heaving up and down through the waves. Even in summer, it was cold here, but he never felt the cold himself, or if he did, he shut it out of his mind. At sixty years old, he woke up every morning with a bone-deep aching in his limbs, but he didn't let it keep him from the chores of the day: shoveling his island driveway, splitting and chopping wood for the fireplace, or lifting weights religiously in his basement gym. As far as Reich was concerned, he might as well have been forty-five.

He wore a brown sheriff's department uniform, which fit perfectly and was pressed into sharp creases. He hadn't gained a pound in years. His badge glinted like gold on his chest, and he shined his boots to a high polish every night, cleaning off the grime of the job, which took him into muddy, dusty corners of the county. His white hair was cropped to a half-inch length and was as flat as it had been in his marine days. He wasn't tall, about five feet eight, but he had fought and beaten men who were thirty years younger and fifty pounds heavier over the years. He figured he still could.

Reich watched the water with a grim expression. You could live here your whole life, as he had, and find something different in the colors of the waves every day. On the horizon, he saw the rocky outline of Plum Island and, beyond it, the low shelf of Washington Island, where he'd bought his home in the 1970s and stayed, alone, unmarried, ever since. He felt a kinship with the island and the rocky passage to the mainland, but he was no romantic about it. Every season, they fished out the bodies of those who underestimated Death's Door.

Not saying a word, Reich sat down on the bench opposite Peter Hoffman, who didn't look at him. Tree stumps dotted the clearing around them. Spidery shadows from the birches made a web in the grass. Pete drank coffee from the plastic cup of a Thermos, and Reich could see steam clouding above the mug. He could also smell whiskey on his friend's breath.

"Pretty early for the sauce, Pete."

Pete held out the Thermos. "You want some?"

Reich shook his head. He liked to drink, but never on duty and never when he was flying or driving—and not at nine in the morning.

"You heard?" Reich asked.

Pete swallowed his doctored coffee and wiped his mouth. His eyes were focused way out in the bay. He nodded, but he didn't say anything.

"Glory Fischer," Reich murmured. "Like that little girl didn't suffer enough."

Pete took a loud, ragged breath. Reich thought his friend might cry. He was worried about Pete and had been for the better part of a year. When they'd served together, Pete had been just like himself, a hard nail you could pound and never bend its shape. That had stayed true for most of their lives. Both of them were natives, which made them a rare breed in Door County. They could practically see each other's homes across the four miles of the passage. They'd hunted, fished, and gotten drunk together more times than Reich could count. They had identical values about God, life, and evil that had stayed rock solid while the rest of the world went to hell.

This was not the Pete he knew, though. The old man drinking on a bench in the early morning. Letting himself go. Drowning in his sorrow. Limping around his empty house, thanks to the bullet he'd taken when he stepped in front of a rifle aimed at Reich in 1969. His rigid bearing had begun to slump, and only his hair, which was still oddly black, resembled the man who had been his best friend for his entire life. Pete was eight years older, and he looked like he, like the water, was on death's door.

"I talked to Delia," Reich told him. "She's in Florida with Tresa and Troy Geier trying to get the local cops off their asses. She'll be home tomorrow. Tresa's not going back to River Falls this term. She's staying here."

"Good thing," Pete rumbled.

"Delia and the cops think it was that son of a bitch who was banging Tresa," Reich added. "The teacher. Mark Bradley. He was down there at the hotel. The cops are pretty sure he was on the beach with Glory."

Pete turned to him with bloodshot eyes. "Is he going to get what he deserves this time?"

"If I have anything to say about it, you're damn right he will."

The two men sat in silence. The wind roared between them, waking up the trees. Early-season birds chattered in agitation. Peter Hoffman pushed himself off the bench, and his body swayed unsteadily. Reich made a move to help him, but Pete waved him away. Pete leaned against a tree stun and overturned his Thermos, letting the coffee splash into a puddle in the dirt. He straightened up as well as he could and looked down at Reich with immense sadness.

"It's going to come up again, isn't it?" Pete asked. "The fire."

"I imagine it will."

"I really thought we were done with it. I thought it was over."

Reich said nothing. He knew the fire wasn't the kind of event that was ever really over. No matter how much you tried to lock the past in a cellar, it found a way to get out. That had been true for Pete since it happened, and it was hard to blame him. He'd lost his oldest daughter. Two of his grandchildren. All of that, the year after his wife succumbed to a slow, horrible disease. It was like having his whole life leveled to the ground with napalm.

"I guess the fire got Glory after all," Pete went on.

Reich shook his head fiercely. "This has nothing to do with the fire or with Harris Bone. Mark Bradley is the one who did this to Glory, and I'm not going to let him throw up a smoke screen."

Peter Hoffman shoved his hands in his pockets and stared at the sky through the tangle of trees. "Harris Bone," he said fiercely.

Reich found himself getting angry with his friend. "We can't change the past, Pete. This is about getting justice for Glory. Okay? We owe it to that girl. We were the ones who found her."

It was over before anyone knew.

It was over before there were sirens and lights and before a single high-pressure fire hose blasted water over the superheated remains. By the time a neighbor near Kangaroo Lake awoke in the middle of the night and smelled the sharp aroma of burning wood in the air, and called 911, the Bone house was gone, its walls consumed into ash, its roof caved in over scorched Sheetrock and stone. The fire was complete in its destruction.

That night, Felix Reich and Peter Hoffman had been playing poker with two of Felix's deputies in a farmhouse east of Egg Harbor. The air had the deadness of summer, humid and warm. Mos-

quitoes and moths clung to the screens.
Their T-shirts were wet with sweat. They
were only three miles west on County
Road E of the home where Pete's son-
in-law lived. Harris Bone was married
to Pete's daughter Nettie, father to his
grandchildren Karl, Scott, and Jen. That
was the man's only redeeming quality
in Pete's eyes.

Reich knew that Pete had little time
for his son-in-law of seventeen years.
Harris had taken over his mother's liquor
store in Sturgeon Bay after she passed
away, but it had failed when a larger
competitor opened in town. Since then,
he had spent most of his life on the road,
scraping together money as a vending
machine salesman around the state of
Wisconsin. Even when he was home,
there was no peace. He and Nettie tore
into each other like feral cats. It was a
house painted over with thick coats of
bitterness and bile.

In truth, Reich knew that Nettie was
no prize, but you didn't say that to a
friend. He'd listened to her pick apart
her husband for years. Harris was a
failure. He wasn't religious enough. He

wasn't successful enough. He didn't know how to work with his hands. He was always wrong. Reich, who'd never wanted a wife and never missed having one, felt the tiniest sympathy for Harris every time he was in the house, listening to the man's ego get chipped away by this tiny, overbearing woman, who dominated his life from her wheelchair. The boys had begun to pick up the same habits, running down their father to win their mother's approval. For Harris, being home in that house must have felt like being in a cage.

Reich knew they would never divorce. Godly couples didn't do that. He had just never imagined where it would all lead when Harris finally snapped.

He heard the call on his radio as the poker game was winding down. The report of the fire. He jumped in his truck to respond, and Pete, who'd driven with him to the game, joined him for the ride. They had no address, but the closer they got to Kangaroo Lake, the more the smoke guided them, until they spotted a black column above the trees that was even darker than the night sky. It had never occurred to either one of them where the fire might be, and it was only when they turned down the road leading to the lake, where Pete's family lived, that Reich began to get a sick feeling. He drove faster, and the loose gravel made a roar under his tires.

He could sense it in Pete, too. The fear. The horror.

When they were half a mile away, he saw the glow of the fire, but it was too late. He parked on the road, and both men got out and ran, but the flames were already smacking their lips, popping and belching as they picked over the remains. A hundred tiny fires glowed throughout the wreckage, spreading across the wooded lot. Reich felt the heat on his face. He coughed violently as he inhaled smoke. He smelled gasoline and wood, and above all that, he recognized a foul odor he hadn't smelled in decades and had hoped he would never smell again.

Burnt human flesh.

Next to him, Pete began to disintegrate. His eyes widened in terrified disbelief, as if he'd been ushered into the belly of hell to witness the conflagration. He moaned his daughter's name and the names of his grandchildren. He crumpled in the driveway and then ran, stumbling, directly for the fiery core where the house had been. Reich chased after him, knowing that Pete wouldn't stop; he would run into the fire and let it kill him. With a shout, he threw himself on his friend's back and drove Pete into the earth, holding him down while he cried and beat the ground. Reich winced, listening to the primal agony screeching out of Pete's throat, hearing it devolve into whimpers of despair.

When Reich got to his feet again, covered in dirt and ash, he saw Harris Bone.

Harris stood thirty feet away, silent, motionless, watching the work of the fire. His Buick was parked in the grass. Sparks flew around him like fireworks, landing in his hair and making black burn marks like cigarette holes on his clothes. He seemed oblivious to the presence of Reich or to the tortured desperation of his father-in-law. Reich approached Harris carefully, and as he did, Reich realized that the man reeked of gasoline, and his face was streaked with soot. Harris's eyes, reflecting the fire, were blank and devoid of emotion.

"What happened here, Harris?" Reich asked.

Harris Bone shook his head and murmured, "I'm sorry."

"Were they inside? Was your family inside?"

"I'm sorry," he repeated, continuing to watch the fire as if it were something distant and detached.

Reich heard Peter Hoffman bellowing behind them. "You did this! You did this!"

Before Reich could stop him, Pete had Harris on the ground. The old man had the younger man's throat in his grip, and he hammered his son-in-law's skull against the rocks as he squeezed off the air from his windpipe. Harris barely struggled to save himself. Reich grabbed Pete's shoulders and threw his friend bodily away and stood in his way to block him as Pete charged for Harris again.

"Pete, stop!"

Crying, breathing hard, Pete backed

off and stood with his hands on his knees. Reich took Harris and pulled him up by the collar of his shirt and held him. Without thinking, he made a fist with his left hand and crashed it into Harris's face, where he heard the snap of cartilage breaking. The man's nose erupted in blood, and Harris staggered back and sank to his knees.

Reich rubbed his knuckles, which were bruised and raw. He cursed himself under his breath for losing control. Pete watched him, saying nothing at all.

That was when Reich heard it. A tiny voice, hidden under the roar of the fire. "Help me!"

He looked up with a sudden urgency.

"What the hell was that?" Reich asked. "Did you hear that?"

Pete shook his head. A mile away, they both heard the sirens of the fire trucks growing louder.

"Someone's alive," Reich told him.

He marched into the grass, dodging pockets of smoldering fragments blown from the house. He scoured the burnt yard, pushing through tall weeds. He listened but didn't hear the voice again.

"Hey!" he called. "Hey, where are you?"

No one answered.

Reich tramped toward the woods on the west side of the house. He made his way around the burnt shell of the old garage, which had disintegrated except for one wall that seemed to defy gravity and cast a shadow into the meadow. He squinted, trying to see through the darkness. The field was a mess of brush and flowers, but just outside the spotty clusters of flames, he saw a flash of pink huddled amid stalks of Queen Anne's lace.

As he watched, the pink bundle moved. He saw a girl's face. Scared eyes. The fire was moving closer to her.

Reich ran.

"I don't want to hear you talking about the fire," Reich told Peter Hoffman.

Pete nodded slowly. "I hear you, Felix."

"Mark Bradley didn't pay for what he did to Tresa, but he sure as hell is going to pay for what he did to Glory. So it's not going to help anybody if you and me start dredging up the past."

Reich smoothed his uniform and headed for his Tahoe, leaving Pete alone on the trail looking out on the water. Before he could climb into his truck, he heard Pete calling after him.

"Felix?"

Reich stopped. "What is it?"

"You know it doesn't matter what we say or don't say. Somebody's going to make the connection to the fire anyway."

Reich said nothing. He knew Pete was right.

"They'll say it was Harris Bone who did this to Glory," Pete went on, and his voice was broken and old. "They'll say he finally came back."

PART TWO

The Ghost

PART TWO

14

Five years ago, the buzz around Hilary Semper's high school in Highland Park was about the hot new substitute teacher who'd joined the district. The grapevine already had him pegged: six feet tall, buzzed brown hair, a golf pro who'd given up the tour because of an injury. Loud, confident, funny. Married once, divorced quickly, now unattached. In a school where most of the teachers were twenty-something blondes looking for a husband, this was big news.

Hilary herself had no interest. It wasn't that she'd had no relationships in her life. She had fallen in love at least twice, but in both cases, she'd realized that she was dating someone who wanted a wife, not a partner. In those days, she had tried to change herself into more of what a man was looking for, but she'd eventually decided that love wasn't worth pretending to be someone else. She knew she intimidated men with her brains. She knew she was outspoken to the point of driving people away. If the man didn't exist who could live with that combination of qualities, so be it.

She was the only one of six Semper siblings who hadn't walked down the aisle. Two had divorced and remarried; three had marriages that had barely survived the arrival of children. They all looked at Hilary at holiday gatherings and asked her in amazement why she wasn't married yet. They weren't amused when she asked them why they were.

In truth, she did want to get married. She wanted to be in love. She wanted kids. If a relationship came, she would throw herself into it. If it never happened, she wasn't going to cry about it or spend time regretting what she hadn't found. She simply went about her life, without wasting her time hunting for a man who might never show up.

Her family, which already looked at her strangely for staying single, hadn't understood her choice to go into teaching, either. She'd graduated from Northwestern summa cum laude with a major in finance. Brokerages and banks in Chicago and New York had dangled six-figure salaries in front of her, and she'd turned them all down. Instead, she did what she'd always said she would do, teach math and dance to high schoolers. It wasn't the road to riches, although her own expenses were low, and she'd invested well. Her loud criticism of everything that was wrong with public schools didn't win her any fans among the school district or the teachers union, but her students loved her. She loved them, too. She was exactly where she thought she wanted to be in life.

Then Mark Bradley became a substitute teacher in her school.

She'd already prepared herself not to like him. The more the naive young teachers swooned over him, the more she'd steeled herself to meet an egotistical womanizer who was overly impressed with his looks. He worked in the district for six months before she got him as a sub. She did what she did with every sub for her class—meet him in advance to go over lesson plans for an hour and a half, map out what she wanted him to do, and provide him with bios on the strengths and weaknesses of every student. All that for two days while she attended an education conference in New Orleans. Most subs groaned at her thoroughness, and few did what she directed them to do in her classroom. She expected that Mark Bradley—English and art major from the University of Illinois, former pro golfer—would be among the worst, with little interest in what she wanted from her math students. She'd already leaped to the conclusion that he was nothing more than a dumb jock.

She knew—because he told her so later—that she'd been rude and condescending to him. She'd barely looked at him, although even a glance was enough to realize that he really was as attractive as the other teachers had said. If he wanted an opening with her, she wasn't prepared to give him one—and she doubted that an ex-athlete pursued by most of the cute twentysomethings at school would have much interest in a tall, pushy teacher in her midthirties, with a handful of stubborn extra pounds on her frame.

Mark surprised her. He kept his ego and his jokes firmly in check when they met and listened to her instructions and took detailed notes. He had a brain and the same kind of passion for kids that she did. When she returned to school after her two-day conference, she was shocked to discover that Mark had followed her guidelines precisely and kept the classes on pace with her lesson plans. She was less surprised that half her girls had already fallen in love with him and were begging her to bring him back.

Later that week, when she did a post-mortem with him in the cafeteria, he waited until the very end of their conversation before asking her out to dinner.

She had to admit to herself that she was intrigued and a little aroused. Even so, she wasn't stupid, and she had no interest in a date where his only objective was sex. So, with her usual bluntness, she'd asked him why he wanted to go out with her. It wasn't exactly a great way to launch a relationship, but it was a great way to cut one off in its tracks. He surprised her again.

"When I golfed, I never liked to play it safe and lay up," Mark told her. "I always went for the green. I figured it wasn't worth it to settle for second best."

If any other man had tried that line with her, she would have written it off as hollow flattery, but she saw something different in Mark Bradley. Sincerity. It was a quality she prized more than just about anything else, and she had been let down by enough people in her life that she thought she could recognize it when she saw it. Mark was a man who meant what he said, who didn't pretend to be someone else for the world. That was her own philosophy, too.

She decided that Mark Bradley was worth the risk. One night. No sex. No strings. She didn't expect it to lead to anything deeper, which was her way of managing her expectations. She certainly never expected that not even two years later, she would be married, and she and Mark would be leaving the Chicago area for the kind of idyllic life they both thought they craved. Moving someplace quieter and emptier. Moving someplace where the roads were lonely and tree-lined and the rest of the world was far away. Giving up old dreams for new dreams. Living in isolation.

That was how it had all started. Five years ago.

Now those dreams were dying.

The calendar said winter was over, but no one had told the weather gods in Wisconsin. The wind off the bay was raw. Snow was expected overnight. The only sign of spring was the expanded schedule on the Northport car ferry, which meant that they could now come and go from the island mostly at will. During the three deepest months of winter from January to March, they were forced to spend weekdays in a small rental cottage near Fish Creek, and they could only retreat to their real home on the weekends. Hilary would be glad to sleep in their own bed every night.

Mark was silent as they drove along the southwest coast of Washington Island toward their home. It had been a long day, flying into Chicago from Florida and driving north for four hours along the coast of

Lake Michigan to Door County. They'd barely made the last island ferry at dusk. They were both exhausted and wanted to do nothing more than sleep.

He drove them along the main road leading through town, which was a generous description of the rural community on Washington Island. There were a handful of shops and restaurants, most of them on the west side, widely separated by farmlands and trees. The island itself was flat as a board, barely thirty-five square miles with dense forest over most of the land and rough water on all sides. Anything that was sold here had to be shipped over from the mainland, and as a result, there wasn't much more than the bare necessities for the residents, particularly in the off-season. The prices were high. Most people waited and did their main shopping once a month at the far southern end of the county in Sturgeon Bay, which was the closest thing the peninsula had to a real city, unless you wanted to travel another forty miles to Green Bay.

They drove past the island's old watering hole, Bitters Pub, and Hilary saw the owner of one of the handful of local motels standing next to his pickup truck with a bottle of beer in his hand. She knew him; he knew them. That was the way it was on an island populated by fewer than seven hundred people. He didn't wave or smile. Instead, he watched their Camry pass, and his face was graven with hostility as he tilted the bottle to his lips. She knew that word had already spread among the locals about what had happened in Florida.

When they'd first moved to the island, they had been welcomed politely, if not embraced. You weren't really accepted if you weren't a native, but people were cordial and helpful, even if they didn't invite you into their lives. Hilary and Mark didn't care about that kind of friendship, but at least they hadn't felt like intruders. That all changed when the story about Tresa broke. From that moment, politeness turned to cold distrust. It wasn't easy living in a small town where you were shunned, particularly a community that was cut off by water from the rest of the world.

She worried what would happen next, now that they all knew about Glory. How far do your neighbors go to tell you they don't want you?

Mark saw it, too. There was a deadly

expression on the man's face in front of the pub.

"Welcome home," he said to Hilary with a weary smile.

He continued up the north coast of the island and turned down the harbor road at the cemetery, which was scattered with gray headstones among the pines and snow. The gravel road led from the grave-yard into the trees, ending at Schoolhouse Beach, one of the most popular gathering spots for tourists during the summer sea-son. During the off-season, though, the cove was deserted on most days. The back porch of their house was a hundred yards from the shore, and during the winter, when the trees were bare, they could glimpse the water.

Rather than turn right on the road that led home, Mark continued to the dead end at the beach. He parked and got out and walked down to the shore, which was made up not of sand but of millions of polished rocks. The sheltered harbor created by the half-moon inlet was calmer than the vio-lent lake just beyond the edge of land, but calmness was relative here. He shoved his hands in his pockets and stared at the whitecaps blowing across the water like tiny icebergs.

Hilary joined him. They stood next to each other, not talking. The brutal wind tossed her hair around her face and made her lips white with cold. The entire curving stretch of beach was empty. In the desolation, they could have been the only two people on the island. That was what they'd wanted—seclusion in the midst of nature, the deserted roads, the silence unbroken except for birds and wind. It had never felt ominous before, but for the first time, she felt threatened by their very remoteness.

"You know what's hard?" Mark said. "I still love it here. This is like the most beautiful place in the world."

"I feel that way, too."

He turned to her and cupped her neck in his palms and kissed her softly but intensely. There were so many kisses you could have as a married couple, the goodbye kiss, the after-a-fight kiss, the love kiss, the bedroom kiss. His cool lips on hers this time felt new, like a kiss that acknowledged they were both in need of rescue and had to save each other. It was a kiss that said *Hang on to me, because this crossing is going to be rough.*

They got back in the car. Their house was half a mile to the north. It was small—a three-bedroom house with matchbox rooms and a screened-in rear porch with wood growing soft with age. The pale blue paint needed a fresh coat. The windows let in the drafts. For its size and age, it had been absurdly expensive, but out here, you paid for the land and the view. They'd scraped together a down payment from Hilary's investments and a nest egg left over from Mark's golfing days, but that still left them with a mortgage that was barely within their reach. Their budget had been based on two jobs. Now there was only one.

Even so, when they turned into the dirt driveway, Hilary felt home. She'd never had that sensation anywhere else. That was why she never wanted to leave, no matter how bad it got, no matter what it took to keep it. When she climbed out and smelled the coming of snow, and felt the mushy, molding leaves under her feet, she felt a sudden surge of contentment. When she glanced at Mark's face, she knew he felt the same way. This was their refuge.

Their escape from reality didn't last.

They left their luggage in the trunk and went to the front door, and Hilary stopped on the porch when she saw the door hanging open. Mark peered into the darkness inside. Mud and leaves had drifted into the foyer. A fetid aroma wafted like a toxic cloud into the sweet, cold air.

"Wait here," he said under his breath.

She watched him go inside. He was tense, his body coiled like a spring. Seconds later, she heard something come from his throat, an exhalation of rage unlike anything she'd heard from her husband before. It was as if his life had been sucked away by whatever he'd found.

"Mark?" she called.

He didn't answer her.

"Is everything okay?" she asked, more urgently.

When he was still silent, she went inside herself. Beyond the hardwood floor of the foyer, she turned into the living room, with its musty carpet and fireplace and furniture gathered from their separate lives before they were married. Mark stood in the center of the room, his face grim with violence. In the gloom of near darkness, she could see the damage. She understood now what was next. She recognized the message that their neighbors were sending.

The house had been violated. That was the only word she could use. Holes had been punched in the Sheetrock with what must have been a baseball bat. Figurines she had collected since childhood lay shattered into shards on the floor. Lamps were overturned and broken. Animal feces had been thrown at the wall and left to sink into vile brown streaks. The cushions of the furniture had been slashed with knives, foam stripped out, littering the floor like cottonwood.

A single word had been spray-painted everywhere. On the walls. On the glass of the windows. On the ceiling. On the floor. It must have been fifty times.

A single word over and over in bloodred paint.

KILLER.

15

I've lived here for twenty years," Terri Duecker told Hilary, as she took the cigarette out of her mouth and watched the smoke dissipate in the cold air. "It never ends. You weren't born here, so you'll never be a local. If you have kids, they'll be accepted from day one, but not you."

The two women sat in the bleachers outside the Fish Creek High School. Both of them wore heavy coats, and Hilary had her hands shoved in the fleece pockets. The grass of the football field was white with frost. The sky overhead was a mottled blanket of charcoal. A row of spruce trees lined the far side of the field like spectators, blocking the view of the Green Bay water past the bluff. Behind them, the school parking lot was wet, thanks to the intermittent sleet that had fallen overnight.

"I don't care about that," Hilary replied. "We knew that coming in, but it's different now. They're trying to drive us out. Scare us away."

Terri shrugged. "Small towns," she said. "If they could, they'd build a wall to keep strangers out. It's worse that you're from Chicago, too. People around here need someone to blame because the whole county is changing, and they figure it's because of rich people moving in from Chicago."

"We're not rich."

Terri shook her head. "It doesn't matter. As long as you live here, people will look at you and see a Land of Lincoln license plate on your car. Once a fib, always a fib. I was lucky. Chris and I moved here from Fargo. We're still outsiders, but at least we're not Bears fans. Even so, you won't find any of the natives spilling their secrets to me."

Hilary glanced at the school behind

them. She saw two other high school teachers chatting on the sidewalk outside the glass doors. She could follow their eyes and the way they turned their heads toward them, and she knew that she and Mark were the topic of conversation.

The school itself, two hundred yards away, was a one-story building, long and low, made of vanilla brick. She heard the American flag snapping in the wind and the flagpole rope banging against the metal. It was a place that could have been any other high school in the country. She could easily have been back in Highland Park, except that there weren't expensive suburban Audis and BMWs in the parking lot. She'd always felt comfortable walking through school doors, smelling the cafeteria food, listening to the thunder of shouts and basketballs in the gymnasium. Now, however, going inside meant being watched by a hundred spies. It was ground zero for the gulf between her and Mark and the teachers, administrators, and parents who wanted them gone.

"So why do you stay here if you feel that way?" Hilary asked Terri.

"We're just like you two. We always

wanted to live in a place like this. You go north of Sturgeon Bay, and it's like going back in time. No chain stores. No fast food restaurants. The views are amazing, and we've got room to breathe. If it weren't for the tourists in the summer, it would be paradise all year. We all know the tourists pay the bills, but don't expect anyone around here to be happy about that."

"Can I ask you something?" Hilary asked.

"Sure."

"Do people around here give you a hard time because we're friends?"

Terri shrugged. "Yes."

"Well, thanks for sticking by me."

"You and Mark remind me of Chris and me when we moved here," Terri said. "We outsiders need to have a community, too."

Terri was a handful of years older than Hilary, but they were good friends. She was a slim brunette whose principal vice was her morning cigarette break on the edge of the school grounds. Hilary often joined her. Terri had taught science at the high school for two decades. She and her husband, Chris, owned a series of guest cottages and condominiums around the Fish Creek area that they rented during the summer, which was their main source of income. Chris managed the properties. During the winter, when most of their units were vacant, they'd allowed Hilary and Mark to rent a cottage from them for little more than the cost of utilities. It was a perfect arrangement. Hilary and Mark could stay near the school and ferry back to their Washington Island home on the weekends.

"What are they saying about us now?" Hilary asked.

"You know exactly what they're saying," Terri replied. Her eyes were sad but hard. "It was the first thing out of everyone's mouths at school yesterday morning. Mark killed Glory. It's not a rumor. It's not suspicion. As far as most people are concerned, it's fact."

"I'm glad I wasn't here."

"They won't say it to your face, but they'll talk behind your back. You're only innocent until proven guilty in a courtroom, Hilary. Not in real life."

"They're going to boot me out, aren't they?" she asked. "I'll never get tenure now."

Terri shook her head. "No, you will. You're a star, and everyone knows it. Plus, you're a woman, not a man, that always helps. I think some people actually feel sorry for you, too. You'll get tenure, but they'll do everything they can to make you so miserable that you don't want to stay."

"Great."

"I'd understand if you and Mark chose to leave," Terri added, "but I hope you won't."

"I get stubborn about other people telling me what to do," Hilary said.

Terri smiled. "Me, too."

"I appreciate your not asking me, by the way."

"Asking you what?" Terri asked.

"Whether I'm sure. Whether I think Mark did it."

Terri stubbed out her cigarette on the metal frame of the bleachers. She squinted at the gray horizon. "You sound like you want me to ask. You sound like you need to say it."

"Maybe," Hilary admitted.

"Are you sure?"

"Yes."

"He didn't do it?"

"No."

"That's good enough for me," Terri replied. "Look, I saw Mark in the classroom. I saw him with the kids. No way he would lift a hand against a teenaged girl. He wouldn't sleep with one, either, because that man loves you. I'm not saying he wouldn't kill someone who tried to mess with either of you, but an innocent girl? Not Mark. Chris and I talked about it. He feels the same way."

"Thank you."

"I wish I spoke for the majority, Hilary, but I don't."

"I know."

Terri checked her watch and shivered. The two women climbed down from the bleachers, taking care not to slip on the damp metal steps. The frost-crusted grass crunched under their feet. They walked back toward the school beside Highway 42, the north-south road that stretched along the west coast of the peninsula. The two-lane road was quiet.

"This isn't just about Mark," Terri confided, speaking louder as the wind roared and covered her voice. "You understand that, right?"

"What do you mean?"

"I mean, it's about Glory, too. It would

be bad with any local girl, but it's worse because it's Glory. We all felt sorry because of what happened to her."

"What happened?" Hilary said.

Terri stopped. "You don't know about the fire?"

"No, what are you talking about?"

"Oh, hell." Terri checked her watch again.

"Tell me," Hilary said. "Please."

"I'll give you the short version. It was six years ago. Glory was ten. You know that Delia has an old place over near Kangaroo Lake, right? Well, she and the kids lived right across the road from a house owned by a man named Harris Bone. Does that name ring a bell?"

Hilary thought about it and shook her head. "I don't think so."

"I'm surprised. I figured it would have made the papers, even in Chicago, because it was so horrible."

"What happened?"

Terri sighed. "Harris Bone was married to a local girl named Nettie. She was a native from a prominent family, the Hoffmans. They go back decades here in Door County. It was kind of an odd match. Harris was an only child from Sturgeon Bay, lived with his mom above a little liquor store there. Not exactly a catch, but he was a good-looking guy, and I think Nettie wanted a mama's boy she could push around. She was a piece of work. Always treated Harris like crap, but it got ten times worse after she wound up paralyzed in a car accident. She got angry at the world and took it out on Harris. I'd hear their kids talk about what it was like in the house. The arguments. The screaming. Not pretty."

"What does this have to do with Glory?" Hilary asked.

"Glory stumbled into the middle of it on the wrong night," Terri replied. "She found a kitten in the Bone garage and began sneaking out at night to feed it. One of those nights, Harris Bone came home while Glory was hiding in the garage. The son of a bitch doused the entire house in gasoline, inside and out, lit up the place like a torch. Nettie and the boys died. Harris sat there and watched them burn. No shame, no regret, no guilt. I remember Sheriff Reich saying it was like he was in a trance."

"What about Glory?"

"Glory was in the garage, and the fire almost got her, too. She crawled out

through a hole in the wall, but she'd inhaled a lot of smoke. She spent weeks in
the hospital. She made it, but that's the
kind of thing that does as much damage
to the head as it does to the body. People
always said the fire made Glory the kind of
girl she was. Wild. Reckless. Promiscuous.
Like she was running from the past."

Hilary found it hard to breathe. Terri was
right. It would have been bad with any girl,
but she understood now what it meant to
this community to lose Glory. She remembered what Delia had said in Florida. *I almost lost her once, and I thought I got a
second chance.*

This was the girl that everyone thought
Mark had murdered.

"I'm sorry," Hilary murmured. "Tresa
never mentioned it to us."

"Well, I'm not surprised. We all treated it
like it had never happened. I think the idea
was, if you didn't talk about it, it didn't exist.
Everyone was trying to spare Glory. Who
wants to remember listening to a family burn
to death?"

"Did she go through therapy?"

"I hope so, but people aren't big on that

around here. It's like a character flaw if you have to see a shrink."

"It must have been hard on Tresa, too," Hilary said.

"Sure it was. She became the forgotten sister."

Hilary shook her head as she considered the wreckage of the Fischers and Bones. People were fragile things. You scratched the surface and found pain everywhere. When something bad happened to someone, it had a ripple effect, washing away other lives as the circles got larger.

The two women continued walking slowly toward the school building. They were already late for the next class.

"So Mark's paying the price for Harris Bone," Terri told her. "That's part of what's happening here. People around here are sensitive to the idea of a man getting away with murder. They don't want to see it happening again."

Hilary stopped and put a hand on Terri's shoulder. "Getting away with murder? What are you talking about? You said they found Harris Bone at the ruins."

"They did. Harris was tried, and he got

life in prison. A lot of people wished we had the death penalty in Wisconsin. Most of us thought life in prison was too good for him."

"That's not the same as getting away with it."

"I know, but Harris escaped," Terri said. "He got away as they were taking him to the Supermax facility in Boscobel. He's been on the run ever since. He's out there somewhere, hiding."

16

Amy Leigh's room in Downham Hall at the University of Wisconsin in Green Bay looked out on the remnants of a cornfield from the previous harvest season. Beyond the rows of broken stalks, she could see the line of barren winter trees marking the Cofrin Arboretum that ringed the entire campus, isolating it like an island protected by an enchanted forest. It was late afternoon on Tuesday, but the ashen sky made the day look later than it was. Classes had begun again, and she had psychology books piled on her bed that she needed to read, but she was finding it hard to concentrate.

Rather than working, she kept looking outside at the desolate field and thinking about Glory Fischer and Gary Jensen.

She'd thought about nothing else but the two of them since the bus arrived back in Green Bay: the girl who'd been found dead on the beach in Florida and the coach who always seemed to be stripping her naked in his head when he looked at her.

"Gary and his wife went rock-climbing in Utah in December," Amy murmured, studying the article she'd pulled up on the Internet. She wasn't even aware that she'd spoken aloud until her roommate rolled over on her back on the opposite bed and groaned.

"Are you on about this again?" Katie asked.

Amy took the pen from her mouth. "His wife died. She lost her grip during the climb and fell more than two hundred feet. There was no one in that area of the park but the two of them. If you wanted to murder someone and get away with it, can you think of a better way to do it? Who knows what really happened out there?"

Katie laid the textbook on her bare stomach. She wore a sports bra and loose-fitting sweatpants. "I remember you telling me that Gary looked devastated when you saw him on campus in January."

"People can fake that. What if she found out the kind of man he was?"

"What kind of man is he?"

"He's a pig. He comes on to all the girls."

"So do half the older men in the world."

"It was in the papers after she died," Amy said. "The police in Utah investigated her death."

"The police are going to investigate any time somebody falls off a cliff. They didn't charge him with anything, did they?"

"No."

Katie sat up and swung her legs over the edge of the bed. "Look, Ames, just because your coach is a jerk doesn't mean he's some kind of serial killer. First he kills his wife and now some girl in Florida he doesn't even know? Does that make any sense?"

"I just wonder if I should tell someone. I mean, I think I saw Gary with Glory Fischer."

"You think?"

"Okay, I'm not sure." She added, "This is personal for me now. Because of Hilary."

"She was your coach. You haven't seen her in years."

"Yes, but you saw the news," Amy said. "They're looking at her husband. He's the prime suspect."

"Well, he knew the girl, and he had a room right near where she was killed, and he had a grudge against the family. Sounds like he deserves to be a suspect."

Amy took a strand of her curly blond hair and twisted it between her fingers. She shook her head. "I remember him. He was a nice guy. Hilary wouldn't marry anyone who could do something like that. She's way too smart."

"Wow, don't tell me you're that naive," Katie said. "If you're going to be a psychologist, you better learn real fast that you can't trust people just by looking at them, you know?"

"Yeah, I know."

Her roommate got off the bed and grabbed a Green Bay sweatshirt from the top of her laundry basket and shrugged it over her skinny torso. She peeled off her sweatpants and squeezed her bare legs into a tight pair of jeans. Sitting on the bed again, she laced up her sneakers. As she bent over, her glasses skidded down her nose.

"I'm going to dinner," she told Amy. "You want to come with me?"

"I'm not hungry."

"You sure?"

"Yeah. You go."

"Okay, whatever. See you later."

Katie left Amy alone in the room. Amy got up and paced back and forth between the walls, then tried to clear her mind with a series of yoga positions. It didn't help. She sat down at the desk again and reread the story in the Green Bay paper about the death of Gary Jensen's wife four months earlier. It was the kind of accidental tragedy that happened every day. There was nothing suspicious about it. She was making Gary into a monster in her head for no good reason.

Amy called up the home page of Facebook on her computer. She had almost four hundred friends on the network, including everyone from her high school class and dozens of dancers she'd met from schools across the country. She did a search and found the profile for Hilary Bradley, who was one of her friends, and clicked over to her former coach's home page.

Hilary's profile photo showed her on a bicycle somewhere on a tree-lined road. She had a big smile, her long hair blew behind her, and her blue eyes were hidden behind sunglasses. She looked happy. Amy figured the photo had been taken where she lived now, in the rural lands of Door County. Hilary didn't look as if she had changed much in the three years since Amy had known her in high school in Chicago. She was pretty and blond, like Amy, and she was tall and full-bodied, which was also like Amy. That was one of the things she'd liked most about Hilary. She wasn't a stick. She didn't make any apologies for her figure. She'd always told Amy that you could be a big girl and still be graceful and sexy.

Amy read Hilary's status on Facebook, which had been posted from a cell phone only a few minutes earlier. Hilary had written: *I'm having the same bad dream, and I'd really like to wake up.*

She didn't have any trouble understanding what Hilary meant. The previous year, she had followed the trail of events on Hilary's page as her husband faced accusations of having an affair with a student. Now it was déjà vu.

Amy clicked on one of the photos on Hilary's profile, which showed Mark Bradley painting on a Door County beach. Amy had barely known Mark in Chicago, but the girls who had had him as a substitute teacher had all fallen for him. He was the kind of teacher who inspired crushes. The strong, sensitive type. Handsome. Creative. He had it all. You wanted romance, but you also wanted someone who would make you feel safe in a dark alley. That was Mark Bradley.

Amy thought about what her roommate had said. You can't judge people just by looking at them. She hated to think that her head was upside down about Glory's death. Gary Jensen might be nothing more than an innocent man whose wife had died in an accident, leaving him alone and bereft. Mark Bradley, solid, sexy, married to Amy's idol, might be the evil one. The killer. That was the obvious answer, and the obvious answer was usually the truth.

You can't trust your instincts. Katie was

probably right about that, too. Amy didn't have anything except her instincts to tell her what to think. She knew Hilary. Through her, she felt as if she knew Mark. She knew Gary, too.

Instincts.

Amy thought about sending Hilary a message on Facebook, to let her know that she was thinking about her and Mark. She wondered if she should mention her suspicions, but she didn't. Instead, she closed her computer and picked up her cell phone from the desk. She hesitated before dialing. Her breathing came faster. She felt the way she did before stepping out onto the floor of the arena for a performance.

"Amy, what the hell are you doing?" she asked herself aloud.

Rather than answer herself, she punched the buttons on the phone and waited. When he answered, she heard the slippery charm in his voice, and her skin crawled.

It was Glory Fischer I saw you with. I know it was.

"Gary? It's Amy Leigh."

Gary Jensen had no problem picturing Amy's face and body when she called.

She was one of the girls he most enjoyed watching during her workouts in the gym. He liked it when her face glowed with the sweat of her routines and her legs and arms bulged with strength. She had full breasts, which were usually the enemy of a dancer, and even a tight bra couldn't stop them from swaying seductively. Her blond hair would grow damp and paste itself to her skin. She was very attractive.

He knew she didn't like him. She'd never made a secret of it. She listened to him and followed his instructions as a coach, but she was cold whenever he talked to her. Most of the girls played the game with him and flirted back at him when he made his advances, but Amy never did. He was surprised and curious to get her call.

"Hello, Amy," he said. "What's up?"

"I have some ideas for new moves," she told him. "Some really hot stuff. I figure we're going to have to take it up a notch to win next year, right?"

"That's true," he said, listening to the pitch of her voice. She spoke haltingly, which was unusual for Amy. She was typically among the most confident girls on his team.

"I was thinking, maybe I could talk to you

about it," she went on. "Maybe we could get together."

"Of course," Gary said. "I'd like that."

"Could we meet somewhere tomorrow?"

"I wish I could, but tomorrow's not good for me. I have a meeting outside the city. What about Thursday night? I'm going to be reviewing videotapes of the competition. Why don't you come by my house, and we'll look at them together? I'd like your input."

He heard hesitation on the other end of the line. Then she said, "Yeah, all right. I'll do that."

"You know where I live, don't you? It's near the end of Bay Settlement across from the county park."

"I know it." He expected her to hang up, but she added after a long pause, "Hey, Gary, I know I should have asked this before, but how are you?"

"What do you mean?"

"Well, it hasn't been very long since you—you know, since you lost your wife, and I know how hard that was. I felt really bad for you. I just wanted to make sure you're okay."

"That's kind of you to say, Amy. I wouldn't say I'm okay, but I'm dealing with it."

"Good."

"I'll see you on Thursday."

He hung up the phone. He stroked his chin with two fingers, thinking about the girl's nervous manner and wondering about her real agenda. Part of him was suspicious at the timing, coming so soon after Florida. She'd mentioned his wife, too. He didn't like that.

He was in the master bedroom of his turn-of-the-century house, which he had bought five years ago when he moved to Green Bay. The wallpaper was a heavy pattern of burgundy and gold. The bedroom set, which came with the house, was made of walnut, with imposing four-poster columns on the queen bed and a matching ornate bureau that stood beside the window like a grim soldier. Michelle had nagged him to sell the furniture, so they could redecorate the room and make it lighter and happier. They'd never had the chance.

Gary peered out through the floor-to-ceiling curtains at the empty road beyond the yard.

He still had flashbacks of Michelle falling. He could see the terror in her eyes as she screamed. He'd cried, seeing it happen, watching her die. At that moment, he'd thought about throwing himself after her. There were still days when the pain and loss were almost impossible to bear.

If only there had been another way. If only she hadn't learned the truth.

Gary dialed his phone and watched the road, which grew darker as dusk fell. When he heard the familiar voice, he said, "It's me. We may have a problem."

17

Mark Bradley wore a white mask as he repaired the damage done to their house by the vandals. He wished the cowards had come while he was home and given him a chance to fight. On Tuesday, while Hilary was back at school, he'd swept up the glass and debris, hauled the broken furniture out to the street, and scraped down the walls. By late Wednesday, he had torn out the carpet and covered the living room in two coats of fresh paint. At least he no longer had the word staring him in the face.

KILLER.

While the paint dried, he grabbed a beer from the refrigerator and took it out to the screened three-season porch at the rear of the house. He sat down in the wrought-iron chaise, which squealed under his weight. With the bottle halfway to his lips, he realized he was still wearing the white painter's mask. He peeled it from his face, tilted the bottle, and took a long swallow. His neck was tired and sore, and he rubbed it with his fingers.

That was when he felt the small bump of two scabs on his skin. Scratches.

Mark closed his eyes and felt a cold sweat of fear form on his body. "Son of a bitch," he murmured.

He remembered Glory on the beach and felt the girl hanging on to him as she wrapped her hands around his neck. Her long nails drove into his skin, hurting him. Leaving a mark.

He knew what that meant.

The police in Florida had gathered skin cells from inside his mouth with a cotton swab and bagged the sample and labeled it. They would hunt under Glory's dead fingernails and find skin there, and analyze the tissue, and match it. One name would come out: Mark Bradley.

They'd know he had been there. On the beach. With Glory.

Mark put the bottle down. His taste for beer was gone. He stared through the dormant trees at the gray water of the harbor a hundred yards away. In two months, when the leaves unfurled, the beach would be invisible behind the birches. He couldn't help but wonder if he would be here to see it, or if they would have arrested him by then.

They can prove you were there. They can't prove you killed her.

He wasn't convinced the distinction would sway a jury if it came to that. When a teenaged girl died, everyone wanted to see someone pay the price.

Mark felt a wave of anger. It was happening to him more and more now. Moments of rage. He was naturally claustrophobic, and when the walls began to close in, he beat on them and tried to fight his way out. If he couldn't find an escape, he wanted to punish the ones who had put him here.

His phone rang on the table beside him.

It was Hilary, and he relaxed when he heard her voice. Sometimes she had a sixth sense for when he needed her.

"I'm in Northport waiting for the ferry," she told him. "I'll be home in an hour or so."

"Good."

"How's it going?" she asked.

"Better. The house is looking better."

She listened to his voice. He could feel her divining his mood. "You okay?"

"Not really."

"What's up?"

"Not on the phone," he said. He was already paranoid, wondering if the police were listening in on their calls.

"Let's go out for dinner tonight," she suggested.

"Are you sure? You know what it'll be like."

He was reluctant to go out anymore in the midst of other people from the island. He was sick of the dark stares and muttered hostility from people around them.

"Screw everybody else," Hilary told him. "We can't let them stop us from living our lives."

He smiled. "Damn right."

"See you soon."

She hung up. He picked up his beer
again and continued drinking. He reminded
himself, as he did on most days, how lucky
he had been to find Hilary Semper. Some
men weren't secure enough to marry a
woman who was smarter than they were,
but he'd had plenty of experience with
women who only wanted him to show him
off to their friends. He'd even married one
when he was twenty-five, a bubbly brunette who had stalked him on the pro tour
and seduced him into bed and then into
the courthouse. He was young; she was
young. She talked a good game about lov-
ing all the same things he did, when all she
really wanted was a ring and a husband
who made her girlfriends jealous.

It had lasted two long years. When he
divorced her, he'd sworn to himself: Never
again.

Not long after the split, he'd had ten
beers too many and driven his car into a
median on the Kennedy Expressway. Stupid. He could have died. Instead, surgery
gave him back his life, but not his career.
After rehab, he had a ninety percent range
of motion in his left shoulder, but a pro
golfer needed about a hundred and ten

percent. A hundred and twenty if you're Tiger. He wasn't going to play professionally again. Golf was dead to him.

What seemed like a curse at the time turned out to be a blessing. He was insanely competitive when he stepped onto a playing field, but he learned that he was something more than a golfer, a competitor, and an athlete. He went back to something he hadn't done since he was a teenager. Painting. He took up reading again and devoured the classics. He found himself attracted to teaching because it was so unlike his prior life and because it gave him time to become someone he liked a lot better than Mark Bradley, pro golfer.

It made him poor, too. That was the downside.

As the money dried up, he assumed the come-ons would vanish, but he discovered that looks were enough for plenty of women of all ages. He could have slept his way to a comfortable lifestyle, but he'd already been through one loveless marriage. He said yes to the occasional fling, but nothing that ever felt serious for either of them. Not until Hilary. Hilary, who was sexy and didn't even have a clue about it.

Hilary, who blew him away because everything she said was so damn interesting, and because she didn't seem to care about what anyone else thought about her.

Hilary. It took his breath away sometimes to think that *she* married *him*.

That was why the anger kept coming back. It was the fear that he might lose everything he had. He had already lost his job, and now he worried that he would lose his house, his freedom, and the one woman he'd ever really wanted.

All because he took a walk on the beach. All because of Glory Fischer.

Mark went back into the house, where the sickly sweet air freshener covered the stench of the filth that had been thrown against the walls. He decided to take a run to off-load his frustrations. For the first time, he took a key with him and locked the front door as he left the house. This was Washington Island. No one locked their doors. There was no one to fear, because the rest of the world was half an hour away across Death's Door.

Not anymore.

He stretched among the dead leaves in their dirt driveway, loosening his muscles.

The forest around him was still. As he bent and touched his fingers to his toes, he noticed his Ford Explorer sagging at a queer angle in the clearing among the trees. When he looked closely, he saw that two of the tires were flat. The rubber had been slashed, and the rusty ax that had done the damage lay next to the truck in the weeds.

They were sending him a message. He could cover it up with paint, but no one was going to let him forget. *Killer.*

Mark picked up the ax, which was heavy and old. He weighed it in his hand. He felt his anger rush back, and he threw the ax at the flaky white trunk of a young birch tree, where it impaled itself, its handle quivering. He dug the ax out and swung it again, making a deep wound in the side of the tree. He did it again and again, wood and bark flying, until he ran out of breath and the immature tree stood on nothing more than a ragged fraction of its trunk. He wrapped his hands around the tree as if it were someone's throat and pushed until the tree groaned and cracked away from its base and toppled into the forest with a crash.

He staggered backward into his driveway.

His chest heaved. His face was flushed. The ax dropped from his hand.

He heard a noise from the road and swung around fiercely, expecting to see them coming for him. The vandals. The punks. He was ready to take them on, hand to hand.

It wasn't anyone from the island.

A purple Corvette was parked at the base of his driveway, looking oddly out of place in the island wilderness. He saw a ridiculously tall man in a business suit standing next to the Corvette's door, leaning on it and watching him from behind sunglasses that made no sense on a dark day. He'd been watching as Mark exploded with rage.

It was Cab Bolton.

Cab climbed back into the rented Corvette under Bradley's hostile glare. He had no interest in having a conversation with Mark Bradley right now, but he wanted the man to know he had followed him home. The investigation wasn't over, and if Bradley thought he had escaped with his freedom that easily, he was wrong. Cab also knew, watching Bradley erupt in fury with the ax, that his original opinion of the man had been correct.

Mark Bradley had a temper. Push him hard enough, and he lost control.

Cab did a U-turn and returned to the road that led past Schoolhouse Beach and out to the island's main highway beyond the cemetery. It occurred to him that he'd been in most corners of the world, and he didn't think he had ever felt quite as remote as he did now, on this island at the tip of the Door County peninsula. The entire stretch of land north of Sturgeon Bay felt as if he were driving through a winter ghost town, with shuttered storefronts and long stretches of forest and dormant farmlands. It was beautiful and ominous, like a transplanted corner of New England where someone had posted NO TRESPASSING signs to keep out the rest of the world.

He'd never spent much time in the Midwest. In his head, he'd always thought of it as a place where winter lasted nine months, the cows outnumbered the people, and the land was flat and endless. Nothing he'd seen so far had changed his mind.

On the way back to the ferry port, he found a Western-style saloon in need of paint, immediately adjacent to the road. The sign read Bitters Pub. When he parked in the gravel in front of the bar, his Corvette stood out like a Hot Wheels play car next to the row of dusty pickups and hulking SUVs. He got out and smelled a waft of pine blowing in with the cold lake air. Inside, the odor of stale cigarette smoke choked the bar. He stripped off his sunglasses. He saw a long oak counter with stools on his left, square card tables scattered across a hardwood floor, and two pool tables at the rear. The walls were crowded with knickknacks like logging saws and skis.

Three men with huge bellies drank beer, played pool, and blew smoke rings. A bored bartender, young and cute, eyed him in his expensive suit with a curious smile. A grizzled fireplug of a man sat at the bar with a mug of coffee in front of him. Cab approached the bar, and the bartender sauntered his way. She had her black hair loose, and she wore a rust wool sweater and frayed jeans.

"Help you?"

"I'm looking for Sheriff Felix Reich," Cab told her. "One of his deputies told me I could probably find him here."

The girl nodded her head at the fireplug seated at the end of the bar. "Sheriff," she called, "somebody's looking for you."

Sheriff Reich's head swiveled slowly, and he took the measure of Cab from head to toe with the pinched expression of a man biting into a lemon. His eyes started at Cab's spiky blond hair and moved down his long body, taking in his pinstripes, tie, and polished loafers, and then traveled back up again, focusing on Cab's manicured fingernails and gold earring. When he was done, Reich turned away to study the steam rising out of his coffee cup, as if that were more interesting than anything Cab was likely to say.

"What can I do for you?" Reich said. His voice was as gravelly as the back roads on the island.

Cab took a seat two stools from the sheriff, with his back to the bar and his stiltlike legs stretched out into the middle of the hardwood floor. He balanced his elbows on the bar behind him. The white cuffs of his shirt, which were closed with onyx cufflinks, jutted out from the sleeves of his suit coat. He was accustomed to looking like an outsider and immune to the stares and silence when he went somewhere he didn't belong. This place was no different from a hundred others.

"Sheriff, my name is Cab Bolton," he said. "I'm a detective with the Naples police in Florida."

Reich, who wore a heavy flannel shirt tucked into corduroys, sighed and slid sideways on his stool. He wasn't a big man, but he was packed tightly into his clothes. His face was weathered, as if he had a permanent case of frostbite, and his blue eyes were hard and impassive.

"A detective?" he asked.

"That's right."

"Well, Detective, if one of my cops came into work wearing an earring, he'd have a choice. He could either yank it out and go home until the hole closed up, or he could quit."

Cab grinned, but Reich didn't smile back. He could see the old sheriff studying his smile and thinking, *Look at how white those teeth are.*

"I guess it's a good thing I don't work for you," Cab told him.

"What did you say your name was?"

"Cab Bolton."

"Cab? What kind of name is that?"

"I was named after my grandfather," Cab replied, selecting a new explanation and a new name to go with it. "Cornelius Abernathy Bolton."

"Abernathy?"

Cab just smiled.

Reich grunted and reached for his coffee. "You here because of Glory Fischer?"

"That's right."

"You planning to arrest Mark Bradley?"

"For now I just want to find out more about him. About Glory, too."

The bartender wandered closer and gave Cab an interested smile. She was about twenty-five, with no ring on her finger. She had big brown eyes and round cheeks. "Can I get you a drink?" she asked Cab.

Reich gestured at the lineup of alcohol bottles behind the bar. "Yeah, what is it you people drink down in Florida? Mojitos?" He pronounced it *moh-jee-toes.*

"No thanks," Cab said.

The bartender winked. "Maybe you want to join the club instead."

"What club?"

Reich snuck a smile at the fat men playing pool. They drifted closer, and the smoke in the bar thickened. "Detective, you're not just in a pub," the sheriff explained. "This is the worldwide headquarters for the Bitters Club."

"Oh?"

"That's right. It was started on the island by Tom Nelsen back in 1899. Nelsen was convinced that Angostura bitters were an elixir of health. Sort of like you Florida folks and orange juice. He drank a pint or so a day."

"A *pint* of bitters?" Cab asked.

"It's not exactly Guinness, but you get used to the taste. It's right up there with motor oil. You don't have to down a whole pint, though. If you can put back a shot glass of the stuff, you're in the club."

Cab wasn't going to let this man win his macho game. "Sure, set me up."

The bartender smirked and reached under the bar. She placed a shot glass in front of Cab and filled it with a black liquid that did look suspiciously like motor oil. Cab brought the glass under his nose and smelled it. Reich eyed him carefully, and so did the others, watching for his face to screw up with distaste. He didn't react, despite the noxious aroma that would have awakened a coma patient. He figured it was all or nothing. This wasn't brandy you sipped and savored. He swirled the liquid in the glass, tipped it to his lips, and gulped down the bitters in a single swallow. His lips pinched together involuntarily. His throat contracted. The taste reminded him of chewing cigarette butts picked out of the gutter.

"Like it?" Reich asked.

"Great," Cab croaked.

"Welcome to the club."

"I'll call my mom," Cab replied.

Reich relaxed and smiled, as if Cab had passed a Door County test of endurance. "So give me the dirt, Detective. What exactly do you have on Mark Bradley?"

Cab played with the empty shot glass. His mouth still tasted like weed killer. "Honestly? Not much."

"I'm sorry to hear it," the sheriff replied. "I couldn't nail Bradley for sexual assault last year, because Tresa Fischer was so moon-eyed in love with the bastard that she wouldn't say a word against him. You ask me, a teacher poles one of his kids, he ought to be hauled off to a pig farm for castration. We wouldn't have to worry about repeat offenders."

"You're sure they were having sex?"

"I read the girl's diary. Her imagination's not that good."

"Can you think of a reason why Bradley would kill Glory Fischer?" Cab asked.

"I can think of lots of reasons. Maybe he tried to rape her, and she fought back. Maybe he just popped his cork and went off on the girl. Take your pick."

"You may be right," Cab told Reich, "but right now, I can't even prove Bradley was on the beach with the girl. We're still running the forensics, and I hope we'll get lucky. Otherwise, we need to find somebody who saw something."

"So what do you want to get done on my turf, Detective?" Reich asked pointedly. "You're going to stir up a lot of people who are already hurting because of what happened."

"I'd like to find out if Bradley had some kind of previous relationship with Glory

Fischer. I'd also like to know if there was anything else going on in that girl's life."

Reich put down his coffee mug on the bar. "What's that supposed to mean?"

"Glory saw someone she knew in Florida. It scared her. I want to know who it was and whether it had anything to do with her death."

"Someone she knew?" Reich asked. "You think it was someone from around here?"

"That's what I'd like to find out."

Reich's lips crinkled unhappily. "My advice is to keep your eyes on the ball, Detective. I spent a lot of time with Mark Bradley last year. Having him in the middle of this thing doesn't surprise me at all."

"No?"

"No. That man is a powder keg."

"What about Glory?"

"What about her?" Reich asked.

"I hear she had problems. Stealing, drugs, sex. Sounds like she ran pretty fast for a nice country girl."

Reich shrugged. "Around here, there's not a lot to do in the quiet season. Kids get into trouble. Glory had her share. People aren't going to take it too well if you start dragging a nice girl's name through the mud. She's the victim here. Don't you forget that."

"I won't."

"Delia Fischer is a good woman. She doesn't deserve to see her kids treated like this."

"You know her well?" Cab asked.

"We're both natives. Those of us who have been around here our whole lives know everybody else, Detective."

Cab got off the bar stool. "I've taken up enough of your time, Sheriff. I've got a ferry to catch. I just didn't want to start nosing around your jurisdiction without introducing myself."

"That was a smart plan," Reich agreed. "If my deputies or I can help you nail Bradley, you tell me, okay? There's bad blood for me on this one."

"I understand." Cab nodded at the shot glass, which contained a residue of bitters. "Thanks for the drink. I'm not likely to forget it."

"I bet not."

"Tell me something, Sheriff," Cab added. "You know pretty much everything that happens around here. Is there anything else I should know about Glory Fischer? Anything that could have led to her death?"

Reich finished his coffee and wiped his mouth. "Not a damn thing, Detective. You just keep your eyes on Mark Bradley."

18

Hilary spotted the purple Corvette in the boarding line for the last ferry of the day and saw a lanky man in a business suit atop a bench in the park by the harbor. She recognized his gelled blond hair and movie star looks, and her hands tightened around the steering wheel with anxiety. She pulled sharply off the road.

Cab Bolton nodded to her as she climbed out of her car. He held a cell phone high over his head, aimed at the sky. "Hello, Mrs. Bradley," he said. "This is a beautiful island, but the cell signal sucks. It's driving me crazy."

Hilary didn't waste time with small talk. "I hope you weren't harassing my husband, Detective."

"God forbid," Cab replied pleasantly. He climbed off the bench and stood up to his full height. Hilary, who wasn't small, wasn't used to anyone towering over her the way Cab did. He gave her a disarming smile and tugged at the sleeves of his suit coat. "Is it always so cold here in late March?"

"If it's too cold for you, go back to Florida."

"Oh, I just like complaining." He glanced around the island at the rocky water beyond the harbor and the thick barrier of evergreens hugging the shoreline. "This is a barren place to live. Why did you and your husband move up here?"

"Not everyone loves the suburbs," Hilary replied.

"Were you running away from something?"

"Yes, we were. Smog. Crowds. Traffic. Concrete. Sameness."

Cab took off his sunglasses and dangled them on his fingers. His eyes were irresistibly blue. "I did my homework on you, Mrs. Bradley. People in the Highland Park schools told me you were one of the best teachers they'd ever had. They hated to lose you."

"So?"

"So I wonder why you'd give it up to work in a small school in the middle of nowhere."

"I love teaching. It doesn't matter whether the school is big or small." She added, "Mark loved it, too, until he got crucified."

"That must be hard going to work every morning, knowing people think your husband cheated on you with a student."

"I don't need your sympathy, Detective."

"I'm still curious about why the two of you moved out here. Did Mark have a problem with girls in the Illinois schools? You may as well tell me. I'll find out anyway."

"There's nothing to find," Hilary snapped. She was tired of having her motives questioned by people who didn't understand them. Cab Bolton wasn't the first, and he wouldn't be the last. Her family. Her colleagues. Her neighbors. They were all the same. They looked at her and Mark and wanted a vote in how they chose to lead their lives.

"You know what my mother said to me, Detective?" she went on. "When I told her that Mark and I were moving to Door County? She asked me how I could be such an independent woman for so many years and then give up everything in my life for a man."

"What did you say?" Cab asked.

"I told her the truth. I wasn't giving up anything at all. Mark and I were making a choice about what we wanted. That's it. That's the big secret. I don't care if you understand it."

"The two of you were just crazy in love," Cab said, and she heard cynicism in his voice.

"Spare me the sarcasm, Detective. I'm not in the mood to play games with you."

"I'm not trying to play games. I like you, Mrs. Bradley. Really. I think you're smart, and I respect that you're ferociously protective of your husband."

"But you think I'm a fool."

"I think people aren't always who we think they are," Cab told her. "While you're protecting your husband, you might start protecting yourself, too."

"If you're trying to make me doubt Mark, you can stop."

"I think you have doubts, but you won't admit them to yourself."

"Then you don't understand what it means to have faith in someone," Hilary said.

"You're right. I don't."

"If that's true, I feel sorry for you."

"Don't worry about me." Cab shoved his hands in his pockets and shrugged his body against the cold. "Look, let's assume your husband told you he was out on the beach with Glory. I'm not asking you to say yes or no, but if he was there with her, there's a good chance he killed her. You're smart enough to realize that. Maybe he didn't mean to do it. Maybe things got out of control. It doesn't matter."

"I can see I'm wasting my breath," Hilary said. "You're like everyone else around here, assuming Mark is guilty. You've appointed yourself judge and jury."

"I don't assume he's guilty, but I don't assume he's innocent, either."

"Good night, Detective." Hilary pointed at the boat, where one of the deck workers waved to attract Cab's attention. "You don't want to miss your ferry. I'd hate to think of you trapped overnight in a barren place like this."

Cab smiled and slid his car keys from his pocket. "I talked to Sheriff Reich. He's not a fan of your husband."

"I'm not a fan of the sheriff, either," Hilary replied. "He hasn't lifted a finger to stop the locals harassing us."

"He says Delia Fischer was right. Your husband was having sex with Tresa."

"Tresa was a sweet, misguided kid. That's all there was."

"Men are awfully easy to seduce," Cab reminded her. "Women usually find a way to get what they want."

Hilary was good at reading people, and she thought she could see past the armor in the detective's blue eyes. His cynicism wasn't just professional. "Is this about me or you, Detective?"

"Excuse me?"

"It sounds like there was a woman who messed with you. You loved her, and she hurt you."

Cab's face darkened. "Now who's playing games?"

"I'm sorry," Hilary said, "but don't take out your past on me and Mark."

"I'm not doing that."

"No?"

"No. I already told you I'm not assuming your husband is guilty. If the evidence points to someone else, so be it."

"If that's true, then tell me something. Did Sheriff Reich mention Glory and the fire?"

"What fire?"

"Glory lived next door to a man who burned down his house with his family in it," Hilary told him. "She was there when it happened. She almost died."

Cab's mouth puckered into a frown. "I didn't know that."

"Neither did I until today. Don't you find that interesting? This girl was a witness to a murder six years ago, and now she gets murdered herself. That's a big coincidence."

She watched Cab working through the implications of this information in his mind. Weighing its significance. Deciding if she was blowing smoke at him.

"Why do you think there's a connection?" he asked. "I'm not sure how a six-year-old crime, even a horrific one, has any relevance to what happened to Glory in Florida."

"Only that the killer escaped," Hilary said. "He's still on the run."

"The man who started the fire is at large? Is that true?"

"It's true. His name was Harris Bone. Look it up." Hilary returned to her Camry and stood outside the driver's door. She was pleased with herself. Looking at Cab Bolton and studying his face, she decided that the man might never be an ally, but he might not be an enemy, either.

"If you can get past your obsession with my husband," she called to him, "you should ask yourself the question that I've been asking myself all day, Detective. What if Harris Bone was in Florida? Think about that. What if Glory recognized him? What do you think he would do to her?"

Night fell on the island two hours later. Without daylight, the temperature dropped like a stone, dipping below the freezing mark. Gusts off the bay blasted the land and made the dark trees sway. No one came or went through the canyonlike waves of Death's Door. The ferries were done until early morning, and the private boats that traversed the passage stayed in the shelter of the harbors. The stone outpost of Washington Island was cut off from civilization, isolated and empty.

He drove without headlights. At night, under low clouds, he could barely pick out the headstones of the island cemetery laid in granite rows beside the road. Where the cemetery ended, the road disappeared into the forest, and he slowed to a crawl. The tires of the stolen pickup crept over the gravel as if it were sandpaper. Ahead of him, he spotted the pale break in the trees where the road stopped at Schoolhouse Beach. He turned right on a crossroad less than a hundred yards from the water and navigated blindly around the curves that hugged the shore. He knew where Mark Bradley lived. It wasn't far. When he was a quarter mile away, he saw house lights glowing out of the black forest like torches. He stopped.

He parked in the driveway of a home that was empty for the winter season. He got out, taking a heavy crowbar with him, nestled in his gloved hand. On the road, he was invisible as he hiked toward the lights. He stayed close to the shoulder, where the birch trees leaned over the gravel and waggled their fingers at him. The wind covered the crunching noise of his boots. Near the house, he veered into the woods, worming his way through spindly branches and mushy ground, until he was barely twenty yards from their windows.

He could see the Bradleys. They were both inside.

Mark Bradley stood by the glass, staring into the darkness directly at him. If it had been daytime, he would have felt exposed, but he knew the window was nothing but a mirror of reflections now. Behind Mark Bradley, he saw the man's wife, holding a near-empty glass of red wine. Hilary Bradley was still dressed for work in a shimmery silver blouse and black slacks that emphasized her long legs. She came up behind her husband and whispered in his ear, but he didn't react.

Hilary finished her wine and squeezed her husband's shoulder, but he remained where he was, a statue. She left the room, and a moment later, light illuminated the small square of the bathroom window down the hall. There were no curtains. In the privacy of the island, there was no one to spy. Except now. He could see her torso framed against the white tile and watched with detached interest as she undressed. She undid the buttons of her blouse and slid it down her arms and hung it on a hanger on the back of the door. Her fingers, which were topped with bright red nails, picked apart the strands of her blond hair, loosening it and letting it fall over her shoulders. She took off and folded her glasses. The effect of the innocent gesture was strangely wanton. With both hands behind her back, she unhooked her bra. The straps slipped down her shoulders, and the cups spilled from her chest. Her breasts were pale, full globes. She unzipped her slacks, stepped out of them, and peeled down her panties, bending over so that her breasts hung forward and swayed. She was naked now, but he could see her milky skin only as far as her hips. As he watched, she stepped into a running shower and disappeared.

Mark Bradley was alone.

He made his way toward the rear of the house. His footsteps were soft on the spongy earth. He felt occasional snow flurries melting on his face. He ducked under the eave and crept sideways. The living room window, which was open two inches, was immediately on his right. He edged his face around the frame to look inside. Mark Bradley was near the fireplace, studying a painting hung on the wall. The canvas was wild with bloodred strokes and strange giant angels. Bradley's back was to him, so he crossed the path of the window with two silent steps. He was near the rear corner of the house now, where a door led into the screened porch. All he needed to do was lure Bradley outside.

He told himself he was doing the right thing. They couldn't afford to be exposed.

The warped door opened outward from the porch, offering him cover. When Bradley pushed the door open, he could take a step and swing the forked tongue of the crowbar squarely into the back of Bradley's skull. One blow. That was all it would take. He'd done much harder things in his life.

He reached in his pocket and dug out a Fourth of July firecracker that was no bigger than a birthday candle. He lit the fuse of the firecracker with a cigarette lighter and flicked it end over end with his thumb. It flew and landed ten feet in front of the porch door, but the fuse fizzled and burned out without triggering a bang. He pawed inside his pocket for another noisemaker. He only had one left, and it was old and just as likely to blow up in his hand. He touched the fuse to the flame and again flicked it away, watching it arc with a tiny glow. It landed, and he could see the wick burning.

Crack.

It went off with a flash of white light, but the pop was oddly muffled. He wasn't sure if it was loud enough. There was a long, tense moment of silence, but then the old house shifted with the movement of cautious footsteps on the porch. Mark Bradley was coming closer, investigating the noise.

He cocked the crowbar in his arm.

In front of him, the porch door opened.

19

Mark?"

Hilary saw her husband in the doorway of the porch. He stopped as she called to him and turned back into the house.

"Is everything okay?" she asked.

"I heard something outside."

He lingered in the door frame. She saw him flexing his hands, as if his protective instincts had been aroused. His tension fed her own anxiety, but when he saw nothing, he let the door bang shut behind him and hooked it closed.

"Anything?" she asked.

"I guess not."

Hilary breathed easier. There were always occasional moments of fear, living in a remote area. It had been an adjustment, going from the suburbs to the island. In Chicago, there were always people around, and as claustrophobic as it had sometimes seemed to her, she realized there was a certain security about it, too. Here, with only a few hundred people spread across thirty-five square miles, there was no one nearby if something went wrong.

She also didn't know if she could trust anyone who did come to their aid now. She'd begun to see everyone as a potential threat.

Mark sensed her unease and embraced her. His presence was strong and comforting, and a little sensuous, too. He kissed her forehead and slid a fingernail down the damp skin of her chest between the silk folds of her robe. He had graceful hands. That wasn't why she'd fallen in love with him, but it was a bonus.

"You look good," he said.

She heard the erotic rumble in his voice. "That's for later. Right now, let's go to dinner."

"I'm not hungry," he said.

"Yes, you are. Go take a shower while I get dressed."

He patted her ass and stripped off his T-shirt as he headed for the bathroom. "Your hair's still wet," he called. "You could join me."

"Go," she repeated.

Hilary padded behind him in bare feet to their bedroom, which was a twelve-by-twelve square, painted in burgundy, with cracks in the old walls. The hardwood floor was cold, and the first thing she did was sit on their queen bed and put on socks. She stuck her legs into bikini panties as she stood up, then shrugged off her robe. She caught a glimpse of herself in the full-length mirror on the closet door: topless, panties, black athletic socks.

"Sexy," she muttered aloud, shaking her head.

By the time she finished dressing, Mark was out of the shower, his hair dripping on the floor. He was naked, just as she'd been earlier. She eyed the bedroom window, where the blinds were up, as they always were. They'd become casual about their se-clusion, to the point of not even thinking about other people when they were in their home. For a woman who used to close the bathroom door when she was alone in a hotel room, she'd become unself-conscious in a few short years. She dressed, undressed, showered, peed, and had sex, all in the belief that there was no one to see her.

Oddly, right now, staring at the window, she didn't feel alone. The sensation dogged her like an unsettling dream. Gooseflesh rose on her skin.

"Let's go," she murmured when Mark was dressed.

They took coats and headed out into the frosty night. She noticed that Mark didn't switch off the house lights and locked the front door behind them. As they drove, steam fogged on the glass, and she found herself shivering in the cold interior. She cupped her hands in front of the vents, waiting for warm air. Mark was silent beside her. She knew the arrival of Cab Bolton had left him shaken.

"You want to talk about it?" she asked.

Mark didn't reply immediately. He flicked on the Camry's high beams to light up the twisting stretch of road.

"I think I should tell Bolton I was out on the beach," he said finally.

Hilary shook her head. "No way."

"If the DNA matches where Glory scratched me, Bolton will find out anyway, and he'll think I have something to hide."

"You remember what Gale told us? There's no case if they can't prove you were on the beach. Period. You can't give up your best legal advantage, Mark. We have to be practical about this. For all we know, they won't be able to recover any DNA because Glory's body was in the water."

Mark's eyes strayed to the rearview mirror. "Glory was talking about fire on the beach," he told her.

"What do you mean?"

"She was humming that Billy Joel song when I first saw her. 'We Didn't Start the Fire.' She mentioned the Robert Frost poem 'Fire and Ice' and talked about the world ending in fire. She asked me—she said, why didn't I want to play with fire? It kept coming up."

"So maybe it's true," Hilary said. "Maybe something happened in Florida that was connected to the fire."

"Harris Bone?"

"It's possible. He's out there somewhere."

"If I tell Bolton what Glory said, maybe he'll realize I'm not the only game in town."

"I know how you feel, but we can't say anything that might put you at risk. Look, I'll find out whatever I can about the fire. I'll try to get Peter Hoffman to talk to me. Harris Bone was his son-in-law. He may know something that would help us figure out if Bone could have been in Florida. If I find something, I'll give it to Bolton. Okay?"

There was no answer from her husband. She realized that his eyes were fixed on the rearview mirror. Hilary twisted around and realized what Mark had seen behind them. Headlights.

Another vehicle trailed them on the highway.

"That pickup's been back there since we left," Mark murmured. "I spotted the lights when we turned at the cemetery."

"Do you have any idea who it is?"

He shook his head. It was unusual to see other vehicles on the island roads at night during the off-season, and there were only a handful of other residents living year-round in the remote lane past School-house Beach. He slowed, drawing the truck closer, until the lights were immediately behind them like giant white eyes. The vehicle made no move to pass.

Hilary squinted into the blinding brightness. "I can't see the driver or the plate."

Mark tapped the brakes and slowed until the Camry was barely doing twenty miles an hour. The pickup matched their speed and stayed on their tail, crowding their rear bumper.

"Hold on," Mark said.

He shoved down the accelerator. The Camry leaped forward, but the engine of the pickup growled, too. The road was dead straight in this part of the island, and Mark accelerated to sixty and then seventy miles an hour before the speed felt unsafe. Despite the burst of speed, the pickup closed on them again, and as it did, the driver switched on his brights, throwing a dazzling light through their rear window. Next to her, Mark blocked his eyes and pushed the mirror aside.

He braked.

The pickup accelerated. Mark barely had time to shout a warning before Hilary felt a bone-rattling impact as the truck hammered into the rear of the Camry. Her head was thrown back, snapping against the seat. The Camry swerved, fishtailing as Mark struggled to keep control. The car veered from shoulder to shoulder, weaving close to the gullies on both sides. Finally, the Camry slowed, and Mark shunted the car onto the right-side shoulder, kicking up dark clouds of gravel and leaves.

The pickup flew past them. Hilary barely saw the shape of the truck; she couldn't pick out its color or see the driver. Ahead of them, she watched its taillights grow distant.

Mark breathed fast. His face was beet red, his body knotted up with fury.

"This ends now," he said.

"Mark, don't."

He didn't listen to her. He gunned the engine and chased the pickup. Hilary clung to the door and bit her lip until she thought she tasted blood in her mouth. She saw the red lights of the truck a mile ahead of them, and Mark gained on the other vehicle a tenth of a mile at a time. The chassis of the Camry rattled. The border of the forest was a wavy blur.

"Slow down!" she shouted. "For God's sake, Mark, you'll get us both killed."

Mark's hands remained locked around

the steering wheel, and his eyes were riveted on the road. The car's engine howled in her ears. Wind sang in the seams of the windows. They were half a mile behind the pickup when the taillights winked out in a single instant. Mark slowed sharply, but he was still going forty miles an hour as the straightaway ended in a rightward curve. The car yawed left. He yanked down on the wheel. Hilary was afraid they would roll, but the tires grabbed the pavement, and he accelerated safely out of the turn.

That was when she saw a huge dark shape immediately ahead of them. The pickup truck was parked sideways, blocking the road at the end of their headlight beams.

There was no time to stop.

"Oh, no," she gasped.

20

Cab drove through the deserted streets of the town of Fish Creek and parked outside the guesthouse near the harbor. It was a quaint village of candle shops and cafés on the west coast of the peninsula, choked with tourists in August, but quiet on a mid-week evening in March. He'd rented a two-story apartment. The smell of the bay was sweet as he got out of his Corvette, but he didn't linger in the freezing air. He let himself inside and climbed the stairs to the main level of the apartment, which had a full kitchen, a fireplace, and a balcony that looked out on the water.

He was paying for it himself. He didn't apologize for the luxuries he'd known his whole life. His money—or his mother's money, to be precise—helped him deal with the ugliness of the world. Sometimes, when he was drunk enough to be honest with himself, he also acknowledged that his money allowed him to build a hiding place wherever he went. A pretty cage.

Cab turned on the oven in the apartment's kitchen. He'd found a restaurant on the north side of town that sold vegetarian quiche, and he'd ordered it to go, along with a bottle of Stags' Leap chardonnay. He deposited the quiche on a foil-lined baking sheet and put it in the oven, then located a corkscrew and opened the wine. He found a glass in a cabinet above the stove and poured the wine almost to the rim. With the chardonnay in hand, he dimmed the lights in the apartment and switched on the gas fireplace. He settled into the leather sofa, put up his long legs, and drank the wine in gulps as he watched the fire.

He thought about calling his mother. They texted each other several times a month, but he hadn't actually heard her voice in six weeks. It was the middle of the night in London, so he used his phone to send her a message instead.

Cold as hell here. Lonely but beautiful. See pic. C.

He attached a picture he'd taken with his phone on the crossing from Washington Island, with the angry water against the gray sky and the forested coastline of the peninsula looming ahead of him. His rented Corvette had been the only vehicle on the ferry. Right now, in the empty guesthouse, he felt like the only man alive in the town of Fish Creek.

He was accustomed to that sense of isolation. He thought of it as being homeless with a roof over his head. If he were back in his condominium in Florida, he would have felt the same way.

His mother had extended an open invitation to join her in London. Neither one of them had anyone else in their lives who really mattered. Even so, he'd resisted moving there, because he didn't know if he was ready to stop running. Whenever he looked back, he saw Vivian Frost chasing him. He still needed to exorcise her ghost. That was something his mother didn't understand, because he'd never told her the truth about Vivian's death.

Cab finished his glass of wine. He got up, checked the quiche in the oven, and poured a new glass before sitting down again. He watched the gas fire, which burned in a controlled fashion, never changing. Fire wasn't like that. It was volatile and unpredictable, twisting with the wind, sucking energy out of the air. It was also, he knew, a particularly excruciating way to die. Hilary Bradley might have been blowing smoke his way with her story about Harris Bone, but she was right about one thing. If you were capable of burning up your wife and children, then you were the owner of a cold, dead soul, and you would feel little remorse watching the life flicker out of a girl's eyes on the beach.

Then again, he'd felt no remorse himself watching Vivian die. Not then. Not until later.

Cab got up restlessly and took his wine with him. He walked to the west end of the apartment and pushed open the glass doors that led to the balcony. He went outside, where the wind shrieked and cut at his face. The empty boat docks of the harbor were below him, and streetlights glowed in halos along the waterfront.

He thought about Hilary Bradley and re-alized he was annoyed with her. He was used to being the smartest person in the room, and he had the sense that she was every bit as smart as he was. He didn't like that she had put a finger squarely on his vulnerability without knowing anything about him. It also bothered him that he ex-perienced a glimmer of jealousy at the idea that she was so deeply in love with an-other man. It was an unwelcome reminder that his own life was emotionally and sex-ually barren. When he did have sex, it was generally the end of a relationship, not the beginning. He'd even gone so far as to pay for sex on a few occasions when he was living overseas, in order to be free of any complications.

"Cab."

He heard the voice, but he didn't move or look around, because he knew it wasn't real. It was just the echo of a ghost. Vivian had always had this way of wrapping her Spanish-tinged British accent around his name, so that it came from her lips like a prayer. She'd said it that way so many times. When she recognized his voice on the phone. When she was under him and her body was arching with one of her violent orgasms. When she was on her knees on the beach, pleading for her life. Begging him to spare her.

Cab.

That was the last word she'd ever spoken.

She disappeared on a Tuesday.

They had planned to meet for paella and Mahou at a street café north of the Diagonal, but Cab sat there alone for an hour, watching the crowds for her face. She never arrived. When he walked to her apartment six blocks away, everything personal about her had been stripped. The kitchen and bathroom stank of bleach. It was as if she had never existed. She left nothing behind.

The next morning, black smoke poured skyward from the shattered windows of the Estacio-Sants train station. Twenty-seven people died.

The Spanish police needed only four hours to identify the terrorist behind the bombing. Cab knew he'd been played

for a fool when he saw the CCTV feed from inside the station. The grainy footage showed Diego Martin, an American fugitive wanted for gang murders in Phoenix, arm in arm with Vivian Frost.

Diego Martin, who had led Cab and the FBI on a chase to Barcelona. Diego Martin, who had used Vivian to spy on Cab instead.

There had never been any love in Vivian's heart. Only sex and betrayal. Only lies.

That night, Cab drove north. He brought his gun. He knew what no one else did; he knew where they'd gone. A few days earlier, he'd found reservations for a rented house on a secluded beach near the rocky coast of Tossa de Mar. It was the ideal getaway for two people to disappear.

Vivian and Diego.

He arrived after midnight on one of the most serene nights imaginable. The gentle breeze off the Mediterranean was warm, the air was scented with flowers, and moonlight flooded the beach. He climbed down the sharp hillside to the sheltered cove and quickly realized that he wasn't alone by the still water. They were there. He could see them on the sand. Entwined. Vivian on top, her back to him, displaying an ivory expanse of skin sloping from her neck to the cleft of her buttocks. He heard the guttural noises from her throat, so intimately familiar to him, and even now, after everything, her abandon could arouse him. They were fifty yards away, in the wet sand, close enough for the surf to lap at their bodies.

He lifted his gun as he walked closer. He thought he had the element of surprise, but he was young and out of his head with anger.

Diego's hand moved with the speed of a snake. Cab dove into the surf as bullets screamed past his head. When he spun back with his own gun, Diego already had Vivian in front of him. His gun was at her temple. Diego lurched out of the sand, dragging Vivian with him.

"You want to kill me," Diego said, "but you have to kill her first."

"Do you think that's a problem for me?" Cab asked.

"I know this woman. I know what she does to you."

"Cab," Vivian pleaded. "Cab, I'm sorry. Let us go."

He stared at her. She was naked, her body lit up by the moonlight, shadows under her breasts. Streaks of sand clung to her damp skin. The natural thing would have been to fold her up in his arms and lower her to the beach and make love to her.

"Drop the gun," Cab said, "or I'll kill you both."

"I don't think you will," Diego replied calmly. "You'd let me kill you if it meant saving this wonderful whore."

Vivian begged. "Cab, please."

He kept the gun steady in his long, outstretched arms. "Viv, you know he's going to kill you, don't you?"

"Cab," she whispered. "Just go."

"Why do you think he brought the gun to the beach, Viv? Just because the police might come? Come on, you're smarter than that. This man travels solo. He was going to let you make love to him one last time, and then he was going to put a bullet in your head."

Diego began to back up in the sand.

"Once he's safe, you're dead, Viv," Cab told her.

He could see her blue eyes. They were always the same—smart, cool, and infinitely calculating. She knew he was right. It made him feel good to realize that she'd been betrayed, too. Her eyes dipped to the sand, and he understood; she was about to drop out of his arms. Her legs buckled, she fell, and there Diego was, head and torso exposed. Cab shot him four times, in his chest, neck, eye, and forehead. What he enjoyed most was the surprise. The disbelief. As if it had never occurred to Diego that this woman could ever betray him.

Diego lay on his back in the water, dead. Vivian sprang to her feet, crying, as if in relief, as if he'd freed her from a monster. "Oh, God, Cab, thank you, thank you."

She took a step toward him, her arms wide.

"Stop."

Vivian froze. "Cab, what are you doing?"

Cab aimed his gun again, this time at

her head. "Get on your knees," he told her.

She stood in the sand. "Cab."

"Do it!" he shouted.

Vivian's knees sank into the dark sand. She squared her shoulders, as if to show off her breasts to him. She was beautiful, even with her white skin splattered with Diego's blood.

"So what happens now?" she asked him.

"Now I take you to the police. Now you spend the rest of your life in a stinking hole."

"You can't do that to me."

"Watch me."

"I lied to you, Cab," she admitted. "I cheated on you. I betrayed you. But the rest? I didn't know. Diego was running from you, but I had no idea what he was planning. I would have told you if I'd known."

"Twenty-seven people died, Vivian. The police won't care. No one will care."

"Just let me walk away. You have Diego. He's dead."

"You can mourn him while you sit in your little box."

Vivian's face screwed up in anger. "Is that what this is about? I fucked you, and now you fuck me back?"

"This isn't about you and me."

"Oh, like hell it's not." Vivian spread her knees wide, exposing the shadow between her legs. She leaned backward, stretching her torso, balancing on her palms. "Is this what you want? You want a last ride, like Diego?"

He felt his fury resurfacing. "Shut up."

"Come on, Cab. I'm just a whore. I'll do whatever you tell me to do."

"Stop it. How could you do this to me?"

"I'm sorry. We were both fools."

"I loved you," Cab shouted. "I still love you."

She bowed her head. Her hair fell across her face. "Then let me go. Don't put me in jail for the rest of my life just because I lied to you."

"I don't have a choice, Vivian."

"Cab," she pleaded again.

He wanted it to be over. He never wanted to see her again. He wanted to begin the process of excising her face from his memory. Cab let his arm fall, pointing his gun toward the beach. He hadn't counted on her desperation, her willingness to betray him again. Vivian grabbed Diego's gun from the sand, taking him by surprise. She didn't hesitate. She wasn't sentimental. In a single motion, she swung her bare arm around and fired.

She missed. She was an amateur. The bullet sang by his ear, but Vivian never made a mistake twice. Her arm shifted, aiming again, and he knew her next shot would be dead square into his brain.

Cab raised his arm and pulled the trigger on the woman he loved. He didn't miss.

Cab's wineglass was empty, and his skin was numb. He turned his back on the harbor and went inside. In the warmth of the apartment, he smelled his quiche burning, and when he opened the oven to a cloud of smoke, he saw that his dinner was charred and inedible. It didn't matter. He wasn't hungry anymore. He poured more wine. More than half the bottle was gone.

His phone rang. He dug it out of his pocket and checked the caller ID and saw that Lala Mosqueda was calling from Florida. He was glad to have a conversation with someone other than Vivian, and the truth was, he missed Lala. He'd felt himself falling for her when they dated. He didn't know if their relationship would have gone anywhere, but he hadn't wanted the risk of leaving himself vulnerable, as he had done once before. That was why he'd pushed her away. As usual.

"Mosquito," he said automatically, and his face screwed up with self-disgust. He was doing it again. "Sorry. Lala."

"Hello, Cab," she replied. "I tried you twice. Where are you?"

"The Arctic, I think. I'm pretty sure I saw a polar bear. Anyway, the signal comes and goes around here. Are you still at the office?"

"No, I'm home."

"Good. You work too hard."

Lala was slow to reply. He knew she was wondering if he would sting her with a joke. Anything to maintain their distance.

"Yeah, well, home's no treat. The neighbor's yipper dog is barking again, and someone didn't take out their trash this week, and the AC is broken, so it's like a compost pile in the rain forest in here."

"Florida," he said.

"Exactly."

"You're welcome to stay at my place while I'm gone," Cab suggested.

Lala was silent.

"It's right on the beach," he added.

"I know," she replied coolly.

"I know you know. I'm just saying. The AC works. You could feed my fish."

"You have fish?"

"Actually, no."

"Are you drunk, Cab?" Lala asked.

"A little."

"So what, is this a game or something?"

"No, I'm serious. If you want to stay there, I have a spare key in my desk. You should do it."

"Thanks," she replied, "but I think I'll pass. We both decided that once was enough when it came to my staying at your place. Remember?"

Cab knew he deserved the reproach. He also knew it was easier to open the door to a woman when he was a thousand miles away. "Sure."

"Nothing personal," she said with an edge.

"No."

"I called to give you an update on this end," she told him.

"Go ahead."

He listened to her quietness on the line. They'd both pushed too far. It had become a sport with them, leaving bruises on the other. He half-expected her to apologize, but she didn't, and he didn't want an apology anyway. That would just make him feel sorrier for himself.

"You made the right choice," Lala said. "Going to Door County, I mean. So far, things are still pointing that way."

"You mean Mark Bradley?"

"Yes, but not just him."

"Then who?"

"The boyfriend. Troy Geier."

"What about him?" Cab asked.

"I tracked down a girl who was at the hotel pool on Saturday night when Glory and Troy were there. According to this girl, Glory was flirting with other boys at the pool, right in front of Troy. I mean, it sounds like she was groping some of them under the water. Troy flipped. He pulled Glory aside, and the two of them went at it. The girl couldn't hear exactly what they were saying, but she got the gist. When Troy stormed away, she said he looked like he was ready to explode. Those were her words."

"Troy didn't strike me as having the guts to stand up to anyone," Cab said.

"Well, what if he woke up in the middle of the night and Glory wasn't back in their room? We know he'd been drinking, and he was already pretty steamed at her."

"True enough. Any word from the ME? Was there evidence of sexual intercourse?"

"He can't say yes or no," Lala replied. "That's the bad news. The Gulf gave her a saltwater douche."

"What's the good news?"

"The good news is that two of her fingers were buried in enough sand that the water didn't wash away all the organic material. He found some skin cells, enough to run DNA matching. Including the sample we took from Mark Bradley. We'll need to get a swab from the boyfriend, too."

"I'll work with the sheriff's department up here," Cab told her. "Just for the hell of it, see if we can get a sample from the bartender. Ronnie Trask."

"Already in progress. Mr. Trask was glad to oblige in order to clear his name."

"Good. Oh, there's something else you can do for me. It looks like Glory may have been a witness at a murder scene several years ago. Sounds bad—a husband torched his house with his family in it. The guy's still at large. His name is Harris Bone. Come up with everything you can on him and the fire, okay?"

"Sure," Lala said. "Is there a chance this guy was in Florida?"

"I don't know. Once we get a profile, let's start comparing it to hotel guests. Glory saw someone she knew, and she got scared. If it was Bone, she had plenty of reason to run."

"Okay." She added, "You want more good news?"

"Definitely."

"I got another call. Another witness."

"Tell me someone saw Mark Bradley on the beach that night," Cab said.

"You lead a charmed life," Lala replied. "This guy had a room on the Gulf side on the tenth floor. He says he couldn't sleep, so he was out on his balcony in the middle of the night smoking a cigar. He saw a man heading out to the beach from a ground-floor room below him sometime after two thirty."

"Could he identify him?"

"No, the man's back was to him, but he said the guy was wearing a bright yellow tank top."

"Did he see Glory, too?" Cab asked.

"Not exactly, but he spotted this same guy down on the beach a while later. He could see the tank top. He couldn't make out everything at that distance, but he's sure the man met up with a girl down there. And get this. He says the two of them were kissing."

21

_____

The Camry plunged into the black side
door of the abandoned pickup.

Glass sprayed. The headlights shattered
and went dark. The chassis crumpled like
an accordion, sucking up the energy of
the crash in a loud, tortured twisting of
metal. The car swung into a dizzying spin
but stayed upright, a mess of folded steel.
Ahead of them, hammered by the impact,
the pickup rolled bottom over top and spilled
into the gully on the far side of the road.

Inside the car, Hilary felt her body snap
forward, airborne. In the fraction of a second before the safety belt seized across

her chest, the air bag exploded at two hundred miles an hour and began to deflate as she crushed against it. The balloon filled her face, and then she lurched backward, tossed between the seat and the strap like a rag doll. It was over as quickly as it began. The spin slowed. The momentum of the car bled away, and it drifted to a stop at an angle on the highway.

She heard a hiss of steam venting, but otherwise, the aftermath was oddly silent. Her eyes were squeezed shut, and she blinked, opening them but seeing nothing. There was a chemical smell in the car. Pieces of the shattered windshield sprinkled into her lap like popcorn, and cold air blew through the gap and stung the abrasions on her cheek. As her eyes adjusted, she saw the air bag drooped over the dashboard. Outside, over the tented metal of the hood, she saw the outline of evergreens beyond the car and a slice of night sky.

"Hilary."

It was Mark. His voice was strangled with fear and urgency. Her brain was rattled, and she momentarily forgot how to speak.

"Hil."

"I'm okay," she murmured.

"Don't move."

She heard him struggle with his door, prying it open. When he spilled onto the road, his knees caved, and he grabbed on to the frame to steady himself. His shoes kicked through metal and glass as he came around the rear of the car. He yanked on her door, and she felt him unlock her belt, and she dissolved limply into his arms. She clung to him as he helped her out of the destroyed chassis. Her legs bent like rubber as they hit the ground.

"You have to sit down," he said.

She didn't protest. They were near the shoulder, and he kept her upright for several steps until she could sink down onto the dirt. Her legs dangled over the ditch. Her hair was plastered over her face. He slid down next to her and supported her back.

Hilary put a hand to her cheek, and it came back wet. "I'm bleeding," she said.

"You have a cut from the glass. That's all I see. How are you?"

She took stock of herself. "No serious damage, I think. What about you?"

"Same."

She eyed the remains of the Camry, which was twisted into an unrecognizable heap almost to the windshield. On the other side of the highway, she saw the upside-down wheels of the pickup jutting out of the ditch.

"God, Hil, I'm so sorry," he told her. "If I'd lost you—"

"You didn't." She added, "Can you walk? We should see if anyone was in the truck."

"I'll check."

Mark pushed himself up. Hilary watched him limp past their car and skid down the side of the ditch near the pickup. She could see his head and shoulders as he examined the truck. When he climbed back to the road, he called across to her.

"It's empty."

He returned to the open driver's door of the Camry and reached down to the floor. She saw the trunk pop with a soft click, as if they were doing nothing but putting groceries inside. He reached into the trunk and extracted a first aid kit and a roadside emergency pack. He dug into the pack, and soon she heard sizzling and saw a fiery red light glowing as he lit a flare to warn oncoming traffic.

He came back and bent down beside her. He'd brought a blanket from the trunk, and he wrapped it around her shoulders. He dabbed at her cheek with a soft cloth, causing her to wince. The cloth came away doused in red.

"Facial cuts really bleed," he said.

"How bad is it?"

"Not bad. Small."

She knew she sounded vain, worried about a scar. She wondered if she would be reminded of this moment every time she looked in a mirror. "I'm still beautiful, right?" she said, cracking a wan smile.

"Gorgeous." He applied a small pad to her face and covered it with tape. He caressed her other cheek with the back of his hand, and she held it there, savoring his touch. His face flickered along with the light of the flare.

"Did you recognize the truck?" she asked.

"No, I haven't seen it on the roads around here."

"Where's the driver?"

Mark shook his head. "I don't know."

"He could still be close."

Whoever had driven the pickup and

then left it in their path had disappeared into the woods and escaped on foot. Or maybe he was still in the trees, watching them. Mark stood up and made a slow circle, studying the forest. Hilary closed her eyes and listened for noises close by, like the sound of branches snapping underfoot. She heard nothing. The sensation of being watched, which had dogged her at home, was gone.

"I think we're alone," she said, "but he was there before."

"What do you mean?"

"At the house. He was at the house, too. Remember? You heard something outside."

He nodded. "Who's doing this to us?"

"I don't know."

"I'll try to reach 911," Mark said. He dug into his pocket for his phone and checked the signal strength. "Thank God for Verizon."

"I love that little guy with the glasses," Hilary murmured.

She waited and listened to Mark estimating their location for the emergency operator. Her body ached, and she was exhausted and hungry. The blanket didn't stop her from feeling chilled, and her pants were cold where she sat on the ground. She closed her eyes.

"Ten minutes," she heard Mark say.

She didn't reply. Her head swam. She was conscious of Mark sitting on the road behind her and of his arms gently taking her shoulders and easing her body back onto his chest. He stroked her hair and whispered in her ear. *I love you. Thank God you're okay.* She tried to say something, to talk, but the signals left her brain and broke into fragments long before they reached her mouth.

She had only one more conscious thought before she drifted away.

Someone was trying to kill them.

22

Cab found Sheriff Reich behind his desk on Thursday morning in the county administration building in Sturgeon Bay, which was the southernmost town on the peninsula. Sturgeon Bay was where people drove to get a taste of the suburbs in chain stores, big box retailers, and greasy fast food restaurants. North of the city, those things disappeared. The hour-long drive from Sturgeon Bay to the tip of the rock at Northport was a journey past miles of gnarled cherry trees, roadside farmers' markets, and sleepy block-long seaside towns. To Cab, it felt like a ship-in-a-bottle world.

Sheriff Reich sat in a leather chair that was oversized for his compact frame. He wore black reading glasses on the end of his stub nose and a white uniform shirt with silver buttons. His brown sheriff's coat, looking starched and perfect, was hung behind the door. On the walls, Cab noted photos and commendations from the man's service in Vietnam and framed newspaper articles of major Door County events from the past thirty years. There was also a WANTED poster featuring the jail-house front-and-side photographs of a fit, balding man in his late thirties.

The name on the poster, in bold letters, was Harris Bone.

Reich, who was poring over paperwork, took off his black glasses and eased back in his chair when he saw Cab in the door-way. "Detective Bolton," he said.

"Good morning, Sheriff," Cab said. "I'm surprised to see you here so early. You have a long commute from the island."

Reich shrugged. "Most days, I fly my Cessna down here. I keep a place in town for the bad weather. Otherwise, I'm not at my desk much. I don't believe a sheriff makes much of a difference when he's stuck inside."

"That's a good philosophy."

"I called your lieutenant about you, Detective," Reich informed him, twiddling his glasses in his fingers.

"That must have been an interesting conversation."

"It was. He tells me you're smart, but you don't play well with others."

"That's fair," Cab agreed.

"He also says you're stubborn, indifferent to authority, and condescending."

"Guilty."

"He told me about your mother, too. That explains a lot. I figured you were either rich or on the take. Most cops don't rent Corvettes."

"They don't own Cessnas, either," Cab pointed out with a smile.

"I'm not saying having money is a crime," Reich replied. "I've got a plane, I've got a boat, a couple of trucks. My family was smart enough to snap up a lot of real estate around here back when it was cheap. I could retire, but I don't want to sit on my ass all day."

"Then we have something in common," Cab said.

"That's about the only thing, Detective. What can I do for you?"

"I heard about the accident on the island."

"You mean the Bradleys?"

"Yes. Are they okay?"

"Bruised but fine."

"Do you have any idea who was responsible?" Cab asked.

"I'm not sure how that concerns you. This is a local investigation."

"Mark Bradley is a suspect in my homicide case."

"Well, it looks like someone almost cut your case short. Some cops wouldn't lose sleep over that."

"I don't want a vigilante killing a man and his wife on the basis of rumors," Cab replied. "If he's guilty, I want to prove it and put him behind bars."

Reich nodded. "I agree."

"Washington Island isn't a big place. No one came or went last night unless they had a big boat, right? With your history around here, I would think you'd already know who did this."

Reich's frown lines deepened into canyons. "You can be indifferent to authority and condescending in your own jurisdiction, Detective. Not with me. Not on my turf."

"Fair enough, you're right. I'm sorry."

"For your information, the truck used in the accident was stolen from an island farm. We're checking it over now. I can think of a couple dozen hotheads who know Delia Fischer and might have done this, but they're not likely to be stupid enough to admit it to me. Don't worry, I'll get them."

"I'm sure you will."

"Is that all you wanted, Detective? Because if so, I'm pretty busy this morning."

"I promised to keep you up to date on my own investigation," Cab informed him. "We've located new witnesses among the people who were at the hotel on Saturday. Apparently Glory had a big argument with her boyfriend, Troy Geier, a few hours before the murder."

Reich snorted. "Troy? You're wasting your time."

"Maybe so, but he wasn't straight with me. I'm going to talk to him again."

"What else do you have?" Reich asked.

"Another witness saw a man on the

beach with a girl in the right location and time frame. They were physically involved. Based on the description, we think it was Mark Bradley. I want to talk to the witness myself, but if it pans out, it's significant. If we can combine it with DNA evidence, we'll be on the way to making a case that hangs together."

"Excellent. I appreciate the update, Detective. As I said, my men and I are happy to help if we can."

"There's something else," Cab told him.

"What?"

"I ran into Hilary Bradley yesterday afternoon. She told me about Glory Fischer and the fire." Cab nodded at the poster on Reich's wall. "She told me about Harris Bone, too."

"So?"

"So I'm surprised you didn't mention it to me, Sheriff," Cab said. "I asked if there was anything else I should know about Glory Fischer."

"I don't see how a six-year-old crime is relevant to your investigation."

"Harris Bone is still at large. That makes him a suspect."

Reich shook his head dismissively. "Harris? A suspect? You think he just happened to be in Florida and happened to run into Glory Fischer?"

"Strange things happen. Glory saw someone she knew. We have a witness who said she looked scared."

Reich pushed his leather chair back and got up. He kept a coffeemaker on the credenza on the opposite wall, and he poured himself a cup in an oversized mug from a restaurant called the Viking Grill. It smelled strong. He gestured at Cab with the pot, but Cab shook his head. Reich sat down and sipped his black coffee.

"What makes you think it was Harris?" Reich asked.

"Frankly, I don't believe it was. I don't believe in straw men when I've got a suspect like Mark Bradley who was out on the beach and has ties to the girl's family. However, I also know what reasonable doubt looks like, and I know what a good defense lawyer would do with this information. If I don't look into it, I'll have to explain why on the witness stand."

"Lawyers." Reich spat out the word.

"Okay, what do you need? What can I tell you?"

"First, I need anything that can help us figure out if Harris Bone was staying at or working in the hotel in Naples under a new identity. Photos, fingerprints, DNA, background, whatever you have."

Reich nodded. "My chief deputy can pull together materials for you from our files. I'll make sure you have it by noon."

"Thank you. Second, I want to know more about him. What happened that night? What kind of man burns up his family?"

Reich studied the poster of Harris Bone on his wall, and his face darkened. "I'll be honest with you, Harris is about the last thing in the world I want to talk about. A lot of people here were hoping we'd finally turned the page on the fire. You know what that kind of crime does to a community. The scars linger."

"I know."

Reich pointed at a 1960s-era photograph near the WANTED poster that showed two dirty men in uniform, their faces green with camouflage, arms around each other's shoulders. "That's me and Pete Hoffman. Pete saved my life overseas. More than once, in fact. Harris killed Pete's daughter and two of his grandchildren, and he did it in a horrible way. Pete never got over it. It ruined his life. I don't like to see my best friend having to deal with that grief all over again."

"I understand. If I can spare him, I will, but I can't make any promises. Right now, the biggest thing standing between me and a case against Mark Bradley is Harris Bone. It may be a distraction, but it's real."

"I hear you. I know how the game is played."

Cab got up and examined the photograph of Harris Bone. The man's eyes were devoid of emotion, like a robot's. He was handsome but empty. "Did you know him well?"

"Who, Harris? Sure, he was a good-looking guy, but mousy and quiet even as a kid. I knew his parents, Lowell and Katherine; they ran a liquor store here in town. Harris took it over when Katherine died, but he didn't have much of a business sense. Pete told Nettie right from the start that the guy was a loser. Nettie didn't listen. Kids never do, right?"

Cab sat down again. "What about his wife? What was she like?"

"Nettie was a pretty little thing. Kind of a God nut, like Pete. Church every Sunday, always reading the Bible to the three kids, hosting prayer groups at their house. Harris played along. I never knew if he believed it or if it was just talk. You could never be sure with him. It didn't stop him from running around, either. Nettie told Pete that Harris was cheating on her. Not that I really blame him. Sounds like Nettie didn't have much interest in sex even before the accident."

"Accident?" Cab said.

Reich nodded. "Car accident. It was bad. Harris was driving, and Delia Fischer's husband, Arno, was in the passenger seat. The wives were in back. They'd all been out to dinner here in Sturgeon Bay and were heading home. They'd had too much to drink. Harris lost control on a slick curve and drove into a tree, full speed. Arno died. Nettie wound up in a wheelchair. Delia was lucky, just a couple broken bones. Same with Harris. After that, Nettie was even worse. She made life hell for Harris."

"Wait a minute, are you saying Glory Fischer lost her father in that accident?" Cab asked. "Harris Bone killed her father?"

"Yeah. Some families get lucky, and some just keep getting hit by lightning. That's Delia. You can understand why I want that woman to get some justice for her daughters."

"This makes it a hell of a lot harder to do that," Cab told him. "The more connections between the Bones and the Fischers, the more a jury might wonder if Glory really did see Harris at the hotel that night. It gives her an extra reason to want to see him captured—and to be afraid of him."

Reich scoffed. "These families were neighbors. They lived across the street from one another. Their kids played together. That's all it was. Glory was too young to understand that her father's death had anything to do with Harris. Even Delia didn't blame him. They'd all been drinking."

Cab wasn't convinced. "Go on," he said. "What about the fire?"

"What do you want to know? You want me to psychoanalyze the son of a bitch? He set the fire and then watched it burn like it was some kind of backyard barbecue.

Nettie and the boys died. If it wasn't for Delia, Jen would have died, too."

"What do you mean?"

"Jen spent the night with the Fischers. Delia knew how bad it was for the girl at home. All the fights. It wasn't just Harris and Nettie, it was the boys. They picked up the poison from their mom. Delia took pity on her, and it's a good thing. Pete still sends Delia flowers every year to thank her."

Cab didn't say anything for a long time. Finally, when he sensed Reich's impatience, he said, "This is ugly, Sheriff. You know how ugly this is."

"I do."

"I came here ninety-five percent convinced that Mark Bradley killed Glory Fischer."

"Trust your instincts," Reich told him.

"That's the problem. My instincts don't like this one little bit. If Glory saw Harris—"

"She didn't."

"Sometimes you bump into your past at the worst possible time," Cab pointed out.

"You said you have a witness. Bradley and Glory were kissing on the beach."

"I still don't like the coincidence."

The sheriff leaned forward with his elbows on his desk. "Detective Bolton, I'm not going to tell you how to do your job. This is your case, not mine. My only interest is making sure that Delia Fischer doesn't have to grieve for her daughter without seeing her killer punished. I'd hate to see the ghost of Harris Bone getting in the way of that."

"So would I."

Reich turned his head sideways. With his index finger, he pointed to a two-inch jagged line on his skull where the hair didn't grow. "You see that scar?"

Cab nodded. "Looks bad. Did you get it in Vietnam?"

"No, I got it in a field about forty miles south of here. That's where Harris Bone cracked my head open with a rock when I let him out of the car for a piss as I was getting ready to dump him in Supermax for the rest of his stinking life. When I woke up, he was long gone. So you know what, Detective? Part of me hopes I'm wrong and you're right. I hope Glory really did see that son of a bitch in Florida, and I hope you find the rock he's hiding under, and I hope you bring him here and leave me alone with him for five minutes. That's all I want, five minutes. Harris Bone and I have unfinished business."

23

Amy Leigh sat on a bench near the trails of the Cofrin Arboretum, unwinding after her run. Beside her, Katie wore sweats and a T-shirt adorned with the school's Phoenix logo. Despite the frigid morning, sweat trickled from her bobbed black hair down the line of her jaw, and her shirt was stained with a triangle of sweat, too. Her glasses kept slipping down her nose. Her roommate lit a cigarette. She always smoked after the two of them jogged, which Amy hated.

Cars came and went on the circular drive around the perimeter of the campus. The school was perched on a bluff a few miles outside downtown Green Bay. The city was gray and industrial, haunted by hardscrabble, beer-drinking cheeseheads who worshipped at the shrine of Lambeau Field, but the university itself was an enclave of green athletic fields and brick academic buildings ringed by the lushly wooded nature preserve.

The two girls stretched out their legs and relaxed. A bright red cardinal flicked among the bare branches of the trees and sang to them.

"You still going to Gary Jensen's house tonight?" Katie asked.

"Yeah."

"You want me to go with you?"

"No, I'll be okay."

"I'm still not sure what you think you're going to accomplish."

"I just want to see how he reacts," Amy said.

"What, you're going to blurt out, 'Hey, Gary, did you strangle that girl on the beach in Florida?'"

"No, don't be stupid. I want to drop some hints and see what he says. I'll know if he's lying."

Katie shook her head. "Some liars are pretty good at it, Ames."

"We'll see."

Her roommate shivered as the cold air began to overtake the warmth of the run. "I did a little poking around on my own."

"About Gary?"

Katie nodded. "I had coffee with a secretary in the Phy Ed department. I said it was for a follow-up story on the dance competition in Florida, but we did a little gossiping, too. Mainly about Gary's wife."

"What did she tell you?"

"Well, the rumor is he was having an affair. Hot and heavy."

"You mean before his wife died?"

"Yep."

"Who was the other woman?"

Katie shrugged. "Don't know. It may not even be true."

"I can't believe no one told the police."

"People aren't going to call the cops about hunches and suspicions. That's all you've got, you know. I haven't found anything to link Gary to Glory Fischer. You saw him with a girl who may have been Glory, but maybe not."

"I heard him coming back to his room late, too."

"Are you sure? My room was a couple doors down, and I didn't hear anything."

"It was him," Amy insisted. "I heard his door open and close."

"It doesn't prove anything."

"I know."

"Did you talk to your old coach about any of this? Hilary Bradley?"

"Not yet. I don't know if I have anything to tell her."

Katie stood up and tugged her damp shirt away from her chest. She stubbed out her cigarette on the ground. "Well, don't make an ass of yourself."

"Yeah."

"You coming back to the room?"

Amy shook her head. "I'll do a couple more miles."

"Jeez, you're extreme. I'll see you later tonight."

"Okay."

Amy watched Katie head across East Circle Drive toward the dorms. She got up and stretched her legs, which had begun to tighten in the cold morning air, and then she followed the path back into the arboretum. The asphalt was slick, and she walked rather than risk twisting an ankle. Fifty yards later, she came to a T juncture where the path ended at a soft trail made of bark, moss, and dead leaves. The trees grew over her head, and the trail was dim and narrow, as if she were disappearing into a train tunnel. Where the trail curved, she couldn't see around the next bend.

She took a few tentative steps, but she stopped with a strange sense of discomfort. The down on the back of her neck stood up, as if the little hairs were iron filings drawn by a magnet. She felt eyes following her from somewhere in the forest.

"Hello?" she called.

Amy turned around slowly. She was alone, but the trees were big and wide enough here to hide someone. Those were crazy-making thoughts; she was letting herself get paranoid. She inhaled, smelling nothing but mold and the dewish sweat of her body. She didn't hear anything.

She waited. Everything was still. *There's nobody,* she told herself.

Amy shook off her fears and jogged. She got into a rhythm as she ran, enough that she could crowd out other thoughts.

Running was pure escape for her, in which she was conscious of nothing but the noise of her breathing and the vibrations as her feet hit the ground. She made two loops around the east section of the arboretum, following the border of the escarpment. It added almost two miles to her route, and when she finished the circle for the second time, she slowed to a walk to cool down. Her face was flushed. Her blond curls were frizzed.

She wasn't far from the trail that led back to the perimeter road when she felt it again. Eyes. Like a voyeur watching her.

She was sure she wasn't alone.

"Who's there?"

Behind her, a male voice growled the way a bear would, and Amy spun with a choked scream. Twenty yards away, a student she knew from one of her psychology classes giggled as she fended off animal kisses from a bearded, long-haired boy. They broke apart when they heard Amy squeal. They were innocent. They were nobody. Amy wanted to laugh in relief, but she was breathing too hard.

"You okay, Amy?" the girl called.

"Oh, yeah, fine. You startled me."

"Sorry."

Amy smiled at them, the couple out for a kissy stroll. She wished she had a boyfriend of her own for that kind of hike. It made her think she should find someone to ask out on a date, but there never seemed to be time, with classes, work, and dance. She knew that was a crock, though. She just didn't want all the hassles of a relationship.

She left the two of them alone. At the juncture, she turned back toward the campus road. It was time to get back to her dorm room. She needed a shower, and she had a class in less than an hour.

Kinesics. Learning to read body language.

Amy was almost at the bench where she'd sat with Katie when she heard a car engine on the shoulder of the road. She emerged from the trees in time to see a Honda Civic hatchback make a fast U-turn off the grass and head toward the Bay Settlement entrance to the campus.

She only caught a glimpse of the side of the driver's face, but she recognized him. It was Gary Jensen. He'd been in the woods with her.

24

Mark Bradley painted on the bone white rocks jutting out into Lake Michigan. He'd been standing in front of his canvas for an hour, and his fingers were numb and raw. It was late morning on Thursday under a cold, weak sun. The wind off the lake drowned out every sound except the screech of gulls, which flocked near the beach and dove into the water for fish. When he looked at the sky between brushstrokes, he saw the rusting white tower of the Cana Island lighthouse poking above the tops of the dormant trees.

He didn't mind that Cana was the most

overphotographed, overpainted landmark in Door County. What he created never looked much like the original subject. His work was dark, with swirls of primary colors and blurry images of angels against black skies. He wasn't religious, unlike Hilary, and he didn't know why his brain told him to paint angels. Even so, he didn't question it.

His family and friends had never understood his art. He was an athlete, and that meant his interests should have ground to a halt at the last page of the daily sports section. One of the qualities that drew him to Hilary was that she didn't put him in a box or maintain a preconceived notion of who he was. She'd never believed he could be one thing and not another.

Mark turned his head, and his neck stabbed with pain. His left shoulder was tender where the seat belt had locked against his torso in the accident. The doctor at the island's medical clinic had suggested that he and Hilary take a day off to recover, but with no serious injuries, they'd both declined. Mark had replaced the tires on his Explorer and taken the two of them across the passage on a midmorning ferry.

Their friend Terri Duecker had offered to lend them a car.

Hilary drove to school in Terri's Taurus. Mark drove to Cana.

He realized he was hungry. He'd packed a lunch in his backpack. He covered his canvas and carried his materials up the beach to the open lawn surrounding the lighthouse. It was immediately much quieter and warmer in the sun. He sat on a red picnic bench on the far side of the lawn, where he took out a turkey sandwich and a bag of grapes. He put up his canvas near the bench and studied his latest painting as he ate.

His sandwich was almost gone when a shadow fell across the brown grass from the trail that led to the causeway. He turned and saw a teenaged girl watching him.

It was Tresa Fischer.

Mark tensed. "Tresa, you shouldn't be here."

"I know."

The girl came closer anyway. The bench faced the lighthouse tower, and she sat down on the same side, inches away from him. She rubbed the red paint on the bench nervously with the pads of her fingers. She wore a loose-fitting purple sweatshirt over her skinny frame, and her wrists looked like matchsticks jutting out of the cuffs. Her shiny red hair covered most of her face in profile.

"No one's around," she murmured. "It's just us."

Mark felt a cloud of mixed emotions. Part of him wanted to get up and leave. Part of him wanted to be angry, but he had no anger against this girl. They'd barely spoken a word to each other since the previous year, when Delia Fischer had forbidden her daughter to see him. The most he'd heard from Tresa was an apology by phone, and he'd told her what he felt—that she had no reason to apologize.

He really liked her. So did Hilary. She was a sweet, smart, sensitive, lonely girl. It was just complicated to realize that she'd done so much to destroy his life. She was still toxic to him, still a danger.

"I'm sorry, Tresa, I have to go," he said.

She turned toward him urgently. Her blue eyes were frantic. She reached out her hands toward him and pulled them back. It was obvious that she was still in love with him, which made it even more important for him to walk away.

"Please. Don't go. I'm not going to cause any trouble for you."

"What do you want?" he asked her.

Tresa stuttered. "I don't know. I heard what happened last night. I'm so glad you guys are okay. It made me feel like—I mean, I just needed to see you, you know? With everything going on."

"I know."

"I told the police in Florida they were wrong. I said you could never, ever hurt Glory. Not you."

"Thanks."

"I'm not sure they believed me. It's like last year. No one believes me."

"It doesn't matter."

"You must really hate me," Tresa said.

"I don't hate you. You shouldn't ever think that, because it's not true." His instinct was to reach out and touch her, but he didn't. He added, "How are you? This must be a terrible time. I'm sorry."

"Yeah, Mom's a wreck. Me, I don't know. Sometimes I cry, and sometimes I get pissed off at Glory." She ducked her head and changed the subject, as if she couldn't bear to talk about her sister. "I like coming out to the lighthouse. It's cool when there's nobody around."

"Me, too."

"Do you ever wonder what it was like?" Tresa pointed at the home attached to the lighthouse tower. "The keeper and his wife and their kids all alone out here. I think I would have liked it."

"It was a hard life."

"Yeah, but you always said alone could be a good thing."

"Sometimes, sure."

"It would have been romantic. Sort of like you and Hilary on the island."

Tresa was still an idealistic teenager, and Mark liked that about her. He didn't want to tell her the truth. Reality had a way of eroding romance day by day, and if you wanted to keep it, you had to cling to it with your fingernails and put on blinders to the tragedy of life.

"I really need to go," he said.

Tresa reached out and covered his hand. Her skin was warm. "Please, not yet."

He gently took his hand away. "Tresa."

"I know." She twisted strands of her red

hair between her fingers and pulled them through her lips. She pointed at his painting. "I like that one."

"Thanks."

"One of the angels, the one near the tower, she looks really, really sad."

"I think you're right," he said.

"I wish I could paint like that."

"You're a writer. I wish I could write like you."

Her face brightened. "Really?"

"Yes. You're very talented. You have a great future."

"Wow. That's really nice." She stared at the bench and murmured, "But those things I wrote about us."

"Let's not talk about it."

Tresa nodded and didn't look at him. "Can I ask you something?"

"Sure."

"You never slept with Glory, did you?"

Mark recoiled. "No."

"Good," she said, looking satisfied. "I didn't think you would, but I know how she could be. Glory had a way of getting what she wanted. She read my diary, and I thought she'd want you just because I wanted you. I'm glad you didn't."

He wanted to steer her far away from the subject of her diary. The explicit descriptions were still vivid, erotic, and horrifying in his mind. "Why did you never tell me about the fire?" he asked.

Tresa cringed. "The fire? I don't know. I wanted to forget it. We all acted as if it never happened."

"You can't forget things like that."

"You can try," Tresa said. "Sometimes you just have to put on blinders, you know? Everybody lost things that day, but nobody ever cared what I lost. I know that sounds selfish."

"What did you lose?" Mark asked.

"You name it. Glory was never the same. Mom kept trying to rescue her, so she forgot about me. Mr. Hoffman shipped Jen out to live with his daughter in Minneapolis, so I lost my best friend. I never really had anybody again. Not until you and Hilary showed up here. Then I went and screwed that up, too." Tresa blinked and wiped tears away from her eyes.

"I'm sorry."

"It's not your fault."

"It must have been a bad night," he said.

"Oh, yeah. We didn't know Glory was

there until Sheriff Reich came and told us. Mom freaked. Glory was just—well, in the hospital, she was all confused, thinking it was *our* house that had burned down, wanting to make sure we were all okay. She blocked it out, but my mom never forgot."

"And your friend Jen lost her family."

Tresa looked away, as if the pain were fresh. "Yeah."

"Did she hate her father?"

"Jen? I think it was harder to lose Mr. Bone the way she did. She loved him. I know that sounds crazy, but the boys sided with their mom, and she always sided with her dad."

"Except if she'd been home, she would have been killed, too," Mark reminded her.

"No, Mr. Bone would never hurt Jen," Tresa insisted. "He knew she was staying with us that night. He talked to my mom."

"Harris talked to Delia?" Mark asked.

"Yes, he was over at our place all the time. I think he wanted to get away from home. You don't know what that family was like. You don't know how bad it was in their house."

"It sounds like you knew him pretty well," Mark said.

"Yeah, I guess."

"Did Glory?"

"Sure."

Mark hesitated. "Do you think she'd know Harris if she saw him today?"

Tresa cocked her head in confusion. "What are you saying?" Then she almost leaped across the bench, taking Mark's shoulders. He winced at the pressure. "Oh, my God, do you think he could have been there?"

Mark watched her hopeful blue eyes. She seemed to be looking for an answer, an explanation, anything to replace the doubt in her brain. He understood. Even Tresa wondered if he'd killed her sister. No matter how much she loved him, or how much she defended him, her heart of hearts told her that he was guilty.

"What would Glory have done if she'd seen him?" he asked.

Tresa bit her lip. "I'm not sure. Wow, I don't know."

"Did *you* see anyone in Florida who might have been Harris Bone?"

"No, no, I would have said something. I hung out by myself a lot. I'm not sure I would have seen anybody at all."

"Okay."

"I'm going to tell my mom. She's got it in her head that it was you, but you're right. Maybe it was Harris. Maybe he was there."

"Don't tell Delia you saw me," Mark advised her. "That won't help either one of us."

The girl nodded. "I understand."

"You should go, Tresa."

"Yeah. Okay."

As if swept up by an impulse she couldn't resist, Tresa wrapped her skinny arms around Mark's chest. Her cheek and red hair rested against his face, and her body pressed against him. She held him there longer than she should have, and he had to push her away. Her face glowed with passion.

"I can still taste your lips," she whispered to him. "Even after all this time."

25

At the end of the school day, Hilary drove north along Highway 42 in the Ford Taurus she'd borrowed from Terri Duecker. She'd popped Advil like candy, but her body still ached. All she wanted to do was take the ferry back to the island and slip into a hot bubble bath and stay there for about three hours.

As she neared the Northport ferry terminal, she remembered that she needed to make one stop before going home. She checked her watch and saw that she still had one more chance to cross the passage that evening if she missed the next ferry. She turned off the highway and backtracked along Port des Morts Drive. At the end of the road, in a turnaround protected by giant evergreens, she parked outside the home of Peter Hoffman.

Hilary wasn't sure if he would talk to her. She knew the rumors about Mark and Glory had made their way through the county grapevine, and Hoffman was close to Delia Fischer. Then again, if there was anyone who had reason to hate Harris Bone and want to see him found, it was the father and grandfather of the people Harris had killed.

She got out of the Taurus and made her way down the muddy driveway. As she approached Hoffman's A-frame home, she saw an older man at work on the wide front porch. She smelled freshly cut wood, and she heard the banging of his hammer. He was on his knees, and he looked up when she reached the steps. He appeared to be nearly seventy years old, although his hair was jet black and looked even blacker against his pale, deeply lined face. He got up slowly, favoring one leg. He wore a flannel shirt with the sleeves rolled up and black cargo pants with years of paint stains on the fabric. His eyes were suspicious.

"Mr. Hoffman?" she asked. "My name is—"

"I know who you are," he interrupted her. "What do you want, Mrs. Bradley?"

"I'd like to talk to you."

Hoffman's face tightened with discomfort. He sucked in a breath and straightened his back. He was a tall man. "About Harris and the fire?"

"That's right."

"There's nothing I can tell you," he said.

"That may be true, but I'd really appreciate five minutes."

Hoffman grunted and laid his hammer on the ledge of the front window. He grabbed a bottle of whiskey from the top of his toolbox and eased himself down on the front steps. Hilary sat down next to him. He unscrewed the top of the flask, and without offering her a drink, he took a long swallow. She could tell from the aroma of whiskey on his breath that he'd already been drinking before she arrived.

"I don't talk about the fire," he said. "You're wasting your time."

"I understand."

"I heard what happened to you, and I'm sorry about that, but that doesn't mean I'm going to help you."

Hilary pulled aside the silk flap of her blouse far enough to show Hoffman the edge of the purple bruise discoloring her chest. "This is from the accident last night. There are people around here who want to give me and my husband the death penalty, Mr. Hoffman, even though Mark is guilty of nothing."

"You believe that, do you?"

"I do."

Hoffman took another drink. "Trust is bullshit."

"I know why you feel that way," Hilary said.

"You don't know a thing."

Hilary let her eyes drift around the huge, forested plot of land. The neat square of lawn and the carefully kept house felt like a tiny zone of order beating back chaos. "Look, Mr. Hoffman, I don't mean to bring up awful memories for you. All I want you to do is consider the possibility that my husband didn't kill Glory Fischer. You don't have to believe it the way I do. You don't even have to believe that Harris Bone was there—but if he was, if Glory *saw* him, we both know he'd have every incentive to kill her to protect his secret."

Hoffman squeezed his knees tightly with his hands. "You're getting me angry, Mrs. Bradley."

"I'm sorry, that's not my intention."

"I know exactly what your intention is. You're trying to exploit the tragedy that destroyed my family, in order to protect your husband, who is most likely a murderer. I won't let you do that."

Hilary recoiled. "I don't want to exploit your grief."

"Don't treat me like an idiot. You don't care about Harris Bone. You don't want to find him. You want him to be a mystery man, so your husband's lawyer can do a dance with a jury and get him off. Don't expect me to be a party to it. I don't need the hope of catching this man dangled in front of my face. You want the truth, Mrs. Bradley? The last person I want to see again is Harris Bone. No one here wants to relive what happened six years ago."

"So he goes free?" Hilary asked.

"I believe in God. Harris Bone will never be free. Not in this lifetime, not in the after-life. I won't let you compound his crimes by using him to help your husband escape punishment for what he did."

"Mark didn't kill Glory."

Hoffman rubbed his jaw with his clenched left fist. He still wore a wedding ring on his finger. When he spoke, his voice was choked with emotion.

"Let me explain something to you," he told her quietly. "Relationships run deep in this part of the world. We have roots. I don't know if someone from the city can under-stand that. The people who grew up here, they look after one another. If it weren't for a good woman like Delia Fischer, the only grandchild I have left would have died in that fire. To me, Delia is an angel. So when she loses her baby girl, it hurts me as much as if Glory were my own daughter. Believe me, I'm not going to let Delia suffer in vain. I'm going to make sure she gets justice."

"Why are you so quick to believe my hus-band did this?" Hilary asked in frustration.

"The better question is, why do you be-lieve he's innocent?"

She shook her head and stood up. It had

been a mistake to come here. "Good-bye, Mr. Hoffman. I'm sorry to have troubled you."

"There are no secrets around here," he called as she retreated down the driveway. "Felix Reich and I go back for decades. He already told me."

Hilary stopped. "Told you what?"

"That detective from Florida, he has a witness. He knows your husband was out on the beach with Glory Fischer."

"Whether he was or wasn't doesn't mean a thing," she said.

"They were kissing, Mrs. Bradley."

The words hit her like bullets. "That's a lie."

"Call the sheriff if you like." He added, "I'm sorry to be the one to tell you this, but you can't live in the dark forever."

Hilary stalked away from the man without saying another word. She didn't want him to see her face. As she retraced her steps, she kept putting her feet wrong, because she had trouble seeing through the tears that clouded her eyes. Her breathing was fast and loud. She got back inside the Taurus, and her fingers trembled as she clung to the steering wheel. Her faith suddenly felt fragile. She thought she would lose it entirely, like a rock skittering off a cliff.

Instead, she thought about her husband. She knew the kind of man he was. Whatever was going on, whatever this person saw, there was another explanation. He didn't touch her. He didn't kill her. Not Mark.

Even so, something new and unwelcome attached itself to her brain and began feeding like a parasite as she drove for the ferry.

Doubt.

Tresa sat by herself at the end of a dead-end road near Kangaroo Lake. She wasn't ready to go home yet. Her heart was still full of Mark Bradley. She hadn't been so close to him in almost a year, and she wanted to remember his face, the feel of his body, and the sound of his voice while it was all vivid to her. The time away at school in River Falls had done nothing to change how she felt. She loved him.

She wanted to save him.

Tresa held her phone in her cold hand. As the sun sank lower, shadows lengthened on the water. She hesitated about dialing, because she hadn't called in almost two years. That was how life worked. People drifted apart. For all she knew, the number had changed like everything else about her friend.

She dialed it anyway. She listened to the ringing and felt oddly anxious, as if she would be calling a stranger. She thought about hanging up, but then she heard the voice on the other end. It hadn't changed. She felt sad and ashamed. All the old guilt flooded over her. She didn't even know if she could speak.

"Hi," she said finally.

There was a long silence as she waited for Jen Bone to sift through her memory and unearth a face and a name from her long-ago past. *"Tresa?"*

"Yeah, it's me."

"Oh, my God. How are you?"

"Okay."

"It's been forever."

"I know. I'm sorry. I didn't want to bother you. You know, new life and all. I wasn't sure you even wanted to remember me. I mean, because of everything."

"Yeah."

"I ask Mr. Hoffman about you all the time," Tresa said. "He keeps me posted on what you're doing, sends me the school newspaper sometimes, that kind of thing."

"I ask him about you, too."

"Oh, yeah? Okay."

"Listen, I heard about Glory on the news," Jen said. "The girls at school were talking about it. I'm really sorry."

"Thanks."

"Your mom must be a wreck."

"Yeah, she is."

"Are you back at River Falls?"

"No, I'm taking the term off. Mom needs me here."

"That's good."

Tresa wondered how to say it. How do you say to a girl who was once your best friend, *If anyone knows where your father is, you do.* She struggled in silence, until it was awkward between them.

"The papers said the police have a suspect," Jen continued, when Tresa said nothing. "It sounded like you had some kind of relationship with him. Is that true?"

"He didn't do it."

She heard the hesitation on the line. "Sure, okay. Whatever you say."

"It's true."

"I believe you." She added, "What do you want, Tresa? Why are you calling me?"

Tresa began, but she stumbled over her words. "It's about Glory."

"What about her?"

"Actually, I guess it's not really about her. Listen, I have to know."

"What?"

Tresa swallowed hard. "Have you heard from your father?"

"My father? Are you kidding? Why?"

"I just wondered."

"No, of course not. He wouldn't contact me. Oh, jeez, you think he did this, don't you? That's what this is about."

"Well, I mean, him being missing and all. The police are still looking for him. I thought if Glory saw him in Florida—"

"That's crazy, Tresa."

"Is it? I don't know."

"He wouldn't do this."

"How do you know?"

She could hear her friend breathing and feel her indecision. Even after all these years, they still had a connection. They'd been as close as sisters. "Look, Tresa, can you keep a secret?"

"You know I can. How can you say that to me?"

"Swear it."

"I do, I do."

"Then listen. My father didn't do this. So don't go spreading rumors like he did, okay? Stop it. I mean, maybe you're trying to help your boyfriend, but I don't need this all thrown in my face again. I've spent too much time getting past it. I'm a different girl now."

"Yeah, but you don't know, do you? I mean, it's possible."

"It's not. Really. The thing is, I know where my father is. He called me last year. He's living in Mexico. He's safe, and I'm safe. I don't want this thing splashed all over the news again and have someone turn him in. You know? So for me, Tresa, please, let it go. My father didn't kill Glory."

26

The bar owned by Troy Geier's father sat at a deserted intersection on County Road T, miles from any of the coastal towns. The low white building needed a fresh coat of paint, as did the two-story farmhouse behind it. Cab parked in the dirt of the highway shoulder and headed for the front of the bar. As he did, he spotted a teen-aged boy hauling two bulging trash bags through the side door. Troy Geier hiked to the rear of the building, breathing loudly, and Cab followed. He heard the clang of metal as the boy threw the bags into a Dumpster, and as Troy barreled back around the corner, he nearly collided with Cab and stopped in surprise.

"Hello, Troy."

Troy adopted a who-cares attitude, but Cab knew it was fake. "I heard you were in town," the boy said.

"Got a minute?"

"Yeah, I guess, but my dad will get pissed if I'm too long."

"It won't be long."

Cab wandered into the middle of the empty road with his hands in the pockets of his dress pants. His tie blew over his shoulder. Troy trailed behind him, his feet shuffling. Cracks ran through the asphalt in the county road. There were no cars in any direction.

Troy smelled of frying grease and stale beer. He wore a Woody Woodpecker T-shirt and blue jeans, and his hands were dirty. His bulging cheeks made him look like a squirrel eating nuts.

"What do you do at the bar?" Cab asked.

"Whatever my dad tells me to do."

Cab nodded. Troy's wavy hair was flat where he'd been wearing a hat, but Cab figured it could have been the giant thumb-print of Troy's dad squashing his boy.

Whether it was his father or Glory, Troy did as he was told.

"I heard you got a witness who can help you nail Mark Bradley," Troy told him.

"Who told you that?"

"Mrs. Fischer talked to the sheriff."

"Well, we've still got a lot of work to do," Cab said. "In the meantime, I need to clear up a few things with you, Troy."

"Like what?"

"Like the argument you had with Glory on Saturday night."

Troy moved his jaw as if he were chewing gum. "I already told you, it was stupid. I wanted Glory to come back to the room with me, and she wouldn't go. So I left."

"I heard it was more than that," Cab said.

"What do you mean?"

"I heard Glory was coming on to other boys in the pool."

"It wasn't like that."

"No?"

"No, Glory was playing games. She wasn't serious."

"If my girlfriend was grabbing cocks under the water, I think I'd be pretty mad," Cab said.

Troy's face reddened. "She didn't do that!"

"We talked to a girl who said you were so mad you were ready to go off like a bomb."

"I was just—that's not what happened. I told you, Glory had been acting weird all day. I was frustrated. It was our last day, and she was ruining it."

"So you left her at the pool with the boys."

"She wasn't doing anything crazy. She was just being Glory. I was mad at first, but I calmed down."

"Did you go straight back to the hotel room?"

Troy nodded. "I watched a movie. I already told you that."

"Then what happened?"

"I fell asleep. That's it. I got up when Tresa woke me in the morning and said Glory wasn't in the room."

"What did you think?" Cab asked. "Did you think she was with another boy? Did you think she'd spent the night with someone?"

"No!"

"Are you sure you didn't wake up overnight and realize Glory was gone?"

Troy shook his head fiercely. "I didn't."

"Would you have gone to look for her?"

"I don't know. Maybe. I don't know. That's not what happened."

"What if you saw her on the beach with Mark Bradley? That would have made you mad, wouldn't it? Particularly if you saw them kissing."

Troy crumpled the collar of his T-shirt in his fist. "Glory wouldn't let him touch her."

"But what if she did? What if you saw her?"

"I didn't! You're trying to make it out like I killed her, and I would never hurt her, never."

"I hear you, Troy. I do. You can help us prove it."

"How?"

"Someone from the sheriff's office is going to pay you a little visit and stick a cotton swab in your mouth."

"What? Why?"

"To get a DNA sample to match against Glory's fingernails. We think she scratched the person who killed her."

Troy's eyes widened. "Yeah, but she was my girlfriend. I don't know, what if she scratched me accidentally that day?"

"Did she?"

"I don't think so, but I don't know. I don't remember."

"Give us a sample. We'll check it and see."

He hesitated. "Yeah, I guess . . . but it doesn't mean—"

"Troy!"

Cab heard a shrill voice from the side door of the bar, which hung open. Delia Fischer stood in the doorway with her hands on her hips. Her face was worn, with suspicion etched in her bloodshot eyes. She shouted again. "Troy, your dad wants to know where the hell you are."

"I have to go," Troy said.

"Sure."

Troy looked relieved to have an escape. He jogged for the bar and squeezed past Delia, who stepped outside and closed the door behind her. She waited for Cab. Her bottle-blond hair hung limply at her shoulders. She wore a roomy polo shirt with the bar's logo on her breast and an apron tied around black jeans. She looked like a woman who had shrunk over the years and was still growing smaller.

"How are you, Mrs. Fischer?" Cab asked.

"How do you think I am?"

"I'm sorry, I know how hard this must be."

"What do you want, Detective? What are you doing here?"

"I'm doing everything I can to find out what happened to Glory," he told her.

Delia's hands were damp, and she dried them on the apron. "Why were you talking to Troy?"

"I just had some more questions for him."

"What kind of questions?"

Cab shrugged. "It's routine."

"The person you should be talking to is Mark Bradley," she snapped.

"Mr. Bradley isn't talking." He added, "It looks like people around here are trying to take matters into their own hands. Some-one tried to kill him and his wife."

"Am I supposed to feel bad about that?"

"If something happens to Mr. Bradley, we'll probably never know the truth about Glory's death."

"People will do what they do. I don't care. That's the sheriff's problem, not mine."

Delia wore her bitterness like a shroud around her tense shoulders. He knew there was nothing he could do to change how she felt. Her mind was made up. She'd settled on one explanation for her grief, and that explanation was Mark Bradley. He'd become the symbol of every wrong turn in her life.

"You work here?" he asked, nodding his head at the bar.

"Yes."

"You wait tables?"

"That's right. I wait tables, and at home, I sell metal jewelry. I scrape by." She eyed Cab's expensive suit with disdain. "I guess you don't know what that's like."

"You're right, I haven't lived that kind of life, but I respect it."

"I don't need your respect or your pity. Some Door County natives, they do pretty damn well. They bought up land decades ago when it was cheap. My parents weren't able to do that. I was just lucky that they paid off the mortgage on their house, so I have somewhere to live. Then I lost my husband, and he didn't have any life insurance, so it was just me and the girls. Now it's just me and Tresa."

"How's Tresa holding up?" he asked her.

"Why? Do you want to interrogate her, too? Do you think she killed her own sister?"

"I just wanted to make sure she's okay."

"That's my business, Detective, not yours. I wish you'd do your job. Instead, you seem to be looking at everyone except the man we both know is guilty. You're badgering Troy, who wouldn't lift a finger against Glory. You're even chasing ghosts."

"You mean Harris Bone?"

"Yes."

"I have no reason to think Harris Bone has anything to do with this case, but I can't ignore the possibility."

Delia shook her head. "Listen to yourself. You're doing exactly what Mark Bradley and his wife want you to do. You're playing their game. If Harris was in Florida, someone would have recognized him."

"Maybe someone did," Cab said gently.

"You mean Glory? If she saw him, she would have called the police. Or she would have called me."

Cab cocked his head with curiosity. "She didn't call you, did she?"

"No."

"But you knew Harris Bone pretty well, right?"

"Of course."

"I'm a little surprised that you stayed friends with him after the car accident that killed your husband."

Delia's mouth tightened, and her lips turned white. "Harris wasn't to blame for what happened any more than the rest of us. We were stupid. It was a tragedy."

"Were you surprised by what he did to his family?"

"I was sickened. Wherever Harris is, I hope he sees the faces of his family every time he tries to sleep. I hope he sees Glory's face, too. That doesn't mean I believe he was in Florida."

"I understand how you feel," Cab told her. "Mark Bradley is the prime suspect, but he's not the only suspect, and if I disregarded other theories of the crime, I'd make it easier for him to get an acquittal at trial. I don't want that to happen."

Delia pressed the heels of her palms against her forehead, as if fighting a migraine that throbbed inside her skull. "I know how it works, Detective. He'll walk away. The people from the city, the ones with money, they hire lawyers, and they get off."

"Not if I can help it," Cab said.

"I've heard it before, Detective," Delia told him wearily, "so don't waste your breath trying to convince me it will be different this time. I'm not waiting around for justice. The police don't do anything. The prosecutors don't do anything. The guilty walk free."

She turned and went back inside the bar and slammed the door.

27

Peter Hoffman parked at the end of Juice Mill Lane, where a rusting metal gate stretched across the old road that led into the forest. He was on the border of Newport State Park, which sprawled across the eastern edge of the NorDoor and jutted into Lake Michigan like the profile of a monster's chin. He still owned several acres of undeveloped land here that had been passed down from his grandparents to his parents over the course of half a century. He rarely visited now. Coming here carried too many memories of time and people passing away.

He was drunk. He knew he shouldn't have been driving, but no one was around to stop him, and the vacant land was only a few miles south on Timberline Road from his own home on the northern coast. He got out of his car. Around him, he saw nothing but winter fields and the tangle of forest behind the gated road. The sun was almost down. The world was getting darker minute by minute.

Hoffman took his half-empty bottle with him. He squeezed past the gate with its NO TRESPASSING sign and limped down the old logger's road. A ridge of dormant grass made a racing stripe between the tire ruts, but no vehicle had traveled this road in years. There were PRIVATE PROPERTY signs posted on tree trunks every twenty yards or so. He'd nailed them there himself. He didn't want hikers in the park drifting onto his land and getting curious.

When he reached the trail that led to his grandfather's hunting cabin, he tried to remember when he'd last been here. Three years, at least. The shack was hidden behind an army of hardwood trunks that were green with moss. He'd spent countless nights and early mornings inside, before the walls had rotted and the roof had caved in during a snowy winter. He'd tasted his first beer there. He'd listened to his grandfather rail against Kennedy. He'd smelled the blood of animals they'd killed. He'd toasted dead friends with Felix in the years since the war.

He'd taken Harris and the boys here once for a man's night in the woods. That had been more than a decade ago. He remembered how content he had been with his life then, surrounded by family, with a wife he loved at home, in a beautiful part of the world, where he had history and friends.

It was all gone now.

He stared at the ruins of the cabin in front of him, and it felt like the ruins of his life. The wilderness was reclaiming it year by year. The windows had long ago been punched out by vandals. Its wooden beams were warped and popped, and the frame, which his grandfather had built by hand, would collapse altogether in another season or two. He didn't plan to be around to see its final demise. It was already a haunted place, and he was ready to become one of the ghosts.

Hoffman uncapped the bottle and drank, not noticing the burn in his throat. He had trouble standing. The cold and wind swirled around his body and picked at his skin. Darkness grew deeper, making the forest a nest of shadows and hiding places. He smelled the wood decaying. As he stood in the clearing, memories stormed his brain. There were good ones and terrible ones.

It would have been easy to kill himself right here. Death had no fear or mystery for him. He'd considered bringing a shotgun and carrying it down inside the musty storm cellar and using his toe to reach the trigger. Eventually, someone would have stumbled upon the ladder in the ground and found him. Eventually, they would all know what had happened.

That was the coward's way. Hoffman had never been a coward. He owed a debt to Delia Fischer and to Glory, and he couldn't run away from it. It was time to face the truth.

The bottle slipped from his numb fingers and landed in the soft ground without breaking, but he didn't pick it up. The amber liquid ran out like a river onto the dirt-covered lid of the storm cellar. He turned, leaving the cabin and all its memories behind. His boots left dents in the earth. He felt at peace for the first time in a long time. He thought that he would be able to sleep tonight, which was something that usually eluded him.

He hiked back along the rutted road until he could see the metal gate at the dead end fifty yards away. The last flicker of daylight made the hole in the woods bright against the gloomy interior of the forest. Sunlight gleamed against something. A mirror. A window. A pair of binoculars.

Hoffman heard the engine of a vehicle. He didn't see it, but he heard it. It was loud but got quieter as it disappeared down Juice Mill Lane with a roar of thunder on the gravel. When he reached the gate, where his own car was parked, he saw nothing but a trail of dust billowing out of the dirt road. The car had come and gone in the time he'd been inside the woods.

Someone had been watching him. Following him.

It didn't matter. He didn't care about the consequences for himself or anyone else. He knew what he had to do.

It had happened when Delia was sixteen. The same age as Glory.

The boy's name was Palmer Ford. That was the kind of name your parents gave you when money was your birthright, when every school you would attend in your life was private and privileged. He was from Kenilworth, one of those rich Chicago enclaves with the gilded estates and the lakeside lots. He was the same age as Delia. That summer, his parents rented a house on Mansion Row in Fish Creek for the last two weeks of July. Palmer had his own car; he was on his own while his parents shopped for art and antiques.

He did what rich boys do in places like Door County. He went to the local kids to buy drugs. Delia met him at a Friday night party on Clark Lake, where stoned teenagers lashed fishing boats together and lay on their backs and watched the stars. Delia and Palmer wound up next to each other, mixing beer and pot and dangling their feet in the cool water. They talked. They laughed. They kissed.

He was tall and handsome, with tight black curly hair, a hooked nose, and a muscular physique. An athlete. He played high school football, and college scouts were already jotting down his name in their rosters. He dressed well, in Izod shirts, khakis, and boat shoes without socks. He threw money around. It was impossible not to like someone who always picked up the check for everyone else. That was what fibs did; they floated in and out of town, skimming the cream, making friends with kids who wouldn't fit in back home.

After that first night, Palmer and Delia spent every evening together. They played miniature golf. They got ice cream. They kissed more, and she let him inside her blouse, where he rubbed her nipples with chapped hands. Delia wasn't a virgin. She'd done it before with two other boys, one a year since she was fourteen. Later, the lawyers made it out like she was a slut who threw it around, but that was a lie. Most of her friends went from boy to boy all summer. Not Delia.

Palmer was a gentleman. That was what she thought. He didn't push her; he stopped when she told him to stop, even though she could feel his erection through his pants like steel against her thigh. On the last night, the night before he would leave her forever and go back to Chicago—which was always how those relationships went—she figured she would give in. Spread her legs, give him his prize for all the money he'd spent on her. She didn't have any illusions that he loved her or that he'd invite her back to Mansion Row to meet his parents. She was summer candy. You unwrapped it, you ate it, and it was gone. That was okay. She didn't expect more.

Delia never got the chance to wait until the last night. Palmer ran out of patience with her. Four nights before the end of his vacation, he pulled onto a deserted side road as he was taking her home at one in the morning. He wasn't satisfied with feeling her breasts; he pushed up her T-shirt and exposed them. His fingers went for the button on her jeans, then the zipper. It should have felt right, but it was all wrong, and Delia found herself feeling terrified and claustrophobic as the weight of his athlete's body held her down. She told him to stop. He didn't.

Twenty-five years later, she could still close her eyes and feel it. The pressure of his chest, making it hard to breathe. His tight hands locked around her wrists, leaving bruises. Her head wedged sideways between the leather seat and the metal car door, her hair across her face. His panting in her ear. The pain, sweat, blood, saliva, and discharge.

The next day, in hushed tones, she'd told the police every detail about the rape. They'd arrested Palmer. Felix Reich, who was a deputy then, not the sheriff, had sworn to her and her mother that the boy would pay for what he'd done. He was young; he was wrong. Palmer didn't pay; his parents did. They bought a lawyer. They bought the politicians and the county attorney. Delia made it as far as the deposition, in which a middle-aged female attorney asked in a horrifying monotone about her sexual history, her period, her drug use, her grades in school, her preference in birth control devices, her experience in oral sex, and how often she masturbated. By the end of that ninety minutes, she felt as if she had been raped a second time. She had a panic attack leaving the attorney's office. She wound up in the hospital.

Palmer Ford was never charged. She

never saw him again. Felix Reich came to their house and apologized to her personally, but she knew it wasn't his fault. You can't fight a system greased with money and power. Rich boys, spoiled athletes, can do what they want. She'd learned a lesson that would be proved again and again in her life.

There was no justice.

Delia thought about Palmer as she stood on the concrete pier that jutted into the rippling waters of Lake Michigan near Cave Point Park. He'd become an attorney, representing victims of sexual harassment in the workplace. That was rich. She wondered what his clients would think if they knew the truth.

She found herself crying. Not for herself, but for Glory. For Tresa, too. All these years later, it was no different. There was still no justice.

Delia heard footsteps behind her. She turned and saw Troy Geier. She hadn't even heard him arrive in his 1980s-era Grand Am, which was parked next to her car in the huge open lot at the end of Schauer Road. She'd been too caught up in her own thoughts. He came and stood beside her, and she was annoyed by his presence. She'd never thought there was any substance to Troy. He was slow and naive, just as his father said. She'd never believed for a moment that Glory had any serious feelings for him.

They stood silently by the lake. The water was nearly black beyond the land. Close in, by the shore, she saw white seashells and slimy colonies of emerald green algae. Waves slurped against the rubber tires fastened to the pier. Her eyes fell on the T-shaped boat ties dotting the concrete, which looked like tiny crosses. It made her think of a graveyard. Delia shivered and grew impatient.

"Okay, I'm here, Troy," she snapped. "What do you want? Why did we have to meet out here?"

Troy glanced nervously behind him, making sure they were alone. "I just didn't think anyone should see us talking."

"Oh, for God's sake. We work in the same bar every damn day."

"I know, but this is different."

"I'm tired. I want to go home and have a drink, okay? Tell me what's so important."

Troy shifted on his feet and adjusted himself in his jeans. She felt guilty about treating him badly, but everyone treated Troy badly. He just made you want to yell at him, because he was such a pussy.

"I'm sorry, Troy," she went on. "I'm just mad at the world. I'm sorry about the things I said in Florida, too. What happened to Glory wasn't your fault."

"No, you were right," he said. "I should have been there for her. I should have protected her."

"Just tell me what you want, so we can both go home."

"I've been thinking about things," Troy murmured. "Nothing's going right, you know? I don't like this detective. He's acting like I did this, which is nuts."

"Cops treat everyone like they're guilty," Delia said. "It doesn't mean anything."

"Yeah, but is he ever going to arrest Mark Bradley? Is that bastard going to pay for what he did?"

Delia thought about Palmer Ford. Harris Bone. People who never paid. "I have no idea, Troy. There's a different set of rules for people like them and people like us."

Troy punched his hand with a plump fist. "Yeah, that's what I'm afraid of. I think he's going to get away with it."

"I hope you're wrong, but there's nothing we can do but wait and pray," Delia told him with a sigh. She felt frustrated. Helpless. "Maybe this time God will come through."

"There *is* something we can do," Troy insisted.

"What?"

"We can take matters into our own hands."

Delia turned from the lake and stared at the boy, whose round face had a childish violence in it that she'd never seen in him before. Her heart pounded. "What do you mean by that?"

Troy's eyes darted around the vacant parking lot again. "All we need is one night where he's alone on the island. I have a buddy who works on the ferry. He'll let me know if Bradley's wife leaves. I can sail over there and take care of it myself. I'd just need an alibi, someone to say I was with them that night."

Delia thought of all the things she should say to him. *You're crazy. This is wrong. Don't ever bring this up again.* She knew she had to cut this off now before it went too far. Before everything got out of control. She had to stop this boy before he made a terrible mistake.

The truth was that she didn't want to stop him.

"When you say you'll take care of it," Delia murmured, "exactly what do you plan to do?"

Troy opened his jacket and showed her. "I have a gun," he said.

28

The downtown street past the White Gull Inn in Fish Creek ended at a beach overlooking the waters of Green Bay. Cab bought a sandwich of brie, sprouts, and focaccia bread and found a bench where he could watch the sun set. He'd finally bought a gray wool overcoat that was intended to reach to his ankles, although it only draped as low as his knees. He was warm for the first time since he'd arrived.

The beach was nothing like the beaches he knew in Florida or Spain, where sun gods lay topless on towels beside water that was still and clear. Instead of flat sand, the wind created a dune of peaks and valleys. Jagged driftwood littered the shore. The water tussled with itself, and waves landed in angry slaps. The disappearing sun looked impotent here, and when it was gone entirely, there was nothing left but a long stretch of melancholy gray.

He felt his phone buzz as a text arrived. When he flipped it open, he saw that his mother had written to him from London, where it was past midnight. His dark mood brightened, thinking of her.

Hello, darling. In a taxi, thought of you, ha ha. When will I see you? We're overdue. Love, T. P.S. Beautiful place you're in, but does anyone live there?

Tarla always had a way of reading his mind. It was disorienting to imagine himself on one corner of the planet, in this solitary place, and to picture his mother across the ocean in the urban lights and noise of London. She was right. He felt as if no one at all lived here. The loneliness was crushing, maybe because the empty land reflected what he was feeling inside. He'd always assumed that seclusion like this was what he wanted, but he had begun to realize that it wasn't healthy. It spread like a virus. He missed his mother in London. He missed Lala in Florida. He wasn't as much of an island as he'd always believed.

"Hello, Detective."

Cab looked over his shoulder in surprise and saw someone who did live here. Someone who claimed to thrive on the isolation that he wanted to escape.

"Mrs. Bradley," he said. He checked his watch. "Shouldn't you be back home by now?"

"I missed the last ferry," she told him. "I have a friend with a rental cottage near here. She lets me stay there."

"How did you find me?"

"I saw you driving through town. Your Corvette is hard to miss. Everyone already knows who you are."

"So it seems."

"Welcome to life in a small town."

"I heard about your accident on the island," Cab told her.

"It wasn't an accident."

"I understand. I'm glad to see you're okay."

"I hurt like hell. I'm staying in bed tomorrow."

"Good for you. Are you hungry? Would you like half of a vegetarian sandwich?"

"Do I look like I eat girly food?" Hilary asked. "You should come back when Still-water's opens for the season and get yourself the world's best cheeseburger."

"I'll take your word for it."

Hilary Bradley sat down next to him on top of the bench. She stared at the horizon, where the blue sky deepened into night. She took off her glasses and brushed a wisp of her blond hair from her eyes, a simple gesture that Cab found oddly erotic. He was uncomfortably aware that he found this woman attractive. He knew what Mark Bradley saw in her. Strength. Determination. Depth.

Even so, her face was troubled. Something was bothering her.

"Are you all right?" he asked.

She gave him a look that said *Why do you care?*

"I'm fine," she replied. "Why do you ask?"

"I assume I would be about the last person on earth you'd want to talk to," he said.

"Sometimes when you live out here, you just find yourself wanting to talk to someone, no matter who it is."

"You have a gift for flattery."

She realized what she'd said. "Sorry."

"Don't worry about it."

Hilary looked as if she were grasping for something innocuous to say. He suspected that was because she didn't want to say whatever was really in her head. "What do you use in your hair?" she asked.

He was amused. "It's a molding gel. My mother sends it to me from London."

"I like it."

"Thank you."

"You're not exactly a typical cop, are you?"

"Not exactly," Cab acknowledged.

"Speaking of your mother," Hilary said, "I didn't realize at first who she was. It took me a while to put together the names. I don't think I've ever seen any of her movies. I go for chick flicks."

Cab cocked an eyebrow. "You?"

"No," Hilary said, smiling. "I already told you, I'm not the girly type."

He was almost willing to believe she was flirting with him.

"It's an artificial life, isn't it?" she asked. "Hollywood, I mean."

"Very."

"Is that why you're not in it?"

"Yes."

"You don't like to talk about yourself, do you?"

"No."

She nodded. "Me neither. I apologize for that crack I made on the island. About a woman messing with you. It's none of my business."

He wondered if she expected him to open up and admit the truth. *You were right,* he would say. *Let me tell you about Vivian Frost.* Instead, he didn't say anything at all. He felt it again, the old instinct to shut himself off from women. He wondered, as he had with Lala, if it was worth trying to get past it. If circumstances were different, Hilary Bradley was the kind of woman he would have enjoyed getting to know. Circumstances weren't different, though. Not for her. Not for him.

"Do you mind if I make a coplike observation?" he asked her.

"Go ahead."

"You don't strike me as a woman who misses a ferry."

She looked uncomfortable. "It happens all the time."

"If you say so."

He gave her a minute of silence. He knew she was tempted to get up and leave. Whatever was bothering her, it made her feel vulnerable, and she was obviously a woman who didn't enjoy that feeling.

"I didn't miss the ferry," she admitted. "I decided not to go home tonight."

"I see."

Her face was haunted, which only made it prettier. He disliked women who wanted you to take care of them, and that wasn't Hilary Bradley at all. She looked as if she could barely get the words out to admit what was in her head.

"Be honest with me," she said. "Do you really have a witness who saw Mark kissing Glory Fischer on the beach?"

Cab understood. The foundation on which she'd built her life suddenly felt weak. Normally, he wouldn't have said a thing about the evidence in the case, but he found himself unable to say nothing. He hedged his words.

"I haven't talked to the witness myself," he said. "I'm going to do that tomorrow. I can't tell you exactly what he saw or didn't see."

"It was dark on the beach. It could still be a case of misidentification."

"I can't say yes or no."

"Things aren't always what they seem," she said forcefully, and he thought she was talking to herself as much as she was talking to him.

"I realize that. For what it's worth, Mrs. Bradley, I hope your husband is innocent. I'd like to think there are a few strong relationships left in this world."

"I thought you only believed in betrayal, Detective." Her voice was cold again.

"I do, but I'd like to be wrong now and then."

Hilary got off the bench and squared her shoulders. "You're wrong now."

"Maybe so."

"Here's what I believe," Hilary told him. "Your witness didn't see what he thinks he saw. Either it wasn't Mark, or he misinterpreted what was happening between them."

"Forgive me, Mrs. Bradley, but if you really believe that, why did you miss your ferry?"

"Fuck you," she snapped, surprising him with her venom. She spun on her heel, then stopped in the middle of the clearing. "I'm sorry. Mark would never kill anyone. That's not the kind of man he is."

"He may not be, but that doesn't mean anything."

"Would you kill an innocent girl?" she asked. "Could you ever do something like that?"

I already did.

"An innocent girl? Of course not."

"Then why do you think Mark could?"

She didn't wait for an answer, and he wasn't going to give her one. She retreated to her car and drove away toward downtown Fish Creek with an angry roar of her motor. He was alone again with the encroaching night and the violent water of Green Bay below him. He didn't like it, no matter how beautiful it was. It felt deadly. Catch-a-Cab Bolton was ready to be anywhere else but here.

29

Gary Jensen lived at a hilltop intersection where five roads came together at the end of the developed area of the city. Across from his corner house, the land gave way to grass fields and farmland. Amy pulled into Gary's driveway after dark under the thick cover of giant oaks and sugar maples crowding the house. She switched off the engine. The radio, which had been playing a moody song by Adele called "Hometown Glory," went silent on the final notes.

She sat in her car and texted Katie. *I'm here.*

Amy got out of the car. Lights glowed on

both stories of the brick house, but the curtains were tightly drawn. Tree branches dangled close enough to scrape the glass on most of the windows. She hiked along the grassy shoulder to the front of the house. A streetlight threw her shadow down the hill behind her on the road that led to the distant bay. Ahead of her, no more than half a mile away, she heard the whine of car motors on Highway 57, speeding to and from downtown Green Bay. She saw a patch of trees diagonally across from the house, marking Wequiock Falls County Park. She'd hiked there to see the waterfall in each of the seasons, not knowing that Gary lived within shouting distance of the trail.

Her phone jangled with music. Katie had texted back. *Don't do anything stupid.*

Amy wondered if she already had, just by being here. She threaded through the maze of fat tree trunks to the front door. When she rang the bell, Gary answered immediately. He'd been waiting for her.

"Amy," he said with a grin. "Come on in."

The house had a shut-in smell of dust

and age, like an old person's house. It smelled the way her grandmother's house always did. The wallpaper was ornate, and it was worn down to the wall in places. The carpet was a dense, plush chocolate brown. Gary led her into a square living room, where the overhead light from an antique brass fixture was dimmed. She saw a piano pushed against one wall, a paisley sofa, and a claw-foot armchair. The room looked out toward the street, but the heavy drapes had been swept closed.

"It's ghastly, isn't it?" Gary said. "I think the Addams Family lived here."

Amy shrugged. "It's just old-fashioned."

"It belonged to an eighty-year-old woman. She lived alone. Probably one of those lifelong virgins who had eighteen cats. The dust was incredible. We bought it cheap because the family was anxious to unload it after she died. My wife figured we'd tear everything out, but we never got the chance."

"I'm sorry."

"Sometimes I think about burning the whole house down," Gary said, "and starting over."

He looked at her as if expecting a reaction. She gave him an uneasy smile. "Guess the insurance company wouldn't like that."

"I guess not." He gestured at the sofa. "Sit down, make yourself comfortable. I'm really glad you came by."

Amy sat on the edge of the sofa with her hands in her lap. She thought she looked like a woman at a tea party, with a yardstick up the back of her dress. *Relax,* she told herself.

Gary sat down in the armchair and crossed his legs. He wore a burgundy button-down shirt, black slacks, and dress shoes. The skin on his mostly bald scalp was suntanned. On his left hand, she noticed the glint of silver where he still wore a wedding ring. He never took his eyes off her. She crossed her arms over her chest when she noticed his gaze drifting to her breasts. It made no difference. She might as well have been stark naked.

"You did really well in Naples," Gary told her. "You bring a real athleticism to your routines. It's a pleasure to watch you perform. I mean, let's face it, there's a sensual quality to dance, and the best dancers know how to exploit it."

"I don't really think about that," Amy said.

"No, of course not, it comes naturally. I can see it in the graceful way you move your body."

Amy played with her curls and felt uncomfortable. "Thanks."

Gary stood up again. "I was about to open a bottle of wine. Would you like a glass? Our little secret."

"Um, sure, I suppose. Not much, though, I still have to drive."

"I'll be right back," he told her. "The TV is inside the big cabinet there. I've got the DVD of the team performances in the machine. Check it out."

"Yeah, okay."

Gary retreated from the living room, and she heard his shoes on the hardwood floor of the foyer. She hurried to the doorway. She heard Gary in the kitchen on the other end of the hallway, behind a swinging door. On her left was a wide winding staircase with a wrought-iron banister leading to the second floor. She noticed a roll-top desk in the foyer with envelopes sticking out of cubbyholes, and she pulled out several of the envelopes to see what they were. Most were bills and bank statements. She wanted something, anything, to connect Gary to Glory Fischer, but she didn't know where to look. Quickly, she yanked his Verizon bill out of the open envelope, but before she could review the dialed numbers, she heard the clink of crystal in the kitchen. She stuffed the bill and envelope back into the slot and ran back into the living room. She could feel a flush on her face, and she was breathing heavily.

Gary strolled into the room with two glasses of wine in his hands. "You didn't turn on the TV?" he asked.

"I couldn't find the remote," Amy said.

"It's right on top of the cabinet," he said, smiling.

"Oh, duh. Sure."

"You okay?" he asked, noticing her jittery demeanor.

"Yeah, I'm fine."

He opened the walnut doors of the cabinet, revealing a wide-screen television inside. He clicked on the power and pushed the PLAY button on the DVD machine. Amy saw the arena at the Naples hotel and heard the chatter of the crowd in the bleachers. On-screen, girls from her Green Bay team were rehearsing before their first event. She recognized herself, doing stretches on the mat, her legs spread apart. Gary's camera seemed to focus on her body.

Gary handed her a glass of wine. "Here you go."

"Thanks."

He clinked her glass. "To you, Amy."

She drank a sip. The wine was cold and dry. "This is great."

"I'm glad you like it."

"That was quite the week in Florida," Amy said.

"I love Naples. Someday I'd love to get a condo down there."

"Yeah, that would be great." She drank more wine in a nervous gulp. "Did you hear about what happened on Saturday night? A Wisconsin girl got killed. Pretty scary."

Gary sat down in the old armchair again and swirled the wine in his glass. "I did hear about it. Terrible."

"She was from Door County. That's not far away."

"No, it's not."

"I saw her picture in the paper. I think I saw the girl in the hotel."

"Really? You saw her?"

"Yeah, what about you? Do you remember her?"

Gary shook his head. "No."

"I suppose when you're around a couple hundred teenaged girls, they all start to look alike."

"If she was on one of the other teams, I'm sure I would have noticed her."

"Yeah, probably. It makes you think, huh? Sounds like she was killed on the beach on Saturday night. I was too keyed up to sleep, so I was just lying in bed. If only I'd been looking out the window, you know? Maybe I would have seen something."

"Well, you can hardly blame yourself, Amy," Gary told her.

"Oh, yeah, I know." She added, "I never sleep well at the end of a competition. What about you?"

"I'm the same way. I toss and turn."

"Yeah, my room was next to yours. I thought I heard you coming in late. I figured you couldn't sleep either."

Gary got an odd little smile on his face. "You must have heard somebody else. I was in my room all night."

"Really? I was sure I heard your door open and close."

"I left to get ice at one point. I forgot about that. That's probably what you heard."

"Sure."

Gary's eyes were steady; he stared back at her without blinking. His voice was calm, not speeding up, not getting louder. He didn't show any outward signs of guilt or suspicion. Even so, Amy was convinced he wasn't telling her the truth. His explanations came too quickly and too easily. It was almost as if he'd been anticipating her questions and had been practicing all the right answers to deflect her concerns.

With each sip of wine, she found herself getting a headache. She didn't drink much, and she put the glass down, not wanting to make it worse.

"It was a beautiful hotel," she continued.

"Gorgeous. Very elegant."

"I was in the pool so much I thought I was going to grow gills," she said, giggling. That was a lame joke. Why did she say that?

"Yes, I remember seeing you there. You look pretty damn good in a swimsuit." He smiled at her. His eyes glittered.

"That was my power bikini," she said, laughing too loudly. "Didn't I see you talking to a girl by the pool on Saturday night?"

"I don't recall."

"It wasn't one of the Green Bay girls, so that's why I noticed."

"If you say so, Amy," he told her, still smiling.

"You were wearing your white Phoenix T-shirt."

"Well, lots of men wear white T-shirts down there."

"Yeah, I guess."

Gary's phone began ringing. He glanced at the caller ID. "I'm sorry, I need to take this call. It could take me a few minutes, do you mind? Make yourself comfortable."

Amy waved a hand at him. "No problemo. It's a great old house. Mind if I look around?"

"Go ahead," he said. "Don't look at the dirty underwear on the floor, though."

He answered his phone as he left the living room. As he had before, he exited through the foyer and headed to the kitchen. Amy followed. She was angry with herself for drinking, because she could feel the wine going to her head. The room spun, and she shook herself in order to focus. She could hear Gary's voice on the other side of the swinging door.

Holding the banister, she ran up the curving steps. She put her foot wrong twice and had to steady herself to keep from falling. At the landing, she swayed. She licked her lips, studying the rooms upstairs. To her left, through an open doorway, she saw a large master bedroom. Like the rest of the house, it had a dark, grim decor, with deep red wallpaper and heavy curtains shutting out the light. A Tiffany lamp by the bed cast a pale yellow glow around the room.

Just as Gary said, the room was messy. His clothes were in a pile near the closet. He hadn't unpacked from the trip, and his suitcase was shoved against a wall. It was open. She bent over it and slid to her knees. Her headache was worse. She rubbed her forehead and realized she was sweating. She dug through the items that had been dumped in the suitcase, pushing through dirty clothes. She saw handwritten notes about the dance competition on a yellow pad. Two hardcover books on sports. A camera. A pair of binoculars.

When she lifted up a pair of men's safari shorts, she noticed a fringe of pink lace pushing out of a side pocket. She used the tip of one finger to extract what was inside, and she discovered a pair of thong panties. They were flimsy and sexy. As she dangled them on her finger, she also noticed the white T-shirt that Gary had worn by the pool on Saturday night. She picked up the shirt and put her nose close to it. It smelled of sunblock and sweat, but more than that, she also caught a strong briny aroma of saltwater.

"Amy?"

It was Gary, downstairs, calling up to her.

"I'll be right there."

She froze with the clothing in her hands, wondering if she should steal it for the police. Sooner or later, he would wash the shirt. The panties? He'd find them and throw them away. She hung on to the clothes as she tried to decide what to do. The gears in her brain weren't functioning. She felt the room spinning again, and she grew dizzy as she got to her feet.

"You okay, Amy?"

"Uh, yeah," she called. "I have to use the bathroom."

She returned to the hallway and saw an open door on the other side of the stairs that led to a toilet. She went inside and closed the door behind her. She nearly fell against the door as she did, and when she tried to twist the lock, her fingers slipped. She winced as her head throbbed. She spotted a floor-length linen closet, and without thinking, she opened the door and shoved the thong and the T-shirt inside, hidden under a stack of clean towels.

Amy dug in her pocket for her phone.

Hilary sat at the kitchen table of Terri Duecker's condo in Fish Creek, with a mug of blackberry tea steeping in front of her, sending up a warm cloud of steam. She knew the rental cottage well. It was their winter residence on weekdays, when the ferries didn't run late enough to take them home. Right now, it felt empty and too quiet, and she was conscious of being alone. She knew she'd made a mistake. An immature, impetuous mistake.

She'd driven to the ferry after meeting Peter Hoffman, but she'd watched it leave, rather than driving onto the deck. Fifteen minutes later, she'd called and lied to Mark and said she'd missed it. Cab Bolton was right. She never missed a ferry. If she was anything in life, she was organized and efficient about her schedule.

Terri had looked at her strangely when Hilary returned to Fish Creek, but she didn't ask any questions. She'd simply said, "Sure," when Hilary asked if she could stay in the condo for the night. Her face full of concern, she'd also asked if Hilary needed anything, and Hilary had lied again and said no. In truth, she needed her faith back. She needed Mark. She needed to know the truth.

He'd called twice, and she'd ignored the call both times. She didn't want to talk to him until she knew what she was going to say. Now, in the silent apartment, with the aroma of her tea wafting through the kitchen, she realized she was ducking the hard path and hiding from what she had to do. She was also making a mistake she'd long ago sworn never to make, by judging Mark based on what someone else said, instead of relying on her own instincts.

She picked up her cell phone, which was lying next to the mug of tea in front of her. She punched the speed dial for their home phone.

"Hey, I've been trying to reach you," Mark said.

"Yeah. Sorry. I was picking up dinner at

a restaurant, and then I was talking to Terri. I couldn't grab the phone."

"No problem. I miss you here."

"Me, too."

"Is everything okay? You sound strange."

"No, I'm fine," she murmured, but she wasn't fine, and she didn't want him thinking that she was. "Actually, babes, it was a tough afternoon."

"How so?"

Hilary steeled herself. *Say it.* That was how it was supposed to work between them. No secrets. "It looks like Cab Bolton has a witness. Someone who saw you on the beach with Glory."

"Son of a bitch," Mark said. "I was afraid of that."

"There's more."

"What do you mean?"

"Well, the witness saw you and Glory kissing."

Mark was silent. She could hear him breathing. Finally, he said, "That's why you didn't come home. You believe it."

"I don't know what to believe."

"Do you need me to deny it? Okay, I'll deny it. It didn't happen. I didn't touch her. But if you're not sure, I don't know if it's going to help for me to say so. How can I prove it to you?"

"You don't need to prove anything to me."

"It sounds like I do." His voice was cold and disappointed.

"I was wrong to doubt you. I was wrong not to come home. It just knocked me for a loop, coming out of the blue. I needed to get my head together."

He was slow to reply. When he did, the angry edge was gone. "Hil, I'm sorry. You've stuck by me in the past year, when most wives would have sent me packing. You've never wavered. I can't blame you for wondering if you've been a fool when you hear a story like that. All I can say is, whoever this witness is, he or she made a mistake. I did not kiss Glory. No way. I told you that she put her arms around my neck and scratched me, because she was drunk. Maybe that's what this person saw. He misinterpreted."

"That's probably it."

"It drives me crazy to have this coming between us, because I can never do anything but ask you to trust me."

"I do."

"You feel really far away," he told her.

"I know. I'm sorry." Hilary heard the beep on her phone that told her another call was coming in. "Can you hang on? Someone else is calling. Don't hang up. I want to keep talking."

"I'll be here."

Hilary pushed the FLASH button on her phone and said, "Hello?"

She heard a young voice she hadn't heard in years. "Hilary? Thank God. It's Amy. Amy Leigh."

Amy spoke in hushed tones into the phone in Gary's upstairs bathroom. What was she doing? Her voice slurred, and she was afraid that Hilary would think she was drunk and playing games with her. A few sips of wine, and she *was* drunk. She tried to concentrate on her words, but she found that her brain and her mouth kept missing each other.

"I was at the—that is, I was down on—in Florida. Last week."

"Yes, I know, Amy, I was there, too. You did great. Congratulations."

Amy tried to think. Tried to figure out what to say. "I know what's going on with you. I'm really apology. Sorry. I mean, sorry."

"Amy, are you okay?"

"I don't know."

"Have you been drinking?"

"I guess. That's—that must be it. My coach."

"What?"

"My coach. My coach. Do you know him?"

"I've heard of him," Hilary told her. "What's his name? Johnson?"

"Jensen. Gary Jensen. Yes. Gary."

"What about him?"

Amy heard his voice again. He was at the base of the stairs. His voice was suddenly low and suspicious. "Amy?" he called again. "Amy, are you up there? What are you doing?"

She heard him climbing the twisting steps. Getting closer to her.

"Florida," she said into the phone.

"Amy, you're not making any sense," Hilary told her.

Amy banged her knuckles against her head. The words wouldn't come. She felt as if she would throw up. Her tongue felt thick. "Gary," she murmured, and then, "Glory."

"What?" Hilary's voice was insistent. "Amy, did you say Glory? Are you talking about Glory Fischer? What about her?"

Amy couldn't feel her fingers. The phone slipped from her hand and dropped to the tile floor. The plastic back popped off, and the battery skidded away. It was dead. She heard Gary knocking on the closed door. He was inches away from her.

"Amy?" he called.

She backed up. The knob turned; he was coming in. She grabbed for the shower curtain, and the rings popped from the rod one by one, and she followed the linen curtain to the floor. The door opened with a squeal of its hinges. He stood there, watching her from the doorway. His face showed no emotion or surprise. He knew; he'd been waiting for this to happen. She had to run. Get up, get past him. Except there was nowhere to go.

Amy crawled two steps, and her knees gave way. She was unconscious as her face struck the floor.

PART THREE

Vengeance is Mine

30

Mark Bradley made the ferry crossing through Death's Door and drove to their favorite open-air market between the towns of Ellison Bay and Sister Bay. It was one of the few farmers' markets that was open year-round, baking hot pies daily and lining the shelves with produce canned in the kitchen at the rear of the store. He loved the smell of sugar and flowers and the samples of mustards and cheeses between the open wooden bins. He carried a paper bag through the aisles, filling it as he went. Some of the locals stared at him, but he shrugged it off. He didn't care what anyone thought of him.

He only cared what one person thought. Hilary.

The morning had felt like a turning point between them after a bad, bad night. He'd slept alone, feeling her absence. He hadn't blamed her for doubting him, but he'd worried that doubt was like a genie you couldn't put back in the bottle once it was free. He feared that every day for the rest of their lives, she would look at him and a single thought would flit through the back of her mind, even if she never said it out loud. *Did he?*

Then Hilary came home. She arrived on the first ferry to the island in the morning. They didn't say a word. Something shook loose in both of them. Her lips were on his, and his fingers were on her clothes, and they stripped on the new carpet he'd laid in the living room and made frantic love, soundless except for the pace of their breathing. The tenderness of their bruises didn't matter. The graffiti hiding under the fresh paint didn't matter. They were alone and connected for the first time in days, and in the aftermath, as he stroked her bare skin, he felt as if he'd won her faith back.

She was sleeping now. He'd left her a note that he was going to the mainland for a few hours.

At the bakery counter, Mark ordered a loaf of rosemary-garlic bread and a cherry pie, warm from the oven. Everything in Door County was cherries. Fresh cherries, cherry pies, cherry soda, cherry caramels, cherry jam, cherry cider, cherry ice cream, cherry wine. There were cherries in tomato sauce, cherries in cheese, cherries stuffed in peppers, cherries stuffed in olives, cherries stuffed in roast beef. He didn't really even like cherries, but that was like living in Chicago and not rooting for the Bears. He'd become a cherry fan out of sheer necessity, because you couldn't escape them here.

He balanced the pie box on his hand. The tin was hot through the cardboard, and he juggled it. At the end of an aisle, he put down his shopping bag and dipped a pretzel stick in mustard. It was cherry mustard. Of course. He actually liked it. He took a jar and put it in the bag.

Mark heard his phone ringing. He had a

special ringtone for Hilary, which was Aerosmith's "Dude Looks Like a Lady." She'd gotten very drunk one night at a bar in downtown Chicago and danced to it solo, and he'd never let her forget it.

"I really needed to sleep," she said.

"I figured."

"That was a nice way to come home."

"Will I get the same treatment tonight?" he asked.

"Come home and see."

"Soon. I'll swing by the Pig for groceries and get some wine at the liquor store and then head for the ferry. Do you need anything?"

"You."

"That's a date," he said.

He hung up the phone and realized he was smiling, because he felt a glimmer of the life they'd enjoyed in their first year. Before Tresa. Before Glory. When they were first living on the island and commuting together to their teaching jobs, he'd wondered what he had done to deserve that kind of happiness. He'd feared in his secret soul that one day fate would want to take it all back and even the score.

Sure enough, fate did.

Even now, he couldn't escape it.

Mark looked up, holding his phone in his hand, still smiling at the thought of going home to Hilary. He found an older man with slicked jet black hair standing in front of him. Alcohol wafted from the man's breath. They were nearly the same height, but the man's shoulders were rounded by age, and he held himself at an angle, as if one leg were weaker than the other. The man jabbed a finger in Mark's face.

"I know who you are," he said.

Mark had no interest in a confrontation with a stranger. He picked up his shopping bag and tried to squeeze past the man in the aisle. "Excuse me," he said.

"Do you know who I am?" the man asked sharply.

"I have no idea."

"My name's Peter Hoffman."

Mark stopped and took a deep breath. "Okay. All right. I've heard of you. What do you want, Mr. Hoffman?"

"I know what kind of man you are," Hoffman snapped. His voice grew louder and more belligerent. People in the market turned to look at them.

"I'm leaving," Mark said, but Hoffman

blocked his way and put his hand squarely on Mark's chest.

"You stand there, and you listen to me," Hoffman told him.

Mark felt his heart rate accelerate. His fist tightened around the phone in his hand. He imagined Hilary standing next to him and what she would say. *Stay calm. Don't make it worse.*

"What do you want?" Mark asked. "Because if all you want is to accuse me of things I didn't do, then you're in a long line, and you'll have to take a number."

"You think you're funny? You think this is funny?"

"No, I really don't."

"Do you have any idea what I lost? My daughter? My grandchildren? Do you know what it's like to watch your family die?"

Mark felt the flush of embarrassment on his face. A crowd was gathering, and he wasn't the sentimental favorite in this contest. "Mr. Hoffman, I do know what you went through. I can't imagine how horrible that was for you. You have my sympathy, you really do."

"I don't want your sympathy."

"Then please move aside, so we can both leave in peace."

"I've killed men, Bradley. More than I want to remember. I did what my country needed me to do, and I don't regret any of it. But you. I don't know how you live with yourself."

"That's all. We're done here."

"Then you have the goddamn nerve," Hoffman continued, his raspy voice growing shrill, "to hide behind the man who killed my whole family. How dare you. I won't let you do it. I won't let you get away with it."

Mark pushed past Hoffman, their shoulders colliding. For an old man, Hoffman was solid, and even drunk, he was fast. Mark never saw the punch coming. Hoffman's left fist shot up from his hips and connected with the underside of Mark's jaw, snapping his head back. Mark staggered. The pie tumbled from his hand, spilling out of the box as it fell to the floor, spraying cherry filling onto the ground like blood. His phone flew. Mark lost his balance, stumbling backward into shelves lined with canning jars. The shelves dropped, and dozens of jars clattered downward and rained a mess of sauce and glass. His face and clothes dripped with stains.

Mark regained his balance. He rubbed his jaw, which was stiff, and ran his tongue along the back of his teeth to see if any were loose. He shook his clothes, and bits of glass sprinkled around him. The crowd in the shop around them froze in silence. Hoffman cocked his fists, expecting Mark to retaliate, but Mark had no intention of hitting an old man. He just wanted to get out of the store.

Hoffman rooted his feet so Mark couldn't pass. "Nobody thinks I've got the courage, but I do. I'm going to make sure you get what's coming to you."

Mark tried to keep a lid on his temper, which raced to a boil. He felt trapped as people closed in between the aisles. "My wife and I almost died yesterday, Mr. Hoffman. I'll tell you this only once. If anyone comes after us again, it will be the last thing they ever do."

"You can't threaten me, and you can't scare me."

"I'm promising you," Mark said.

"I'm not afraid of someone who messes with teenaged girls."

Mark was tired of denying it. Tired of pro-testing his innocence. Angry with the world. "Get the hell out of my way," he snapped.

"Your wife knows the truth. I told her. She knows what kind of man you are."

Something snapped in Mark. He couldn't stop himself. By mentioning Hilary, Peter Hoffman stepped across a line that no one could cross. Mark's muscles wound up into knots, ready to burst. He backhanded his left arm like a club into Hoffman's chest and shoulder. Despite his military bearing, Hoffman was no match for Mark's strength. The blow lifted the man off his feet and drove him sideways, where he crumpled into a card table that collapsed under his weight. Hoffman dropped, hitting the floor hard. Broken glass scored the man's face and drew blood.

"Shit," Mark hissed under his breath.

The older man squirmed to get up, but he couldn't get his balance. Mark bent over with an outstretched hand to help the man up, but Hoffman swatted the hand away. Mark saw rage and humiliation in the man's face.

The crowd closed in on all sides, rum-bling with menace around him. Mark's claustrophobia increased, and the store suddenly felt small. He needed to get out. He needed a chance to breathe in the open air. He felt arms grasping for him, trying to wrestle him to the ground like a prisoner, but he pushed past the people in the store and bolted for his truck.

31

Hilary hung up her phone with a pang of worry. She'd tried to reach Amy Leigh in Green Bay half a dozen times since the previous night, and each time, the call had gone straight into voice mail.

Wherever Amy was, she wasn't answering her phone.

She knew it didn't mean that anything was wrong. The girl had sounded drunk during her odd phone call. It was possible that Amy was embarrassed about making the call and was now ducking Hilary's attempts to reach her. Things like that happened at college parties. You drank too much, and you no longer knew what you were doing or why. Even so, that wasn't the girl that Hilary remembered.

Her former student had always reminded Hilary of herself in her high school days: confident, bubbly, determined, and sometimes naive. The girl was self-conscious about her larger frame and determined to make everyone forget it when she was on the dance floor. Amy was religious, just as Hilary was, and she came from a solid Chicago family. On the other hand, she was also young, and fun, and prone to impetuous mistakes, like any student away from home.

Hilary just wanted to make sure that Amy was okay. She dialed again. Voice mail. She left another message. "Amy, it's Hilary. Listen, sorry to be a pest, but could you call me back? I'm a little concerned."

She wouldn't have made a big deal of Amy's strange call, but the girl had talked about Florida in the midst of her ramblings. More than that, she'd said the one name that made Hilary sit up and take notice.

Glory.

Hadn't she? It had all happened so fast on the phone, and Amy's voice was a drunken whisper, and Hilary had barely understood the words. Amy had been talking about her dance coach, Gary Jensen. Then she'd said it. Glory. Or maybe Hilary had simply had Glory on her own mind, and when Amy said Gary's name again, she'd heard Glory instead. Maybe she was hearing what she wanted to hear. Maybe.

Hilary padded into the kitchen and poured herself a third cup of coffee from the pot. She wore a roomy sweatshirt, running shorts, and white socks. Her blond hair fell loosely about her shoulders; it was clean and wet from her shower. Her body ached, but it was mostly a pleasant ache now. A postsex ache. She'd come home not realizing how badly she and Mark needed each other, like both of them grasping for a lifeline. The result was a wild, almost animal coupling, the way it had been in the early days, when they were getting to know each other's bodies. She could still feel him where he'd held her and been inside her.

It made her believe in him all over again. He couldn't fake what he felt for her. There had been a time when she, like Amy, was naive about relationships, but she'd left that part of herself far behind in her twenties. She had open eyes about men and about Mark. If Cab Bolton had a witness, then the witness was wrong. Whatever had happened in Florida, it wasn't what everyone else thought.

Florida. *Glory.*

Hilary was sure that Amy had said Glory's name.

She took her coffee into their bedroom, booted up her desktop computer, and logged into her Facebook home page. When she called up a listing of her online friends, she found Amy Leigh on the third page. She clicked on Amy's profile and saw that the girl had updated her status at 6:47 P.M. the previous day.

Amy's status read: *I'm going into the lion's den.*

Hilary didn't think that Amy sounded like a girl heading for a college party. She reviewed the rest of the girl's profile page and noticed a comment from another Green Bay student that had been posted earlier this morning. *Hey, Ames, missed you in class today.*

Hilary didn't like that at all.

She replayed the brief, hushed phone

call from Amy in her head. She didn't know if there was anything she could glean from it. The call itself had only lasted a few seconds. Even so, whether Amy had said Gary or Glory, she had definitely mentioned Florida, and more important than that, Amy had been *in* Florida when everything had happened. She was a dancer, like Tresa. So maybe she saw something. Or maybe she knew something. What?

Amy talked about her coach. *My coach. Do you know him?*

Hilary knew most of the college coaches who worked with dancers in the Midwest, because she'd had to counsel students on choosing colleges, mostly in Illinois, Michigan, Wisconsin, and Minnesota. She knew the name Gary Jensen, but she'd never met the man. His name had made its way around the dance grapevine when he'd been hired as a physical education instructor at Green Bay and been put in charge of the dance team. She didn't know much about his background, but from what she'd seen, he'd done well with the girls. She remembered an e-mail from Amy two years earlier in which Amy talked about the enhanced physical training regimen their coach had implemented, which was something Hilary always emphasized herself. It wasn't just about coordination and practice; it was about conditioning.

She also remembered something Amy had said in her e-mail back then. It was the kind of throwaway line that a college girl would use. *He's a good coach, if you can get past the creepy factor.* That was the word she'd used. Creepy.

Hilary wanted to know more about Gary Jensen.

She visited the UWGB Web site and scrolled down to the athletics page. She found a link to the coach's biography in the faculty roster. The first thing she noticed was that, unlike most instructors, Jensen had no photograph posted on his page. His bio indicated that he'd taught at the school for four years, and she thought it was odd that he'd managed to duck the photo shoots for so long.

His bio said little about his past. He had a bachelor's degree in physical education and a master's in educational leadership, both from the University of Alaska at Anchorage. Based on his years of graduation, Hilary calculated that Jensen was in his midforties. At Green Bay, he taught physical education classes for freshmen and coached dance and wrestling. What was missing from his bio was detailed information about his work experience prior to his arrival in Green Bay. The summary was vague: "Gary has been an adjunct professor and coach at colleges in Alaska, Oregon, South Dakota, and Canada."

Despite the lack of specifics, his bio raised no red flags. Even so, Hilary kept digging, looking for more information about Jensen's past. She found references to him—or to someone with his name—in articles about sports teams in Anchorage and Portland, but most of the articles were more than ten years old. The name was also common enough that she found thousands of pages on men named Gary Jensen who had no connection at all to Amy's coach.

Then she found a headline on one of her searches that caught her attention.

COACH'S WIFE DIES IN FALL.

She read the brief article from the Green Bay newspaper. Not even four months earlier, Gary Jensen had lost his wife during a rock-climbing vacation in Zion National Park. The couple had been married only three years. Jensen was described as devastated. Heartbroken. The Utah police had investigated the incident and found no evidence to suggest the death was anything other than what Jensen described. A terrible, tragic accident.

Hilary wondered. Two violent deaths in four months, and both times, Gary Jensen was nearby. A coincidence?

She of all people knew that smoke didn't mean fire when it came to guilt or innocence. Mark had suffered when others jumped to conclusions. She had nothing specific to feed her suspicions about Jensen. No connection to Glory. Nothing in the man's background. Just Amy's unsettling phone call . . . and a dead wife.

Hilary returned to Amy's profile page. She knew that Amy posted photographs compulsively, and she found an album dedicated to the girl's dance activities. The album included nearly one hundred pictures of Amy and her college teammates in performances and competitions over the past three years. Hilary went through the pictures one by one, eyeing the backgrounds, trying to find a photo in which she could spot Gary Jensen.

She found three pictures. Jensen wasn't the focus in any of them; he was standing behind the girls. When she enlarged the photos, she was only able to obtain two-inch by two-inch squares on her screen, not enough to see his face in detail. She squinted, focusing on his balding crown of hair and his narrow face. One of the pictures was in profile, and she could see the sharp V-angle of his nose. He looked fit and fat-free. She printed out the best of the pictures, and then she ran another search.

This time she hunted for a photo of Harris Bone.

A man with no identity could be anyone at all, she reasoned to herself. *Even a fugitive with another dead wife in his past.*

The newspapers had all used the same photo of Bone at the time of the fire, a face-front shot from his arraignment. Hilary printed that photo and compared the two. The results were inconclusive. There were some similarities between the two men, but Hilary couldn't be sure if she was looking at a ghost or a stranger. If Gary Jensen was Harris Bone, then he'd lost weight in the last six years and probably had some surgical work done to his facial features. The most she could say was that it wasn't impossible. On the other hand, the faint resemblance might have been nothing more than her own wishful thinking.

Hilary frowned and rocked back in her chair. The only way to be sure was to know what Gary Jensen was doing six years earlier, before he arrived at Green Bay, when Harris Bone was burning down his house in Door County. She ran another search, and this time she found a brief notice about Jensen's hiring. The article was no more than three paragraphs long, but it provided her with the one fact she needed. The university had hired Jensen away from a coaching position at a private high school in Fargo.

One of Hilary's best friends at Northwestern was the director of financial affairs at the same school.

She dialed the phone. She hadn't spoken to Pamela Frank in almost three years, but they still sent Christmas cards and the occasional e-mail. When she reached Pam at her desk, she was relieved to discover that news of Mark's problems hadn't made its way to Fargo. The last thing she wanted to do was rehash the events of the past week. Instead, after five minutes of small talk, she got to the point.

"Listen, there's a name I want to run by you," Hilary said. "Someone who may have been a coach or teacher at the school a few years ago. Gary Jensen."

Pam was silent on the phone for a long while. "Okay."

"Do you know him?"

"I remember him, sure."

"How long was he there?" Hilary asked.

"Three or four years, as I recall." Pam was oddly closemouthed.

"What do you remember about him?"

"Why do you want to know?" Pam asked. "Is this in conjunction with some kind of employment application?"

"No, nothing like that. It's personal."

"Oh." She sounded relieved. "I have to be careful what I say, Hilary. It's too damn easy to get sued."

"You know me, Pam. This goes no farther."

"Let's just say we weren't unhappy when he left us to go to Green Bay. That was about four years ago."

"What was wrong with him?" Hilary asked.

"We didn't have any real evidence," Pam said. "It was just rumors."

"Rumors about what?"

"Sex with students," Pam said in a clipped tone. "We investigated but couldn't prove anything. The law says we can't talk about unproven allegations in a reference check, so there wasn't anything we could say to the folks in Green Bay, but it was solid enough that his wife divorced him."

The second wife wasn't so lucky, Hilary thought.

"What's going on?" Pam asked. "Is Jensen in trouble again?"

"I don't know."

"Well, you said it was personal. I assume you're not involved with this guy?"

"God, no."

"Good. I never heard anything bad about his work as a coach, but if you ask me, he was creepy."

"I appreciate the information, Pam."

"How's Mark?"

"Great. Just great."

"Tell him I said hi."

"I will."

Hilary hung up the phone. She didn't know how to interpret what she'd found.

Pam knew Jensen from his years in Fargo, which overlapped with the timeline of the fire. That meant one thing: Gary Jensen was not Harris Bone.

So who was he?

Amy and Pam had both used the same word to describe him. *Creepy.* If Pam was right, the coach also had a history of sexual relationships with underage girls.

Like Glory.

Hilary stared at the fuzzy image of Gary Jensen in Amy's photograph. She wished that the phone call with Amy hadn't ended so abruptly.

She wished she knew where Amy was.

32

Amy awoke to find that her senses had been stripped. She opened her eyes and saw nothing. She tried to scream, but her mouth was stuffed with a wadded-up cloth that made her cough and choke. When she moved, she found that her wrists and ankles were tightly bound. She was on her back on what felt like a soft mattress below her. When she turned her head, her brain was still dizzy with pain. She tried to piece her memory together, but her mind was blank, and she struggled in confusion and panic before she remembered Gary Jensen.

He'd done this to her.

He handed her a glass of wine, and she drank. That was when it all started, when she'd become disoriented. He'd put something in her wine. Stupid, stupid, stupid. She'd heard all the stories about date rape drugs, but she had taken the wine without even thinking about it. She wondered what he'd given her. Ecstasy. GHB. Whatever it was, the effects lingered. She kept feeling her head float away.

Think.

She had no sense of time or how long she'd been lying here. It could have been night or noon outside. She breathed through her nose and tried not to think about the saliva gathering in the back of her throat that made her want to gag. The aroma that she smelled was of flowers and dust. It was the same Victorian home smell from last night, and she realized that she was still inside Gary Jensen's house.

Amy heard the noise of the furnace and felt warm air from a vent near the bed. Outside, as the wind blew, a ghostly rattle scraped across the roof above her. She was upstairs. The noise was caused by tree branches rubbing on the metal gutters.

Inside the house, below her, she thought she heard voices. It might have been the radio or television, but she felt the floors shudder, and she knew she wasn't alone. Gary was still in the house with her. She didn't know how much time she had before he returned.

There was no way to free herself. Pulling at the tape on her wrists and ankles only made it tighter. She tried to spit out the scratchy cloth in her mouth, but tape on her face held the gag in place. The only noises she could make were stifled, guttural groans, and she was afraid the effort would cause her to vomit and strangle herself. In frustration, she squirmed frantically on the bed, struggling against her restraints, and she felt the whole structure lift off the ground and bang on the floor.

Shit. He'd heard her.

Footsteps moved below her, coming closer. She heard him on the stairs. In the hallway. Outside the door. As he came inside, she lay completely still, playing possum with her eyes closed, but she knew she wasn't fooling him. She could sense his presence looming over her. She heard him breathing and smelled the musk of his cologne. He switched on the bedroom light, and she reacted involuntarily, opening her eyes and squinting.

"Hello, Amy," Gary said. His voice was hushed and sounded almost sad. "I'm glad you're awake."

She struggled, desperate to escape.

"I'm going to take off the gag now, so we can talk," he continued. "Don't scream. No one's going to hear you, and I'll have to get mean, and I really don't want to do that."

She felt his fingernails on the side of her face, digging under the tape. "It's better if I do this quickly," he said. In the same instant, he ripped the tape from her face, and she moaned with the pain of her skin tearing away. He pulled the long ribbon of cloth from inside her mouth, and she gulped air. Her cheeks burned, and she tasted blood in her mouth.

"You fucking bastard!" she screamed. *"Let me go!"*

His palm flew across her face, shocking her into silence with a stinging slap. "Please don't make this harder than it has to be, Amy."

"What the hell do you want?" she demanded, squirming against the restraints.

Gary dragged a wooden chair from the opposite side of the room and sat down near her. They were in a guest bedroom, dark and brooding like the rest of the house. "I like you, Amy. I really wish you hadn't put yourself in the middle of this."

"The middle of what?" Amy asked.

He didn't answer. The back of his fingers caressed her face and under her chin. She turned her head to get away from him, but she couldn't. He touched her lightly with the fingertips of one hand, making a line between her breasts and then following the slope to her right nipple.

"Stop it," she hissed.

He let his palm rest on top of her breast. "I have to tell you, you were one of the girls I fantasized about. I dropped hints, and I always hoped you'd take me up on it."

"Dream on."

"Was it because I was older? A lot of girls seem to find that exciting."

"I'm sure you were a pervert when you were twenty-one, too."

His fingers tightened until she gasped in pain. "Be nice, Amy." He released her from his grip, and she breathed heavily.

"What do you want?" she asked.

"I have some questions for you. Mainly, I just want to know who you told."

"Told what?"

"For starters, you saw me with Glory Fischer in Naples. Who else knows about that? Who did you tell?"

Amy froze. Her roommate's face flashed in her mind. *Katie.* He was going after her. She also remembered—or thought she remembered—making a phone call to Hilary before she collapsed. Oh, God, what had she done? She'd put them both in danger.

"The police," she said. "I told the police."

He chuckled. "Nice try."

"It's true. I have a friend who's a Green Bay cop. I told him I was coming here, just in case you did anything."

"Really? What's his name?"

"You'll find out when he knocks down your door, asshole."

"That's clever, but he's not coming. You didn't call the police. I want to know who you did tell."

Amy sighed. "Okay. You win. I didn't tell anyone. No one knew."

"I'd like to believe you, but I don't."

"I didn't tell anyone else. I didn't even

know I was right, you idiot. You could have lied, and I would have believed you. You didn't have to do this."

"The hard part is, I know you, Amy," Gary said. "I've seen you practice and perform. You're determined. You don't let go of something until you get it right. It doesn't matter what I told you. You wouldn't quit."

"So tell me why you killed Glory."

"It won't make you feel better to know what happened, Amy. Believe me. Glory Fischer was just in the wrong place at the wrong time. She saw something that it would have been better for her never to see, and like you, she wasn't going to keep the secret. Sooner or later, she was going to tell someone. So let's try this again, Amy. Who did you tell? Do you have a room-mate? Do you have a friend on the team?"

"No one else knew."

"I'm only going to ask once more. Who knew you were coming to see me last night?"

"**Nobody.**"

"God, I hate to do this, Amy." He took his hands away from her body. Sharply, fiercely, he hit her again, his fist nearly breaking the bones in her face and wrenching her neck sideways. She heard him wince himself from the force of the blow. Her cheek and eye throbbed, and she started crying involuntarily.

"Stop," she begged him.

"Let's go another way. Who did you call? What did you say last night on the phone?"

"I don't remember," she sobbed. Her emotions soared between helplessness and fury. Her head spun with pain.

"I have your phone. I know the number you called. Who was it?"

"I don't remember making any call."

"I heard you talking in the bathroom. What did you say? Did you mention my name?"

"You drugged me. I didn't know what I was doing."

Gary sighed. "You could make this a lot easier on yourself, Amy."

"I don't remember anything."

She did remember, though. Through the haze of the drug, she remembered the sound of Hilary's voice, and she remembered telling her about Gary. About Glory. She hoped that Hilary hadn't written off the call as drunk ramblings from a former student; she hoped that she would tell someone, send someone. That was the only thing she could pray for. Help.

Katie would wonder where she was. Hilary would try to reach her. One of them, both of them, would send the police here. She had to stay alive until then, and that meant not giving Gary what he wanted.

It was as if he could read her mind.

"Rescue's not coming," he told her. "If that's what you're hoping for, give it up. By the time you're missing long enough for the police to care, this will all be over. I don't want to be ugly. Sooner or later, you'll tell me the truth, so you're only hurting yourself the longer you wait."

"Go fuck yourself."

Amy cringed, expecting another blow, but it didn't come. He sat in the chair silently, not moving.

"Unless you tell me, I'll have to start choosing for myself. I'll start with the people you care about. Your parents. Your friends. Maybe you don't care what happens to yourself, but what about them? Do you want them to suffer, too? They don't have to, Amy. You can spare them. *Tell me*."

"I didn't tell anybody. That's the truth."

"You're lying," Gary said. "That's not going to save you."

"Why the hell are you doing this?" Amy asked him. She felt blood bubbling out of her mouth. "Why? Is it because of your wife? You killed her, too, didn't you?"

Gary inhaled loudly. "I loved my wife."

"So you pushed her off a cliff. Did Glory find out about it?"

"Don't try to understand me," he advised her. "This isn't psychology class. This is about life or death for the people you love. Believe me, I know how painful it is to watch someone you love die."

"Everyone knows you were having an affair."

Gary leaned in closer. "Everyone? Who's everyone? Who told you that?"

Amy bit her lip and said nothing. She cursed herself in her head. She didn't want to give him a road map that would lead him anywhere near Katie. Or Hilary. *Tell someone, send someone.*

"Okay, Amy, we'll do it the hard way."

He stood up, and she could feel his presence above her, growing more ominous. She tensed, waiting for whatever was coming next, knowing it would be bad. Even so, she swore to herself that she wouldn't cry and she wouldn't beg. Not to him. Not in front of this monster. She just had to buy time and hope that someone would look for her. Come to the door. Find her.

At that moment, someone did.

Downstairs, she heard a muffled noise, and she realized it was the sound of the antique doorbell chiming. Gary flinched. Amy sucked in a breath to scream, but he anticipated her intention and was on her immediately, clapping a hand over her mouth. He squeezed her jaw, forcing her lips open, and jammed the ribbon of wet cloth back inside, choking her, cutting off any sound from her throat. When he was done, he slapped tape back across her mouth. She was mute again, other than a low squealing through her nose.

"I'll be back," Gary said. He slammed the door of the room shut as he left.

She heard his muffled footsteps as he ran down the stairs. She fought, trying to move the bed and make noise that would be heard below her, but she was running out of strength. She kept breathing through her nose, struggling to swell her lungs, but she began to cough bile into the thick gag. Panic made her gasp for air. *Help me.*

Somewhere in the house, she heard him talking. Gary had answered the door. She wanted to cry, knowing help was so close and yet out of her reach.

Find me.

33

Cab held up the folder with his Florida badge to the man who opened the door.

"Mr. Jensen? My name is Cab Bolton, with the Naples police. I'm investigating the murder that occurred at the hotel where you were staying last Saturday. I believe you talked to someone in my department about the events you witnessed from your room that night."

Gary Jensen looked flustered by Cab's arrival. His face was flushed, and he peered nervously over his shoulder. "Oh. Oh, yes, Detective Bolton, of course. You took me by surprise. Your people told me that there would be a follow-up interview, but I just assumed it would be by phone. I didn't think you would come all the way up here to talk to me in person."

"The victim in this case was from Door County," Cab told him, "so I've been conducting an investigation in that area. Since you're only an hour away, I thought it would be easiest to talk to you face-to-face."

"Yes, of course."

"I stopped by the university, and they told me you were home today."

"Right. Good. I'm glad you found me."

Cab stared past Gary Jensen at the gloomy interior of his house. "Do you mind if I come in?"

"Oh, yes, yes, I'm sorry. Please. Come in."

"I apologize if this is a bad time. I should have called you first. It's a bad detective's habit, I'm afraid. We show up unannounced."

"No, come in. This is fine."

Jensen swung open the door and gestured with his hand. Cab stepped over the threshold into the foyer, which was dimly lit. Ahead of him, twisting stairs with an ornate iron banister wound to the second level. He saw a living room furnished with dark wood and heavy furniture immediately on his left, but Jensen pointed the opposite way down the hallway. The walls were lined with framed photographs of college teams in action.

"I could use a Coke while we talk," Jensen said. "I'm pretty dry. Do you mind?"

"Not at all."

Jensen led him through swinging doors into a compact kitchen with dated yellow appliances. He checked his watch and switched on a radio as he passed the counter, and Cab heard the dialogue of a sports talk program. The volume was oddly loud. Jensen opened the refrigerator and popped a can of Coke and gestured at Cab.

"You want one?"

"No, thanks. Do you mind turning down the radio?"

Jensen made the volume marginally lower. "Sorry, the spring training report is coming up next. The Brewers are in Maryvale."

Cab shrugged but didn't protest further. He took a seat at the kitchen table and pointed the chair outward where he could extend his legs. Jensen took a seat opposite him and drank his Coke straight from the can. The man acted uncomfortable, but Cab wasn't surprised. Most people lost their bearings when a police officer showed up on their doorstep. He liked the element of surprise, before witnesses had a chance to practice their story.

Other than his demeanor, there was nothing unusual about Gary Jensen. He was middle-aged but athletic, with a narrow face and a pointed chin. There was no pouch of fat on his neck. He wore a navy blue fleece hoodie and mesh sweatpants and brightly colored Nikes. It was easy to imagine him as a college coach, intense and competitive, hollering on the sidelines at students who were substantially taller and larger than he was. The longer Jensen sat with Cab, the more the man made a show of relaxing. He eased back into the chair. A smile came back to his mouth, but it felt artificial and forced.

"Am I keeping you from something, Mr. Jensen?" Cab asked.

The coach shook his head. "Not at all."

"I appreciate your calling us about what you saw."

"Of course. I would have called sooner, but our bus left early in the morning on

Sunday, so I had no idea that something had happened at the hotel. I saw news reports during the week, and I realized I should get in touch with your department."

"I'm glad you did. I'd like to go over some of the details again, if you don't mind."

"Yes, sure."

"Are you a full-time employee at the university?" Cab asked.

"That's right."

"Do you do anything other than coach?"

"I also teach physical education."

"Did any other university employees participate in this trip to Florida?"

Jensen shook his head. "No, it was just me and the students. We contracted with a local bus service for a vehicle and driver."

"Did anyone else share your hotel room with you in Florida?"

"No, it was just me."

Cab's eyes flitted to the ring on Jensen's left hand. "Your wife didn't come with you?

"Sorry, I'm no longer married," Jensen explained, twisting the ring. "My wife passed away last year."

"I'm very sorry."

"Thank you."

"So on Saturday night, you were alone in your room?" Cab asked.

"That's right."

"Tell me what happened."

Jensen took another swig from his can of Coke. "I couldn't sleep. You know what hotel beds are like. Around two thirty or so, I took a cigar out on the balcony and figured I'd relax with a smoke. My room faced the Gulf. Great view. Big moon. I think I was on the tenth floor. Anyway, I sat outside for about half an hour or so. I don't know what time it was, but at some point, I saw a man walking from the hotel down to the beach right below me."

"Can you describe him?" Cab asked.

"I wish I could. It was pretty dark. He looked like a fairly big guy, but from that height, it's hard to tell. All I saw was his yellow tank top. It was bright, so it was easy to spot. I'm not sure I would have remembered him, but I saw him again a while later, down close to the water. It looked like he was making out with a girl."

"Where did this girl come from?" Cab asked.

Jensen shook his head. "I don't know."

"Did you see her leave the hotel?"

"No, I only saw the guy. I noticed her for the first time when the man approached her on the beach. He came from the north, and she was already there when I spotted them. I couldn't see anything about her, other than it was a girl in a bright bikini."

"Are you sure it was the same man you saw leaving the hotel?"

"Well, it was the same shirt," Jensen said.

Cab stopped and looked up at the water-stained ceiling as he heard a heavy thud on the floor overhead. Jensen's face seized with dismay.

"I'm sorry, did you say you live alone now?" Cab asked.

The coach looked embarrassed. He spread his hands as if to say: *You caught me.* "I live alone, but I'm finally at a point where I don't always sleep alone, Detective."

"Ah."

"You can see why I was a little surprised when you showed up. I was sort of occupied, if you know what I mean."

"I understand," Cab told him. "Just to

confirm, you didn't have anyone in the hotel with you in Florida. Right?"

Jensen nodded. "That's right."

"What happened when this man in the yellow shirt approached the girl on the beach?" Cab asked.

"They talked for a while," Jensen said. "Then it was more than talking."

"Meaning what exactly?"

"I could see them kissing."

"Are you sure that was what they were doing?" Cab asked.

Jensen hesitated. "I just assumed it was what they were doing. Their arms were wrapped around each other, so that's what it looked like. You don't think he could have been hurting her, do you?"

"You tell me."

Jensen rubbed his hands over his balding head. "I'm really not sure. I mean, you see two people together like that, you assume they're making out, but now that I think about it . . ." His voice trailed off, then he started again. "I don't know, maybe she was struggling. I hope I'm wrong. I hate to think I was watching him kill that poor girl, and I didn't do anything."

"What happened next?" Cab asked.

"I went back inside and went to bed."

"You didn't stay on the balcony and watch?"

Jensen smiled. "I'm not a pervert, Detective. I wasn't going to hang around to see if they had sex. Besides, by that point, I could barely keep my eyes open."

"What time was this?"

"It must have been a little after three. I remember noticing the clock shortly after I got back in bed, and it was just about three fifteen."

"Could you identify the girl or the man you saw?" Cab asked.

"No, as I told you, it was too dark."

"Have you seen a photo of the girl who was killed?"

Jensen nodded. "Yes, I've seen photos of her in the paper."

"Do you remember seeing her at all during the time you were in Florida?"

"No, I don't. I'm not saying I didn't, but there were teenaged girls all over the hotel. I don't remember her specifically."

"Have you told anyone else about what you saw?" Cab asked.

"No, I didn't give it a thought until I saw

what had happened. Then I called your department."

"What about the girls on the Green Bay team? Did any of them mention seeing anything unusual in Florida? Have you heard any discussion among them about the murder or about the girl who was killed?"

"No, I haven't."

"I'd like a list of the girls who were on the school trip with you. As long as I'm in the area, I'd like to interview them personally."

"You mean today?" Jensen asked.

"If that's not a problem."

"No, no, no problem. I could just jot down a list from memory right now, if you'd like. I don't have their contact information, though. You'd have to get that from the university."

"That would be fine," Cab told him.

"It'll take me just a minute."

Jensen got up and opened a kitchen drawer and retrieved a notepad and a pen. He scribbled names on the paper, then hesitated with his pen poised in the air, as if he were trying to remember. "I heard you have a suspect," he told Cab. "Is that true? Is that the man I saw?"

"I can't comment on that," Cab said. "It would be much better if you didn't read any more articles about the case, Mr. Jensen. You shouldn't talk to anyone about it, either. If this goes to trial, you'll need to testify, and you'll be asked about things that might have influenced your memory."

"I understand."

He finished writing, tore off the page from the pad, and handed it to Cab, who studied the list of names.

Tracey Griffiths
Bracey Berard
Katie Baumgart
Nancy Gaber
Sally Anderson
Paula Davis
Michelle Palmer
Lenie Korbijn
Laura Hansen
Carol Breidenbach
Deb Bodinnar

"This is the whole team?" Cab asked.

Jensen nodded. "Those are my girls."

Cab folded the paper and slid it into the pocket of his suit coat. He stood up. "Thank you for your help, Mr. Jensen. I think that's all for now. If I have any more questions, I'll give you a call."

"Of course."

Jensen led him out of the kitchen. As the coach opened the front door, Cab glanced up the stairs, and Jensen followed his eyes and gave him an awkward smile.

"I'll let you get back to what you were doing," Cab told him.

"Thank you. Good luck with your investigation, Detective."

Jensen closed the door, and Cab ducked through the swaying trees to the Corvette. He climbed inside, eyeing the dirty sky, which promised to open up in heavy rain before it was night. The wide street was empty of traffic. The upstairs level of Gary Jensen's house was barely visible through the thick web of maple branches, but he could see curtains drawn across all of the windows.

He wasn't impressed with Jensen as a witness. The man qualified everything he'd seen with "maybe" and "I'm not sure," as if he'd begun to regret opening his mouth in the first place. A smart defense attorney like Archibald Gale would shred him on a witness stand. There was also something about Jensen's demeanor that made Cab uneasy. He didn't like him.

He retrieved the coach's list from his pocket. He wanted to know what the rest of the Green Bay dance team had seen in Florida. He was ready to drive back to the university, but before he pulled away from the curb, his phone rang.

Cab heard a raspy voice when he answered. "Detective, my name is Peter Hoffman."

He searched his memory and was coming up blank when the man added, "My son-in-law was Harris Bone."

"Yes, of course, Mr. Hoffman," Cab said. "What can I do for you?"

"We need to meet."

"I know. You're on my list. Where do you live?"

"I'm not far from the ferry landing in Northport. When can you be here?"

Cab checked his watch. "I'm about ninety minutes south of you right now, Mr. Hoffman. I'm in Green Bay, and I have some other interviews to conduct in the next few hours. Can I come by your place first thing in the morning?"

"This can't wait," Hoffman told him curtly.

Cab paused. He was curious. "What is it you want to talk about?"

"I have information for you, Detective. It's urgent."

"What kind of information?"

Hoffman practically spat into the phone. "I can help you prove that Mark Bradley is the man who killed Glory."

34

Mark waited at the pier in Northport for the three o'clock ferry back to Washington Island. He couldn't see the boat out on the water through the fog and haze. His jaw ached where Peter Hoffman had connected with an uppercut of his fist, and he worked it carefully with his hand, feeling a loose molar. He sat and fumed, angry at himself for losing control. It didn't matter that he'd been assaulted and provoked by the old man's threats. He wished that he had ignored Hoffman and pushed his way out of the store. Instead, news of their altercation was probably already flying through the county.

Impatiently, Mark got out of his truck. His Explorer was the second vehicle in line for the ferry, and no one had pulled up behind him. It would be a quiet ride back to the island. He walked with his hands in his pockets down to the end of the pier, where he stared out at the white boulders of the breakwater and the choppy waves in the passage. The island wasn't even five miles away, but it was invisible on the mist-shrouded horizon. The afternoon sky was threatening and black. It mirrored his mood. The bright spirit in which he'd started the day, in Hilary's arms, had descended into a storm of depression.

He realized that he hadn't called Hilary yet to tell her what had happened between him and Peter Hoffman, but he wondered if she already knew. Their friend Terri in Fish Creek was a lightning rod for gossip, and if word of the fight had reached her, her first call would have been to Hilary. On the other hand, if his wife knew, she would have called him. His phone hadn't rung all day.

Things were going from bad to worse. Their lives were spinning out of control. He didn't know how to stop it.

Mark reached into the pocket of his jacket but discovered that his phone wasn't where he usually kept it. He patted all of his other pockets and couldn't find it. Thinking that he had left it on the passenger seat of the truck, he tramped back from the shore to his Explorer. He checked the front seat and the glove compartment and then under the seats, but his phone was missing.

He remembered that he'd dropped it in the farmers' market when Hoffman hit him. In the confusion, he'd never picked it up again. He cursed and shook his head. There was no time to drive back to Sister Bay. If he skipped the three o'clock ferry, the last ferry of the day wasn't for two more hours. He'd have to let his phone go until tomorrow.

He walked twenty yards to the ticket booth for the ferry. The crews on the boats and at the pier all knew him. In the old days, they'd shared jokes and talked sports with him while he waited, but not anymore. They were like everyone else now, believing the rumors. The fat man in the booth, Bobby Larch, slid open the customer window when Mark tapped on it. He was reading a copy of *Playboy,* eating fries from a foam box, and drinking a bottle of Baumeister's cherry soda. His daughter Karen had been in Mark's English class during his first year teaching in Fish Creek, and Bobby had told Mark back then how much Karen had raved about his class. He was her favorite teacher.

None of that mattered now. In the days since Tresa, every parent looked at him as a predator.

"Hey, Bobby," Mark said.

The man barely looked away from his magazine. "What do you want?"

"Can I borrow your phone?"

"Why?"

"I lost mine," Mark told him. "Come on, Bobby, I want to call my wife."

Bobby shrugged and dug in the pocket of his dirty jeans. He handed a Samsung flip-phone to Mark. It was warm and greasy.

"Thanks," Mark said. He added without thinking, "How's Karen doing? Is she in college now?"

Bobby didn't answer and slid the booth window shut with a bang.

Mark dialed their home number. The phone rang over on the island, but after four rings, the answering machine took the call. He left a message. "It's me. I lost my phone if you've been trying to reach me. I'll be on the three o'clock. I'll see you soon."

He decided to dial his own mobile number to see if someone had found his phone and turned it in at the market. He wasn't anxious to be showing his face in there again after what had happened.

Mark dialed.

A man answered on the second ring and said in a gravelly voice, "Who is this?"

"This is Mark Bradley. I think you've got my phone."

"Bradley," the man said. "I was wondering when you'd call me."

Mark recognized the voice now. He wished he hadn't dialed the number. It was Peter Hoffman. The old man must have picked up his phone at the store and kept it. Instinctively, Mark's temper, which he'd tried to tame all day, flared again. He struggled to keep a lid on his emotions.

"Mr. Hoffman, I'm sorry about what happened between us. Really. I hope you're okay."

"Don't you worry about me, Bradley. I just hope that glass jaw of yours is broken."

Mark didn't take the bait. "I didn't call to pick up where we left off. I just want to get my phone back."

"I've got it right here," Hoffman said.

"I don't know why you took it with you. I wish you'd left it at the store."

"I could have done that, but then you wouldn't have had to face me again, would you? If you want your phone back, you can come and get it."

Mark checked his watch. The ferry was due in ten minutes. Hoffman's home wasn't far, but he doubted that he had time to go to the man's house and make it back to the port in time. He also didn't think it would be a simple matter of Hoffman handing him the phone. The man wanted another confrontation.

"I have a ferry to catch."

"In other words, you don't have the guts to look me in the eye. I suppose tomorrow you'll send your wife to collect it."

Mark grimaced, because that was exactly what he'd planned to do. Hilary wouldn't let him cross Hoffman's doorstep. Not with what had already happened.

"Good night, Mr. Hoffman," he said.

"Yeah, you hang up, Bradley," the man

interrupted him. "Go back across Death's Door and get a good night's sleep. But let me tell you something. I already talked to that detective in Florida. He's coming to see me."

"Good for you."

"When he knows what I know, he'll be heading out there to arrest you, Bradley."

Mark slapped the phone shut, cutting off the abuse from Hoffman's mouth. He got out of the truck. He smelled the approaching downpour in the thick air. He shivered and hiked to the ticket booth, where Bobby Larch slid open the window and took back his phone.

"Thanks," Mark said.

"Whatever."

"Is the ferry on time?"

Bobby shook his head. "Nah, it'll be ten to fifteen minutes late getting in."

Mark returned to his Explorer. He switched on the radio, and the local rock station was playing a song by the Black Eyed Peas. That wasn't his kind of music, and he normally would have changed the station, but as he listened, the beat of the song thumped in his head. The refrain, re-peated over and over, was the title of the song, and he found himself responding the more he listened to it.

Let's get it started.

That was right. He wasn't going to lie down for anyone anymore. Whatever happened would happen.

When Mark checked his watch, he saw that the ferry delay gave him time to drive to Peter Hoffman's home and see the man face-to-face. He pulled out of the ferry line, did a sharp U-turn, and shot through the flat ribbon of curves toward Port des Morts Drive.

35

The house was dead still, the way it always was.

Peter Hoffman sat at the butcher block table in his kitchen and drank whiskey straight from the bottle as he listened to the silence. His need for quiet was a holdover that he'd never been able to shake from his days in the war. He never played music. He rarely watched television. He wanted to hear exactly what was happening outside so that he could detect anything out of place. His ears were attuned to every sound that the house made, every trill of every bird, every shriek of wind, hiss of snow, and drumbeat of rain. There were times when his wife had insisted on playing symphonies on the stereo, but he'd found that he couldn't stay in the room with the noise. Since she died, he'd lived in silence, listening and waiting.

Forty years had passed, the war was long gone, and he still expected an enemy to come from somewhere. If they did, he'd hear them.

Hoffman had a map of Door County laid out in front of him. Next to it was the metal ring on which he kept his bulky set of keys. He held on to keys long after he didn't need them anymore, but he couldn't bring himself to remove them from the ring and throw them away. He still knew the lock associated with each one. His 1982 Cutlass. The strongbox where he'd kept his insurance and mortgage documents, when he still had a mortgage. Nettie's house, Nettie's garage, before the fire.

He picked up the ring and found the key he was looking for. It was a small silver key, the kind that opened a heavy padlock. It was in good condition, but the lock to which it belonged was dirty and rust-covered where it lay in the dirt, exposed to the fierce elements. In the early days, he'd gone there every few months to check on it, but he'd never opened the lock. He'd tugged on it to make sure it held good, and then he had left. Eventually, he'd realized there was no reason to keep coming back. All he was doing was torturing himself.

Hoffman separated the key from the others on the ring. He undid the latch and extracted the key and dropped the ring back on the table. He held the key and rubbed it until it was warm between his fingers. It was horrifying, the vivid memories you could find in a shiny piece of metal. When he couldn't stare at it anymore, he slid the key inside his pocket.

It was next to Mark Bradley's phone.

He pushed himself up from his chair. As he did, a shiver of pain coursed down his leg like ice. His bad leg, where he'd taken a bullet for Felix Reich in a fetid jungle, had stiffened since the fall at the store, and now it was almost immovable. His calf was swollen and purple and tender to the touch. He suspected he had broken a bone. They'd wanted to call an ambulance for him, but he'd refused, even though now he could barely walk. It didn't matter. He had other things to do.

Cab Bolton would be here soon.

Hoffman clung to the kitchen counter and grabbed his cane. He leaned into it, supporting his weight. With his other hand, he picked up the map from the table and slid it under his arm. Step by step, he limped from the kitchen into his bedroom, where he kept his desk and a printer that doubled as a copy machine. He fumbled with the map, unfolding it and laying it on the glass. He punched the COPY button, but when he saw the page that printed, he realized that he had misaligned the map. He moved the paper, tried again, and decided that the image was too small. He set the machine to enlarge.

It would have been easier to drive along with Cab Bolton to show him the way, but Hoffman knew he couldn't walk that far in the cold and rain. He didn't want to go back there anyway. He had faced evil things in the past, but some evil was too much to bear.

He made several more copies before he was satisfied with the result. He crumpled the other pages and dropped them in the trash basket next to the desk. He left the map where it was on the glass. With the copy in his hand, he staggered back to the kitchen, biting his lip at the shooting pains running up his leg. He lowered himself into the chair with a groan. He searched on the desk for a pen and squinted at the copy of the map.

He listened.

Outside the house, above the tremors of wind, he heard a sharp snap, like the crack of a bullet. Someone's footfall had broken a branch. He had a visitor approaching his house through the woods, someone who was trying not to be heard.

Hoffman wasn't surprised.

He folded the copy of the map and slid the paper into his pocket along with the key and the phone. He pushed himself up with both hands flat on the glossy wood of the table. This time, he didn't bother with the cane, and the weight on his calf nearly made him collapse with his first step. He dragged his leg behind him, making stutter steps toward the closet near the front door. The short distance felt endless. At the closet, he reached inside to find his shotgun, which he always kept oiled and ready. He reached up for a box of shells from the closet shelf and spilled them like marbles as he loaded the gun.

He closed the door and sagged against it, breathing heavily, almost weeping as pain knifed his leg. Leaning his shoulders against the wall, keeping his foot off the ground, he slid along the walnut paneling to the front door. He twisted the knob and nudged it open. Outside, on the porch, he smelled dead leaves. The forest was alive, twisting and knocking bare branches together. The dirt driveway was damp with mud. He looked for fresh footprints from the road and saw none.

Where was he?

Hoffman gripped the door frame and hung on as he cradled the shotgun under his other arm. He studied the forest, just as he'd done years earlier, through the misery of drowning rain and voracious insects. He didn't have to see anyone, or hear them, or smell them, to know he wasn't alone.

"I know you're here," he called into the woods.

There was no answer. The wind roared. He tasted the damp mist on his lips.

"It's time to end this," he shouted, but no one replied. The trees cackled as if they were taunting him. *We know what scares you, old man.* He should have listened to their warning.

Hoffman heard a noise inside the house. He'd forgotten the cardinal rule: Always watch your back. The footsteps on the wooden floor were so close that he expected to feel breath on his neck. He tried to turn, to wheel the gun around, but he didn't have enough strength or time. Strong hands took hold of his shirt collar and yanked him backward into the foyer. He fell like a stone drops, his leg caving under him. As he collapsed, the shotgun was peeled from his hands. He hit his head on the floor. He squirmed like an insect on his back, unable to get up.

In every battle, there was a winner and a loser, and he had lost.

"Close your eyes," the voice said above him.

Hoffman didn't. Not now, not ever. The twin barrels of his own gun dug into his forehead, and he left his eyes wide open to see the end when it came.

Hilary's car smelled of freshly ground coffee. She'd emptied their supply with the last pot of the morning, and so she decided to make a pilgrimage to the small shop by the harbor before Mark arrived home. As she drove back, she heard her phone ringing. She pulled off the road rather than navigate with her phone wedged at her shoulder.

"Is this Hilary Bradley?" It was an unfamiliar girl's voice.

"Yes, who is this?"

"My name is Katie Monroe. I think you know my roommate, Amy Leigh."

Hilary heard Amy's name, and her stomach turned over with anxiety. "Is something wrong? Is Amy okay? I've been trying to reach her."

"You have?"

"Yes, Amy called me last night. It was a strange call. I've called her several times since then, but she's not answering her phone. I'm worried."

Hilary heard the girl breathing into the line.

"She didn't come back to our room last night."

"Is that unlike her?"

"Some girls stay out all night, but not Ames."

Hilary yanked off her glasses and closed her eyes as she thought about Amy's call. "Listen, Katie, Amy mentioned the name of her coach when she called. Gary Jensen. Does that mean anything to you?"

The girl paused. "Son of a bitch!" she exclaimed.

"Did she tell you anything about him?"

"Amy told me she was going to talk to Gary last night. She was meeting him at his house. I haven't been able to reach her since then."

"Did you call the police?"

"I called campus security, but they blew me off. They all know Gary. They told me I was crazy. A college girl not coming home overnight isn't a big deal to them."

"You should go to the police," Hilary repeated.

"And tell them what? My roommate didn't sleep in the dorm last night? They'll pat me on the head and tell me to come back tomorrow. I can't do this alone." Katie stopped and then spoke again in a rapid voice. "Listen, you're just over in Door County, right? That's why I called. If you drove down here, we could talk to the police together."

Hilary checked her watch and frowned. "I'm on Washington Island. There's only one ferry left for the day. I'm not sure I can make it."

"Please," Katie insisted. "If we do this together, they'll take us seriously. Otherwise, they won't start pushing papers around for a couple days, and I'm afraid that Amy is in trouble right now."

Hilary hesitated. She knew they had nothing of any weight to tell the police. Gary Jensen might have been creepy, but creepy wasn't a crime. Even so, she shared Katie's fear that something was wrong. If Amy was at Jensen's house when she made that odd call, then she might be in danger, particularly if Jensen was in some way connected to Glory Fischer.

"Okay," Hilary said. "If I make the ferry, it'll still take me a couple of hours to get there. In the meantime, don't do anything, okay? Just wait for me."

"Call me when you're getting close," Katie said.

Hilary hung up. She glanced at the foreboding sky and realized she'd be driving into heavy rain as she neared Green Bay. A wicked storm was coming. She turned the car around and accelerated toward the ferry harbor. As she drove, she punched the speed dial for Mark's number. The phone was already ringing when she remembered the message he'd left on their answering machine.

He'd lost his phone.

She was about to hang up when someone answered on Mark's line. It wasn't Mark.

36

Cab found the dead end at Peter Hoff-man's house and followed the edge of the dirt driveway toward the house. He brushed past tree branches, and his black shoes sank into mossy ground. He noticed boot prints in the mud of the driveway; some-one else had come and gone recently. The house was situated in a clearing that had been carved out of the woods, in the mid-dle of a lawn littered with leaves, acorns, and branches. The log beams of the home glistened. Steam from the furnace spewed out like smoke from a pipe through a white exhaust vent. Behind the house, where the woods began again, Cab could see a glimmer of the blue water beyond the cliff.

He noticed something else, too. From the woods at the rear, a second set of footprints made impressions in the long grass leading toward the back door.

Two visitors. One in front, one in back.

Cab approached the porch warily. He saw tools strewn across the floor and patches of sawdust. The front door was closed. He climbed the stairs, but he couldn't see inside, because the drapes were swept closed across the windows.

He rang the bell. When no one answered, he pounded loudly.

"Mr. Hoffman!" he called. "It's Cab Bolton."

There was no response from inside.

Cab nudged the door with his shoulder. When it didn't open, he took a handkerchief from his pocket and carefully twisted the knob. The door was locked. He stood on the porch, hands in his pockets, and surveyed the yard. To his left, beyond the house, he saw a detached garage. The door was open; a car was parked inside. Rutted tracks led in and out, but they didn't

look recent. Hoffman hadn't driven anywhere today.

His gut sounded an alarm. He reached
inside his coat and extracted his service
Glock, which he cradled loosely in his hand.
He descended the steps and followed the
house to the rear, noting the footsteps in
the grass, which were mostly indistinguish-
able, with no visible tread marks. The rear
door of the house was ajar. Beyond the
door, the frame of the roof angled upward,
and huge windows looked out on the water.
In the yard, he saw a lonely deck chair laid
out beneath the shade of a mammoth oak
tree, near the sharp drop-off to the shore.
In the stretch of gray-blue on the horizon,
he spotted a dot of white where a ferry
cruised through the passage toward Washington Island.

Cab approached the open door and
called again. "Mr. Hoffman!"

The door led into the dinette area of the
kitchen. At the doorway, he stepped out of
his loafers and crossed the threshold in
black socks. He was near a butcher block
table placed in front of the windows. The
kitchen was on his right. The house was

warm, and in the shut-up space, he smelled the metallic smoke of gunpowder. Above it was something fetid, a dead smell of excrement and blood.

Cab swore under his breath.

He followed the hallway toward the front of the house, passing doors for two bedrooms on his right and stairs to a loft. At the end of the hallway, the house opened up into a large living room with a high ceiling. He saw the body lying halfway onto the carpet behind the front door. Unspent shotgun shells gleamed on the floor. Blood made a spider on the tile of the foyer and soaked into a pool on the fibers of the carpet. Peter Hoffman was a limp mess of sprawled limbs. He had no face. The blast from the gun had obviously been dead-on into his skull while the man lay on the ground.

Cab reached for his phone. He was about to call Felix Reich when he stopped.

He knew what would happen when the crew from the sheriff's department arrived. Reich would take a statement and get him out of the house, which was exactly what Cab would do if it was his own turf. Before he was banished, Cab wanted to know if

Hoffman had left behind any clues about what he intended to tell him. Whatever information the man had, it had been enough to get him killed.

He backtracked to the kitchen. Based on the cane and pushed-back chair, he concluded that Hoffman had been sitting at the dinette table before he made his way to the front door and was shot. There was nothing on the table except a pen and an open bottle of Jameson's. On the kitchen counter, he saw the man's bulky key ring and a pair of glasses. He checked the master bedroom, which was impeccably neat, and spotted a computer and printer on one wall. When he lifted the top of the printer, the glass was clear. The wastebasket beside the desk was empty. He pulled open the top drawer and found pens, paper clips, staples, and a neatly folded Door County map. That was all.

He did a quick review of the filing cabinet near the man's desk, but the folders mostly revealed tax and property records, which would take hours to study in detail. He nudged the computer mouse with the knuckle of his finger, but the computer had been powered down.

Cab frowned. Nothing.

He checked his watch and knew the clock was ticking. He needed to call the sheriff. He made his way back to the living room and stared down at Peter Hoffman.

"What did you want to tell me?" he said aloud to the corpse at his feet.

At that moment, the body began to sing to him in Steven Tyler's voice. It was an Aerosmith song. "Dude Looks Like a Lady."

Cab started in surprise before realizing that the music came from the dead man's pocket. It was a phone. Cab bent down and used two fingers to reach inside Hoffman's right pocket and slide the phone into his hand. He answered neutrally. "Yeah?"

"Hello? Mark? Who's this?"

"You first," Cab said.

"This is Hilary Bradley. I don't know who you are, but I think you've got my husband's phone."

Cab shook his head in sad disbelief. This wasn't going to be a happy call. "It's Cab Bolton, Mrs. Bradley."

"Detective?" He could hear her freeze with shock and surprise. "How on earth did you get Mark's phone?"

He didn't answer her question. "Do you know how he lost it?"

"No, I don't."

"Where is your husband now?"

"As far as I know, he's on the ferry back to the island. What's going on? Where did you find his phone?"

"I can't tell you that right now."

"Excuse me?"

"You won't be able to get it back."

"Why not?"

"I'm sorry," Cab said. "That's all I can say."

"Is something wrong?"

"I'm sorry," he repeated. "I have to hang up now. It would be better if you didn't call this number again."

He ended the call before she could say anything more. She'd know what it was all about soon enough. The sheriff was going to be out for blood, finding Mark Bradley's phone in the pocket of Peter Hoffman, lying dead in his own house. Peter Hoffman, who was Reich's lifelong friend. Peter Hoffman, who swore he had information that could help put Mark Bradley behind bars.

He bent down next to Hoffman's body. As he slid the phone back into the dead man's pocket, his fingers grazed something else. Paper. He extracted a single folded sheet with his fingertips, and when he unfolded it, he found an enlargement of a map showing a small portion of the Nor-Door section of the county stretching west to east from the town of Ellison Bay to Newport State Park. Nothing was written on the page itself.

Curious, Cab reached into Hoffman's pocket again and dug to the bottom. This time he found something metal. He pulled it out and cupped it in his hand.

It was a key.

37

Hilary saw Mark's face as he drove off the ferry and knew that something had gone terribly wrong. He drove by her, oblivious to everything around him. His face was pale. His eyes were blank and distracted. She hit the horn to get his attention, and he pulled off the road when he spotted the Taurus. He got out and walked toward her. He climbed into the passenger seat, but when she hugged him, he sat motionless, not responding.

"What is it?" she asked. "What's wrong?"

"Peter Hoffman's dead," Mark told her.

"Oh, my God, what happened?"

"I don't know, but I know who they're going to blame for it."

Hilary stared at the ferry port. They were behind schedule, and she knew they'd be rushing to get the half-dozen cars on board. "Back up, back up," she told him. "What the hell's going on?"

Mark ran his hands through his hair. "Hoffman confronted me at the market. He was spouting off about how I'd killed Glory. It got physical. He hit me. Cracked me right in the jaw."

Hilary closed her eyes. "What did you do?"

"I pushed him, and he fell. Everybody saw it happen."

"You mean he died? Right there?"

"No, no, no, no, but everyone knows there was a fight."

"Mark, you're not making any sense. What happened to your phone?"

"I dropped it at the store when Hoffman hit me. When I realized it was gone, I called my number, and Hoffman told me he had it. So when the ferry was delayed, I drove to his house. I wanted to apologize, get my phone back, and get the hell out of there. He was dead. Someone blew his head off.

It was so recent that I could still *smell* it. It must have happened in the fifteen minutes or so between when we talked and I drove over there."

"What did you do?"

"I left. I ran." He added, "I didn't kill him, Hil. It wasn't me."

Hilary cupped her hands in front of her mouth. Her mind raced. "They already found your phone," she murmured.

"What?"

"I called you. I forgot about your message. Cab Bolton answered. He must have been at Hoffman's house, which means he found the body *and* your phone."

Mark shook his head. "They're going to crucify me."

Hilary wanted to tell him he was wrong, but she wasn't going to fool either of them with false hope. He was the obvious suspect. The accusations, the fight, the phone calls, all of it played against him, and all of it could be proved by witnesses and records. She felt a sense of uneasiness herself, however much she tried to pretend she was immune. Hesitation. Doubt. Every time she quelled it, something happened that pushed her deeper into shadow.

He saw it in her face. "Even you're wondering if I'm a murderer."

"I'm not."

"You're thinking, *He's got a temper. Hoffman pushed him too far, and he lost it and killed him.*"

"Don't talk that way, Mark." She didn't want him to know what was in her head. He *did* have a temper. He *had* been pushed too far. None of that mattered now.

Mark reached out and covered her hand. "I'm not lying. I didn't do this. Any of this. Not Glory. Not Hoffman." He stared at her and added, "Not Tresa, either."

"Tell me exactly what you did at Hoffman's house."

"I wasn't there for more than a minute or two. I drove to his house from the port. I walked up the driveway, and I saw that the front door was open. I called Hoffman's name, but he didn't answer. I went inside and found him in the hallway on the floor."

"What did you do next?"

"I got the hell out of there. I slammed the door behind me, and I ran to the car and went back to the ferry port."

Hilary glanced at Mark's hands. He was

wearing leather gloves. "Did you have the gloves on when you went inside the house?"

"Sure."

"So you didn't leave fingerprints?"

"I guess not."

"What about footprints?"

Mark nodded. "I left plenty."

"Get rid of your shoes," she told him.

"What?"

"Drive to a deserted beach before you go home. Throw them into the lake as far as you can. Make sure no one sees you."

"That's crazy. I'm not going to do that."

"Mark, we can't let them prove you were there. The footprints are the only things to put you at his house. Get your clothes in the washer, too. You may have tracked blood from the scene."

"Hil, forget it. I borrowed a phone at the pier. I called my number, and I pulled out of the ferry line. You don't think people will remember that? If I try to cover it up, it will only make me look guilty."

He was right, but Hilary didn't want to hear it. Her voice rose as she felt anger and despair carrying her away. "You can't give them rope to hang around your neck.

They're not going to care about the truth. All they want is to put you in prison. They want to take you away from me, and I am *not* going to let that happen."

Mark reached out and embraced her. She felt as if they were holding on with nothing but their fingertips, slipping out of each other's grasp. To make it worse, she was about to leave him alone for the night.

"Call Gale," she told him, "but don't mention the shoes. A lawyer can't advise you to destroy evidence. I still think you should get rid of them."

"That's like admitting I killed him."

"Why are you fighting me on this?"

"Because this time, I think you're wrong, and if I do it, there's no going back."

"How long were you gone from the ferry line when you drove to Hoffman's house?" she asked.

Mark shrugged. "Ten minutes. Maybe fifteen."

"That's not much time."

"They'll say it's plenty of time to get to his house, argue, struggle, and kill him."

"For God's sake, Mark, whose side are you on?"

"Ours," he said, "but I'm not going to pretend. I'm in trouble. Lying and hiding won't get me out of it."

Hilary saw the crew at the ferry dock waving to her. The other cars had already pulled ahead of her and boarded. She checked her watch; it was two minutes before four o'clock. The boat was leaving.

"I have to go," she told him.

"What? Why? Where are you going?"

"Amy Leigh is missing. I got a call from her roommate at Green Bay. She hasn't seen Amy since last night, and Amy's not answering her phone. I'm going to Green Bay. We're going to talk to the police."

Mark blew out his breath in disappointment. "Of all nights, Hil. I really need you with me."

"If something happens to Amy, and I didn't do anything to stop it, I'd never forgive myself. She called *me*. She reached out to me. I've got to do this."

"Let me come with you."

"Not in those shoes. Not in those clothes. Go home and call Archie Gale."

"Hil, let it go. I'm coming."

She shook her head. "Look at yourself,

Mark. You're not in any shape to do this now. Plus, if you're there, the police will make this about you, not Amy."

He opened the car door. Wind rushed in. "Okay. Go."

"This might be our one chance to find out what really happened to Glory," she told him. "To prove it wasn't you. This coach that Amy talked about, Gary Jensen, I called a friend of mine at the school where he used to work. He was suspected of having sexual relationships with teen-aged girls."

Mark climbed out of the car and leaned back in through the door with a sad smile. "So was I."

"Damn it, Mark, don't talk like that."

"I'm sorry, I can't help it." He pulled her face closer and kissed her. His lips were cool. "I love you. Don't forget that."

"I love you, too."

He shut the door and walked away. After an instant of doubt, she put the Taurus in gear and drove onto the ferry. With the car parked, she got out and climbed the steps to the passenger deck. She stayed outside, hanging on to the railing as the boat eased away from the island. Beyond the shelter of the harbor, the wind on the open water intensified, and the ferry swayed under her feet. Back on the shore, in the parking lot, she could still see Mark's truck. She waved, and she saw the lights of the Explorer flash on and off. He was inside, watching her go.

Inside the bridge cabin, on the top deck of the ferry, a nineteen-year-old man named Keith Whelan watched Hilary at the railing. He was as thin as a telephone pole, with shaggy black hair. He'd worked on the ferry runs for two years. The pilot at the wheel glanced away from the water and followed Keith's eyes to the woman on the deck.

"There's nothing sexier than a woman in the wind," the pilot said. "Especially that one."

Below them, Hilary turned and disappeared inside the passenger compartment. The deck was empty. They could barely see the land of the NorDoor five miles away.

"I see that woman going back and forth every day," the pilot said, "and I never get tired of the view."

"Whatever." Keith rubbed his nose and tugged at the crotch of his jeans. "Gotta piss."

"Sure, go."

Keith left the shelter of the bridge and took the steps down one deck. The boat rolled, but he didn't notice it anymore, even in the worst weather. He ducked through the door to the passenger space, where half a dozen drivers read magazines and gabbed into their phones while they still had signal. Hilary Bradley stood off by herself, staring out the window. Their eyes didn't meet. With her glasses, she looked stuck-up and brainy. Keith didn't like women who pretended they were smarter than he was.

He slipped inside the phone-booth-sized toilet and locked the door. He grabbed his cell phone and punched in a number.

"It's Keith," he said. "You wanted a heads-up, right? She's on the four o'clock heading to the mainland. No way she's going to turn around and go back on the five. I'm telling you, she's sleeping somewhere else tonight. He'll be alone in the house. If you want him, this is your chance."

38

I'm sorry, Sheriff," Cab told Felix Reich. "It's hard to lose a friend this way."

Reich sat in the driver's seat of his Chevy Tahoe in the turnaround at the end of Port des Morts Drive. His hands were on the wheel, and he stared into space down the tree-lined road. His chest rose and fell with fierce precision. After a long silence, Reich's head swiveled on his neck, and Cab saw a fury so deep and bitter that blood vessels pulsed in the man's eye.

"Let me tell you something, Detective Bolton," the sheriff growled. "I hate to say anything bad about a brother behind the shield, but you know what? I don't like you. You race your Corvette into my county with your expensive suits and your spiky hair and your earring, and the next thing I know, a friend of mine is dead. I blame you."

"I understand you're hurting, Sheriff, and I respect that, but let's lose the guilt trip, okay? I don't need it."

Reich clenched his fists so tightly that his knuckles turned white. "Here's the way we're going to do this, Detective. You're going to tell me everything you know like a witness at a crime scene, which is what you are. When we're done, you're going to drive down to your luxury apartment in Fish Creek and pack your bags. Tomorrow I want you to get the hell out of Door County."

"Threats just make me more stubborn," Cab replied.

"I gave you free rein in my jurisdiction because you were investigating a murder. Now so am I, and you're in my way. Go home."

"If our cases are connected, we should work together."

"If our cases are connected, it's because you didn't listen to me about Mark Bradley. He's mine now. You're going to have to wait your turn, and that'll be a long time coming."

"You're convinced Bradley did this?" Cab asked.

"I've assembled more evidence in an hour on this case than you've gathered since you arrived. When you live in a place your whole life, people trust you. They become your eyes and ears. They tell you things. You didn't know that Pete had a fight with Bradley near Sister Bay today, did you?"

Cab raised an eyebrow. "No."

"I got four calls about it. Pete swore in front of a dozen witnesses that he was going to make sure Bradley paid for his crimes, and Bradley threatened to kill Pete. Bradley was also spotted in the ferry line at Northport at two forty-five. He borrowed a phone and made a call, and then he took off at high speed and came back fifteen minutes later. Guess who he called? His own phone. The one you found in Pete's pocket. This is the end of the line for that man."

Cab wasn't convinced, but he didn't say so. "I wish you luck, Sheriff."

"Remember what I said. I want you heading home to Florida in the morning."

"I'll keep that in mind, but I have one question first. What did Peter Hoffman know about Bradley?"

"I don't follow you."

"Hoffman said he'd make sure that Bradley got what was coming to him. He told me he could help me *prove* that Bradley killed Glory. I'd like to know how he planned to do that."

"If I find out anything about that, you'll be my first call."

"I was wondering if you knew what it might be."

"I have no idea."

"You can't keep secrets in a small town. Somebody knew something."

"Pete didn't talk to a lot of people."

"What about Delia Fischer?" Cab said. "Hoffman was close to the Fischer family. Maybe he had information about Glory. Or Tresa. Something that would tie Bradley to one or both of them."

"Leave Delia out of this," Reich snapped. "I don't want you bothering her. Is that clear? Anything that involves Peter Hoffman is part of my investigation now, not yours. Stay out of my way."

"Whatever you say," Cab replied.

He pushed open the door of the Tahoe, but Reich reached across the truck and stopped him with a powerful hand on his shoulder.

"Before you leave, find one of the evidence technicians and give them a fingerprint sample. Shoes, too. We'll need to clear your prints on anything we find inside and outside."

"Of course."

"Talk to one of the deputies and go over your movements in detail."

"Sure," Cab said.

"What are we going to find?" Reich asked.

"Meaning what?"

"Meaning, what did you do before you called me? You knew you wouldn't get another shot at Pete's house. I assume you tried to figure out what he was going to tell you."

Cab smiled. Reich wasn't a fool. "I opened a few drawers. I looked in the file cabinet. That's all."

"Did you find anything ? If you did, you better tell me now."

Cab had been hoping to hide behind a vague denial, but Reich wasn't giving him the chance. The smart thing to do was to hand over what he'd found in Hoffman's pocket. The enlarged section of the Door County map. The key. If he didn't, he was committing a crime. If he did, it was also the last time he'd see the evidence, and he wasn't ready to take himself out of the chase yet.

"I didn't find a thing," Cab told Reich. "Nothing at all."

39

The tiger-striped cat sauntered across Delia's path as she sat on the rocking chair on
the front porch. It perched on its haunches
next to her and watched her with its serious dark eyes. Delia stretched out her foot
and stroked the cat's short-haired back.
The animal slid down onto its side and offered up its plump stomach for attention. It
squirmed and purred as Delia's stockinged
foot rubbed its fur, and Delia only stopped
when she realized that tears were stream-
ing down her cheeks. Part of Delia loved the
cat, because she couldn't see it without

thinking of Glory. Part of her hated the cat for the same reason.

Glory had named the cat Smokey, which she said was because of the swirls of black in the cat's fur. Delia knew better; the kitten had smelled of smoke for days after the fire. Smokey was bereft now and was constantly near Delia seeking comfort. The cat had slept in Glory's arms every night, and it didn't understand why the girl was gone. It kept looking out windows and doors with confused longing, as if it expected her to come back.

Delia wiped away her tears and continued with her work. She had a wooden tray draped across her lap, where she crafted her costume jewelry. She'd cut narrow strips from cans of Dr Pepper and Orange Crush, and she had a pliers on the tray to bend and twist the strips together into two-tone spiral earrings. She wore a magnifier on a headband over one eye for the close work. She'd done it so many times that the process was mindless now, making metal curls and buffing the edges with steel wool. On eBay, she could sell a pair for ten dollars. The local gift shops charged more, but she had to give the storeowners a cut of the money. In the past year, she'd netted almost two thousand dollars, which was a welcome boost to a budget that never seemed to be in balance. There was always one bill too many.

Even with her extra income, it would never have been enough for Tresa's college tuition. State school or not, she couldn't afford it. Thank God for Peter Hoffman. He'd paid for everything, tuition, room and board, books, spending money. He'd told her he would do the same for Glory when it was her turn, but Delia had never believed that Glory was college material. Tresa was the serious one, the introvert, with the brains to make something of herself. Glory had no patience for school. Delia had grown up the same way. A party girl. Maybe that was why she had always favored Glory, not only because of how the girl had suffered, but because Glory reminded Delia of herself in a way that Tresa never did.

Tresa reminded her of other things. Bad things.

When she saw Tresa, she still thought of Harris Bone, and she wondered. Agonized. Doubted. She'd never pursued the truth, because she didn't want to know one way or another. Some things were better off as questions without answers. She could remember, though, the times that she'd watched Tresa and Jen Bone together as teenagers. The two girls were best friends, inseparable, almost like sisters. She'd tried to see the likeness in their faces.

She'd tried to decipher whether Harris was father to both of them.

The affair with Harris had been an on-again, off-again thing over the years, but when she'd become pregnant with Tresa, it was during a period when they were sleeping together regularly. Delia had never thought of sex with Harris as cheating. After her own rape, she had disconnected sex from her emotions. She'd never really loved her husband in a romantic way; he'd been convenient, a provider, sweet and reliable. When they had sex, it was to fill his needs, not hers. Harris was different. She'd understood him as a man, or she'd thought she had, until the fire. He'd spent his whole life under a woman's thumb, first with his mother, Katherine, and then with a wife who was just as controlling. The only person to whom he ever confided his frustrations was Delia. She'd enjoyed being his confidante, not realizing that there were emotional strings attached to his secrets. Their relationship had spilled over from soul-sharing to bed-sharing in no time at all, and for years, they had used each other in bad times for physical and spiritual release.

People wondered how she'd been able to forgive Harris for the accident in which her husband died. The truth was that his death had been an economic loss more than an emotional loss. She'd felt sorrow but not devastation. In the aftermath, she'd relied on Harris even more for all of her needs. So had the girls. Glory and Tresa loved him, and he loved them back. Delia knew the sacrifices Harris made every day, going on the road for a job he hated, coming home to a wife and sons who despised him. He did it without complaint, and that was what made the end so shocking. In all the time they'd spent together, sharing secrets and having sex, he'd never given her a hint of what he was planning. She hadn't seen how close he was to the breaking point.

She hated Harris now, not just for what he had done, but for leaving her alone in

the process—and Tresa and Glory, too.
He'd abandoned them, just as he'd abandoned his own daughter. All Delia wanted
to do was forget him. She'd never breathed
a word about the affair to anyone. She'd
never given Tresa any reason to wonder
who her father really was or to fear that
she had bad blood in her. No one needed
to know, especially not Peter Hoffman. If
he had known the truth, he never would
have been so generous with her and the
girls. He would have blamed and resented
Delia, rather than using her to massage
his guilt and grief.

Now even that source of security had
been taken away. Peter was dead. He'd
written his last check to her. She wondered
how she would break the news to Tresa that
she no longer had money to send her back
to school. It was one more body blow in a
lifetime of disappointments and betrayals.

Delia removed the magnifier from her
eyes as she saw an old Grand Am turn
from the road into the bumps of their driveway. Troy Geier got out like a plump clown
and jogged for the house. The wooden
steps, which needed repairs, groaned under his weight. He was breathing hard,

gulping down air. She could tell, looking at Troy, that the boy was scared.

"What do you want?" Delia asked impatiently. She wasn't in the mood to deal with his naive gallantry today.

Troy peered through the screen door into the house. "Is Tresa here?"

"No, she went to the grocery store. Why?"

"I don't want her to hear this. You know how she is about Bradley."

Delia's eyes narrowed. "What's going on?"

The boy gestured to the house. "Let's go inside, okay?"

Delia sighed and handed her jewelry tray to Troy as she pushed herself out of the rocker. Smokey scampered between her legs and disappeared through the cat door into the house. "Take off your shoes," she snapped. "I don't want you tracking dirt on the carpet."

Troy kicked off his shoes on the mat. He followed Delia inside, and she led him back to the kitchen. She needed to get dinner started. She opened the refrigerator and pulled out an egg and a package of ground beef and dumped it into a metal bowl, where she separated the meat with her fingers. She cracked the egg into the bowl and poured in bread crumbs.

"So what do you want?" she asked Troy again.

Troy sat at the kitchen table and fidgeted. "You heard about Peter Hoffman?"

"Of course."

"The word is Bradley did it."

"I heard about the fight. So?"

"We have to do something," Troy said.

Delia shot him a look of disdain. She didn't need false hope now. "Troy, do you really think you're some kind of hero? You? Let it go. Leave this for the men."

"I can do this," Troy insisted. "Bradley has to be stopped."

"And you're the one to stop him?"

"Yes."

"Oh, quit kidding yourself and go home," Delia said.

Troy shook his head. "I'm going to do this, and it has to be tonight."

Delia stopped kneading the beef. "What are you saying?"

"My friend Keith called. He saw Bradley's wife leaving the island on the four o'clock ferry. He's going to be alone."

Delia realized that something was different about Troy. He was older. Determined. She'd assumed all along that the boy was puffing out his chest with his threats, but now he'd gone from talk to action.

"Troy, you don't know what you're saying," Delia said, hesitating. "This isn't a game. It's serious business."

Troy reached inside his coat and laid his gun on the table. It was the same gun he'd shown her at the lake, a silver revolver with a fat black grip that must have been thirty years old. "I am serious."

"All you're going to do is get yourself killed. That gun looks like it would blow up in your face if you pull the trigger."

"It's old, but it works fine. Look, I know where I can steal a boat from a summer house, and I can get to the island myself. I'll stay overnight at Keith's and go back in the morning."

"Why are you telling me this? Do you want me to talk you out of it?"

"No, I want you to get rid of Tresa tonight. Send her to a friend's house for a few hours. Whatever it takes. That way, you can say I was here with you. We were talking about Glory, looking at pictures. If anyone tries to point a finger at me, you can back me up."

Delia's fingers were thick with raw meat. She pulled them out of the bowl and ran them under hot water in the sink. When they were clean and damp, she wiped them with a towel. She studied Troy, who was watching her intently, his face hungry and mean. He was still just a boy, but he was also big and strong enough to go up against a man. She'd known him since he was a baby, and she knew his father had never stopped treating him like a kid in diapers. He'd always been desperate for approval. Desperate to prove himself. He was going to do this whether she said yes or no.

She spotted Smokey in his cat bed on the floor. The cat was curled into a ball, but its eyes were open, watching the two of them like a co-conspirator. It was as if he knew. It was as if he understood. This was about justice for Glory. That was what they all wanted.

"Okay, Troy," Delia told him in a quiet voice. "If you think you can do this, then you go do it. Go get that son of a bitch."

Tresa backed down the hallway in silent horror. Her blue eyes grew huge. She was careful not to make a sound so her mother and Troy didn't realize she was there. She let herself out through the screen door and closed it quietly behind her. She pulled up the hood on her sweatshirt and hurried down the steps. Her mother's car was next to Troy's Grand Am, where she'd parked it moments earlier. She got inside, threw the plastic grocery bags on the passenger seat, and veered backward onto the road.

Her heart was clear; she had to get to Mark right now. She had to warn him.

She sped down County Road E where the bridge crossed over Kangaroo Lake, and then she swung onto Highway 57, heading northwest toward the top of the county. The last ferry for the island departed in less than half an hour. She didn't know if she had time to make it through the upper towns of the NorDoor.

Her fingers clawed the steering wheel. She thought the tires would fly.

"Stupid, stupid, stupid," she murmured to herself. She couldn't believe what Troy and her mother were trying to do. *They want to kill him.* She wouldn't let them get away with it. She'd be there to stop them.

Desolate farmlands whipped past her in the late afternoon gloom. There was almost no traffic, but she studied the dashboard clock with nervous impatience as the minutes ticked closer to five o'clock. In Sister Bay, she passed the wavy harbor on her left, where a handful of early sailboats bobbed in the slips, and then she accelerated onto the empty road heading north. The sky felt low over her head. She passed ruined barns in overgrown fields, where flocks of birds screeched into flight at the noise of her car. On her left, she saw the soldierlike rows of trees guarding the bluffs over the bay.

She still had fifteen minutes' drive ahead of her and only ten minutes before the ferry left the dock.

Tresa continued deeper into the countryside on the huge zigzag that marked the last miles leading to the port. Headlights beamed ahead of her. She hugged the right shoulder as a car passed her heading south. Almost immediately, another car followed, and then another, and then another. She knew what it meant to see so many vehicles in quick succession. The ferry had landed, belching out cars onto the mainland. They'd be loading up for the last journey of the day. She was running out of time.

She saw the last car in the parade. Her eyes caught a glimpse of the driver behind the headlights, and she realized it was Hilary. She braked and leaned on her horn to attract her attention, but when she looked in her rearview mirror, the car had disappeared into the shadows. Hilary was gone. She slowed, debating whether to turn around, but if she took the time to chase her, she lost her chance of getting to the island. Mark would be alone.

A mile later, Tresa reached the band of S-curves leading to the ferry pier. Her tires squealed as she spun the wheel back and forth, but finally, she saw the open water and the boat dock dead ahead. The ferry was still in port, but she saw the gate lifting on the boat behind the last vehicle. She hit the horn, blaring it over and over, and flicking the high beams on her headlights on and off. Her car skidded to a stop twenty feet from the ferry deck, and the rear of the car swung wide on the concrete. She shoved the car into gear and climbed out, waving her hands.

Tresa saw Bobby Larch near the boat. She'd gone to school with his daughter Karen. The large man jogged over to her car, his face pink with anger. He wasn't happy with her.

"Tresa, what the hell do you think you're doing?" Bobby shouted. "Are you crazy? You could kill somebody driving like that."

"Mr. Larch, I'm sorry, I'm sorry, please, I really need to be on that ferry." She fumbled in her purse for cash and held out several crumpled bills. "I've got the fare right here, but this can't wait, it's an emergency."

"We're closed up, Tresa, that's it. Catch the first one in the morning."

"I know, but the boat's right there, please. You only have a couple cars, there's plenty of room. *Please.*"

Larch let out an exaggerated sigh through his rounded cheeks. He waved at the bridge, making a downward swing with his arm. Tresa breathed with relief as the gate descended again, opening up a path for her car. Larch took her money and pointed at a gap on the port side of the deck for her to park.

"Next time, Tresa, you're out of luck," he told her. "Remember that."

"You're the best, Mr. Larch, thank you!"

Tresa drove onto the ferry with a loud metal clang. She got out of the car and tottered on the balls of her feet on the open boat deck. She hugged herself in the cold, feeling scared, sick, and alone. Her stomach lurched. The boat rolled and then slapped with a downward dip into the waves as it churned beyond the breakwater into Death's Door. When she checked her cell phone, she saw that she had already lost signal out on the water. She couldn't even call Mark to warn him. Instead, she had to hope that she was well ahead of Troy crossing the passage.

Tresa felt a splash of water on her cheeks. She looked up and saw rain descending in silver threads out of the dark sky.

The storm that had been threatening all day had finally begun. It would only get worse.

40

The ferry was well into the channel as Cab arrived at the Northport pier. He watched the boat disappearing into the milky haze. He sat in his car in the deserted port, with the Corvette's engine idling like a caged cat, and pulled out the section of the Door County map from his pocket. It told him nothing. The page showed a vacant stretch of northern land, populated by a handful of dead-end roads with colorful names. Lost Lane. Juice Mill Lane. Wilderness Lane. Timberline Road. There was nothing written on it to give him a clue about what this section of the county had meant to Peter Hoffman.

Cab caught a glimpse of movement in his sideview mirror. A fat man with his stomach bulging out of a Packers sweatshirt tapped on the door of the Corvette. Cab lowered the window, letting in the drizzle. The man carried a clipboard and wore an employee name tag with a Washington Island ferry logo. The badge read THOMAS LARCH.

"Nice car," the man told him. Water dripped from the brim of his baseball cap.

"Thanks."

"You need some help here?" he asked.

Cab shook his head. "No, I came by in case the ferry was late, but I missed it."

"Yeah, the next one is at eight o'clock tomorrow."

"Thanks."

It didn't really bother Cab that he'd missed the boat. He'd only wanted to see Mark Bradley that night to study the man's face when Cab showed him the key he'd taken from Peter Hoffman's pocket. To see if there was any reaction or recognition there that Bradley couldn't hide.

Someone in Door County knew what that key was and what it meant.

"You're that cop from Florida, right?" Larch said.

"That's right."

"Yeah, I already talked to the sheriff. Mark Bradley was here a couple hours ago. He borrowed my phone."

"So I hear. You want to get out of the rain for a minute, Mr. Larch? I have a few questions for you."

"I'll get the seat wet."

"It's a rental."

"Well, sure."

Larch walked around to the other side of the Corvette and climbed inside. He brought a damp, mildewed smell with him like a wet dog. He ran his hand admiringly over the dash and the buttery leather of the seats. "What does one of these things cost?"

"A lot."

"I'll bet."

"So Mark Bradley used your phone this afternoon?" Cab asked.

"Yeah, sounds like I'll have to give it to the cops. Evidence, huh? Just like *CSI*. Guess they'll buy me a new one. That's pretty sweet."

"Bradley left the ferry line and then came back?"

"Yup. After he used my phone, he sped off like he was in a big hurry."

"How long was he gone?"

Larch scratched his chin. "Ten minutes maybe? Could have been shorter, could have been longer. But hey, Pete lived just down the road."

"So you heard about Peter Hoffman's murder."

"Oh, sure. Word travels fast around here."

"Did you know him well?" Cab asked.

"Who, Pete? Well enough. He's lived here forever. Tough old guy. Sucks, what happened to his family."

"Did you ever see him with Mark Bradley?"

"Pete and Mark? Don't think so."

"I just wonder why Bradley would have killed him," Cab said.

"Word is that they had a fight."

"About what?"

Larch shrugged. "You're the cop."

"Do you have any guesses?"

"Beats me. I mean, you think you know people, but you don't. I thought Mark was cool. My daughter liked him as a teacher.

Then all this shit with Tresa happened last year. Like I say, people surprise you."

"Peter Hoffman must have been pretty upset about the accusations involving Bradley and Tresa. He was close to Delia Fischer, wasn't he?"

"Oh, yeah," Larch agreed, bobbing his head. "Pete was like a guardian angel to Delia and the girls. It's going to be hard on her with him gone. I hope he left her a little something in his will, you know?"

"What about Glory?" Cab asked. "What was the buzz about her?"

Larch's brow furrowed into large wrinkles under his cap. "I'm not sure what you're getting at."

"I heard she liked to walk on the wild side."

"Sure, Glory could be a handful. Hard to believe her and Tresa were sisters, you know? Tresa's a bookworm, and Glory was a party girl. That doesn't mean she was asking for trouble."

"Of course not." Cab added, "Were there any rumors about Glory and Mark Bradley?"

"What, you think he was doing them

both? That's news to me. Anything's possible, but I never heard about it."

"What about Peter Hoffman? Could he have known whether something was going on between those two?"

Larch shook his head. "If Pete knew that, he would have taken Bradley's head off. He would have told Delia and the sheriff, too. It would have been all over the county."

Cab nodded. Larch was right. "I appreciate your talking with me."

"No problem." Larch opened the door of the Corvette, and the rain was loud outside. He climbed out and then bent down to shove his head in the car again. "Hey, you really need to get over to the island tonight?"

"Why, can you take me?"

"Sure, I do private fishing charters all the time. It'll cost you, though."

"How much?"

"Two hundred bucks. I'll take you round-trip, or I can drop you and you can spend the night." He added, "Or you could let me take the Vette out for a spin, and then it's no charge."

Cab grinned. "I don't really need to go over there tonight. It can wait."

Larch pulled a ferry brochure from his pocket and slid a pen from the top of his clipboard. He scribbled something on the brochure and handed it to Cab. "That's my phone number. If you change your mind, give me a call. I live over in Gills Rock. I can have you there in less than an hour."

Cab glanced at the sky. "It'll be dark soon."

"Night doesn't bother me. That's when you get the biggest walleyes." Larch winked. "Mark Bradley would be pretty surprised to see you at his house tonight."

"What's that mean?"

"Hey, she's over eighteen now, so it's not like there's anything you guys can do about it. Even so, it tells you what a piece of shit he is."

Cab's eyes narrowed. "I'm still not following you."

"Let's just say Mark probably has some company in his bed tonight," Larch told him. "His wife came over on the four o'clock. She's gone for the night. So who races up to the dock like she's a NASCAR driver to get on the last ferry? Tresa Fischer."

"You're telling me that *Tresa* went over to the island tonight?"

Larch nodded. "That's right. Makes you wonder, doesn't it?"

Water pummeled Troy. Water was everywhere.

The twenty-footer clawed into the waves, but beyond the top of the peninsula, the boat rocked like a toy in the ocean. The headwind bit at his exposed skin, and the sky gushed rain down as heavy as a waterfall. He stayed west beyond the worst currents of the passage, but even in the calm of Green Bay, swells rose up and slammed the boat down so hard that his jaw hurt as the bow landed. His progress was excruciatingly slow. After ten minutes, he thought he'd spent an hour on the bay.

He was cold to his bones. He wore long underwear under his jeans and a heavy wool sweater over his jersey, and he was covered head to toe in oilskin camouflage gear he'd borrowed from his father's closet. None of it kept him warm. His toes were numb inside his boots, and he clutched the wheel so hard he couldn't feel his fingers. Beads of rain squeezed inside through the gaps at his collar and trailed down his back like icy fingers.

The black sky felt as opaque as night. He had to keep wiping his eyes to see the land looming on the horizon ahead of him, seemingly as far away as when he'd started. To his northeast, the Plum Island lighthouse blinked out of the gloom. With every minute, he thought about turning back, but if he did that, he would prove what his father had always said about him. He was a failure. A coward. If Glory was looking down at him in the middle of the water, he didn't want her thinking he'd abandoned her.

Troy churned through the passage. He fought to keep the nose pointed toward the bulk of the island as the current swept him nearly in circles. The up-and-down hammering made a relentless thump, vibrating through his body. Even his breathing felt strained as rain flooded his nose and mouth. He had to cover his face and swallow air openmouthed to keep from choking. As bad as it was, he barely noticed when the water finally grew steadier around him. The boat picked up speed. When he glanced eastward, he realized that Plum Island was behind him now. The land mass of Detroit Island, which stretched like a finger below Washington Island, acted like a reef to cut the chop from the lake.

His adrenaline soared. He'd survived the worst of the crossing. The island grew large less than two miles ahead of him.

As he neared land, Troy stayed west of the main harbor where the ferries came and went. He didn't want to be spotted there. He hugged the shore and turned north along the island's jutting index finger, where he could make out individual trees, the white paint of houses built on the water, and deserted beaches. Ahead of him, near the rounded end of the finger, the green trees stopped at the water's edge, and the vast bay took over, reaching twenty-five miles to Michigan's Upper Peninsula coast.

He followed the land as it turned back south into the deep inlet in the island's coast known as Washington Harbor. A long white beach tracked the water. The base of the inlet, Schoolhouse Beach, was made not of sand but of millions of ivory rocks polished smooth by the currents.

He'd gone there with Glory many times in the summers. If he looked hard enough, he could picture her there, in her bikini on a red beach towel, or skinny-dipping in the cool water on a late weekday afternoon. None of that mattered now. What mattered was that Mark Bradley lived on the east side of the beach, in a house hidden inside the trees.

Troy aimed for a forested stretch of shore, out of view of any of the beachfront houses. Most were unoccupied now anyway. Looking down, he saw the water growing shallow. He raised the motor and drifted. As he neared the beach, he climbed over the side and dropped into the knee-deep water, which knifed him with cold. He splashed onto the rocks, dragging the boat with him, until it was far enough out of the water that it was too heavy to move. He left it there. He wasn't sure if he'd go back for it or if he'd slip onto the ferry in the morning with Keith's help.

With any luck, no one would have discovered Mark Bradley's body by then. He'd be free to escape back to the mainland.

Troy climbed the beach to the edge of

the trees and followed the curving shore-line to the east. Heavy rain continued to dimple the half-moon of harbor water, caus-ing overlapping circles. The wet rocks scraped under his feet. He was wet and frozen, but he was determined. He checked the silver revolver under his jacket. It was heavy in his hand. He'd found the gun a year earlier in one of the abandoned barns that he and Keith explored in the off-season. Something about having a weapon made him feel strong. He'd cleaned the revolver as best as he could, oiled it, and tested it. A few times, he and Glory had slipped into empty fields and fired at pop cans placed on barbed-wire fences. She liked the power of the gun, too. She said it turned her on.

Troy reached the beach road that led from the water to the island cemetery. There was a park here, which was crowded with picnickers during the summer. Now, in the rain, as night fell, it was deserted. He chose a bench and sat down to wait. He was only a few hundred yards from Mark Bradley's house, and he could travel along the beach and arrive through the trees. No one would see him. He could creep up next to the house where he had a good shot and squeeze the trigger. That was all it would take. A split second to get justice.

Beyond the trees, on the beach, it rained and rained. It would be dark in minutes. When he had the cover of night, he would move.

PART FOUR

Ashes to Ashes

41

Hilary was near the city of Green Bay on Highway 57 when Katie called her.

"I wanted to make sure you were still coming," the girl said. "Are you getting close?"

Hilary squinted through the windshield at the highway signs. The road was slick, and visibility in the driving rain was poor. She'd already had a near-collision with a deer bounding across the highway lane. "I'm about five miles from the university. Where should I find you?"

There was a long pause. "I'm not actually on campus right now," Katie admitted.

"Where are you?"

"I'm parked across the street from Gary Jensen's house."

Hilary tensed and almost dropped her phone. "What the hell are you doing there?"

"I'm sorry. I needed to do something, so I followed him. I'll explain when I see you."

"Stay where you are, and I'll meet you. Where is this place?"

"If you're close to the university exit, you can't be far. You can take a right turn off the highway toward Wequiock Falls Park. That's where I am. Jensen's house is diagonally across from here."

"I'll be there soon," Hilary said.

She saw a sign for the county park two miles later, and she braked and turned sharply right. One long block from the highway, five roads came together at an intersection like a giant starburst. Telephone wires crisscrossed the sky overhead. The land around her was open; she was at the flat summit of a hill above the bay. A cornfield was on her left. The dead-end road into the park was on her right. On the opposite side of the intersection, she saw a two-story redbrick house shrouded by mammoth trees.

Jensen's house.

Hilary turned into the park and spotted a red sedan parked off the grass in the shelter of an oak grove. She pulled in behind it. When she got out, she peered through the rain-streaked driver's window and saw nothing inside. Her heart leaped with concern.

"Hey."

Hilary heard a hushed call. Near the intersection, under the shelter of one of the trees bordering the crossroad, she saw a girl waving her arms. Before Hilary could move, the girl jogged across the wet grass and joined her by the cars.

"Katie?"

The girl nodded. Her short dark hair was plastered to her skin, and her glasses were dotted with rain. She was medium height and bony, with a nervous twitch to her limbs. She wore a black jacket zipped to her neck and black jeans. She smelled of fresh cigarette smoke.

"You're soaked," Hilary said. "Let's sit in the car."

They got into the Taurus, which was warm. Hilary swung into a U-turn leading back toward the road that led to Highway

57. When she found another break in the trees on the shoulder of the park road, she pulled to her left and stopped. The car was mostly hidden by trees, but they had a view diagonally across the intersection to the brick house.

Beside her, the girl's fingers jerked in a nervous rhythm. "Do you mind if I smoke? I'm so keyed up."

"Put the window down," Hilary said.

Katie did, and she extracted a damp cigarette pack from her jacket and lit up. She blew the smoke out the window. She calmed down as she inhaled, and she closed her eyes briefly.

"I'm so glad you came," she said.

"What's going on? Why are you here?"

Katie tapped ash outside the car. "I couldn't sit in the dorm and do nothing. I'm a reporter, so I figured I'd follow the story, you know? I went to the athletic department to find out if Gary was at work today."

"Was he?"

The girl shook her head. "He called in sick."

"And you still haven't heard anything from Amy?"

"No, I've called and texted her, but nothing. I think he's got her, the bastard. Jeez, I was stupid."

"How did Amy get involved in this?"

"We were in Florida with the dance team. Amy found out about the girl who was killed down there. She said on the bus that she saw Glory and Gary together, and she heard Gary going back to his room late the night she was killed. There are a lot of rumors around town about Gary's wife, too. She died in an accident, but some people aren't sure it was an accident. Anyway, Amy got it in her head that Gary may have been involved in Glory's death."

Hilary nodded. "Were you in Florida with Amy?"

"Yeah, I snuck along for the ride, but I didn't see anything weird down there. I hung out with the dancers during the competition so I could write a story for the paper."

Hilary stared at the house tucked among the trees. She couldn't see lights inside.

"You said you knew Gary was inside," Hilary said. "Have you seen him?"

"Yeah, I told you I checked out the athletic department, right? He was sick? Well, when I got back to the dorm, I saw him coming out of the front door at Downham. That's *our* building. He didn't look sick."

"Did you talk to him?"

"Sure. I played dumb, because I'm not sure if he knows that I'm Amy's roommate. I mean, I know him, and he knows me, because of my job at the paper, but that's it. At least I was able to ask him why he was at the dorm."

"What did he say?"

"He had a good excuse. Like he'd been working on it. He said Amy came over to his house to talk about dance strategies, but she said she wasn't feeling well, and she left right after she arrived. So he came by to see if she was okay."

"He could be telling the truth," Hilary said.

"Yeah, or he could be giving himself an out."

"Did you spot her car?"

"No, I drove around and looked. It's not here. He could have ditched it somewhere. Or maybe it's in his garage."

Hilary frowned. "Let's go talk to the police, but I'm not sure they're going to do anything. Not yet."

"We're running out of time," Katie told her, grabbing Hilary's arm as she placed it on the wheel. "If Amy's alive, we need to do something now."

"What do you mean?"

The girl flicked her cigarette out the window into the wet ground. She took a deep breath and coughed into her sleeve. "After I saw Gary at the dorm, I followed him. He made one stop, and then he came back here. That was an hour ago. If you didn't get here soon, I was going to go over there myself."

"Don't be crazy," Hilary said. She looked at Katie's face and then added: "Where did he stop? What did he do?"

"He stopped at a hardware store," the girl told her. "He bought a large roll of plastic sheeting and a shovel."

Delia grew nervous when Tresa didn't come home.

She dialed her daughter's cell phone number, but there was no answer. She called the store in Egg Harbor where she'd sent Tresa for groceries, and the manager told her it had been more than an hour since she left. Tresa should have been back long before now. It wasn't like her to be late without calling.

Delia stood outside on the porch, watching the empty driveway and the rain falling on the unkempt yard. She struggled with a horrible sense of anxiety. Part of it was her grief over Glory, which triggered an immediate, irrational fear when Tresa was overdue. Part of it was guilt, as she wondered what awful chain of events she had set in motion because of Troy.

Vengeance was so seductive. She was tired of the world taking things from her and offering no retribution. Mark Bradley deserved no mercy, not after what he had done to her and her family. Troy killing him would be a way to right the scales. One man would finally pay the price for the others who had escaped.

It was a simple thing, but she knew it wasn't simple at all. She could hardly breathe. Her mind cascaded through all the things that could go wrong before this was over. Troy was a fool. He would be caught before or after he'd used his gun; he'd go to jail for years. Or he'd be killed in the attempt. She didn't want the boy's life on her conscience. Too many people had died already.

Delia made a decision. She dialed Troy's phone. Wherever he was right now, on the boat or on the island, she had to get a message to him: *Stop. Don't do this.* She needed to end this craziness before it started, but her call went nowhere. Troy had switched off his phone or was without signal. It was already too late; the wheels were grinding forward, and she couldn't stop them. She was in the middle of it now, leaving an electronic fingerprint that tied her and Troy together.

Her phone rang.

"Thank God," Delia murmured. She assumed it was Troy calling back. Or it was Tresa. Either way, she felt a glimmer of hope. Maybe she could put the demons back in their box.

"Yes, hello, who is it?"

"Oh, hi, is this Delia? Delia Fischer?"

The voice was familiar, but she didn't recognize it. "Yes, that's me."

"Delia, hello, this is Bobby Larch. You know, up in Ellison Bay? Our daughters went to school together."

Delia sighed and grew impatient. People were always calling about community activities. School meetings. Fund-raisers. Right now, she didn't want to have anything to do with anyone. "This isn't a very good time, Bobby."

"I'm sorry to bother you, but this has been weighing on my mind. I'm a parent like you, and I figure I'd like to know if my daughter was doing something like this. It doesn't matter how old they are, they're still our kids, right?"

Delia was distracted, and she had trouble following his words, but then her brain caught up with him. *Tresa.*

"What is it, Bobby? What are you saying?"

"I work up in Northport at the ferry dock. The thing is, right as the five o'clock ferry was getting ready to go, your daughter, Tresa, came racing up, saying it was an emergency and she had to get on the boat. I suppose if I'd been thinking, I would have said no, but I let her drive on. It may not be anything important, but I also know that Mark Bradley's wife left the island on the previous boat, so the more I thought about it, the more I figured it was something you should know about, what with everything that happened last year and all. I know you'd want her to be safe."

Delia struggled to find her voice. "Yes. Yes, I do appreciate the call, Bobby. Thank you."

She hung up without letting him say anything more. Her chest felt heavy, as if a fist were constricting her lungs. She should have guessed immediately. Tresa had seen Troy's truck. Her daughter must have crept inside and heard what they were discussing, and now she was there, on the island. With Mark Bradley. In the line of fire when Troy made his way to the house. *Tresa, Tresa, what were you thinking?*

Delia pulled at her hair in panic. She beat her forehead with closed fists, trying to decide what to do. She clutched her phone and dialed Tresa again, and then Troy, and both times she got nothing but the infuriating loop of voice mail. She was helpless. Cut off.

Just like Harris, she'd lit a fire, and now it was out of control.

There was only one option. One way to stop this. She had to get help. Delia dialed another number, and this time she felt a huge relief when the sheriff answered immediately.

"Felix? Oh, God, Felix, it's Delia. Are you back on the island yet?"

"Yes, I just got home. Why?"

"You have to help me. I've made a terrible mistake."

42

Most of the back roads on the northern tip of the peninsula dead-ended in the woods or at the lakeshore. Cab drove back and forth along narrow trails with names like Europe Bay, Lost Lane, Timberline, Juice Mill, and Wilderness, and he saw the same things: farm buildings, locked gates, boat launches, and hiking trails, all of them deserted. None of it meant anything to him, and all the while, it got darker around him. It was already night inside the trees. The relentless rain poured down over the car.

He parked on the road to the state park and turned off the engine. He knew he was wasting his time here, going around in circles. Running blind.

Cab glanced at his phone and saw that he had a single bar of signal. He didn't know how long it would last. Signal came and went with the wind here. Quickly, before the air currents switched directions, he called home to Florida. It was odd that his brain supplied the word. Home.

"Lala, it's Cab," he said when she answered.

"Well, well," she said. "The tall blond stranger."

Hearing her voice, he could picture her face. Her dark skin. Her fierce eyes. Ebony hair. The last time they'd talked, he'd been drinking, and this time, she was the one who sounded buzzed, with a mellowness in her voice. It was softly sensual. It reminded him of the one time they'd made love and how oddly vulnerable she'd been in his bed, not wild and uninhibited as he would have expected. He could picture her naked body and remember the tiny flaws—the freckles, the scar on her knee, the barest pooch—that made her not perfect but more beautiful for being that way. They had danced around that night ever since, with Cab doing what he did best. Running blind.

"Where are you?" he asked.

"I'm in your condo," she told him. "I hope you don't mind."

He was surprised but pleased. "Not at all. I told you to go there."

"My air conditioner still isn't working. I felt like I was back in Havana. I had to do something."

"It's fine."

"I'm drinking your wine."

"Good."

"It's really, really good wine."

"I know."

"I've had a lot of it."

"That's why it's there."

"I suppose you want to talk about the *case,*" she said, drawing out the word with a snarl.

He did, but he didn't. He needed her help, and he didn't know how long his cell signal would last before it evaporated into the sky. Even so, he simply liked hearing her voice out here, in the middle of nowhere. "What else did you want to talk about?" he asked.

"I did something bad," she said.

"I doubt that."

"No, no, I did. I went through your night-stand drawer. I told myself I was looking for a rubber band for my hair, but I was just snooping."

"What did you find?" he asked.

"A picture."

Cab knew which one. "Okay."

"She's pretty."

"Was."

"Was. Sorry."

"Her name was Vivian," he said.

"You want to tell me about her?"

Cab took a long time to reply, and Lala let him off the hook.

"Never mind, you don't owe me your life story. I like the idea that some woman was able to get to you. I sure couldn't."

"Not true," he said.

This time Lala was the one who was slow to answer. "Did she break your heart, Catch-a-Cab?"

"Something like that."

"So now all of us have to pay, huh?"

"Something like that," he repeated.

"That's pretty screwed up."

"Yeah."

"I'm saying things I shouldn't," she said. "I'm sorry. It's the wine. I better shut up."

"Don't."

Lala hesitated anyway. "There's something I never told you."

"What?"

"Shit, what am I doing?" she murmured.

"Tell me."

"I don't hook up," she said.

Cab tensed. "I don't understand."

"I don't do it. Some women do. Not me."

"I'm still not sure—"

"Couldn't you tell?" she interrupted him. "I've made love to three men in ten years. I was engaged to one. I thought I was in love with another. Then there's you."

She'd been right. He wasn't ready for this. "Lala."

"You don't have to say anything."

That was a lie. She wanted him to say something. He needed to say something. He kept looking for a door. Looking for a key. That was the irony, because he had a key in his pocket, and he needed a lock to go with it. *Say something.* He didn't, though, and he waited too long.

"I'm going to press the reset button on this conversation," Lala told him, sounding more sober and sad. "Okay? Reset. Beep. This is Mosqueda. Is that Detective Bolton? What can I do for you, Detective Bolton?"

"Lala," he repeated lamely.

"A report? You want a report? Because I have information for you."

Cab sighed and played the game. "What did you find out?"

"Enough to think that something's not adding up. Enough to think we have a problem."

"Go on. Tell me."

"I started thinking about Glory on Friday night," Lala continued. "When she ran into our bartender friend, Ronnie Trask. I tried to nail down the exact time it happened. Trask said he took his break before stopping at the hotel restaurant to stock up on wine for the bar. Then he went straight from his near-collision with Glory back to the pool bar. He figures he served a drink within two or three minutes of getting back. I checked the invoices and was able to calculate what I think was his first sale. Based on that, I have a window of about five minutes or so when Glory came running from the event center."

"Good work, but I'm not sure where you're going with this," Cab told her.

"Hang on. I called the woman who coordinated the entire dance competition and had her check that time against the performance schedules. Here's what I found. Tresa Fischer would have been in the lineup immediately before that time window. Makes sense, huh? Glory would have been in the arena to watch her sister."

"Sure. Mark Bradley was there, too, so Glory could have bumped into him during the break."

"Yes, but the *next* scheduled performance after Tresa's team was the team from Green Bay. So there were a lot of people with Wisconsin connections hanging around the event center. I started calling people from Green Bay who were staying in the hotel to see if anyone remembered Glory freaking out. I talked to a parent of one of the dancers, and damned if she didn't tell me she remembered a girl losing it outside the event center and go running off."

"Did she know why?"

"No. She said that Glory was standing in front of a window in the corridor and suddenly she screamed and bolted."

"What's on the other side of the window?"

"A patio."

"I don't suppose we have any idea who was out on the patio."

"Actually, we do. This woman's daughter was out there, along with the whole Green Bay team. They were getting a pep talk from their coach, who happens to be Gary Jensen. Ring a bell?"

"Oh, shit," Cab said. "Our witness?"

"That's him. Call me cynical, but I don't like the coincidence."

Cab didn't like it either. "Are you digging into Jensen's background?"

"I'm doing that right now."

"Could there be a connection between Jensen and Glory?" Cab asked.

"That's the million-dollar question."

"Could Gary Jensen be this missing fugitive from Door County? Harris Bone?"

"That was my first thought, too," Lala said, "but no. Unless Bone managed one hell of a sophisticated identity theft, Jensen's got a paper trail that goes back for years. Of course, there could be some other connection between him and Harris that we haven't found yet."

"Keep at it," Cab said, "and keep me posted. That's great work."

"Thanks."

"You've earned the wine," he said.

"I thought so."

"Listen, about what you said," he began. "Before."

"Forget it."

"Lala, you took me by surprise. It's not that I don't—"

"Forget it," she insisted. She added, "Why did you call, Cab? You obviously wanted something."

I wanted to talk to you. I wanted to hear your voice. He didn't tell her that; instead, he explained where he was and what he was doing. The map. The key. The roads that led nowhere. What he didn't say was that he was tired and lonely, and he'd run out of ideas. "It's dark," he said finally. "There's no point in doing anything more tonight. I'm heading back to the apartment. I'll call you in the morning."

Lala didn't let him go. He wondered if she wanted to hear his voice, too. "Have you checked property records in the area?"

Cab glanced around at the dark parkland. There were no houses to be seen. There were hardly any houses anywhere among the roads he'd traveled here. He hadn't thought about people owning the land, because there seemed to be nothing to own. "No, I don't have a laptop with me."

"I can run some searches for you. Give me a second." He heard the clink of crystal as Lala put down her wineglass, then, seconds later, the tapping of keys. "Okay, hang on a second. Here we go, Door County real estate records. All nicely online. You want to give me some street names?"

"Europe Bay Road," Cab said.

"Sounds rustic. I'm getting about a dozen parcels and owners. You want names? Two parcels for Waters, then Petschel, Clark, Moore, Barrick, Sawyer, Lenius, Haines, Mikel, Knoll, Heinz. Any of those mean anything to you?"

"No."

"Next?"

"Wilderness Lane."

"You're kidding."

"No."

"Wilderness. Lots of parcels, one owner. Royston."

"Lost Lane."

"Where the hell are you, Cab?"

"Lost."

Lala was quiet. Finally, he heard her typing. "No parcels on that one."

"Juice Mill."

"I've got the Nature Conservancy owning a parcel, then individual owners Gunn, Kolberg, Dane, and Hoffman."

Cab had closed his eyes, and now they sprang open. He straightened up in the car and banged his head on the roof. "Did you say Hoffman?"

"Yes."

"Peter Hoffman?"

"That's him. The fire address is 11105 Juice Mill Lane."

"Anything about the property?"

"I can tell you what he pays in taxes, the value of the land, and the value of the improvements."

"Improvements?" Cab asked. "There's a house there?"

"Something's there, but the improvements don't even total ten thousand dollars. The land around it is worth a lot more."

"Okay, I'll see what I can see. Thanks, Lala."

"Call me tomorrow, and I'll tell you what else we know about Gary Jensen."

"Good." He added, "Hey, you want to know something?"

Lala didn't answer. He took her silence as an invitation.

"I miss you," he said.

She still didn't answer. He heard nothing from her at all. He wondered if he'd crossed the line, or if she simply didn't know whether he was serious. When Lala was still silent, he glanced at the phone and realized that the wind had changed, and his signal had vanished into the frigid air. She was gone.

43

Mark followed his headlights into the driveway and immediately realized that something was wrong. He'd switched on a lamp in the living room before he left the house, but there was no light shining behind the curtains now. The house was dark.

He climbed out of the Explorer and waited next to his truck. He couldn't see. Rain trickled through the tree branches, splattering on the dirt and covering up other noises in the woods. He ran his hands along the damp metal of the chassis, hunting for the handle of the rear door. When he found it, he opened the door and leaned inside and searched on the floor. His fingers closed over the forked head of a hammer. He grabbed the tool by its wooden handle and shut the door quietly.

Mark felt as if he were blindfolded. Night on the island was black under the hood of trees, and the thick clouds made the sky moonless and starless. He made his way with his hands, creeping toward the house. He felt flagstones under his feet, marking the path. When his outstretched fingers found the front door, he turned the handle, which twisted easily; the door was open. He shoved the door inward and clutched the hammer tightly. Squatting, staying low, he crept into the hallway of his house.

He left the lights off. Light painted him as a target. He peered around the wall that led to the living room and could make out the shapes of the furniture. The walls still smelled like fresh paint. The room was empty. He sidestepped down the hallway, his knees bent, and passed the open door to their bedroom on his left. He lingered there, watching and listening, before he continued to the kitchen and then the den. He ducked into the porch and checked the door leading outside, but it was locked and deadbolted. He began to relax, but as he did, a noise startled him. It sounded like the casters of their bed scraping across the hardwood floor, the way it did when he banged the frame with his knee.

Mark retreated toward their bedroom but stayed in the hallway. In the glow of the clock on his nightstand, he could see that their closet door was ajar, which wasn't how he'd left it. He gripped the hammer and sprang off his knees and charged. He leaped across the short space and threw himself past the door into the belly of the tiny closet. His shoulder slammed the wall, cushioned by the fabric of Hilary's dresses.

He heard running feet and twisted around in time to see someone rolling across the bed on the way from the bathroom to the bedroom door. He jumped, and the two of them collided, landing together in a heap on the floor. Something metallic skidded away into the wall. He expected a fight and didn't get one. The person in his arms was bony and fragile. He smelled girlish perfume. He held her shoulders to the ground, and she whimpered as his weight overwhelmed her.

"Don't hurt me, don't hurt me. Christ, Troy, it's me, Tresa."

Mark couldn't see her face, but he recognized the shape of her body and her familiar long hair. "*Tresa?* What the hell are you doing here?"

She almost seemed to be holding her breath as he spoke. It took her a moment to say anything. "*Mark?* Is that you?"

"Of course it is."

Tresa threw her arms around his neck. "Oh, thank God you're okay. I've been waiting forever. Where were you?"

"I went out to dinner," he replied. "Tresa, what's going on?"

She breathed heavily, still holding him. When he peeled away her arms, she touched his face in the darkness with her fingertips. Her perfume filled his nose as she leaned in and pressed her lips to his.

"Tresa, stop," he said.

She backed away. "I'm sorry. I'm just so glad it's you."

"I'll turn a light on," Mark said.

Tresa grabbed his shoulder. "*No.* Don't. Leave it dark."

"Why?"

"He could be out there. We can't let him see us."

"Who?" He thought about what she had said as he landed on her. "Why did you think I was Troy?"

Tresa leaned against the bed. She held his hand, and her skin was moist. "I overheard Troy talking to my mom. He has a gun, the stupid bastard. He knew Hilary was gone tonight. He said he was going to sail over here and kill you."

Mark swore to himself. "Did you see the gun? Are you sure he really has one?"

"I saw it."

"Do you know when he was planning to come here?"

"No, but he must be here by now. He must be close by. If he saw you come home—"

"Take it easy, Tresa," Mark told her. "I'm not sure Troy's got what it takes to pull this off. It's one thing to think you can shoot someone, but it's different to actually pull the trigger."

"He'll do it, Mark. You should have seen his face."

"I understand, but you shouldn't have

come here. You should have called and told me."

"I know, but I thought—I wanted—that is, I figured maybe Troy would listen to me."

Mark heard guilty embarrassment in her voice. It wasn't just that she was afraid of what Troy would do, or that she thought she could talk him out of it. She wanted to be the one to save Mark. She wanted to rescue him. That was what you did for someone you loved.

"How did you get here?" he asked.

"I drove my mom's car. I parked it down the road. I didn't think you'd want anyone to see it in your driveway—you know, because of what people would think. I mean, Hilary's not home, and here I am."

He knew she believed it. *See? I'm trying to protect you.* Even so, her voice had a breathless quality to it, and he was conscious of the warmth of her body pressed against him.

"Do you know anyone else on the island?" he asked.

"No."

"I'll take you to one of the motels. You can spend the night there, and you'll be safe."

Tresa clung to him fiercely. "No way. I'm not leaving you alone."

"I'll be fine."

"No, Mark. I'm staying here."

She had a childish determination. Part of him wondered if the story about Troy was really true, or if she had made it up as a way to bring them together. He didn't know how far Tresa would go. She'd taken the ferry to be here on a night when Hilary was gone, and he'd found her hiding in his bedroom. He couldn't help but wonder if this was a fantasy, like the sexual encounters in her diary. A fairy tale. It started with Mark being in danger, and it ended with her seducing him.

Or was she telling him the truth?

"Did you call the police?" he asked.

"I couldn't do that. I don't want my mom getting in trouble."

Don't call the police. Mark wondered: Did she really want to protect Delia? Or did she want to protect herself from another lie? He'd been fooled by this girl and her desires before. He liked her, he felt sorry for her, but he had to keep reminding himself that she'd nearly destroyed his life once already.

"Let's go, Tresa," he said.

"Wait! Did you hear that?"

Mark listened. The rain beat on the roof. That was all he heard. "There's no one outside," he said, but he had the same feeling he'd had earlier. Something was wrong. He looked around the bedroom, trying to pinpoint his anxiety, and realized that the clock on the nightstand was dark. Moments earlier, it had glowed with white numbers.

"Stay right there," he told her.

He pushed himself off the floor, but despite his warning, Tresa got up with him and clung to his side. Her arm wrapped around his waist. He felt the speed of her breathing as her chest rose and fell like a scared animal. She wasn't acting. This was real.

Mark groped for the light switch on the wall, and when he found it, he flicked it upward and downward several times. Nothing happened.

"The power's out."

"Oh, shit," Tresa murmured. "He's here."

44

Cab found an old steel gate at the dead end of Juice Mill Lane, where it butted up against the western land of the state park. He examined the gate in the darkness with the beam of a Maglite. Two dented signs hung over the top rail, tied with rusted wire. One said NO TRESPASSING. The other was a number stamped like a license plate in faded white letters. 11105.

This was Peter Hoffman's land.

He studied the rutted road beyond the gate that disappeared into the thick of the forest. The ground was a muddy mess of dirt and grass. He didn't see footprints, which told him that no one had been here in the rainy hours since Peter Hoffman's death. That was good. If Hoffman had a secret that had gotten him killed, and if this land was part of that secret, then Cab didn't want to wait until morning and give someone else a chance to visit overnight.

The rain kept on like Chinese music, making a plink-plink rhythm on the roof of the forest. He walked around the gate. The ground had a damp, wormy smell. He saw one fat worm in the light, stretched out like pink candy among the old leaves. He picked his way along the path, noting PRIVATE PROPERTY signs with reflective letters shining among the wet, glistening trees. Far from the old gate, he spotted vines draped over a narrow trail, where an ash had fallen, blocking the way with a mossy trunk. He stepped over the tree and followed the trail away from the road, sweeping the dirt with a back-and-forth arc of his flashlight. Fifty yards inside the forest, he spotted a glint of glass reflecting from the ground. Standing over it, he saw an open, empty bottle of Jameson's whiskey. The glass was clean; it hadn't been lying here for long. It was the same brand he'd found on the kitchen table at Peter Hoffman's house.

Hoffman had been here recently.

Cab lifted the flashlight and saw the remains of a cabin in front of him.

The dilapidated structure was quickly disappearing back into the arms of nature. Snow and rain had punched the roof downward, leaving gaping holes. The walls bowed inward, specked with remnants of red paint. Popped, rusty nails lined the beams like broken teeth. The door hung open, rotting away from its top hinge, and the chambered windows were broken into jagged fragments. Shredded yellow curtains billowed into the rain. Weeds grew as high as the gutters.

Cab walked up to the door and exposed the interior of the ruins to his light, scattering red-eyed mice. He saw an old stove, its door hanging open, with a rusted grate still inside. Two wooden chairs lay in broken slats on the floor, and bricks from the chimney had crumbled forward into scattered rubble. Rain splattered into puddles through the open roof, and he saw black pellets of feces. Old spiderwebs hung like lace across the windows. Other than the animal presence, the cabin had been unoccupied for many seasons, left to fend for itself in a losing battle against the elements.

Peter Hoffman had been planning to send Cab here to this spot with the section of map in his pocket. Cab was sure of it.

Why?

He followed the damaged walls of the ruins. When he'd made a complete circle, he took a cautious step inside. Debris sprinkled from the gaps in the roof. His foot sank through a rotting beam, trapping his ankle between jagged spikes until he bent down and pushed aside the splintered wood to free himself. He cast his light upward into the rafters, where he saw deserted bird nests and wasp hives.

Cab backed out of the cabin. He studied the trail, which petered out amid a solid grove of pines. In the cone of light, he spotted the empty bottle of Jameson's again, and he made his way there to stand where Peter Hoffman would have stood. When he squatted down, he saw a brown puddle in the belly of the bottle. He followed the beam of light from the bottle's neck into an open patch of dirt where nothing grew. The tall grass and weeds made it almost invisible. He kicked at the mud with his toe and found that the ground at his feet was actually metal. He bent down and scraped aside the dirt until his fingers were black and found a corrugated metal door, two feet by two feet, built into the earth inside a concrete border. It was a tornado shelter.

He saw thick hinges where the door was secured to the concrete foundation. Opposite the hinges, he saw a heavy padlock that kept the hasp of the steel door clamped shut.

The padlock needed a key.

Cab dug in his pocket. He extracted the key he'd taken from Peter Hoffman's body and got down on all fours. He didn't care about the knees of his suit getting sodden and dirty. He balanced the flashlight on the ground and took hold of the lock and used his thumb to clean the key slot, which was caked with grime. When he saw the opening, he inserted the key and twisted.

The lock snapped open.

"I'll be damned," he said aloud.

Cab crouched there, breathing heavily, not daring to move. His wet hair was pasted to his forehead. He turned the shackle sideways and squeezed it out of the staple and put it aside on the ground. With the edge of his fingers, he pried at the hasp, but it had rusted shut with disuse and wouldn't move. He grimaced, tugging harder. When it resisted, he dug out his own keys and wedged one of them under the hasp and yanked again. This time, it sprang open with a bang, scraping Cab's fingers and drawing blood.

He forced his nails under the edge of the metal door. He lifted, but it was heavier than he expected, and it slipped out of his wet grasp and clanged shut. He tried again. The hinges, which hadn't moved in years, groaned and refused to turn. He worked his palm under the narrow opening and pushed, winning a few more inches. This time he used both hands, breaking through the accumulated rust bonding the steel together and forcing the lid open. It fell backward, and Cab fell with it, nearly tumbling down into the shelter.

He righted himself and stared into the blackness of the square opening. A metal ladder disappeared below. Pent-up smells of must and decay bloomed out of the hole. When he pointed his flashlight downward, he saw a dirty concrete floor ten feet below him, where the shelter opened into a larger space. He couldn't see anything beyond the tunnel leading into the cellar.

Cab laid his flashlight on the ground. He took hold of the metal ladder and tested his weight on it. The braces clamping it to the concrete wall wobbled but held. The steps felt secure. He turned off the light and shoved it in his pocket, and he was blind as he took the next step down into the hole. It was dark above him, around him, and below him.

He descended into the belly where Peter Hoffman kept his secrets.

He supposed everyone had such a place, real or imagined, a black cave where you buried the things you wanted to forget.

His feet landed on the concrete floor of the storm cellar. Spiderwebs clung with sticky fingers to his skin and his hair, and he spit strands from his mouth. He felt the dampness of the earth in the porous walls and rain dropping through the hole into a pool where he stood. The opening at the top of the ladder looked small above him.

He switched on his flashlight.

The space was tight. No more than ten

feet separated him from the opposite wall. As he shifted the beam of light, he saw metal shelves lined with canned goods buried in thick dust and plastic jugs of water. Bottles of beer, too, cloudy and stale. Black mold covered the wall like burnt eggs. He saw hundreds of worms, most of them dead on the floor. More cobwebs sagged from the ceiling, clinging to the corpses of bugs like treasure.

He saw a single wooden chair in the middle of the room, as if someone would come here to do nothing but sit and think about his life passing. He tried to imagine why Peter Hoffman came here.

Cab shifted his light and illuminated the last dark corner of the shelter.

"Son of a bitch," he said.

45

We have to do something right now," Katie said. Her breath, when she exhaled, reeked of nicotine. The window beside her was open, and rain sprayed across the girl's arm.

"There's someone I can call," Hilary said.

"Who?"

"His name's Cab Bolton. He's the Florida detective who's investigating Glory's disappearance. The local police will listen to him. They'll send a car out here, and we can talk to them."

Katie wiped steam from the glass with her elbow. "They'll ring Gary's doorbell, and he'll give them a song and dance, just like he did for me at the dorm. Amy needs us *now*. You said you'd help me."

"We can't deal with this alone. Cab's smart. He'll know why this is important."

Hilary dug out her phone and hunted in her purse for the card with Cab Bolton's number. Before she could dial, Katie covered the phone with her hand and stopped her.

"I've got a better idea."

"What is it?"

"Let's give the police a reason to go inside."

"I don't understand," Hilary said.

Katie pushed open the door of the Taurus and climbed out into the rain. Hilary reached across the seat and grabbed her arm.

"What do you think you're doing?"

"I'm going to Gary's house."

"No way. Get back inside."

Katie pulled free. Water dripped from her face and hair. "If the police knock on Gary's door now, he can slam the door in their face, and they won't be able to do a thing about it. But he'll let me in. He has no reason to think I know anything."

"What do you expect to accomplish?" Hilary asked.

"I'm going to force his hand."

"How?"

"I'll tell him the truth. Amy thought he was a murderer. I'll say I'm going to the police."

"You're *not* going to do that," Hilary insisted. "If he really has Amy, all that does is put you in danger."

Katie's head bobbed. Her glasses slipped down her nose. "If he grabs me, great. He doesn't know you're out here. If I'm not back in ten minutes, then you can call 911, and you've got an excuse for the police to storm the place. Otherwise, they have nothing, and we both know it."

"In the meantime, you could be dead."

"He won't do anything to me that fast."

"You can't take the chance."

"Too late," Katie said. "Give me ten minutes."

The girl slammed the door and ran across the wet grass of the park. Hilary got out of the Taurus to chase her, but Katie was already too far away, running through the driving rain. Hilary wanted to shout after her, but she bit her lip and said nothing.

As she clung to the top of the car door and watched her, the girl dashed across the empty intersection into the glow of the streetlight. Katie disappeared behind the towering maple trees that guarded the front of Gary Jensen's house.

Mark heard a muffled splintering of wood as someone forced open the door leading to the back porch. He clapped a hand over Tresa's mouth to squelch her scream. He put his lips against her ear and whispered.

"He's in back. We'll go out the front. Don't make a sound."

He pulled Tresa toward the hallway, and with his body blocking her, he guided them toward the front door fifteen feet away. The distance felt long, and he was a big target if anyone took a chance by firing a shot from behind. He kept his hands firmly on Tresa's shoulders. The girl trembled, and he hoped she wouldn't panic and run, giving away their location.

The door was ajar. When the wind blew, he could taste the rain. He winced as the door moved an inch, its hinges making a sharp squeal. Ahead of him, Tresa froze and sucked in a breath. He put pressure on her back and bent down so that his face brushed her red hair.

"Keep going."

They squeezed through the narrow gap. They were still blind, but the night air felt like freedom. Mark guided them toward his truck, feeling his way to the end of the wall where the living room jutted out beyond the front door. When they reached the driveway, he let go of Tresa's hand and stopped to slide his keys out of his pocket into his fist. He reached out to take Tresa's arm again.

She wasn't there.

He spread out both of his arms. The girl was gone.

"Tresa?" he hissed, as loud as he dared.

Mark heard the squish of her running footsteps. He turned, and she collided with him hard. She bounced off his chest and stumbled backward and fell. He bent down to reach for her, but she jumped up at the same time, and this time, she clutched at his arm, and his keys flew from his fingers. So did the hammer.

Twenty feet away, the car alarm of the

Explorer whooped. The headlights flashed on and off like a strobe. The horn blared a warning. The light caught them in its blinking glare, exposed and vulnerable. Mark scanned the ground for the keys and didn't see them, and he didn't have time to search in the dirt. He grabbed Tresa and pulled her toward the far side of the house.

"Come on, we'll head for the beach."

Beyond the wall, protected by the house, the night was pitch black again. The alarm wailed behind them. He didn't care about the noise they made. He charged through the trees, stumbling over rocks and roots, shielding his face with an outstretched hand as branches clawed for his skin. He clung to Tresa's hand, dragging her in his wake. Ahead of them, he could make out the paleness where the forest ended at the rocky beach near the half-moon bay. He burst from the trees with Tresa on his heels. The rain and wind found them. The water lapped at the shore.

Running on the rocks was loud and difficult. He turned west, and they tramped up the beach along the outskirts of the woods, using the shaggy branches of the evergreens for cover. He wrenched his ankle as he put his left foot wrong, but he didn't slow down. Shivers of pain shot up his leg as they ran. They reached the dirt road that led from the beach into the campground and then to the island cemetery.

"I know where to hide," he told her.

He followed the road into the campground. The trees were tall here, and the land was flat, with straight narrow trunks blocking the way like soldiers. He guided them through the darkness and nearly collided with the cinder-block wall before he saw it. It was one of the changing rooms built for summer bathers, like a small cottage tucked among the trees and picnic benches. He felt for the wooden door and prayed that it was unlocked. When he tugged the wet handle, the door slid silently open. He and Tresa crept inside, and he closed the door behind them. Even in the winter season, the dank space smelled of sewage. He felt his way forward on the concrete floor, and his fingers brushed the metal wall of a toilet stall. He pulled Tresa inside, leaving the door unlatched.

The interior was cold and damp. The

girl was shivering. He slid off his coat and draped it around her shoulders. Outside and inside, he heard water dripping.

"Now what?" Tresa whispered.

"Now we wait," Mark said.

46

After half an hour on the black, rolling water, the lights of the Washington Island harbor looked like salvation. Cab was green, but Bobby Larch looked unconcerned as he throttled back the engine of his fishing boat and drifted into the calm shelter past the breakwater. Cab could see the outline of the ferries where they were docked for the night. As they neared the shore, he heard something odd and out of place. Jazz music. Somewhere in a harborside restaurant, a live band drummed up applause from the crowd of locals.

Cab didn't think he had ever been happier than when the boat nudged gently against the pier. Larch saw it in his face.

"Hey, I said I'd get you here," he said.

Cab stepped off the boat onto the dock, and his knees were wobbly as the ground stopped swaying under his feet. His skin was icy and wet. His suit and coat were thick with grime. "Yeah."

"So why'd you change your mind about coming over here tonight?"

"Long story," Cab said.

A long story buried in a hole.

It was a story of vengeance and justice. Cab knew why Peter Hoffman was dead. He knew Mark Bradley would most likely be dead by morning, if he couldn't stop it. He knew things he wished he didn't know at all.

"I need a car," Cab said. "You know where I can get one?"

"You got a hundred bucks?"

"Yeah."

"Then I know where you can get one."

Cab peeled off a bill from the inside of his wallet, and Larch snapped it with a smile and strolled away from him down the dock. Cab followed as far as the parking lot. He

saw Larch disappear inside the harbor restaurant, hearing the music get louder as
the door opened and closed. Larch was
gone for two minutes. When he returned,
he flipped a set of keys through the air. Cab
caught them.

"Here you go. It's a black Nissan around
back. You'll have it back by morning, right?"

"Right." Cab added, "How much did you
give your friend?"

"Fifty."

"You're a good businessman, Bobby."

Larch winked. "Good luck, Detective."

Cab had no trouble finding the Sentra
parked behind the restaurant. It was old
and crusted with road spray, and it smelled
like sweet pine thanks to a Christmas tree
air freshener dangling from the mirror. He
adjusted the driver's seat as far backward
as it would go and shot down the harbor
road. He switched on his high beams to
light up the narrow lane between the trees.

The town was empty. The handful of
year-round residents were down at the harbor listening to jazz, or guzzling beer at Bitters Pub. Heading north, he sped into the
lonely land away from the shops. He almost
missed the cemetery, where he turned

toward the water, and then he turned again on the dirt road toward Mark Bradley's house. He slowed to a crawl, scanning the woods for the man's driveway.

When he found it, he parked in front, blocking the way out.

Cab got out, bringing his flashlight with him. As he walked toward the house, he lit up the Ford Explorer parked diagonally on the edge of the clearing and then the ground surrounding the truck. His light glinted on something shiny, and he saw a set of keys dropped in the mud. He picked them up, shook off the dirt, and deposited them in his pocket. He saw a mess of footprints in and out of the house. When he turned the flashlight toward the front door, he saw it standing open.

"Shit," Cab muttered.

He was too late. He reached inside his jacket pocket and slid his Glock into his hand.

He took a chance by shouting, "Bradley!" Then, a moment later, he called, "Tresa!"

He listened, but no one answered. Water dripped through the trees, and wind rushed in whistles through the branches. He used the flashlight again, hunting on the ground and in the woods. He knew what he was looking for in the sodden earth. Bodies. He was relieved when he found none.

Cab called again. "Bradley!"

He followed the perimeter of the house, tracking footsteps along the eastern wall. He came upon the screened porch at the rear of the house, and through the mesh, on the other wall, he saw another open door and the jagged splinters where the lock had been yanked out of the frame. He circled the porch and let himself inside through the broken door. The house was cold where the night air had been blowing through the open space. There was no smell of fresh blood. He checked the kitchen, then illuminated the hallway in the cone of light.

He spotted an open bedroom door and tightened his grip on his gun as he moved inside. He checked out the closet and saw clothes lying in piles on the floor. The bed was made, but the comforter was rumpled. On the wall, half under the bed, he spotted a cell phone, and he squatted down and flipped it open to look inside. The photo on the screen showed a girl in the wind, her long red hair blowing across her eyes, her face sad and contemplative.

Tresa.

Tresa had been here. In the bedroom. He half-expected to smell the musk of sex lingering in the air, and he realized that the relationship between the two of them was still a mystery. He didn't know if the affair between them had been real or a product of the girl's erotic imagination. All he knew was that she'd come to the island as soon as she found out that Hilary was gone for the night.

Now Tresa and Mark Bradley were both gone.

He also wondered for the first time: Where was Hilary? Why wasn't she here?

Cab slid the phone into his pocket and got to his feet.

As he turned, the air around his head whistled with motion. He flinched instinctively, knowing what was coming. Something rock solid hammered the base of his skull, where bone met muscle. The blackness of the night turned hot and orange behind his eyes. He had an instant of pain, and then he was falling, but he was unconscious before the weight of his body collapsed on the floor.

Ten minutes passed, and Katie hadn't returned.

Hilary got out of the Taurus and walked through the mushy grass to the trees near the road. She took cover and eyed the dark house across the street. She saw nothing. She heard nothing. She danced with impatience and indecision. When she checked her watch, more time had ticked away.

Katie might be inside, in danger. Or maybe, like the smart, manipulative girl that Hilary suspected she was, Katie had never gone inside at all. She might simply be hiding outside, waiting for Hilary to call the police.

Hilary started across the street. The light overhead cast a yellow glow in a pool on the asphalt and turned her shadow into a black giant. She passed through the light quickly. At the corner, under sagging telephone wires, she studied the brick house, which was almost invisible behind the trees. She sheltered herself under the low-hanging branches. On the front wall, a faint light glowed behind the curtains upstairs and downstairs.

"Katie," she whispered.

If the girl was nearby, she was silent. Hilary fingered her phone.

She hiked toward the rear of the house. Beyond the bushy arms of a huge arbor-vitae, she found a gravel driveway and ducked into it, steps away from the down-stairs windows. The curtains were drawn here, too; she couldn't see inside. She saw the garage ahead of her, its white door shut. The driveway was lit by a dim fluo-rescent bulb, and she felt exposed stand-ing there. If anyone looked outside, she was visible.

Hilary crept around the side of the ga-rage. The brick wall was built with a single window, tall and narrow, and she put her face close to the glass and peered inside. As she stood, framed by the window, the garage was flooded by light.

Gasping, Hilary threw herself to the ground. She heard the grinding of the ga-rage door and the click of a car door as it opened and shut. An engine caught. She kept her chest tight to the wet ground, and she saw a Honda Civic back out of the garage toward the street. Its bright beams passed over her head. The car turned into the street, and as it headed east toward Highway 57, she heard the garage door groaning downward.

She acted on instinct before her brain could stop her. She pushed herself off the grass and ran for the corner of the house. Only six feet separated the bottom of the garage door from the concrete floor. She got to her knees and rolled under the door, scraping her hands on loose rock. The old door didn't have a safety mechanism. It slammed shut, nearly pinning her leg, which she scooted into the garage under the metal skirt at the last second.

Hilary was alone in the empty garage.

She hurried to the door leading to the interior of the house and turned the knob silently. She pushed it open and felt warm air and saw the darkness of the kitchen. She listened, not knowing if the house was empty. She didn't hear voices or the sound of a television, only the hum of the furnace. The kitchen smelled like burnt tomato sauce.

Hilary crept inside. A voice in her head screamed, *What the hell are you doing?*

She swallowed down her fear. She'd given herself an opportunity to see if Amy was in the house. Katie was right. That was something the police couldn't do.

Where was Katie?

Hilary had a sickening thought, as she considered the possibility that Katie was in the back of the Civic that had just left. Tied up. Or dead. She'd been a fool not to stop her. One domino fell, and suddenly the others began to fall, and you couldn't prevent them from tumbling down.

She left the kitchen through swinging doors and followed the hallway to the living room. The hearth smelled of a recent fire. The television was on, which made her freeze with concern, but the sound was muted, and the room was empty. It occurred to her: *Jensen isn't going to be long.*

She rushed through the downstairs rooms. The dining room. The bathroom. The library. The pantry. It was a big house with odd corners and Victorian spaces. There were nooks and crannies where you could hide things. Everywhere she went, the curtains had been swept shut. The house felt Gothic. Haunted. Even so, the rooms were empty and innocent, as if she'd made a mistake.

She found the basement. Her heart was in her mouth as she descended the wooden steps. Here, belowground, she felt comfortable enough to turn on a light. The sprawling underworld was twisted, with concrete-block walls, pipes and ductwork nestled among pink insulation, and corners and turns that mirrored the layout of the house above it. She practically ran, conscious of time passing, of minutes ticking away before Jensen came back. The basement was like a maze, and she had to open steel doors and peer behind stacks of boxes and into crawl spaces to make sure he hadn't built a killing ground for himself in the cold dampness down here.

Nothing.

Hilary returned carefully to the main floor. She breathed heavily as she ran up the twisting staircase to the second story. There was a hallway that broke off like a Z in several directions, and the doors were all closed. Too many doors. All she could do was check them one by one. She went left and tore each door open and swung it shut. Bathroom. Linen closet. Nursery. Master bedroom.

She began to think this was all a fool's errand. A misunderstanding. She had to get out.

Hilary retraced her steps and quickly investigated the other side of the house. Bedroom. Bathroom. Bedroom. All of them empty and mostly unused. She found a spur hallway leading to a last bedroom that overlooked the rear of the house, and as she headed for the closed door, she heard a sickening noise.

The rumble of the garage door. Gary Jensen was back.

"Oh, no," she murmured, freezing in her tracks.

She almost quit right there. She almost didn't open the door, so she could run downstairs and let herself out the front of the house before Jensen made his way inside through the kitchen. Instead, she twisted the knob and pushed her way into the last bedroom, and immediately something was different.

She smelled a pungent mix of sweat, urine, and perfume. It all added up to fear. Someone was here in the darkness.

Hilary turned on the light, and her hands flew to her mouth. She was there. Spread-eagled, tied to the bed. Gagged. Eyes wide. Pleading. Awake. Alive.

Amy.

47

In the dark shelter, Mark heard only the hushed in-and-out of Tresa breathing and the rustle of her clothes as she shivered. They were both wet and freezing. Sharp pain shot from his ankle to his calf, more often the longer he stood, and when he couldn't lean against the metal wall anymore, Tresa got up and forced him to sit down. She sat down again, too, balanced on his knee. She wrapped her arms around his neck and buried her head in his chest. He couldn't see her at all. She was invisible. He could only feel her huddled against him, her fingers clinging tightly to his skin, her damp hair nestled against his chin.

"I'm sorry," she whispered. "This is my fault."

"Don't say that."

He didn't think anyone would hear their low voices through the stone walls. They were in a black cocoon, just the two of them.

Tresa was silent, and then she said, "I still think about it, you know. You and me. On the beach."

Mark knew exactly what she meant. Weeks before Delia Fischer found her daughter's diary, before his life began to crash down, there had been the kiss. It had happened not far from here. They'd been on the beach in the moonlight behind his house, warmed by flames licking from a fire pit. Hilary had left them there as it got late and gone to bed. She trusted him, the way she always did, more than he trusted himself. He and Tresa had talked for two more hours, well past midnight, although Tresa was the one who did most of the talking. She told him about her dreams, fantasies, life, guilt, hopes, fears, and loneliness. Then, as they stood up and he poured dirt on the fire, she'd gotten on her tiptoes and kissed him, not a girl's kiss, not an innocent kiss, but a kiss with all the eroticism a teenager could bring to it.

She'd said what she wanted. "Will you make love to me?"

Now, holding her, he could feel her arousal again, the heat through her clothes. This was romance to her, not life and death. Her rescuing him. Him rescuing her. He felt her shift on his lap, and though he couldn't see her face even an inch away from his own, he knew that her cool lips were about to find him with the same urgency, the same passion, as they had a year earlier. She wanted him to touch her. Undress her. She wanted to be the heroine in the novel.

He stopped her with a gentle pressure on her cheek. "We can't."

Tresa tensed. He felt her disappointment. She eased away from him and stood up in the cramped space.

"I've tried not to love you," she murmured, "but I can't help myself."

"Tresa, don't."

"I'm not a kid. This isn't a crush. I know I

can't have you, and I know I'm a fool, okay? I never meant to hurt you and Hilary. That was the last thing I wanted. Really. Except here I am, doing the same thing all over again."

Mark said nothing.

"At least tell me you were tempted, huh?" she went on. "A little?"

"Tresa, there isn't any way that I would have let something happen between us. It's not just that I love my wife, and it's not because you aren't a sweet, beautiful, amazing girl. It's because I care about you too much. A girl like you falling in love with your teacher is absolutely innocent. A teacher who perverts that love for his own ends is sick. I wouldn't do that to you."

"Oh, shit, you think I'm a child," Tresa murmured, with a grievous hurt in her voice, as if it were the worst thing he could have told her.

"That's not what I mean."

"You're wrong," she told him. "I'm not innocent. Do you think I didn't know exactly what I wanted on the beach with you?"

Her voice grew loud enough that he worried she would be heard outside.

"You read what I wrote in my diary," she said. "I know the positions, okay? I know where things go. I know I was asking you to cheat on your wife. I still am, and I hate myself for it. I don't care. I'd take off my clothes for you right now and get on my knees. That's me being innocent, Mark."

He realized he was making the same mistake with Tresa all over again—treating her like a girl in women's clothes when it was the other way around. She could be naive and seductive all at the same time. Just like Glory.

"All right, yes, of course, I was tempted," he told her. "I'm human, but I wasn't going to wreck both of our lives. Okay?"

"Say yes now."

"You know I can't do that."

"It doesn't have to be anything more than right now. One night."

"Tresa, no."

He felt her bitterness and disappointment emanating out of the darkness. When she spoke, her voice was thick with betrayal. "Were you human with Glory?"

"What?"

"Did you say yes to her?"

Mark heard the echo of Glory whispering to him on the beach. *No one will ever know.*

"Nothing happened between me and her."

"You were out there with her, though, weren't you? Just like everybody said. You and Glory. Together."

"It wasn't like that."

"Be honest with me."

"Yes, I saw her on the beach," he admitted. "That's all."

"Did you arrange to meet her?"

"No. It was an accident. I went for a walk, and I found her there."

"Did she try to seduce you?" Tresa asked quietly.

Mark hesitated. "Yes."

"That bitch. I knew it."

"She was drunk. She was upset. It wasn't deliberate."

"What did she do to you?"

"It doesn't matter."

"Did she kiss you? Did she go down on you? What?"

"No, nothing like that."

He could hear the rattle in her voice as

she battled between anger and tears. "You know what, Mark? You know what I really think? I think you fucked her, and you don't want to admit it to me."

"That's crazy."

"You're lying, aren't you?" she demanded breathlessly. "Glory got whatever she wanted. It's true, isn't it? Everybody's right. You had sex with her, and then you killed her to cover it up."

"No."

"I don't know what's worse. The idea of you killing my sister, or the idea that you wanted to have sex with her, not me."

"Tresa, listen to me. Stop and listen. You're wrong. I didn't have sex with Glory. I didn't kill her."

"So what happened to her?"

"I don't know."

"Do you think I killed her myself? Are you trying to protect me?"

"You didn't kill her."

"If I saw the two of you having sex, I swear I would have strangled her."

"I know you, Tresa," Mark said. "I know you didn't do this."

Tresa sobbed quietly. She shuffled closer, bent down, and threw her skinny arms around his chest. "I'm sorry. I'm such a complete fool. I'm saying whatever comes into my head."

"Tresa, you have to believe me. I didn't kill Glory."

"I know. I'm just as bad as everyone else. I'm the one who's supposed to trust you, and I was ready to say you did it, too."

"I was in the wrong place at the wrong time," Mark said. "That makes me the only suspect, at least until Hilary gets back from Green Bay."

Tresa stiffened and pushed away. "What did you say? Why is Hilary in Green Bay?"

"There's a man there who was in Florida last week. Apparently he's got a sexual history with teenagers, and he may be involved in a girl's disappearance. Hilary thinks the police should be looking at him."

"He's in *Green Bay*?"

"That's right."

Tresa climbed off his lap and paced between the tight walls of the stall.

"What's wrong?" Mark asked.

"I don't know. I guess it's just a creepy coincidence."

"What is?"

Tresa stopped and squatted in front of him and held on to his knees. He could feel her entire body trembling. "A girl disappeared there? What's her name? Who is she?"

"Amy Leigh. Hilary coached her in high school in Chicago."

"Amy Leigh," Tresa repeated, rolling out the name as if she were searching her memory and coming up with nothing.

"Do you know her?"

"No, I've never heard of her."

"Tresa, tell me what's wrong."

"Nothing. I just can't believe—"

"What?"

Tresa reared back so hard and fast that she stumbled against the metal door. "Wait a minute, you said Hilary coached her? This girl's a dancer?"

"That's right."

"Was she in Florida?"

"Yes, she's on the Green Bay team."

He heard Tresa breathing openmouthed.

"Oh, shit," she murmured. "It has to be her."

"What are you talking about?"

Tresa ignored him. "How did Hilary get

mixed up in this? Please, tell me what happened."

"Amy called Hilary yesterday. It sounded like she thought her coach might have had something to do with Glory's death. Now Amy's missing, so Hilary drove down there to talk to the police. She's worried this guy may have grabbed her."

"This guy you're talking about, is he the Green Bay dance coach?"

"I think he is, why?"

"What's his name? Do you know? Is it like Jerry something?"

"It's Gary Jensen."

"Oh, shit, that's him, that's him. I forgot all about it. I'm so stupid! Peter Hoffman said I'd want to see it because I was a dancer. Shit!"

"Tresa, you're not making any sense."

Her voice was urgent. "Mark, we have to get out of here. Please, we need to go. We have to warn Hilary."

He felt his adrenaline and fear accelerate as he heard Hilary's name. "Warn her about what?"

"She has to stay away from there," Tresa moaned. She crumbled, losing control.

"Tresa, Hilary's not going anywhere near Gary Jensen."

"No! No, no, no, you don't understand. What have I done?"

The metal door swung open, and Tresa rushed out of the stall. Her panicked sobs bounced between the concrete walls as she stumbled for the way out. When she found it, she tore open the outer door and let it bang shut behind her. Mark chased blindly in her wake, heading into the woods outside the shelter, where the rain and wind swallowed the noise.

"Tresa, stop!" he hissed. "It's not safe."

For a moment, somewhere close by, he heard her running footsteps and the choked gasp of her cries, but he couldn't see through the darkness to follow her. Soon he didn't hear anything at all.

"Tresa," he called again, as loud as he dared.

She was gone.

Cab awoke with his blood dripping from his face to the floor. It made a pool around the tips of his fingers. The pain in his head was like a nail hammered through the back of his skull and driven out between his eyes.

When he pushed himself up on his fore-arms, a wave of dizziness and nausea almost made him vomit and collapse. He stayed on his hands and knees until his head cleared, then stood up slowly, supporting himself against the bedroom wall. He touched the back of his head tenderly and winced as he felt the swollen bump, which was damp with blood. He had no idea if he'd been unconscious for a minute or an hour, but his flashlight was still lit, shooting a tunnel of light toward the bed. He squatted carefully and retrieved it.

When he listened to the cold, quiet house around him, he concluded that the assailant was gone. So was Cab's Glock. It was missing.

He staggered toward the bathroom and turned on the water at the sink. He grabbed a hand towel from the rack, soaked it under the water, and dabbed it against his skull, wiping the blood. He opened the vanity cabinet under the sink and used the flash-light to find a box of gauze bandages and medical tape. Positioning a pad at the base of his skull, he added tape until the mesh stayed tight against his hair and skin. It was a crude job, but he didn't have time to waste.

Before he left the bathroom, he opened a bottle of Advil and took five of them to battle his monster headache.

Cab made his way out of Mark Bradley's house and tramped through the muddy driveway to the black Nissan, which was parked where he'd left it. He leaned against the car, letting the waves of pain in his head dissipate. Whoever had assaulted him couldn't be far. Neither could Mark Bradley and Tresa Fischer. He just didn't know where to find them. They could be anywhere, hidden by the night.

He opened the car door.

That was when he heard it. A sharp crack sizzled through the noise of the rain. The echoes bounced around him, but the ripples of sound started at the beach.

A gunshot.

The world spun as Cab ran for the water.

48

Hilary ran to Amy on the bed.

As she did, her cell phone rang, and the music was jarringly loud in the silence of Gary Jensen's house. She fumbled with the buttons to answer the call before the coach heard the ringing downstairs.

"It's Katie," Amy's roommate whispered as Hilary pressed the phone to her ear. "Gary's back! Where are you? Are you inside?"

"Call 911," Hilary hissed. "I found Amy. Get the police here right now."

She slapped the phone shut before Katie said another word. She didn't have time to wait. At the bed, she cupped Amy's cheek and then clawed with her fingernails at the tape that bound the girl's wrists. The tape was tightly wound in layers and was slow to fray as she picked at it and pulled it away from the down on the girl's skin. Behind the gag, Amy whimpered, partly in pain and partly in relief, but Hilary quieted her with a gentle hand at her mouth.

"Shhh."

Hilary succeeded in freeing Amy's right wrist, and the girl's arm flew around her neck and pulled her close. They couldn't stop for emotion. She disentangled herself and set to work immediately on Amy's other wrist. This time, her progress was faster, and in less than a minute, Amy's arms were both free, and the girl immediately ripped off the tape from her mouth with a gasp and dug out the cloth bandage that had been stuffed inside, choking her. Her face was blistered and red.

Amy flew up at her waist and again hugged Hilary in an embrace so strong she could barely breathe. "Thank God, thank God, oh, Hilary, thank you," she murmured in a rush of words.

Hilary peeled the girl's arms firmly away. "I know, kiddo, but keep quiet, he's downstairs. We have to hurry. Help's on the way."

Hilary grabbed her car keys out of her pocket and sawed at the tape on Amy's left leg with the jagged edge of one key. The threads split apart, and she tore it away, making the girl's skin bleed. Amy winced and bent her leg at the knee to jump-start her circulation.

Hilary quickly freed her other leg.

"Let's go," she whispered. "Let's get the hell out of here."

Amy swung her legs off the bed, but her knees gave way as she stood up, and she collapsed heavily into Hilary's arms.

"I'm dizzy," Amy said.

"I know. Try again."

Hilary slid an arm around the girl's waist, and Amy draped her left arm around Hilary's shoulder. Amy swayed as the two of them took a step together, but she didn't fall.

"Stay quiet," Hilary whispered. "The front door is at the base of the steps. We'll go straight down and out, okay?"

"Hell yeah."

With each step, the girl grew stronger. Her young body shrugged off the aftereffects of the drug and the long stretch spent prone on the bed. She let go of Hilary, balancing one hand on the wall of the hallway. They reached the stairs leading back to the ground floor, and Hilary went first, with Amy at her heels. Freedom felt close; she could almost smell the rain and pine outside. The staircase wound like a corkscrew, and as they followed the iron railing around the curve, the front door beckoned to them from across the marble tile of the foyer.

She wanted to run. In ten seconds, they could be through the door and safe. She reached behind and took hold of Amy's hand.

Hilary glanced back at the girl. Their eyes met. She gave Amy an encouraging smile, and the girl's face glowed with confidence as she smiled back. Then, as Hilary watched, the smile vanished, and Amy's expression bled into terror. Hilary looked downstairs and understood why.

Gary Jensen stood at the bottom of the stairs, waiting for them. Hilary's eyes followed the length of his right arm and saw that he was holding a gun.

Amy screamed in panic, yanking Hilary's hand and dragging both of them back up the twisting staircase. The girl's speed took Jensen by surprise, but they were only a handful of steps ahead of him as he charged in pursuit. At the top of the stairs, Amy sped left through the open door to the master bedroom. Hilary cleared the doorway behind her, slammed the door shut, and pushed the surface bolt into place just as Jensen's shoulder collided with the heavy door.

Hilary longed for the sound of sirens, but she heard nothing outside. She dug out her phone and punched in 911 on the keypad. On the other side of the door, Jensen hammered and kicked. The lock shivered under the impact, the screws loosening. She heard the phone ring once, twice, then three times, with excruciating slowness.

Jensen kicked again.

"911 Emergency," the operator finally answered.

"Get the police here, we've got a man trying to kill us."

Her panic didn't rattle the operator. "Ma'am, this is a mobile phone. I'm showing this phone registered to an address in Washington Island, Wisconsin. What is your current location?"

Jensen kicked again, and this time the lock hardware exploded off the door, and the door itself spun around on its hinges and banged into the wall. He surged through the doorway with his gun extended and his finger on the trigger. He pointed the barrel at Hilary's head.

"Ma'am, what is your location?" the operator repeated.

"Hang up!" Jensen whispered.

Hilary hesitated. The operator spoke urgently into her ear. "Ma'am? Are you okay? Are you still there? Ma'am, what is your location?"

Jensen shifted and pointed the gun at Amy's head, not even two feet away. *"Hang up!"*

Hilary clapped the phone shut. She let it fall from her hand to the ground.

"Don't be stupid," she told Jensen. "The police are already coming. You may as well let us go."

She watched his face. His eyes darted

between them, and his hand squirmed on the gun, which slipped in his sweaty fingers. She realized he was paralyzed. He didn't know what to do.

"Give it up," she urged him. "If you harm us, you only make it worse."

At Hilary's feet, her cell phone began ringing.

"See?" she said. "They know we're here. They're already tracking the pings on the phone. It won't take long."

Jensen squatted and took the phone in his hand. He flipped it open, not taking his eyes off the two of them, and switched the phone off.

"Get on your knees," he said. "Both of you."

Amy glanced at Hilary, who nodded. They slid down to their knees on the bedroom floor, next to each other. Jensen towered over them, shifting the gun back and forth between their faces.

"You killed Glory, didn't you?" Hilary asked, stalling for time, praying for the police to hurry. "That's what this is all about."

Jensen laughed, but it was manic and strangled, like a man who laughs at things he can't see in the darkness. Things that scare him. He pointed the gun at Hilary's head.

"Please don't do this," she said.

The gun trembled in his hand. His finger moved onto the trigger, and she knew she had to jump for the gun. If she jumped, if she got in his face, then she gave Amy a chance to survive.

Hilary thought about Mark. She saw his face and felt his touch, as real as if he were here with her. She thought about the faces of the children they would never have. She thought about how you can go from life to death in an instant.

She readied herself to leap, but before she did, she spotted movement in the hallway behind Gary Jensen. She didn't dare look away from Jensen's eyes, but in the dim light beyond the doorway, she realized that someone was creeping down the hallway toward them. A teenaged girl stalked Jensen's back with a finger pressed over her lips for silence.

It was Katie.

49

The shot went wild, careening into the treetops.

Troy cursed silently to himself. He'd heard Bradley's voice in the woods above the beach, but he was aiming like a blind man. His nerves made him careless. Now, with a foolish shot, he'd warned Bradley away.

He hiked up the dirt road away from the beach. He hoped the patter of the rain covered the slow crunch of his footfalls. He had the uncomfortable feeling that he was being watched, but he couldn't see anything in the darkness, and he was confident that no one could see him. Even so, he didn't feel alone. The woods felt alive. He told himself that it was his imagination creating monsters in his head, but every scrape of tree branches as the wind blew made him twitch with fear.

He wanted to quit. He wanted to hike to the main road and call his buddy Keith, who would pick him up and smuggle him onto the ferry in the morning. They could spend the night in Keith's basement, drinking beer and playing pool and surfing porn. Forget about Mark Bradley. Forget about the gun in his hand.

He thought, *Glory's laughing at me.*

Maybe she was the one watching him; she was the spirit he felt. Her ghost. If he listened, he could hear her voice. *You can't do anything right.*

He was angry at Glory. Angry at himself. All of that anger still had a focus that made him stay where he was, rooted to the ground. Mark Bradley. He wasn't going to give up while Bradley was alive.

"Where are you, you bastard?" he murmured aloud.

Like the answer to a prayer, Bradley revealed his location. No more than two hundred yards away, Troy saw a stream of light splash through the woods. It was deep in the trees in the campground between the beach and the cemetery. He stayed on the road and hustled, eating up the space between them. Based on the direction of the light, Bradley was heading toward the graveyard, and Troy realized he could get there ahead of him and be waiting for him when the man emerged into the open ground.

Troy splashed through huge puddles in the road, sprinting south. A quarter mile farther, he broke from the trees and found himself in the sprawling grass of the cemetery. He had enough light under the open sky to see rows of stones poking out of the earth. He bent low, moving from tomb to tomb, eyeing the woods. The telltale light came and went, flashing on and off, and Troy was directly in its path. Mark Bradley was heading straight for him.

He stopped behind a grave marked with black marble only fifteen yards from the brush where the forest ended. It was slick with rain, and the grass was sodden as he crouched near the tomb. He clutched his gun, smelling burnt powder on his hands.

He watched the trees, hunting for the shadow of a man arriving at the long carpet of headstones. His heart thumped so fast he thought he would die before he sprang up and pulled the trigger.

Troy took a deep breath. He lifted the gun.

Mark couldn't find Tresa. She'd been swallowed up by the night. After the boom of the gunshot rose above the rain, he knew that Troy was out there, firing blindly at anything that moved. The boy was a menace, and if Mark didn't do something to stop him, someone was going to get killed. He picked his way through the forest, breaking branches, not caring about the noise he made. If Troy was here, he wanted the boy to hear him and follow him. He wanted to draw him away from Tresa.

His ankle was swollen where he had twisted it. Each time his heel landed on the uneven ground, he grimaced. He headed south, but it was nearly impossible to keep a sense of direction inside the trees. He wished he had a flashlight to guide his path. Where the forest ended, he planned to cut across the cemetery ground to the main road. He had little hope of flagging down a car on a deserted night, but he could follow the road toward the center of town until he reached the house of one of the year-round residents, and then he could finally use a phone.

Call the police. Call Hilary.

To his left, he spied a beam of light in the maze of trees. It came and went, on and off, as someone maneuvered through the forest. It had to be Troy. They were on parallel paths, both heading toward the cemetery.

Mark pushed past the trees at the border of the graveyard, and a moment later, he was free of the dense, grasping grip of the woods. The sky opened up over his head. Rain swooped down in sheets, and he wiped his eyes with his sleeve so that he could see. Triangle-shaped pines and skeletal oaks dotted the land. He looked for the warning glow of the light he'd seen before, but the forest was dark. He eyed the trees and graves for a moving silhouette, but as far as he could tell, he was alone.

"Troy!" he shouted.

His voice fought with the storm.

"Troy, it's Mark Bradley. I know you're here. I want to talk to you."

He wandered deeper into the cemetery land. He looked down, but he couldn't see the names on the stones.

"Troy, listen to me. Tresa's here, too. Neither one of us wants her to get hurt."

Forty yards away, not far from the woods, Mark saw a headstone grow into a large shadow, as if a ghost were rising from the earth. The silhouette detached itself from the grave and walked toward him. Mark recognized the bulky outline of Troy Geier, and he saw that the boy had a gun outstretched at the end of his arm. Troy marched closer until he was no more than ten feet away. The gun was pointed at Mark's heart.

"I'm here," Troy said.

"So am I," Mark replied.

"Where's Tresa?"

"I don't know. She ran. I didn't want you shooting her accidentally."

"I wouldn't hurt her. This is between you and me."

"I understand."

Troy was silent. Mark could see his gun arm shivering.

"Listen, Troy," he went on, "Tresa knows you're here. If you kill me, you'll go to jail. You'll be throwing away your life."

"I don't care."

"I know you think you're doing this for Glory."

"That's right. I'm doing it for her and for Mrs. Fischer and for Peter Hoffman and for Tresa, too. You're going to pay the price. I'm not letting you get away with everything you did."

"What did I do?" Mark asked.

"You killed Glory."

"No."

"You killed Peter Hoffman."

"No."

"You think I believe you?" Troy demanded loudly. "You're a liar trying to save his skin."

"Troy, listen to me. I didn't do those things."

"Bullshit. Everybody knows you did."

Mark spread his arms wide. If Troy wanted to be a man, then Mark would treat him like one. "Okay, you better shoot me. If I really killed them, I'm a monster, and I have to be stopped."

Troy hesitated. "You don't think I can do it, do you?" he asked, his voice puffed up with nervous bravado.

"I know you can," Mark told him. "If you really believe that I could do those things—that I could strangle your girlfriend on a beach in Florida, that I could take a shotgun and blow off an old man's head—then you need to shoot me now."

Mark could barely see the boy's face in the darkness. He couldn't see if he was reaching him. He watched the gun, which was still aimed at his chest at point-blank range. One pulse, one twitch of Troy's finger, and the bullet would sear through Mark's body.

"I—I don't know," Troy murmured.

"This is what men do, Troy. We do what's right. We take responsibility. You need to look into my eyes and tell me you *know* that I'm guilty. After that, it's easy. After that, you won't have any doubts."

"Mrs. Fischer, she said—"

"I don't want to know what Delia thinks," Mark told him firmly. "This is between you and me. What do you think?"

"It had to be you. It had to be."

"If that's true, then pull the trigger."'

Troy's arm fluttered as if he couldn't hold it steady in the wind. He took a step toward Mark. "I'm going to do this."

"I know."

Mark couldn't take his eyes off the barrel of the gun. He wondered if he would see the flame or if he would hear the explosion, or if it would all happen in silence and darkness before his brain could process the shot. He would simply be standing here in one instant and lying on his back in the next instant, unable to draw a breath, feeling the warmth of blood on his chest.

Troy was crying. Mark could see the boy's chest heave.

"I have to do this," Troy said.

"I'm not going to stop you."

There were no easy choices. If Mark moved, he died. If he stayed where he was, he died. Troy tightened his grip on the slippery butt of the gun. As he hesitated, poised to fire, a bright beam of light speared through the night and caught the two of them in its glare like deer on the highway. Mark instinctively shielded his eyes with his palm. Troy spun in shock, taking the gun with him.

"Troy, put that gun down right now," a man barked.

Like a child, Troy complied. His arm sagged; the gun pointed at the ground.

Mark recognized the voice and saw the man's squared shoulders and squat legs in the light that bounced off the dirt.

Sheriff Reich marched toward them from the edge of the forest.

Tresa huddled in the trees above School-house Beach. She shivered, her arms wrapped around her knees. Her red hair was plastered to her face. She could barely feel her fingers and toes. She felt paralyzed by what was happening. By the gunshot. By everything that Mark had told her. By her fears of what was about to happen.

By the past.

She'd kept the secret for too many years. She'd willed it out of her mind as if it had never happened. She'd told herself that she was wrong, but now Glory was dead, and Mark and Hilary were both in danger, and it was all because she'd pretended she didn't know anything at all. She'd allowed everyone around her to believe a lie.

She should have known what had really happened in Florida. She should have suspected the truth.

Tresa stared at the water, which was a black sheet merging into white rocks. Part of her wanted to walk down into the lake's cold embrace and keep walking until the waves closed over her head and she was numb. Her guilt overwhelmed her, and she wanted to drown in it. Her eyes got lost in the dimpled surface of the bay. The raindrops hypnotized her. Only the silhouette of the man hiking on the beach awakened her from her trance. He came from the east near Mark's house. He hugged the woods, twenty feet from where Tresa was hiding. At first, she saw only that he was absurdly tall and lean, but then, as he drew near, she recognized Cab Bolton.

Gathering her courage, Tresa bolted from her hiding place. "Detective!"

He didn't look surprised to see her. "Tresa, are you okay?"

"Yes." She saw ribbons of blood on the detective's neck. "You're hurt."

"I'm fine," he said, but his face was ashen. "Where's Mark Bradley?"

"He's in the campground. We were hiding from Troy."

"What the hell is Troy doing here?"

Tresa hesitated, but she was done hiding and pretending. "He came here to kill Mark. I tried to stop it, but I've made a mess of everything. I don't know what to do."

Cab put an arm around her shoulder. "Come on, stay with me. We have to find them. Troy isn't our only problem right now."

He pulled her along the fringe of the beach, but Tresa stopped and held Cab's arm. "Wait."

"What is it?"

She tried to breathe. She tried to get the words out.

"I know who killed Glory," Tresa told him.

50

Troy, you stupid ass," Reich snapped. "What the hell do you think you're doing?"

Troy shrank like a wilted flower in front of the sheriff. The boy opened his hand, and the gun dropped to the wet ground of the cemetery. It might as well have been on fire. "I just—I mean, I thought I could make things right for Glory, you know?"

"You?"

"Yeah. I thought if no one else could stop him, then I could."

The sheriff marched so close to the boy that he was practically in his face. "Then do it already," Reich told him.

Troy cocked his head in confusion. "What?"

"Shoot the fucker."

Mark wasn't sure he'd heard the words come out of Reich's mouth. Reich wasn't joking. He was dead serious. When Troy stood frozen in disbelief, Reich squatted and retrieved the gun and stuffed it back into the boy's hand. Like a robot following orders, Troy turned back toward Mark, but he could barely hold the butt of the gun steady. Panic and fear made his entire body quake.

"Do it," Reich ordered him. "You pussy, get something right for once in your life. We'll ditch your boat, and you can go hide in my basement, and we can figure out what to do with you. We're going to have to get you seriously lost."

"Sheriff, what are you doing?" Mark asked.

"Shut up, Bradley. I'm waiting, Troy. Pull the trigger. Do it now."

"I don't—I don't think I can," Troy murmured, his voice broken.

Reich stepped in front of Troy impatiently and stripped the gun out of the boy's hands. "Like I thought, no balls. Jesus, what a waste."

"I'm sorry."

"Get the hell out of here," Reich told him.

"Where do I go?" Troy asked plaintively.

"My truck is on the highway. It's parked off the shoulder a hundred yards east of here. Climb inside and stay out of sight. Stay right there until I get back, got it? Do not move."

Troy did as he was told. He ran, tripping over the ground like a clown, through the cemetery land. He never looked back. Reich followed Troy's progress until he couldn't see the boy anymore, and then he reaimed Troy's gun at Bradley's chest. Unlike Troy's wobbly hand, Reich's grip was solid and assured, and his arm was rigid.

"Now it's just you and me, Bradley," Reich said.

"Sheriff, are you out of your mind?"

"Where's Tresa?" Reich asked.

"I don't know. She ran. Sheriff, if this is a joke, it's not funny."

"It's no joke."

Mark could see that it wasn't. Reich's intentions were deadly.

"Why are you doing this?" Mark asked.

"Because as long as you're alive, people are going to keep digging up ghosts. Once you're gone, you can take the blame for everything. If you'd died in that car accident like you were supposed to, the case would already be closed."

"I can't believe you'd kill an innocent man," Mark told him.

"I've killed plenty of men. They were innocent. You're not. Don't bother pleading for your life. I'm fresh out of mercy."

"I didn't kill Glory."

"Now you're just making me mad," Reich growled.

"I don't care. I didn't do it."

"Pete knew you were a liar."

"I didn't kill Peter Hoffman, either."

Reich nodded grimly. "That's the first true thing you said, Bradley, but it doesn't matter. I killed Pete. You gave me no choice."

Mark felt the breath leave his chest. He knew with a terrible clarity that there was really no hope now. No chance of this ending well, of him walking away alive and free. Reich was no immature kid like Troy who was in over his head. When the sheriff ran out of bile, the gun in his hand would spit a bullet into Mark's heart.

"He was your best friend," Mark said.

"That's right, I killed my best friend because of you."

"Because of me?"

"Because you're a liar," Reich told him. "Because you had to hide behind a ghost in order to cover up your own crime. Pete was willing to give up everything to make sure you paid the price. I couldn't let him do that, but I'll make sure you pay. That's what Pete would want. That's why I can live with what I've done."

Mark shook his head and slowly held up his hands. "Sheriff, I swear I don't know what the hell you're talking about."

"He's talking about Harris Bone," Cab Bolton said.

Reich whipped his light toward the voice that rose from the cemetery graves, but he didn't take his eyes off Mark or lower the gun even an inch. In the beam, Mark saw Cab Bolton ten feet away, next to the gray tower of a bell-shaped tombstone. Tresa huddled next to him, her face red with anger and tears.

"Bolton," Reich hissed.

"What now, Sheriff?" Cab demanded. "Are you going to kill me, too? First Hoffman, then Bradley, then me?"

Reich's eyes darted furiously between Mark and Cab. He was a man looking for a way out and not finding one.

"The girl, too?" Cab went on. "Could you shoot the girl? How many more people are you willing to kill to keep the secret?"

"Get the hell out of here," Reich ordered him. "Take Tresa with you. You have no idea what this is about."

"Harris Bone," Cab repeated. "That's what this is about. Peter Hoffman couldn't handle the guilt anymore, could he? When he thought Bradley was hiding behind Harris to get away with murder, he decided to tell the truth. Hoffman wasn't about to let Delia Fischer get robbed of justice. He wasn't going to let some defense attorney use Harris to get an acquittal. He knew Glory didn't come face-to-face with Harris Bone in Florida. That was a lie. That's what he wanted to tell me."

"Goddamn you, Bolton," Reich said. "You couldn't let it go, could you? What the hell did you do?"

"I found him, Sheriff," Cab replied. "I found him in that hole where the two of you left him to rot. Harris Bone never escaped. He never ran. You and Peter Hoffman killed him."

In the miles since they left the county courthouse in Sturgeon Bay, Harris Bone hadn't said a word. He sat silently in the back of the squad car, his balding head hung forward, his hands and ankles cuffed. His jail clothes were baggy on his frame. Harris had never been a large man, but he'd shrunk inside his skin in the months since the fire, until he was almost a skeleton.

Reich watched his headlights tunneling through the night. He was south of Kewaunee in the midst of flat, dormant farmlands. It was January, during one of the frigid winter stretches, with temperatures falling into the teens below zero when the sun went down. The season had been mostly snowless, leaving the ground barren, swept clean by the bitter wind.

He glanced in the mirror with hard eyes.

"You should look outside, Harris. You won't be seeing open country again for the rest of your life. Just eighty square feet of concrete for twenty-three hours a day."

Harris didn't acknowledge him.

"I'd watch my back in there if I were you. Big-ass gang killers don't like a man who burns up his wife and family."

Harris finally looked up with sunken eyes. "Shut the hell up, Felix."

"Oh, don't start mouthing off. That's a bad lesson. You shoot off your mouth in there, and bad things are likely to happen."

"Thanks for the advice."

Reich heard the sarcasm, and he didn't care. "A lot of people think you're getting off easy, sitting on the taxpayer's dime for the next forty years. That doesn't feel like justice."

"Is that right? What do you think, Felix?"

"If it were up to me, we'd gather volunteers and stone you."

"Too bad it's not up to you."

Reich nodded and studied the empty highway. "Yeah. Too bad."

Behind him, Harris closed his eyes, and his head fell back against the seat.

"I always felt sorry for you, Harris," Reich called to him. "Nettie was a bitch. Not that I'd ever say so to Pete. But there are some lines a man doesn't cross, no matter how much he hates his life. There are some things that when you do them, you stop being human."

Harris leaned forward until his weary face was pressed against the steel mesh. "What does that make you, Felix? How many babies did you kill during the war?"

Reich gripped the wheel fiercely. His lip curled into a snarl. "Are you suggesting I'm the same as you? Is that really what you want to say to me?"

"I'm saying you can spare me the morality shit. I don't need it."

Harris sank back and pretended to sleep. Reich studied the man's face and saw tears slipping down his cheeks. It didn't matter. He felt nothing for him. It was just as he'd said: There were lines a man didn't cross. There were also things a man had to do when justice demanded it.

He was close to the rendezvous. Through the headlights, he spied the intersection at the county road, and he checked the odometer to count off one point seven miles. There was nothing but frozen land on either side of the vehicle. He and Pete had scouted the terrain weeks earlier as they made their plans.

Where to meet. Where to stage the escape.

Reich spotted the driveway leading to the farmhouse, miles from anything else around it. He slowed sharply and turned. In the backseat, Harris felt the change in direction and opened his eyes.

"What's going on?"

Reich said nothing. He drove into the rutted cornfield bordering the house and steered around the rear of the detached garage, where he parked the squad car with its right-hand door butted against the wall. From the highway, the car was invisible. It would be days before anyone found it.

"What the hell are you doing, Felix?"

Reich heard it in Harris's voice. The first tremors of fear. The first horrified realization of what was about to happen to him.

Justice.

Reich got out of the car. The wind was ferocious, and the cold bit through his coat like a man-eater. He opened the rear door and dragged Harris Bone into the night by the cuff of his shirt. Harris, who wore nothing except his prison scrubs, howled as the frozen air knifed his skin. The bound man hunched his limbs together. Reich yanked a billy club from his belt and swung it across the man's skull. Harris collapsed to his knees. Reich laid a boot on the man's back and crushed him forward onto the rock-hard dirt, where he twitched from the pain and cold. Harris tried to crawl, but Reich held him down.

"Hello, Felix," Peter Hoffman said. He was waiting for them beside the garage.

"No mercy tonight," Reich replied.

"None."

The house and land belonged to a retired couple who were away in the sunshine of Mesa and wouldn't be back in Wisconsin until after Easter. Reich had checked the house and garage three weeks earlier and found the couple's Accord parked inside for the season. Keys on a peg board by the door. He loved midwesterners.

"Let's get it over with," Pete said.

Reich marched to the side door of the garage. He didn't notice the cold, other than the prickly bite of ice crystals in his nose when he breathed. He cocked his leg and smashed the door inward with a swing of his boot. Just like Harris Bone would do. Inside, he pushed through spiderwebs and heard the scurry of rats in the rafters. He returned to find Harris on the ground, curled into a ball, and he lifted him bodily with both hands and threw him toward the garage door. Harris tripped in the shackles and fell with a whimper. Pete stepped over him into the garage, started the engine of the Accord, and popped the trunk. Reich grabbed Harris and pulled him, heels dragging, to the rear of the car, where he dumped him in.

He slammed the trunk shut, locking Harris inside.

"Come on," Reich said. He dug in his pocket for the keys to his squad car and threw them on the ground. He handed the keys to the cuffs and shackles to Pete, who stood by the driver's door with his hands in his pockets. "You having second thoughts?" he asked.

"You know me better than that, Felix."

Reich stared into his friend's face for a long time in the shadows. "Okay, then."

Pete drove. They headed north on the deserted roads, back toward Door County. Ten miles from the farmhouse, they passed a bar with a handful of pickups parked outside the door. Pete continued past the bar for a quarter mile until no one who ventured into the winter air would see them, and then he pulled onto the shoulder. Both men got out.

The wind poured over their bodies with an unforgiving fury. Pete dug his chin into his neck and pulled down his wool hat. Reich simply walked down the gully from the road into the dirt of the field. He wasn't even wearing a hat to cover the steel wool of his hair. His skin was already numb and white, but he didn't care.

Pete followed. "You sure about this, Felix?"

"Just do it." Reich squatted and found a fist-sized clump of earth that had frozen into jagged edges. "Here."

"I wish there was some other way," Pete said.

"Hit me. Hard. You only get one try."

Pete reared back with the rock and swung his gloved hand into his friend's forehead. The frozen spikes cut through Reich's skin, erupting in blood. Reich stumbled back at the force of the blow and nearly fell. He staggered. Pete dropped the rock and reached for his friend, but Reich shrugged him away.

"Get the hell out of here."

"Can you make it to the bar?"

Reich touched his hand to his cheek, where the warm blood was already freezing. He felt his words slurring as he tried to talk. He tasted copper on his lips. "Just go. I'll join you as soon as I can, and we'll finish this. It's for Nettie and the boys, remember?"

Reich stayed where he was, bleeding in the field, until Pete climbed the shoulder and drove away. The car disappeared, its taillights winking out, leaving Reich alone. He was losing blood fast. He took two clumsy steps toward the bar, which looked impossibly far. Briefly, he wondered if it would be better to lie down among the broken cornstalks and give himself up to the winter. He had a vision of his future, and it wasn't pretty.

Maybe Harris was right. Reich had been the one to cross the line tonight, and there was no going back.

Even so, he quashed his doubts and marched for rescue like a wounded soldier.

"I saw what was left of him, Sheriff," Cab said. "The two of you didn't just kill him. You tortured him."

"Torture is burning to death," Reich replied. "I've seen it happen to people I considered my enemies, and I didn't even wish it on them."

"I saw the broken bones. The bullet holes."

Reich shrugged. "I don't regret what I did. Sometimes you have to take justice into your own hands."

"Peter Hoffman regretted it, though, didn't he?"

"Pete got soft," Reich said. "He got old. The booze took over."

"Or maybe he finally realized the two of you had become the monsters you were trying to destroy."

"We did what we had to do," Reich said.

"If you're so sure about that, why kill Hoffman to cover it up? Why not tell the world?"

"People like you don't understand," he snapped. "They don't appreciate the tough decisions that others make for them."

Tresa pulled away from Cab and marched toward Reich through the wet ground. She swept the red hair from her face. "You son of a bitch," she hissed.

"Tresa, stay out of this," Reich told her.

"All this time I thought Harris was alive. That made it okay. Now I find out you killed him. You bastard!"

"This doesn't concern you."

"Who else knew?" she demanded. "Did my mother know?"

"No one knew. Look, Tresa, you were a kid. Your father was dead, and Harris was there for you. That doesn't change what he did."

Tresa pushed in close enough to spit in Reich's face. "You're always right, aren't you? You're right about everything. You didn't believe me about Mark, either. You wouldn't listen when I told you that nothing happened between us. Instead, you had to go about ruining his life."

Reich wiped his face with his free hand. "I'm sorry you had to find out about Harris, but if there's one good thing to come out of this, at least now you know what kind of a man Mark Bradley really is." He jabbed a finger at Mark across the dark space between the graves. "He wanted you to think Harris Bone killed your sister, didn't he? Now you know that's a lie. He was the one out on the beach with her. He was the one who killed Glory."

Tresa shook her head. "You stupid macho jerk. All of you. You. Troy. Peter Hoffman. Everybody."

She walked toward Mark. Reich shouted to stop her, and Mark put his hands up to warn her away, but Tresa put herself squarely between Mark and the sheriff, in the path of his gun, and spread her arms wide. "If you want to kill him, now you'll need to kill me, too."

Reich's face pulsed with fury and frustration. "He's as evil as Harris was, Tresa. Don't be fooled."

"You're the evil one," Tresa said. "You're the one who murdered an innocent man."

"What the hell are you talking about?" Reich growled.

"Don't you get it?" Tresa screamed at him. "Harris Bone didn't kill his family. It wasn't him. He didn't start the fire."

51

Gary Jensen heard Katie in the hallway.

His shoulders swiveled, and his eyes flicked away. That was Hilary's chance. She charged from her knees and leaped across the space between them, driving Jensen backward into the wall. Her knee spiked into Jensen's groin, and he doubled over. She dove for his gun hand, but he swung the butt of the gun and caught her on the bottom of her chin. The impact of metal on bone ricocheted in her brain. She staggered backward, tripping on the bed and falling as her left leg gave way beneath her.

Jensen, still bent over, aimed the barrel at her chest. Hilary was dizzy, but she saw his finger slide over the trigger. Just as he fired, she heard a shout and saw a blur of motion. Amy threw herself into Jensen's body, and as they collided, the gun went off with a deafening blast. The bullet tore into the wall over the bed, blasting through Sheetrock and kicking up a cloud of white dust. Amy and Jensen toppled onto the floor. They rolled over each other into the doorway, and Amy clutched Jensen's gun arm with both hands, holding it down. Jensen pummeled the girl's kidneys with his other fist, and Amy, who was still weak, lost her grip. Hilary climbed to her feet as Jensen broke free. She dodged sideways just as a second bullet narrowly roared past her ear, so close she felt a searing heat on her hair.

Jensen tried to get up, but Amy threw her dancer's leg backward, landing her heel on his wrist. His fingers went numb. The gun spilled from his hand and twirled as it skidded down the hallway. It landed in front of Katie, who picked it up. The coach threw an arm around Amy's neck and yanked the girl into his chest, squeezing off her air.

"Stop!" Katie screamed.

She stood over them, the gun in her hand. Jensen loosened his grip. Coughing, Amy crawled away and pushed herself to her feet. Jensen stood up, too, and fell heavily against the bedroom wall. He looked bruised and beaten.

Amy limped for Katie and threw her arms around her neck. She hugged her roommate with a smile of relief and then turned back toward Hilary.

"The two of you saved—" Amy began, but she never finished.

Katie lifted the gun and brought the butt down solidly onto the back of Amy's skull. Amy took two shaken steps in confused disbelief, crumbled to her knees, and pitched forward onto her face, unconscious.

"Katie!" Hilary screamed.

The girl quickly aimed the gun at her. "Don't move. Stay right there."

Katie slid an arm around Gary Jensen's waist as he stretched his stiff muscles and twisted his neck. She pressed a quick, passionate kiss on his lips. "You okay?"

"I'm fine."

"Katie, you're being a fool," Hilary warned her. "Don't trust this man. I don't know what he's told you, but he's dangerous."

The girl gave her a peaceful smile. "You've got Gary all wrong."

"He's using you."

"No, he's protecting me," she said.

"Protecting you from what?"

Katie stared at Amy on the floor, and the smile washed away from her face. "From who I was."

Jensen checked his watch and tugged Katie's arm. "The police will be here soon," he said. "We should go."

"There's something we need to do first," she told him.

Jensen stiffened with unease, and Hilary tried to read his face. She realized for the first time that she had it wrong. Jensen wasn't the one in control. He was in thrall to this girl. It was Katie whose eyes betrayed a terrible detachment. It was Katie who looked like fragile china, riven with cracks, ready to break apart.

"Katie, we don't have to do this," Jensen said. "Not now."

"We don't have a choice."

"Yes, we do. Forget about them. We can run."

The girl's lips tightened into an angry line. "I've been running my whole life. I'm done with it."

"Give me the gun. I can protect us."

"No, you can't." Katie kissed Jensen again and pushed him toward the bedroom door. "Don't lose your nerve now. We've come too far. Go downstairs and grab gasoline, liquor bottles, whatever you can carry."

"Katie, *stop.*"

"You know what we've been through. It's just one last thing. Then it's over. Then we're free."

Hilary saw something in Jensen's eyes. Self-awareness. Self-hatred. He couldn't say no to this girl. A man who had destroyed his first marriage seducing teenagers had been seduced and manipulated himself.

"Hurry," Katie told him, her voice insistent.

Jensen vanished toward the stairs without further protest. Amy remained motionless on the floor. Hilary was alone with Katie. The girl cradled the gun loosely in one hand and chewed a fingernail on the other. Her glasses slipped down her nose, and she stared at Hilary through the rain-dotted lenses.

"What's this all about?" Hilary asked.

Katie shrugged. "Glory saw me in Florida."

"Glory saw *you*?"

Her head bobbed. "She started to remember everything. I knew she wouldn't let it go. She'd tell someone. Gary didn't want me to do it, but I couldn't take the risk. I had to stop her."

"You killed Glory? Katie, why?"

The girl got a faraway look in her eyes. "Everyone used to call me Jen back then, but my father always called me Katie. That was my grandmother's name. I was Jennifer Katherine. That's the only part of me I have left from those days."

Hilary's throat went dry with despair. "You're Jen Bone. Harris's daughter."

"I was. I stopped being that girl that night in Door County. I thought I would never have to be her again. Really. It was over and done. Then Glory saw me, and it all came back to her. She remembered being in the garage that night. She saw me light the fire."

52

I never wanted to believe it," Tresa said. "I convinced myself I was wrong, you know? Everybody said Harris did it. He confessed. The thing is, I knew he would have done anything for Jen. He must have known she did it, but he took the blame. To protect her."

Cab drew closer to the three of them, conscious of the gun in Reich's hand. He didn't know how far Reich would go to save himself. When he studied the sheriff's heavily shadowed face, he saw someone who was staring into the maw of a black hole, the way Cab himself had done in the storm cellar. He wondered whose face Reich saw looking up from the darkness. Harris Bone, screaming in agony for his life. Or Peter Hoffman, staring into the eyes of his friend as Reich shot him to death.

"Sheriff, put the gun down," Cab said.

Reich ignored him. "I don't believe this shit. Harris Bone was *there.* He admitted it. This is another of your fantasies, Tresa."

"Jen was with me that night," Tresa went on. "We were up late writing our stories together. She was really keyed up. I'd never seen her so out of control. When I woke up in the middle of the night, I saw that she was gone. I figured she couldn't sleep, you know? Then I heard her come in. She was naked. She'd taken a shower, and her hair was wet, but I could still smell it."

"Smell what?" Reich asked.

"Smoke."

Reich's arm slowly sank, as if under a great weight. The gun slipped downward. He ran a hand over his bottlebrush hair, and his eyes were wide. "Jesus," he whispered.

"I didn't tell anyone. I mean, by morning, I wondered if I'd dreamed it. Everyone was saying Mr. Bone was the one. I wanted to be wrong, you know? I did just what Mr. Bone did. I protected Jen. Even after what Glory told me."

"Glory?" Bradley asked her. "What about Glory?"

Tresa nestled closer to him. "We were in the hospital. Glory and me. She told me what she saw. It was Jen, through the window of the garage, lighting a cigarette. That was the only thing she remembered. I knew she'd seen her. She'd seen Jen starting the fire." The girl bowed her head and stared at her feet. "I convinced Glory she'd imagined the whole thing. We never talked about it again. Not ever. Glory never talked about the fire or told anyone what she saw. It was like it had never happened, you know?"

"What about Florida?" Cab asked.

"Jen must have been there," Tresa said. "I never thought that was possible. I mean, she's not a dancer, you know? I never dreamed she would do something like that. I still don't know why."

She saw someone she knew, Cab thought.

Jen Bone. Through the looking-glass of

the window at the hotel. The memories must have stormed back, carrying Glory away like a tsunami. He felt sorry for the girl, coming face-to-face with everything she'd spent six years trying to escape. Remembering what had really happened at the Bone house.

"When Mark said Hilary was in Green Bay, I knew," Tresa murmured, "I just knew. Jen goes to Green Bay. That man Gary Jensen, she wrote an article about him for the school paper last year. Peter Hoffman sent it to me. He thought I'd want to see it because it was about dancing. He told me Jen's roommate was a dancer just like me. It must be this girl Amy. The one you said disappeared."

Bradley picked up Tresa under her shoulders and lifted the girl away from him, protecting her with his body. He was inches from Reich. "Are you going to shoot me, Sheriff? If so, you better do it now, because if not, I'm leaving. I have to get the police to find my wife."

Reich stared blankly at him and didn't move or raise the gun. He was in shock. Cab waved at Bradley, telling him to go, and the man took off limping through the cemetery. Running for a phone. Cab beckoned to Tresa. He took her hand, and he put out his other hand toward Felix Reich.

"Bradley's right," Cab said. "We need to call the Green Bay police right now. We don't have much time. Let's go, Sheriff."

Reich said nothing at all. Cab gestured with his hand again.

"Sheriff? Come on, it's over. You're too honorable a man for more violence. It's time to surrender."

"Take the girl and go," Reich murmured.

"What?"

Reich looked up, and his face was as dark and dreadful as a corpse. Their eyes met. Cab saw that the sheriff wasn't staring down into the hole anymore. He was inside it, consumed by the mold, dampness, worms, and stench of the burial ground. Reich withdrew Cab's own gun from his pocket, the one he had stolen when he assaulted Cab at Bradley's house, and threw it at his feet.

"Take Tresa with you, Detective," he repeated.

Cab wrestled with his conscience. Stay or go. "Sheriff?" he murmured, his voice a question and a warning at the same time.

"The living are more important than the dead," Reich told him.

Cab retrieved his gun. As he did, Reich deposited his flashlight on the flat top of the headstone beside him. He turned his back on Cab and Tresa without another word and marched away, heading back toward the thick curtain of the forest. He still had Troy's gun in his hand. The night swallowed him in seconds, and he disappeared, and so did the wet sucking noise of his boots in the grass. Cab tugged at Tresa's hand.

"We have to hurry," he said, pulling her toward the road.

"Are you just going to let him go?" Tresa asked. "He'll escape."

"Nobody escapes," Cab said.

Reich was right. The living mattered now. Hilary Bradley. Cab hoped they were in time. He grabbed the flashlight and ran, fighting down the waves of pain in his skull, and Tresa ran beside him, her young body quick and graceful. She guided him more than he guided her, urging him to go faster when he slowed down. They fought through the pools of standing water toward the bay. From there, when they could see the beach ahead of them, they followed in Mark

Bradley's path on the dirt road toward his house.

That was when Cab heard the single gunshot behind them.

He'd been waiting for it. Expecting it. The noise was loud and sharp as it pierced the forest, growing softer with each successive echo. Tresa flinched and looked in the direction of the shot, but he dragged her away. The waves of sound took several seconds to fade completely away, which was long after the bullet had traveled through Felix Reich's brain and long after the sheriff had fallen where he stood, an old soldier dead in the jungle.

53

I needed a cigarette," Katie explained. "I was on the patio with the Green Bay team while Gary gave one of his rah-rah speeches, and I wandered over by the hotel window and flicked my lighter. I heard a girl scream inside. Crazy. I knew Tresa was at the hotel, and I'd been avoiding her, but I never thought Glory would be there, too. It must have triggered something when she saw me. The brain's a funny thing."

Hilary watched this pretty young girl talk clinically about her crimes, as if they had sprung from someone else's hand.

"I never wanted this to happen," she

went on. "I'm Katie Monroe now. I've spent six years trying to forget that I was Jen Bone or that I ever lived in that house."

"You murdered your mother and your brothers," Hilary said. "You burned them all to death."

Katie's eyes flashed. "Did you live there? Do you know what it was like? Do you have any idea of the things they did to me? I wanted to erase them and that house and everything in it. I wanted it to be like none of it had ever existed. I didn't feel guilty. I still don't."

"But you let your father take the blame."

Katie's face went cloudy. That was the first real emotion Hilary had seen in her. "Dad got home while I was watching the place burn. He acted like he was *sorry.* Can you believe it? I was doing both of us a favor. With them out of the way, it was finally going to be just the two of us, but Dad didn't understand. He sent me back to Tresa's house, and he stayed there to wait for the sheriff."

"Has he contacted you?"

Katie shook her head. "He's dead. If he wasn't dead, he would have gotten in touch with me. My aunt was always telling me I didn't have to be scared of my father coming back. Like she knew something. Like it was a secret I should keep."

Hilary wanted the girl to keep talking. She wanted time for the police to find them. "So is Gary Jensen supposed to take your father's place?"

"What does that mean?" Katie retorted. "Do you think I was sleeping with my father? You think he was abusing me? Is that what you think?"

"I have no idea."

"You're the one with the husband who screws teenaged girls."

"That's a lie."

"Oh, you think so? You're like every wife, loyal and stupid. Gary's wife was the same way, until she found pictures of me on his phone. He convinced her he'd dumped me, but he dumped her instead. Off a cliff."

"Mark's not Gary."

"Yeah? I followed Glory out to the beach that night, but your husband got in the way. They put on a hell of a show."

"Don't play games with me," Hilary snapped.

"Glory took off her top, and then she got

on her knees. Do I need to spell it out for you?"

"Shut up."

Katie shrugged. "You know I'm telling the truth."

Hilary saw Gary Jensen reappear behind Katie. He clutched bottles of rum and vodka in one hand and a plastic gallon jug of gasoline in the other. His jaw was tight with dismay. He hovered in the doorway, unwilling to enter the bedroom. Katie gestured at him, and her face betrayed a growing agitation and impatience. She was losing control.

"Pour the gasoline around the room," Katie told him. "Quickly."

Gary didn't move. "We don't need to do this."

Katie reached out and caressed his cheek. "There's no going back now. It's too late. If you'd gotten rid of Amy fast like I told you, then we would have been fine—but you let the cat out of the bag, lover. We could have contained the damage if it was just Amy, but not anymore. By the time the police sift through the ashes, we'll be in Canada."

Jensen opened his mouth but said nothing. He crouched down and laid the bottles at his feet. He unscrewed the cap on the plastic jug and hesitated over the prone body of the girl on the floor.

"Pour it over Amy," she instructed him. *"Do it."*

With a long glance at Katie, Jensen turned the jug upside down, letting the gasoline spill out in spurts, covering Amy. Her hair. Her shirt. Her arms. Her jeans. Her feet. As the strong fumes gathered in her nose, Amy began to stir. Hilary heard her moan, but the girl's eyes were still closed.

"Now the rest," Katie told him. "Do the whole room. The curtains. The carpet. And don't forget Hilary here."

Jensen's eyes awakened with a kind of shock. He started pouring, but then the jug dropped at his feet. Gasoline spilled out in a growing puddle. "Jesus, how did this happen to us?"

"Hurry. We're running out of time."

"My wife. That girl in Florida. Now we have to kill two more people?"

Katie picked up a bottle of Stoli and shoved it into his hand. "This is the only way."

Jensen slowly twisted the cap. When the bottle was open, he dropped the cap to the floor and watched it bounce and roll. He took a stuttering step toward Hilary, and then he stopped and shook his head.

"No."

Katie clenched her fist. "Gary, please."

"I won't do this."

"I told you, this is the last time. Once it's done, we're free."

"You said that about my wife. You said that about Glory."

"I know. I never meant for any of this to happen."

"Let's get out of here," he said. "You and me. Right now."

Katie kissed his cheek and exhaled in a slow, sorrowful sigh. "Okay. You win. Sure."

"Really?"

"Whatever you want, Gary. You know I love you."

Katie gently pried the vodka bottle from his hands. She upended it to her lips and took a burning swallow. When she was done, she wiped her mouth, pointed the gun at Gary Jensen, and fired into the center of his forehead.

Hilary screamed. The explosion sounded

like a bomb, rattling her head. Blood and brain matter blew out the back of Jensen's skull in a chunky spray and painted the wall. Jensen's body dropped straight down like an imploding building with its columns knocked out. He crumpled into a dead pile. The smell of charred metal was like sulfur in Hilary's nose.

Katie bit her lip unhappily, staring down at his body. She blinked rapidly, as if even she were surprised at what she'd done. As if it were an impulse she couldn't resist, like scratching an itch. The echo of the shot died, and in the terrible silence, they all heard a rhythmic wailing, rising above the wind. In the distance, sirens grew louder and closer.

Multiple sirens, overlapping, from police vehicles racing toward them.

"It's over, Katie," Hilary said softly.

Katie listened to the shrill sirens, her face stricken with indecision.

"It's over," Hilary repeated. "It's too late."

Hilary pressed her hands into the bed and tried to stand up without alarming the girl. Katie swung the gun, which was still smoking, and pointed it at Hilary's face.

"I swore to my mom I was going to burn

the house down," Katie said. "She laughed. She didn't believe me."

"Don't do this."

Katie ignored her. Her mind was made up. She swung the vodka bottle into the corner of the door frame, and it shattered across the floor in razor-sharp fragments. She jerked the open, jagged body of the bottle toward Hilary, letting the alcohol splash across Hilary's face and soak through her blouse to her chest.

Katie shoved a hand in her pocket and pulled out a cigarette lighter.

"Don't worry," the girl told her. "I've done this before."

54

On the floor, Amy Leigh's hand shot out.

Before Katie could react, Amy locked her fingers around her roommate's ankle and yanked Katie's leg into the air. Katie flew, crashing backward onto broken glass. Sharp fragments stabbed through her clothes and impaled themselves like arrowheads in her skin. The gun broke loose from her hand.

Amy lunged for Katie, leaping past Gary Jensen's corpse and landing on the girl's chest. She drove the air out of Katie's lungs, and Katie rasped for breath, pinned underneath her. Katie's fingers twitched on the cigarette lighter. She cocked her elbow and pressed the lighter against Amy's gasoline-soaked clothes. Hilary shouted a warning, but before Amy could react, Katie's thumb flicked the wheel, spinning it, striking the metal against the flint.

Amy pushed Katie down with a shout. Her eyes locked on the purple plastic cylinder in Katie's hand. She waited for a cloud of flame to billow over her body, but Katie spun frantically in a series of empty clicks without triggering a spark. The mechanism was wet and useless.

Katie's fingers unclenched, and she dropped the lighter, but she reached out in the same instant and scooped the butt of the gun back into her hand. Amy grabbed the girl's arm and hung on. They rolled, scraping across glass, mingling gasoline, alcohol, and blood. Hilary saw the gun caught between the two girls and threw herself hard toward the wall as the flying barrel pointed toward her stomach. The gun didn't go off. Instead, as Katie squirmed away and aimed from her knees, Amy caught Katie's hand and grabbed her index finger before the girl could slide it onto the trigger. She bent back hard, snapping the bone. Katie screamed. The gun fell like a stone, and as the two girls struggled, Amy kicked it, and the gun slid across the floor and bumped into the far wall.

Hilary rolled across the bed and collected the gun. She pointed it at the ceiling and shouted at the two girls, who were entwined on the floor.

"Stop! Stop it now!"

Amy scrambled to her feet, pulling Katie with her. She threw Katie against the wall, and Katie landed with a groan, holding up her hands, crying with pain. Amy backed away toward Hilary, who trained the barrel on Katie as the girl bent over with her hands on her knees and tried to catch her breath.

Outside, the sirens soared in volume, seemingly from every direction. Police cars sped toward them down all of the side streets, converging on the house.

"That's it, Katie," Hilary told her. "No more."

Amy slid an arm around Hilary's waist and leaned into her, weak and exhausted. She had enough strength to stare at her friend and the wreckage around her. The broken bottle. The bloodstained glass. The body of Gary Jensen, on his back, eyes open, a burnt red hole in his forehead.

"How could you do this?" Amy whispered.

The air wheezed in and out of Katie's lungs. The girl squatted and retrieved an unbroken, unopened bottle of 151, which was tipped on the floor at her feet. Hilary gestured at her with the gun.

"Stop."

Katie picked up the bottle and shrugged. "Go ahead, fire. One little spark will turn all of us into a fish boil."

"Put the bottle down," Hilary repeated.

Katie rested her head against the wall with her eyes closed. Her face was streaked with blood. Her clothes were torn. She twisted the cap off the bottle, breaking the paper seal, and drank, not caring as overproof rum dripped out the sides of her mouth. As she finished, she hung on to the full bottle by its neck, letting it dangle at her side.

"I heard them screaming," Katie said. "As the fire got them. You never forget."

"Turn around, Katie. Start walking. We're leaving the house."

"Dad said I should have killed him, too,"

Katie said. "I didn't understand back then. Now I do."

Katie splashed rum at her feet and down her jeans and across her bare, bloody arms. She drizzled it over her head. She soaked the carpet, which was already sodden with gasoline. Fumes rose in invisible waves around her, billowing into the shut-up room. The smell alone was enough to make Hilary's head swim.

The girl lopped off the neck of the bottle with a quick swing. She dug in her pocket and came out with another cigarette lighter in her hand. "I always have a backup."

"Katie, don't do this," Amy told her.

Katie's face was blank, like a bone white, empty page. She didn't even seem to be in the same room with them; she was in a different house, with her dead family. She extended her arm, her thumb poised over the sparkwheel. Hilary aimed the gun at her, but she couldn't risk pulling the trigger. Katie cocked her thumb without looking at them or seeing them. With a sad smile, she spun the wheel and lit the flow of butane with a single, deadly flick.

A tiny flame popped from the top of the lighter. There was an instant in which the entire room was nothing but that insignificant fire, no greater than the light of a candle. Then the flame found the gathering fumes, and the first fireball erupted, wispy and gaseous, burning itself out in an orange burst. Hilary and Amy leaped back. Katie held the lighter upright, still lit, and she tilted the broken neck of the rum bottle downward. The liquid became a silver waterfall splashing toward the flame.

"Get down!" Hilary screamed.

She threw herself and Amy toward the floor just as the alcohol struck the lighter. The flame defied gravity and shot upward in a burst of lightning into the bottle and turned it into a bomb. The weak glass blew outward in a lethal explosion of needle-sharp shards. Katie's face and torso were instantly shredded. The fire latched onto the gasoline on her clothes and skin and turned her into a column of flames. She spun like a dancer, her flesh charring, her body consumed. She screamed like a dying animal, but only until the fire sped down her throat and began eating her from inside out, choking off her voice as her lungs melted.

Hilary dragged Amy toward the windows

on the opposite side of the room. She tore off the curtain rod, and the heavy fabric rippled to the ground. Outside, through the glass, the world glowed with the revolving red lights of police cars driving onto the lawn around them. Inside, the doorway leading out of the bedroom was engulfed in fire and impassible, as Katie's dying body became a pyre. Sparks arced toward the bed, smoldering on the linens.

Hilary tried to pry open the lock on the window, but it was painted shut and wouldn't move. She looked around the room and saw an antique brass lamp on the nightstand closest to her. She grabbed it with both arms, dragging the cord out of the socket and winding up as if she were holding a baseball bat.

"Duck!" she shouted at Amy.

The girl dropped to the floor. Hilary threw the lamp into the window, and it burst with a singing clatter. The lamp disappeared down to the ground below them, leaving jagged knives of glass clinging to the wooden frame. Air rushed in, feeding the fire, which gnawed closer to them as it spread across the bed and climbed the walls. Searing heat burned their faces. Sparks exploded like fireworks to the ceiling and fell inches away at their feet.

Hilary bunched the fallen curtains around her hands and knocked the remaining fragments from the window. She looked out through the open square, seeing lights and vehicles drawing closer, feeling the cold wind and the wet rain tease the heat of the fire, and seeing the waving branches of the nearest maple beckoning to her like a rescuer. The ground was a long distance below them.

She thrust Amy toward the window. "Jump! Jump for the tree!"

"What about you?" Amy shouted as she squeezed her body into the frame.

"Jump!"

Amy leaped forward, hands outstretched, and disappeared into the arms of the air. Hilary glanced over her shoulder in time to see the entire room burst like a red ball and surge toward her. She forced her torso through the window opening and wedged her foot on the bottom of the frame. She felt a scorching heat erupt on her back, and she knew she was on fire. She didn't look down.

Hilary jumped.

She felt the tree branches stabbing her. Her fingers grasped like claws, and she found one thick branch with her hand, only to have it peeled away by gravity as she fell. She clung to another for a split second before her weight dislodged it, and it broke with a crack, sending her downward. Another branch stopped her with a hammering blow to her back, and she ricocheted forward, falling again, her clothes tearing, her skin peppered with scrapes and punctures.

She landed hard on her side and rolled through the mud, and when she stopped, she found herself on her back, staring up at the web of branches that had saved her. Fire spat through the broken window overhead like the tongue of a devil. Rain gently poured through the light and cooled her and washed away the blood, and the mud and puddles stamped out the flames that had licked at her back. She tried to move, to pull herself away to a safe distance, but her pummeled muscles refused to budge. All she could do for now was lie on the ground and wait.

She felt a hand on her cheek. When

she turned her head, she saw Amy hovering over her, propped on one elbow. The girl's face was dirty, but her eyes were bright and glassy with tears that streaked down her skin along with the rain.

"You okay?" Amy asked.

Hilary gave a weak smile. "Yeah. You?"

"I'm all right."

Amy sank against Hilary's shoulder and put an arm protectively around her and held on tight. The girl closed her eyes. Hilary did, too. Their chests rose and fell in unison as they breathed. Hilary heard the splash of boots as men drew closer and the comforting shouts of their voices. They talked to her like the angels in Mark's paintings, but she couldn't answer, even as she felt strong arms lifting her and carrying her. All she could do was give herself up to sleep.

55

As the ferry drew closer to the mainland, Cab felt the turbulent waters of the Death's Door passage settle into bobbing swells. The stubborn rain soaking the peninsula had broken up over the past three days and drifted east across the lake, leaving blue skies and mild temperatures in its wake. The magic of the view made him finally understand why there were people who would choose to live nowhere else but in this remote, beautiful land.

Cab's phone rang on his belt. It was Lala calling from Florida. He'd barely spoken to her since she guided him to the body buried on Peter Hoffman's property. They'd only had time for brief conversations as the local police wrapped up their investigations in Green Bay and on Washington Island.

"So what's the deal, Cab?" Lala said. "Are the loose ends tied up?"

"Most of them."

"No more dead bodies?"

"Not today."

"That's good. Try to keep it that way, okay? You're making the lieutenant nervous."

Cab smiled. "I will."

"I read your report. I guess you found what you were looking for. With the key. At the bottom of that hole."

"Yeah, you're right. I did." He added, "It's scary what people keep hidden under the ground."

"It is."

He heard the unspoken questions in her voice. *What about you, Cab? What are you hiding?*

"So where do you go next?" Lala went on, with a casualness that sounded false. "Do I win the bet?"

"What bet?" he asked, but he knew what she meant.

"The pool, remember? I figured this was the week that Catch-a-Cab Bolton would head for the horizon. I have a lot of money riding on you."

"How much?"

"Ten whole bucks."

"You must have been pretty confident."

"No, I was pretty cynical. I'm actually starting to feel bad about that."

"Don't."

"It sounds like Door County needs a new sheriff," Lala reminded him. "Do you want the job?"

Cab laughed. "This place is too cold for me. What's it like down there?"

"What else? Hot. Humid."

"That actually sounds nice," Cab admitted. "I'll be back home tonight. I guess I owe you ten bucks."

"Keep it," Lala said. "You've got a surprise waiting for you down here."

"What is it?"

"I got out of your shower this morning, and guess who was waiting for me in the living room of your condo? Your mother."

"My mother's in Florida?"

"Tarla Bolton in the flesh. Actually, I was the one in the flesh. We were both pretty damn surprised to see each other."

Cab laughed again. It felt good. "What did she say?"

"She said her son has good taste."

"Well, that's true."

"She also brought enough luggage to completely fill your second bedroom."

"She's *staying*?"

"Looks that way. She said something about the mountain coming to Mohammed."

"I guess I better hurry," Cab said.

"I guess. I'll get my stuff out of your bedroom and rinse off your toothbrush."

"You're funny. You know, there's no rush, Lala. Is your air-conditioning fixed?"

"No."

"So stick around a few days. Take a vacation. I need one, too. Besides, my mother is more than any one person can take alone."

"I'll think about that," she said.

"Hey, do me a favor, okay?" he asked.

"What?"

"Take some cash from my nightstand and go get a very, very expensive bottle of red wine. Tonight, you, me, and my mother are going to drink it on the beach."

"How often does a girl get a romantic offer like that?" Lala said.

"I'd like to tell you both a story."

"What kind of story?"

"It's about a girl named Vivian," Cab said.

There was a long silence from Lala on the line. "I'll buy the wine."

"Thanks."

"Travel safe, Cab."

"Bye, Lala."

He hung up the phone and felt an odd heaviness in his heart.

It occurred to Cab that he had never known what homesickness was before, not about people, not about places. He felt restless as the boat nestled against the dock in Northport. He jogged down the steps to the lower deck, climbed into his car, and drummed his fingers on the steering wheel until the deck attendant waved him off the ferry. He was first in line. His Corvette growled with impatience.

As he drove with a thump onto solid land, he saw a long string of cars in the return line, waiting to head back across the blue waters under the blue skies toward

Washington Island. That was how it always was here—people coming and going, heading in opposite directions. The lead car bound for the island, bound for home, belonged to Hilary Bradley. He recognized her, and she recognized him. She waved at him as if he were a friend.

Cab pulled off to the side of the pier, letting the other cars form a convoy away from the ferry. When there was a gap in the traffic, he ran on his storklike legs to the car parked in front of the on-ramp to the boat.

Hilary rolled down the window and leaned out. The warm wind mussed her blond hair. "Hello, Detective."

"Mrs. Bradley. How are you?"

"Better," she said. "Much better. So's Amy Leigh."

"That's good."

"The police in Green Bay treated us well."

"My lieutenant and I made some calls to make sure they did."

She took off her sunglasses and smiled at him. He could see cuts and bruises lingering on her face, but she still managed to look pretty. Her mood matched the lightness of the weather.

"Are you heading back to Florida?" she asked.

"I am."

"I'm glad I had a chance to see you before you left. To say thank you for what you did. For going over to the island that night. Without you, I probably would have lost Mark."

"I should be thanking you," Cab told her. "I feel guilty that it took a schoolteacher and a college girl to expose what really happened on that beach in Naples. I would have felt even worse if either of you had been seriously hurt."

"That wasn't your fault."

"You probably also owe me an 'I told you so' for wrongly suspecting your husband. I'm sorry. I made a mistake."

"You don't know him like I do," Hilary said.

"Well, I told you before that I hoped you were right—and you were."

"I've been wrong many times, but not about Mark. Trusting someone doesn't necessarily make you a fool, Detective."

"I'll try to remember that," Cab said.

He heard a whistle and saw that the

belly of the ferry was empty. One journey was done; the next was in waiting. Hilary Bradley turned on the engine of her car, and he could see in her face the same impatience he felt. To finish the ride. To be home where you belonged with the ones you loved. He envied her for having things in her life he was just beginning to find.

"I have to go," she said, extending a hand through the window. He shook it. Her grip was firm, but her skin was soft.

"Good luck in all things, Mrs. Bradley."

"Thank you, Detective. The same to you."

She drove onto the ferry, and Cab returned to the Corvette. He gunned it and headed south without a backward look at the water and the island. He had a long drive ahead through the small towns of Door County, but it was a perfect day to travel back to reality. He could drive as fast or as slow as he liked on the empty roads. For the first time in a long time, he didn't feel like he was being chased.

Even so, he had somewhere to go, and he was anxious to get there.

Hilary broke through the trees onto Schoolhouse Beach behind their house. Mark was waiting for her. So was Tresa, sitting on a bench beside him, her red hair tied in a ponytail. Sunshine spilled across the expanse of the horseshoe bay and left it flecked with gold. The season was still too early for tourists, and they had the rocky stretch of shoreline all to themselves.

When the two of them saw her at the crest of the slope, Tresa ran. Mark lingered on the bench by himself, letting the girl go first. Tresa greeted Hilary with a huge smile and threw her arms around her in a hug that seemed impossibly strong for her skinny arms.

"I'm so glad you're safe," Tresa whispered.

"Me, too."

"Mark told me you were coming home today. I really wanted to stay and see you."

"I'm glad you did."

Tresa leaned in, hugging her as fiercely as before. When she let go, she ducked her head into her neck. "I'm so sorry about Jen. I mean, Katie. I should have done something. I should have told someone about the fire."

"You were a kid back then, Tresa," Hilary said.

"I still feel like a kid."

"You're not."

"Mark thinks I am."

Hilary didn't answer, and Tresa bit her lip and shoved her thumbs in the pockets of her jeans. "Well, I'll leave you guys alone."

The teenager brushed past her, but Hilary stopped her with a hand on her shoulder. "Tresa, wait. There's something else."

"What is it?"

"You did a brave thing by coming here that night like you did. You risked your own life. Thank you."

"I couldn't let anything happen to Mark," she said.

"I know that, and I'm grateful," Hilary went on, "but I also have to tell you something. Woman to woman."

Tresa hesitated. "Okay."

"You can't spend any more time alone with my husband," Hilary said.

Tresa's eyes widened. "What? I mean, yeah, I—I understand. I'm sorry. He told you what happened, huh?"

"Of course he did."

"I'm really sorry."

"Girl crushes don't bother me, Tresa, but you're not a girl anymore."

She nodded. "Sure. You're right."

"It doesn't mean we never want to see you again."

"No, I get it." Tresa took a long look over her shoulder at Mark. "Thanks," she told Hilary.

"For what?"

"For saying I could actually be a threat. That's cool."

Hilary smiled. "Take care of yourself, Tresa."

"You, too. You're lucky, you know?"

"I know."

She watched Tresa disappear inside the trees, and then she turned with a strange sense of anxiety and relief toward Mark, trying not to run. He climbed off the bench as she drew near. Their faces told the story. They didn't need to speak. His arms enfolded her, and she grabbed him hard, and they kissed with an outpouring of love and longing that left her fighting back tears. It was as if everything in her life had come within a breath of slipping away, and then, suddenly, miraculously, she had it all back in her grasp. They stood there in silence for long minutes, clinging to each other, still somehow afraid that they would be torn apart. When they finally let go, they walked back to the bench hand in hand and sat, still not speaking, listening to the steady beat of the water on the rocks.

"I thought I'd never—" Mark began, but she stopped him firmly with a hand over his lips.

"Don't. Don't say it."

He nodded and let it go. She didn't want to talk about fears or nightmares. She didn't want to talk about what might have happened or how close they'd both come to the edge of the precipice. The only thing that mattered to her was that they were still here and still together.

"I got a call from the principal at the high school," Hilary told him.

"Oh?"

"It sounds like the last few days have made a lot of people rethink what happened last year. Or maybe they got nervous and called their lawyers. I think they're going to offer you your teaching job back."

Mark's head bobbed in surprise. "Seriously?"

"Looks that way. Do you want it?"

"After everything that's happened?" He hesitated, and she assumed he was about to say no. Not ever. Not again. He surprised her.

"Actually, yeah," he continued. "I do. All I ever wanted was the life we had before."

She smiled at her husband. He was the idealist of the two of them. He thought things could be the way they were again, as if the horrors had never happened, as if the injustices had never been perpetrated. She wasn't so blindly optimistic. Life didn't go backward. She prayed that she could look in the mirror one day and see the same two people who had come to this place to escape, that she could live in peace among the neighbors who had wronged them, that she could find a way to heal the wounds in her soul.

Something had been taken from her, and she didn't know how to get it back. She would never admit it to him or anyone else, but when she was alone, she still heard Katie taunting her. *You're like every wife, loyal and stupid. Do I need to spell it out for you?*

She saw Mark and Glory. On the beach. *No one will ever know.*

Hilary told herself for the thousandth time that nothing had happened between them. Mark was an honorable man, and Katie was a sociopath playing with her head. Yet still she wondered. She was human. It was a seedling of doubt she wouldn't water, in the hope that it would wither and die. That was all she could do. You push aside your fears and hope there are no monsters waiting behind them. You live your life. You trust. You have faith.

"So do you want to stay here?" she asked.

"I do," Mark said. "Don't you?"

Hilary nodded. What they had, what they wanted, was worth fighting for.

"I don't want to be anywhere else," she said.

JOIN BRIAN'S COMMUNITY

You can write to me at brian@bfreeman books.com. I welcome e-mails from readers and always respond personally. Visit my Web site at www.bfreemanbooks.com to join my mailing list, get book club discussion questions, read bonus content, and find out more about me and my books. You can join me on Facebook at www.facebook .com/bfreemanfans.

ACKNOWLEDGMENTS

I lost a dear friend during the writing of this book. Gail Foster sent me my very first "fan" letter in 2005 before the release of my debut novel, *Immoral.* As we got to know each other, she became a sounding board and advance reader for my manuscripts, and I always looked forward to her feedback and reflections on my work. Marcia and I had the good fortune to meet Gail several times and to become friends with her and her family. We miss her greatly.

This book is in your hands because of the efforts of many people around the world. I am grateful to everyone in the publishing industry who has been so supportive of my career throughout the past six books. A special thanks to my agents, Ali Gunn, Deborah Schneider, and Diana Mackay—and the agents in many countries who work with them.

Of course, I'm particularly grateful to my readers. I grew up enjoying entertainment from many wonderful authors, and it is an honor to play the same role for my readers. Keep writing to me and sharing your stories. I always appreciate it. A very special thanks to my advance reader, Mike O'Neill, for all his support and insights.

This would be a lonely business without family and friends. My own family in California has been with me every step of the way, even when we are separated by long distances. I'm also blessed with wonderful friends. Many thanks to people like Barb and Jerry, Matt and Paula, and Keith and Katie, for the ways you enrich our lives.

Every book is dedicated to my wife, Marcia. Those of you who have met her know that she is (as one bookseller described her) "the icing on the cake" at book events. Actually, that's not true—she's the cake, too! Whenever I get invited back to a bookstore or library, I can count on hearing the question, "You *will* be bringing your wife, too, won't you?" So the biggest thanks of all to Marcia for twenty-six years of marriage and for joining me on this roller-coaster ride.